Final Destination
A New Homeland

Beca Sue

Final Destination

A New Homeland

Final Destination a New Homeland
Copyright 2015 Beca Sue
All rights reserved

Cover design: Timothy L. Bean

ISBN: 978-0-9961575-5-1

This book is dedicated to Ewald Grieb, who lived through many of the events in this book, and to Ewald's wife, Patricia, who put his memories on paper.

Pictured: Jacob, Magdalena, Erhard, Ewald, and Werner Grieb

Family Tree of the Grieb and Wallentine Families

October 1939

Gottlieb and Rosina Wallentine   **Jacob and Juliana Grieb**

Children: **Children:**

Rosa   Jacob
Magdalena   Albert
Emelie   Olof
Otto   Mathilda
Jacob   Maria
Edward   Hulda
Emil

Jacob and Magdalena (Wallentine) Grieb

Children:
Erhard
Ewald

Albert and Emilie (Wallentine) Grieb

Children:
Albert
Richard
Erwin

ACKNOWLEDGMENTS

Thank you to family and friends who have encouraged me along the way and helped me by reading and critiquing the manuscript of this book. The support I have received with this project is just one of the many ways God has blessed me.

Chapter One

October 1939

German Colony of Hoffnungstal

Bessarabia, Romania

Rosina Wallentine sat in a chair staring out her bedroom window. Five letters were lying in her lap. The most recent letter was over a year old; the oldest 26 years. They were all from the same person, though only two had been signed. How could things have gone so wrong? If only Rosina could have known what was to come, she would have had a better argument, been more convincing in her pleas. Maybe she would have the person sitting here with her now, instead of a pile of letters in her lap.

Rosina thought back to how her family came to live in this area. The story had been kept alive from one generation to the next, through telling it again and again. The thought now crossed Rosina's mind that maybe she should write the story down, just in case there was no one left to remember. She shuddered as that thought took root. Would the new turn of events cause the situation to become as difficult for the Germans living here in Bessarabia as it now was for the Germans who lived in Russia under Communist rule?

Germans had begun to migrate to Russia as early as the 1760's, but Rosina's ancestors didn't make the trek until 1818. Leaving Kassel, Germany, they made their way southeast toward the Black Sea. At the time, the economy of Europe had been struggling, and in Germany, there just wasn't enough land for all the farmers. Also, the Lutheran church had produced a new hymn book, thought to be heretical by more conservative religious groups. So, religious freedom had also played a role in the decision to migrate. Those leaving Germany chose to sing a new song during their worship and the conservatives were happy to see the troublemakers leave, taking their new hymnal with them.

Alexander I was the Tsar of Russia in 1818 when the move occurred, and he had made it very lucrative for the German peasants to pack up and leave their homeland. The Tsar offered large parcels of land, support money for the move, livestock and farm implements. It was all too good to pass up. The Tsar had empty land he wanted filled and the German peasants needed land to farm. Everyone was able to satisfy a need and life had been good for about one hundred years, until the Great War ended.

Rosina's ancestors ended their journey to the west of the Inguletz River, becoming part of the Bessarabia colonies. One hundred years later they would realize the importance of being to the west of that river! Sixty-four families formed the village of Hoffnungstal. Many families produced grain crops but the Wallentine family planted a vineyard. The vines were still visible from the window she looked through now. Six weeks ago they had been laden with fruit but now were just empty vines, waiting for the resting period of winter. Rosina couldn't help but wonder if it would be their family who pruned the vines when early spring arrived. Would they still be living in Bessarabia? And if so, would they still enjoy the freedom of governing their own colonies? So much could change in just a short amount of time. The letters she was preparing to read spoke to that truth.

Rosina's husband, Gottlieb, had been the youngest son of his family. Therefore, he had inherited the land and the vineyard. The vineyard had provided them a good living, along with giving other families employment at its busiest times. The wine produced was of very good quality and was sold throughout the Black Sea region. He was a good leader and kept the village running smoothly. He had earned great respect and the people of Huffnungstal trusted him to make decisions with their best interest at heart. Rosina's days were kept busy with being a school teacher during the winter and feeding everyone who worked on their farm during the summer. It was a busy life but one Rosina thoroughly enjoyed. She wanted to grow old here, living the life she loved. She prayed she would be allowed to do just that, but with the new threat that had just become known, the future of the colonies in Bessarabia were in jeopardy. This beautiful view from Rosina's bedroom window could become a memory, something that could only be seen when she closed her eyes and dreamed.

Rosina thought back to the time during the Great War when they had been forbidden to teach in the German language at their schools, in their churches or any gathering. Russian had become the primary language for every German within Russia's borders. However, that all changed once the Great War ended and Bessarabia was blessed with becoming part of Romania, instead of remaining part of Russia. With that turn of events, Rosina's life had been lived much differently than those who lived to the east of Romania. In Bessarabia, the Germans were allowed to reestablish their own government and have complete control of their churches and schools. German again became the primary language and the Romanian government left them to their own way of life. The only worry now was if the Romanians possessed the military strength to defend against an invasion. Rosina was sure that very question was being asked at the village meeting, which was taking place at this very moment.

Rosina allowed her thoughts to continue down memory lane, back to the first child her and Gottlieb had. Her little grave was in the Lutheran church cemetery. Such a sad time it had been for them. On some days, Rosina didn't know if she would push through the grief. Time has a way of healing though, and soon there were other children; two daughters and four sons. Such a blessing! Rosina's two youngest sons, Edward and Emil, still lived at home and helped their vater with the vineyard and other farming. Her two older sons, Jacob and Otto, had recently married and lived in neighboring villages near their wives' families. Rosina's daughters, Magdalena and Emilie, were both married and had families of their own. They had married brothers, Jacob and Albert Grieb. Jacob and Magdalena had two sons, Erhard seven and Ewald three. Albert and Emilie had three sons, Albert, Richard and Erwin.

The Griebs owned a grocery store, mill and dairy farm in Hoffnungstal. The work was hard but they made a good living. Magdalena and Emilie helped out at the store as needed or with the dairy, making cheese and butter to sell at the store. There was very little time to just sit and think, as Rosina was doing now, and to reread letters that had been kept safe in a trunk for many years. Looking down, Rosina decided to begin the heart wrenching task of reliving the past. Isabella's neat handwriting stared back up at her. Rosina could still vividly remember the conversation she and Isabella had when Isabella announced her decision to leave Bessarabia.

"Daniel Gingrich has asked me to marry him and go back to Kronau to live," Isabella had whispered in Rosina's ear during service at the Lutheran church.

"You told him no, right? Didn't you tell him no, Sister?"

Isabella shook her head, indicating that she had definitely not said no.

"What am I going to do without you near?" Rosina questioned, tears pooling in her eyes.

"You'll be okay. You have Gottlieb and precious Magdalena who's slumbering in your arms as we speak," Isabella answered.

"But we've been so close all our lives, like twin, since there is only ten months between us. It will be like losing a part of me."

"I love him, Rosina. We have spent the summer getting to know one another as he worked in the vineyard. It's like he came here just to marry me," Isabella whispered.

"We'll continue this discussion after church," Rosina hissed.

"Okay," Isabella agreed, *"but I won't change my mind. You've been married nearly three years now. I'm almost twenty and will soon be considered too old to marry. If I turn Daniel down, there may never be another man who is interested in me. Besides, we can come back and visit every once in a while."*

"It's over a hundred miles from Hoffnungstal to Kronau! I will never see you again!"

As heads turned in our direction, Rosina knew she had spoken way too loud. Bowing her head in embarrassment, she vowed to change her sister's mind after church, but it didn't happen. Love won out but oh, what a high price poor Isabella paid.

Picking up the letters, Rosina decided to start with the oldest one, written in March, 1914.

Dear Rosina,

I just had to tell you first. Daniel and I are expecting our first child! I cannot wait to hold the little one in my arms, though it will be six months until I am due. It seems like such a long time. It's the same amount of time I've been gone from Hoffnungstal, and I miss you terribly.

I pray everything is well with you and your family. I trust the grape juice is fermenting into the fine wine the Wallentine's are known for, after the good production of grapes last fall. Daniel is proud that he had a hand in producing that crop. Maybe a bottle will find its way to us in a few years.

Daniel and I farm a fine piece of land with his brother and grow wheat and barley. We also have a small dairy herd and we use the milk to make butter and cheeses which we sell to our neighbors, adding to our income. It all keeps me quite busy but we both know I'm used to the work, just as you are. It's just our way of life; farmers forever.

Daniel read in the Burgerzeitung, a newspaper out of the colony of Alexandrovsk, that the workers in the cities are very disgruntled. The Tsar is under attack again and there are rumors there could be another revolution like in 1905. The unrest has Daniel worried, and he is concerned about all Germans living in Russia. If the Tsar is overthrown, he wonders if a new government will be receptive to the Germans. I hope things improve and we are not threatened or made to leave.

Well, enough about such dreary stuff! The sun is shining and spring is in the air. The wheat is starting to grow after a long winter and looks like it will produce a good crop. There should be plenty for our needs and to add to the communal storage bins for the drought years. We will concentrate on the good and pray about the bad. I have no more time to write now but will send a letter as soon as the baby is born.

Love, Isabella

Rosina folded the letter and placed it on the bottom of the pile. So much had happened soon after that letter arrived, the first event being on August 1st, 1914, when Germany declared war on Russia. Suddenly, the Tsar was loved and men were ready to go fight for their country. However, the Russian Germans were hated. They were seen as spies, even though some of the families had lived in Russia since the 1760's. It did not matter that 250,000 young Russian German men were fighting shoulder to shoulder with the native Russians against the German forces. The Germans had always stayed in colonies, speaking their native language in their churches, schools and government meetings. It was as if they had stayed true to the fatherland, Germany. That was not really the case. It was more about preserving heritage, but to the Russians, it was viewed as being sympathetic to the invading German army. Almost overnight, the German language was forbidden to be used in the schools, press or government. Church services could no longer be in German, either. Those clergy who chose to disobey were deported to slave camps in Siberia, never to return.

The war had raged on, with Russia losing many battles. In March of 1917, the Tsar abdicated from power after 80,000 metal workers in Petrograd rose up a revolt. Even the soldiers sent to break up the demonstration ended up joining the workers against the Tsar, Nicholas II. There had not been enough food for the military or the city workers for quite some time. Adding to these problems, the Russian people were just weary of fighting the war. Rosina recalled the feeling of uncertainty as all of these events took place. That same anxiousness threatened to overwhelm her now as their peaceful lives were again in jeopardy.

When the new government came to power after the Tsar stepped down, it brought excitement for most of Russia. The Germans were again allowed to use their native language in their colony schools and churches. Newspapers printed in German began pouring from the presses for the colonist's information and enjoyment. The fear of being deported had subsided. However, it was short-lived. On November 7, 1917, Vladimir Lenin and his political group, the Russian Social Democratic Party, had a successful coup and took over the government. Thus began Russia's Communist era.

Rosina could not give enough thanks to God for being in Bessarabia when the war ended. The Great War and Russia's own civil wars had caused Russia to lose vast amounts of territory. The Brest-Litovsk treaty confirmed the independence of Finland, Estonia, Latvia, and Lithuania. Poland also regained independence, after fighting a civil war with Russia until 1920, something Poland had lost in the 18th century. And blessing of blessings, Bessarabia became a Romanian province. The "iron curtain" dropped just to the east of Hoffnungstal. The next letter Rosina prepared to read was about what happened on the other side of that "iron curtain". As heartbreaking as it was, it was not the worst of the letters.

Dear Rosina,

I write this letter in hopes of somehow, someway getting it into your hands. So much has happened since I last wrote. Today's date is September 15th, 1917. The Tsar has stepped down from command and a new government is being formed. For this reason, I believe I can send word to you. We have been allowed the freedom of using German again, and newspapers in our native language have begun rolling off the press. With these new freedoms, after three years of being hated and silenced by our fellow countrymen, I am hoping to send word of how things are here.

Daniel and I celebrated the birth of our child on September 15th, 1914. His name is Stefan and he turned three years old today. He looks so much like Daniel it brings tears to my eyes. Daniel was able to enjoy the first month with his new son before joining the Russian armed forces. I have not seen or heard from him since. I have been living with my brother-in-law and sister- in-law until Daniel returns. It seemed the wisest choice, given how cruel the Germans have been treated the last three years. Did you ever think you would see such hatred in this country we call home? It's the only place we have ever lived. How can they accuse us of being spies for a country we know nothing about nor ever lived in? It makes no sense to me.

I miss you and our family so much. I am including a letter for Mutti and Vater, if you would please see that it gets to them. I probably should just travel home until the war is over and Daniel comes back, but I want to be here when he returns. Besides, even though things are better right now, they could change for the worse again. I would hate to be in Bessarabia and not be allowed to return here to Kronau. Such a state of threat and worry we have become! Please pray, Rosina, for Daniel's safe return and for better days ahead. I will be praying for you and yours, too.

I will close for now but will write again soon, hopefully with good news of Daniel's return.

I love all of you and miss you dearly!

Your sister, Isabella

Rosina folded the letter and placed it at the bottom of the pile. She didn't know if she had the strength to read the next three, but realized she needed to as a reminder of what the Soviet Union, Russia's new name, was capable of. The next three letters were proof that they had no mercy for Russian Germans, or their own native citizens, for that matter.

Rosina rose from her chair and made her way downstairs to the kitchen. The sun was sinking low in the sky by now and she wondered what time Gottlieb would return from the village meeting. What would the German colonies of Bessarabia decide to do? They could flee Romania, but where would they go? The way Rosina saw it, they really had no choice but to wait and see what the Soviet's next move would be.

Reaching the kitchen, Rosina made a nice cup of tea and grabbed two cookies to relax her anxiety. Why she thought putting sugar into her body would help calm her nerves made no sense, but the joy of eating them occupied her mind for a moment. She kept telling herself that God was still in control but was reminded that evil still reared its ugly head and bad things still happened, even to people who lived Christian lives. The remaining letters were a testament of that. God had not promised that there wouldn't be trials, just the help to get through them.

Making her way back upstairs, Rosina enjoyed the cookies and tea, relaxing in the view of the sun setting on the vineyard. This place was truly beautiful, and she could hardly bear the thought of having to leave. She hoped it didn't come to that. To never see the sun set on the vineyard again would be one of the things she missed most. Takin her eyes from the window and getting comfortable in her chair again, Rosina picked up the next letter and began to read.

January 1918

Dear Sister,

I will use no names in this letter for fear it will be traced back to one of us. I probably should not even pen it, but I am so scared and fear I will be dead soon. I just want you to know what has happened. It seems a man by the name Nestor Makhno believes everyone should have land, whether they worked for it or not. The peasants here have banded with him and have been taking our land, livestock, food, and even our clothes by force. The house my husband and I lived in is now occupied by peasants.

My husband's father tried to fight for his property and now he lies in the graveyard, along with his wife and two youngest children. It is like something I could never imagine happening! I saw the peasants coming toward our home and ran with my child to a neighbor's house. The neighbors are very poor and the peasants are not interested in their humble abode or very small piece of ground. My brother-in-law and sister-in-law and their two children have joined me here, as the peasants have taken their home, too.

I don't know how I will get this letter to you and maybe never will, but it gives me some comfort to pour out my heart and fears on this piece of paper. Pray, Sister, please pray!

May 1918
   Dear Sister,

   It has been four months since I have written on this letter. I have not been able to find a way to get it sent but feel I must add to it. The German troops have moved in and brought us some peace. We have been able to go back to our houses and speaking our native German language! Hopefully this is a sign of better days!

November 1918
   Dear Sister,

   The German troops are leaving our area. I fear for what is to come! Without their protection, I know the peasants will begin terrorizing our colonies again. Please pray! I will try to get this letter to a departing German soldier in hopes it finds you. I will write your name and address on a separate piece of paper, in case this letter falls into the wrong hands and can be traced back to me. I will surely be killed for exposing such cruelty of my fellow countrymen to the outside world.

   I love and miss you. Please tell Mutti and Vater the same.

Rosina placed the letter under the rest and wiped the tears from her face. If only the German army could have stayed and helped the Ukraine with its independence! Things would have turned out so differently. As it happened, Isabella and her family found themselves in a hostile country, living in constant fear. They were forbidden to leave of their own choosing and had never found a way to escape. It was a nightmare, but their eyes were wide open.

Rosina picked up the next letter deciding to just push through. The words that had been penned on these sheets of paper were very painful reminders of how cruel humans could be, but she needed to read it all again. She needed to be prepared for decisions that may lie ahead. These letters reminded Rosina that as sad as leaving Bessarabia might be, staying might be worse.

My dearest Sister,

I will begin with the good news. The date is June 3, 1922. The American Relief Administration has been allowed to come in and bring us much needed food. We were all starving before these angels of mercy showed up.

After the Austrian and German troops pulled out, Makhno's bandits came with fury. There was no one to stop them. They murdered colonists, burned our homes and raped the women. The horror I have witnessed gives me nightmares. I'm sorry to tell you these terrible things, but someone on the other side of the "iron curtain" needs to know the cruel things that are happening here.

My husband did return, but it was to desolation and famine. The Red Army took our crops and the grain in our store houses and shipped it to other places within Russia, leaving us with no food. After that, we searched for any morsel of food we could find. The situation became very desperate. We even ate rats trying to stay alive. Gross, disgusting rats, Sister!

All of our rights have been stripped from us. Our churches are now social gathering places and we can no longer have worship services. There is an article to the Soviet Union constitution stating "the separation of the Church from the state and the school from the Church", and we have all been made quite aware of it. There is no religion allowed in the schools and clergy are not allowed to teach religion to anyone under the age of 18. Unfortunately, there are very few clergy left to teach religion to anyone, no matter the age. They have been arrested and executed or deported to a slave camp, whether they were guilty of anything or not. Everything has been in an upheaval since the war ended. I truly wonder if things will ever be right again. How can someone expect to run a country without the help of God?

My husband brought a story back with him of the Volga Germans plight. It seems our Black Sea colonies are not alone in the persecution. As with us, the Red army came and took all their grain. The Volga Germans were finally pushed to their limit and formed a retaliation troop of their own, along with other Russian peasants. They went from village to village killing Communist supporters and commissars who had taken all their grain and left their families starving. The Red Army showed up within a few weeks. Hundreds were condemned and executed for their uprising. The Mariental colony decided to resist the army, resulting in over 200 men being killed on the spot and 270 being shot after a mock trial. Not even the parish priest was spared!

The White Army attempted to fight the Red Army and the peasant bandits to give us some relief from the constant persecution. They had little success and finally gave up. All of this turmoil has made it impossible to plant or harvest crops, which has greatly added to our food shortage problems.

As for our child, he could not survive the long days without food. We tried everything, but he took ill and had no strength to fight. I mourn the loss daily but know he rests in the arms of Jesus and the cruelty of this place can no longer touch him.

I will close on the good note again that the American Relief Administration has been allowed to bring us food. Without that, we would have surely died. Maybe one of the relief workers will do me a favor and get this letter into your hands. If not, I know you are still praying, as I am, too. I must admit, however, sometimes I just pray for God to take me from this world, so I can leave all this madness behind. I am confident of this, though; they may take God out of our schools and restrict our worship, but they can't take him out of the hearts of man.

Love,
Your Sister

Rosina folded the letter and placed it at the bottom of the pile. She buried her face in her hands, mourning for her sister and all she had been forced to endure. The last letter would have to wait. Rosina just could not bear reading it this evening.

Chapter Two

Magdalena Grieb carried a sleeping Ewald to his bed and tucked him in. His brother, Erhard, was already asleep in his bed next to Ewald's. At seven, Erhard was getting old enough to follow his father around and learn about the ways of a German farmer. The day began early with cows to milk, followed by daily chores of running a mill and grocery store. It was enough to make Erhard fall into bed and fast asleep soon after supper each night. Ewald was only three and still had a few years of staying close to his mother.

After placing Ewald in the bed, Magdalena made a cup of warm milk and went to sit on the front porch to wait for her husband, Jacob, to return. He had gone to a village meeting that her father, the mayor, had called. The news that had been reported today on the radio was troubling and plans needed to be discussed. Magdalena prayed that a decision could be reached that wouldn't force them to leave their home here in Bessarabia. She had always thought her children would be raised in this German colony, becoming the next generation to work the land. The land would then be passed on to their children, the way it had happened for over one hundred years.

As dusk fell on the October evening, Magdalena could see the men heading toward home. Since the Grieb family ran the mill and grocery store, their house was in the middle of the colony and the comings and goings were easily viewed. The road through the village ran from east to west with many thatched roof homes along it. Each house had a nice yard and a barn in the back to house the livestock and equipment each farmer owned. The Grieb's barn was quite large to accommodate the milking stanchions needed for the dairy herd and the extra hay and grain required to keep them fed through the winter.

Rising from her rocking chair, Magdalena went in to warm Jacob some milk and placed a plate of cookies on the table. Jacob always talked the best when his sweet tooth had been satisfied. It had been one of the first things Magdalena had discovered after their marriage. It had helped smooth over the many disputes they had faced at first, due mostly to Magdalena's bullheadedness. The fact she admitted she had been the cause of the disagreements did not change her attitude much. She was just a strong-willed woman and always would be.

Some German men kept their wives out of their affairs, not wanting women to have any opinions about important issues. This was not the case with Jacob. He included Magdalena in every aspect, even in the business of running the grocery store and mill. Jacob's father, whose name was also Jacob, had not been so considerate with his wife. She was kept out of her husband's dealings and business ventures. But Jacob, Magdalena's husband, thought it best she know about such things in case she found herself on her own and needed to make important decisions.

For this reason, Magdalena chose to wait up for her husband's return. She knew he would be honest and forthright with what had been discussed at the meeting. Jacob had even joked one time that he should just take her with him to the meeting so he didn't have to repeat it all, but he knew that would never be accepted by the other men, especially his father-in-law, Gottlieb, who was the mayor. It would not matter that it was Gottlieb's daughter who was in attendance. She would be sent home and Jacob would become a laughingstock for the other men, like a chicken with two heads.

As Jacob came through the door, Magdalena was pouring warm milk into a mug for him and poured another for herself. The cookies were on the table and Jacob snagged one immediately. It was exactly what Magdalena knew he would do, and she smiled at being able to guess his action before he even thought to do it. This knowledge came from working side by side each day and becoming aware of each other's ways, knowing the other's wants and needs without speaking a word.

"Hullo, wife," Jacob mumbled around his mouthful of cookie, "nice of you to have a snack waiting for me."

Magdalena came to the table with the mugs of milk and placed one in front of Jacob. "Just knew you would enjoy some milk and cookies before bed." A small smile played upon her pretty face.

"You can't fool me, woman," Jacob said with a chuckle.

"So, what did you learn at the meeting?" Magdalena asked eagerly.

"I usually get to enjoy at least two cookies before I begin," Jacob grumped.

"Yes, but this was the most serious meeting you have ever attended." As Magdalena looked with anticipation at Jacob, she knew all joking was over. The meeting had been a serious one, one that might change their lives forever. She watched the emotions cross Jacob's face as he prepared to tell her about the meeting.

"The German army has indeed invaded Poland," Jacob began. "They have advanced halfway across the country, and Russia has invaded from the east. Poland has surrendered to the two invading forces. It seems the non-aggression pact that Hitler and Stalin signed had some secret provisions. The two men actually signed a Frontier and Friendship Treaty upon completing their invasions."

"I knew there had to be some reason Hitler and Stalin had become friends," Magdalena interjected. "They have been bitter enemies since Hitler came to power in 1933."

"Yes, it's a troubling situation, one that raises many questions. What is the Soviets next move? Will they try to take back Bessarabia, since they lost this territory after the Great War? Does the Romanian army have the power to prevent the Soviets from invading? Do we try and flee now, or wait and see what happens next?"

"Why would we leave this area? It has been our home and our ancestors' homes since 1818. Besides, where would we go? Germany? We know nothing about Germany."

"This is true, but one thing we do know; our ancestors left Germany because there was not enough land. That situation has not changed. Maybe we should leave for America."

"America! We know no one who lives there or anything about America!"

"We know it's the land of opportunity," Jacob replied. "If we have to leave Bessarabia, our sons will have nowhere to call home. There will be nothing to pass down to them. No land, no mill, no dairy herd, and no grocery store. We will have to start over again somewhere. Why not start over in America?"

"Do you believe the Red Army will invade Bessarabia?"

"I do not know, but right now the colony has decided leaving is not the answer. I can assure you, though, if we think that the Soviets plan to invade Bessarabia, we will be packing and leaving, with or without the rest of the colony. Where we will go, I do not know. What I do know is this; we cannot stay here if the Soviets invade. We do not want to come under the persecution the German colonies on the other side of that "iron curtain" have been forced to endure."

"Yes, avoiding that "iron curtain" is foremost in all our minds. The letters from my Aunt Isabella is proof that we do not want any part of that," Magdalena concluded.

Magdalena stared into her empty mug, thinking of all Jacob had revealed. What was to become of them; of their children? She remembered her aunt's letters, the ones her Mother allowed her to read a few years ago. To think that those horrors might become a reality for her and her family sent a chill down her spine.

"Don't worry, Magdalena," Jacob said softly. "Just pray for our safety."

"I will, Jacob, but it will be hard not to be anxious about all this. We have two beautiful boys to worry about, not to mention all of the rest of our families. I don't want to leave here, but I know we can't stay if there is a threat of Soviet invasion."

"We will take it one day at a time and do what we must to protect our families. It's what our ancestors have done since coming to this beautiful land," Jacob replied softly. "Let's get some rest. Things always look better after a good night's sleep. Besides, cows don't like to wait to be milked and that will begin with the first light of dawn."

"Yes, things will look better in the morning," Magdalena agreed, trying hard to convince herself of the fact.

****

Magdalena set three year old Ewald on the floor behind the counter with some wooden blocks. Grabbing a rag, she began to straighten and dust the shelves of the grocery store. It was her afternoon to run the store and things had been quite slow. It had given her mind way too much time to think about what might lay ahead for her and her family. Not even the mill wheel was turning to keep her company, beating out its rhythm as the water pushed across it. In early summer, when grain was being harvested, it made a constant clatter. The power for the wheel came from the stream that ran through Hoffnungstal, as it cut a path toward the Black Sea. The door of the grocery store opened, interrupting Magdalena's thoughts. She looked up to see her mutti walking through it.

"Hullo, Mutti," Magdalena cheerfully greeted, glad to have some company.

"Hullo, Magdalena," Rosina answered as she went around the counter to scoop Ewald up in her arms.

"Oma!" Ewald exclaimed.

"How is Oma's big boy today?"

"I'm building a giant barn with my blocks," Ewald informed her.

"And what will you put in the barn?" Rosina asked.

"Lots of cows and horses, and of course hay and grain," Ewald explained.

"What, no fine wine? Your Opa would be upset with this news," Rosina teased.

"Well, then I better add a cellar under the barn," Ewald quickly decided.

"Gut idea," Rosina agreed, chuckling as she placed him back in front of his block barn.

Rosina made her way to the shelf Magdalena was straightening to get to the point of her visit. The store was empty and it would be a good time for a discussion of last night's meeting. Gottlieb was a bit tight lipped when it came to telling his wife about his business, but Rosina knew Jacob was a bit more forthcoming. She hoped she might glean some extra information from Magdalena.

"Did Jacob speak with you when he got home last night?" Rosina began.

"Yes. The Red Army invading is a real threat," Magdalena said. "Jacob is very concerned for the safety of Bessarabia."

"I reread four of your Aunt Isabella's letters while I waited for your vater to return," Rosina confessed. "We cannot wait too long and chance ending up in the situation Daniel and Isabella are in."

"I know, Mutti, but to leave all we have here, to go to a place we know nothing about? Life is good here. I want my sons to grow up working this land, running the mill and grocery store, planting and harvesting grain. It breaks my heart to think of all those plans changing."

"I want that for them, too," Rosina said softly. "Let's just pray we will be kept safe, like when the Great War ended. I admit I do not want to leave the vineyard. I watched the sun set from my bedroom window last night. I can't imagine ever finding a prettier view."

"Yes, the vineyard is truly beautiful," Magdalena agreed. "I have wonderful memories of my childhood, playing with Emilie among those vines. I want Ewald and Erhard to have those same memories of their childhood, memories of growing up among family and making a living from the land."

"Where is Erhard?" Rosina inquired.

"Out being Jacob's shadow," Magdalena chuckled.

"This is gut. He will learn to be a good farmer by following in his vater's footsteps," Rosina said.

"Yes, very gut. Hopefully, he will have a son someday and teach him the same things on this very piece of land. It's what I'm praying for."

"It's what we all hope for, Magdalena," Rosina sighed.

"Jacob mentioned us moving to America," Magdalena whispered, not wanting Ewald to hear the conversation.

"America," Rosina hissed. "Why would he consider such a thing?"

"If we have to leave Bessarabia, Jacob wants to be able to give Erhard and Ewald the opportunity to make a good life. There will be nothing to pass down to them," Magdalena said.

"Do you really think you would have to move to America to make a new life?" Rosina asked.

"I didn't say I wanted to move to America," Magdalena replied. "That's Jacob's idea, but you know how he is once he gets something in his head."

"Yes, I do," Rosina said, "and that's the reason I'm

concerned."

"Hopefully all this worry is for nothing," Magdalena said, trying to calm her own nerves. "Maybe Stalin is happy with getting part of Poland and the surrounding area back. Bessarabia is such a small area. He may just leave us be and allow us to remain part of Romania."

"I hope you're right, Daughter," Rosina replied. "However, the Stalin Isabella writes about doesn't seem to be a man content with having part of something if he thinks there's a chance he can have it all."

At that moment, a customer entered the store. Rosina knew her and Magdalena's conversation had come to an end. Anything more that they wanted to discuss on the subject would have to wait until later. Turning back to Magdalena, Rosina said, "I need a can of milk, if Jacob would be so kind to deliver it later. I need to make some cheese. I will pay you now, so that part is taken care of."

"Okay," Magdalena answered. "I will tell him to take you a five gallon can after the evening milking."

"Thank you, Daughter," Rosina said, as the two walked toward the counter so Rosina could pay.

Rosina slipped back behind the counter to inspect Ewald's progress on his barn while Magdalena waited on the customer. As she looked at his creation, she smiled with satisfaction. The child definitely had a talent of being able to build things. It was a gift that Rosina was sure would come in handy throughout his life.

"Look, Oma, I added a cellar," Ewald said proudly.

"Yes, Ewald, your Opa would be proud," Rosina replied laughing. "I will tell him tonight of what a fine grandson he has."

Ewald beamed up at his Oma, glad to make her and Opa proud.

"Oma is going home now. Opa gets upset if his supper is not on time, and it's getting late. I will see you soon."

"Gut bye, Oma," Ewald chimed. "Thanks for stopping to see me."

As Rosina made her way home, she thought about Ewald and his grand barn ideas. She also thought about Erhard learning in the shadow of his father, Jacob. It was all as it should be, father to son, generation to generation. She just hoped and prayed it continued to be so.

****

October turned chilly. The winter wheat that had been placed in the soil in late September was emerging like small blades of grass. It gave hope of a good harvest come early summer. The Germans depended on the grain crops to feed their families, livestock and for income. The thought at the back of each colonists mind was whether or not they would still be in Bessarabia when it came time to harvest the grain. No one wanted to speak the thought aloud, hoping their fears were just a result of living too close to the "iron curtain" and knowing how quickly the Red Army could be on their doorstep. The village chose to live life as normal as possible, though outside of their cozy colony, Europe was falling apart.

After taking care of things in the East by signing the Frontier and Friendship Treaty with the Soviets, Germany had turned their attention to the countries to the west and south of them. The Soviets, not being satisfied with just getting half of Poland back, chose to invade Finland. Finland had been a territory of Russia until the end of the Great War, just as Bessarabia had. The question was, would the Soviet Union attempt to take back all of the territory it lost at the close of the Great War? The question hanged heavy among the Germans in Bessarabia and was whispered amongst close family members.

The battles of the war were reported on the radio and in local newspapers. The Germans in Bessarabia listened and read intently, looking for any sign that they might become the next target in the Soviets quest to regain what had been taken from them. As long as the Red Army was detained fighting Finland to the north, the Germans in Bessarabia could feel a small sense of security. If Finland fell to the Soviets, then all of Bessarabia would be on high alert.

"Jacob, what do you think Hitler's plans are?" Magdalena questioned one evening, after the boys were fast asleep.

"I really don't know," Jacob sighed. "He seems to be taking control of all the countries to the west of Germany."

"The store buzzed about it all day," Magdalena said. "It seems it was too cold outside for any real work, so the men gathered around the stove and discussed the two wars being fought by Russia and Germany. By closing time, my nerves were shot, just thinking of all that could happen."

"You mustn't worry, Magdalena," Jacob soothed. "You're in a delicate state."

Magdalena unconsciously touched her abdomen where a bump had not even begun to show yet. She had just told Jacob two weeks before and had now shared the news with her mother and sister, Emilie. Emilie was already six months along in her fourth pregnancy, hoping for a daughter after already birthing three sons.

"Yes, I know and it will do no good to worry," Magdalena admitted. "I just need to put it in God's hands and leave it there."

"It's what we all need to do," Jacob confirmed.

"I will admit, though, bringing a child into the world during such an upheaval is almost as scary as thinking about being invaded," Magdalena sighed.

"A child is always a good thing. They are a precious gift from God," Jacob reminded gently.

"I know, Jacob, and I truly am excited. I just wish it were a peaceful time, like when Erhard and Ewald were born."

"I do too," Jacob admitted, "but we don't get to choose these things. So, what news did you hear in the store today?"

"It seems the German colonies in the Baltic have been invited back to Germany. Hitler wants them to return to the Reich."

"Really?" Jacob questioned in disbelief. "I suppose since they are threatened with an invasion by the Soviets, they may just take Hitler up on the offer."

"What choice do they have, Jacob? It's either return to Germany or be under Communist rule. I believe we have all heard enough horror stories to make us pack up and run from the latter."

"That's certainly true," Jacob answered thoughtfully.

"Do you suppose if the Soviets invade us, Bessarabia will be given the same offer?" Magdalena asked.

"I don't know, but it's worth putting some thought into."

"The strange thing about it is that Stalin has agreed that the Baltic Germans may return, without any fight whatsoever," Magdalena added.

"Now that is interesting," Jacob responded, turning to look at Magdalena in surprise. "What exactly are Hitler and Stalin up to, do you suppose?"

"I cannot imagine, but as I said before, they had been bitter enemies since Hitler came to power. The fact that they are now friendly to one another cause much alarm."

"Well, enough worrying for now," Jacob said, getting up from the kitchen table where most of their discussions took place. "It's time for bed. Dawn comes early and brings with it a full day of work."

Stifling a yawn, Magdalena agreed by clearing the mugs and now empty cookie plate. Placing them in the sink, she blew out the lamp and followed her husband to bed. As she curled up next to him seeking his warmth, she couldn't help but wonder about what the future held. If they couldn't stay in Bessarabia, where would they go? She knew she did not like Jacob's idea of moving to America, but it would certainly be better than falling under Communist rule. But how could they travel to America with her expecting a baby? Who would deliver it when the time came? Her mutti had delivered Erhard and Ewald. To think of it being any other way brought tears to Magdalena's eyes. She could not bear the thought of never seeing her family again. Surely there would be some other option for them if they had to flee Bessarabia, an option that didn't require them crossing the Atlantic Ocean.

Chapter Three

Winter of 1940 marched in with a fury and so did the German and Soviet armies throughout Europe as they attempted to add more territory. The Soviets fought the Finns all through the cold, icy months. Finally, on March 12, 1940, Finland ceded the northern shores of Lake Lagoda and the small Finnish coastline on the Arctic Sea to the Soviets. Germany had turned their attention to France and Great Britain. The two countries had declared war against Germany after Germany invaded Poland. The world watched and wondered exactly what Hitler and Stalin were up to.

It was Magdalena's afternoon to work at the grocery store the day Finland ceded to the Soviets. Several men had been gathered in the store around the radio to listen to updates on the war. The grocery store was one of the few places in the village with electricity and the only place with a radio. If you didn't hear it on the radio, you had to wait until it was reported in a newspaper. Jacob was among the men with his ear bent toward the radio, along with Magdalena's father, Gottlieb, and Albert, Jacob's brother.

"Gottlieb, what do make of this?" Albert asked.

"We have no choice but to wait and see what the Soviet Union's next move will be," Gottlieb replied patiently. "I know we're all anxious, but where would we go if we chose to leave now?"

"We could try to get visas and go to America," Jacob replied, causing all heads to turn his direction.

"America! How do you plan to move over 90,000 souls from Bessarabia to America?" Gottlieb huffed.

Jacob looked around at the stares he was receiving. He wished he could just eat the words back up, keep his opinion and hopes of one day going to America to himself. He knew no one else in Hoffnungstal shared his dream of such a journey. They were content to allow the Red Army to invade and do nothing to get their families out of harm's way.

"Brother, I don't think you mean this," Albert said. "Why would you leave our colony to travel to a place you know nothing about?"

"I know there is plenty of land and opportunities in America. Here in Bessarabia we live just to the west of a country that persecutes the German colonies under its power. Those Germans have been stripped of all religious freedoms, had their women raped, and thousands of them have ended their days in slave camps. All their crops they produce have to be shared with the rest of the Soviet people. It's not something I want any part of. In America, everyone is free to pursue whatever kind of life they choose."

"So they say," Albert retorted. "You've always been a dreamer, Jacob. Besides, Gottlieb's right. How could we move 90,000 people at once to a place so far away?"

Jacob knew there was no point in answering and the men went back to discussing the loss the Finns had incurred after such a harsh winter war. Jacob got out of his chair to help his wife with a customer, making sure she did not lift anything heavy. Little Ewald had been perched on his father's knee, while Erhard had listened intently at his father's shoulder. Jacob placed Ewald on the floor with his toys and went to retrieve the 25 pound bag of flour the customer had requested. Erhard was at the counter gathering the other items. Father and son carried the purchases to the waiting wagon.

"Would we really go to America, Vater?" Erhard asked when they were outside.

"If it meant keeping all of you safe, then yes, we would leave for America," Jacob answered without hesitation.

"But what about Oma and Opa Wallentine and Grieb?" Erhard questioned.

"Well, if they choose not to go, we would have to leave them behind," Jacob answered softly.

"And all my aunts, uncles and cousins, too?" Erhard asked.

"Yes, them too," Jacob replied. "Things are changing, Erhard. I feel a real sense of danger approaching. Of course, we cannot do anything until after the baby is born."

"Mutti looks pale," Erhard said.

"She hasn't felt well, Erhard, but she will feel better soon. Just three more months and the baby will come."

"Okay," Erhard answered, not sure if his vater was right.

Jacob and Erhard returned to the store and Erhard joined the men around the radio again. Jacob went to stand beside Magdalena, looking at her closely. Erhard had been correct. Magdalena was pale and appeared to be worn out.

"Are you feeling okay?" Jacob asked Magdalena, looking into her eyes for a truthful answer.

"Yes, I'm fine," Magdalena replied, trying to convince her own self along with Jacob. "Why do you ask?"

"You look a bit tired," Jacob replied.

"I didn't sleep well last night," Magdalena admitted, "and now with the recent radio report..."

"It will do no good to worry," Jacob reminded.

"I know, but I can't help but wonder if Romania will be the Soviet's next target," Magdalena said softly.

"We could be the Red Army's next target," Jacob replied, "but worrying over it won't change a thing. The store closes in fifteen minutes. You and Ewald go ahead home and I will lock up."

"There's no need for you to do that," Magdalena argued.

"I want you to go home and lie down," Jacob instructed, leaving no more room for discussion. "Erhard and I will do the evening milking when we leave the store, so we will be home in a couple hours. I want you to rest until then."

"Okay," Magdalena replied, thankful to be heading home. She gathered her coat while Jacob helped Ewald put his own coat on.

"Are we leaving, Mutti?" Ewald asked.

"You're going home," Jacob replied, "and I want you to allow your mutti to rest. Do you understand?"

"Yes, Vater," Ewald said. "I'll be very quiet so Mutti can rest."

"Good boy," Jacob said, opening the door of the store and sending his wife and son toward home.

Jacob locked up the store and he and Erhard started toward

the barn to do the evening milking. Albert fell in step with them, since he always shared in the chore. When they reached the barn, Albert's oldest son was already there waiting for them to arrive. The men and boys each knew their responsibility, and before long the rhythm made by streams of milk hitting the buckets could be heard. The cows added to the music by chewing their grain and mooing softly to their owners. The timing was a bit off, but the song was familiar.

Magdalena and Ewald made it home, and Magdalena sank onto a kitchen chair. Her back had ached through the night and all day today. Removing her shoes, Magdalena placed her feet on another chair. The pain subsided a bit and after twenty minutes, Magdalena decided a cup of tea would be nice. She would go lie down after she drank it, just as Jacob had instructed.

As she filled the kettle with water, a sharp pain shot through her abdomen. Placing the kettle in the sink, Magdalena grasped the edge of the counter until the pain passed. Was that a contraction? Surely that was not a contraction. It was way too early for her baby to be born. Stumbling back toward the kitchen chair, Magdalena grasped the back of it for stability.

"Ewald," Magdalena called to her small son who had gone to play in his bedroom.

"Yes, Mutti," Ewald answered.

"Please come here," Magdalena requested trying to remain calm.

Ewald hurried into the kitchen to see what his mutti needed. Even through his young, innocent eyes, Ewald could see something was wrong. Coming to her side, Ewald looked into his mutti's pale face. Her hands gripped the chair so tightly that her knuckles were white.

"What's wrong, Mutti?" Ewald asked.

Before Magdalena could answer, another pain gripped her. Clutching the chair and bending forward, Magdalena clenched her jaw to keep from screaming. She refused to scare Ewald more by giving in to the pain. As the contraction eased, Magdalena felt the unmistakable wetness of her water breaking. There was absolutely no doubt left of whether or not she was in labor and no hope of preventing a delivery.

"Mutti?" Ewald questioned, fear in his little voice.

"Ewald, Mutti needs you to do something for her," Magdalena said in gasps. "I need you to go to the barn and get Vater. Tell him I need him quickly, please."

"Okay," Ewald agreed. "I'll run fast, Mutti. You know how fast I can run, don't you?"

"Yes, Ewald, you're fast and I need you to hurry," Magdalena said through clenched teeth. "Now go!"

Ewald stared at his mutti for just a second. She rarely raised her voice, so he knew it was important he get his vater quickly. Rushing out the door, his feet barely touched the ground as he ran for the barn. Jacob heard Ewald hollering before his small son appeared. He knew something was seriously wrong and headed toward the barn entrance. Flinging the door open, Jacob saw Ewald running toward him at full speed.

"Vater, Vater, please come quick! Something is wrong with Mutti!"

Jacob wasted no time running toward the house with Erhard and Ewald on his heels. He found Magdalena gripping a kitchen chair with a puddle of water around her feet. Her face was pale and contorted with pain. There was no need to ask what was wrong. The anticipation of joy a new baby would bring was destined to end in sorrow. There would be no way to save this child who was making an entrance three months too soon.

"Erhard, I need you to go tell Oma Wallentine to come to our house. We need her immediately. Take your brother and leave him with Aunt Emilie. You go help finish the milking after delivering the message to Oma."

Erhard did as his vater instructed him without any questions. He did not understand what was happening but he knew his vater was frantic and needed him to obey immediately. Grabbing Ewald's coat and shoving his arms into it, he took one last look at his mutti before leading Ewald out the door. Running to Aunt Emilie's, Erhard quickly explained that something was wrong with his mutti and he needed to go get Oma. Emilie ushered Ewald in the front door and told Erhard to please hurry.

"Magdalena, I'm here," Jacob soothed, touching his wife's shoulder.

"The baby, it's coming," Magdalena said, the fear evident in her eyes. "My water has broken and there is nothing we can do to stop it!"

"Shh," Jacob comforted. "Erhard has gone for your mutti. She will be here soon."

Another contraction gripped Magdalena and she doubled up from the pain. Jacob rubbed her back and tried to comfort her, praying Rosina would come quickly. When the contraction ended, Jacob carried Magdalena to their bedroom. There, Jacob helped her change into a dry nightgown. Turning the covers back, Jacob held Magdalena's hand as she lowered herself on the bed. The contractions continued as did Jacob's prayers. Jacob had assisted with many births among the farm animals but this was different. He had no idea how to help his wife, and he couldn't even give words of encouragement that everything was going to be fine. They both knew it was much too soon for this little one to be born.

Rosina came through the kitchen door at a sprint. Going to the bedroom, she found Magdalena sobbing from the pain and sorrow that her baby was coming too soon. Taking charge, Rosina sent Jacob to gather towels and heat some water. As small as the baby had to be, she knew the delivery would probably be a short one.

Two agonizing hours later, Rosina delivered her first granddaughter. She was perfect in every way, except she was too young to survive. She never took her first breath. Rosina wrapped the baby in a blanket and handed her to Magdalena. Leaving the room, she called for Jacob to go to his wife. Together, they said good bye to their third child, a beautiful girl. Rosina walked down the street to get the pastor. He would need to record the birth in his records and prepare a burial.

On March 13, 1940, the colony of Hoffnungstal circled a very small grave. The wind blew cold and blustery as the pastor spoke words of comfort to the grieving family. Magdalena stood with Jacob's support, though her mother had told her to stay in bed, her sadness threatening to overwhelm her.

****

The reports on the radio and in the local newspaper continued to add to the uneasiness of the Germans in Bessarabia. On April 9, 1940, Germany finally decided their next course of action. They invaded Denmark and Norway. Denmark gave up immediately, but Norway chose to fight. The battle raged until

June 9th, when Norway fell to the Nazis.

Hitler did not waste any time in his quest to gain territory for his Greater Germany. On May 10th, even before Norway was defeated, the Nazis invaded France and the neutral Low Countries, who had not declared war. Victory came for the Nazis on June 22nd, just a few days after Norway ceded. France lost the northern half of its country to Germany on June 22nd, while Italy invaded the southern portion on June 21st. World War II was in full swing, with Japan causing unrest in the Pacific.

In Bessarabia everyone was on edge. Soviet forces were placed all along their eastern border, ready for the attack. The Romanian government was in a frenzy knowing they did not have the power to fight off the Red Army.

"The Red Army is sitting at our back door, and still your vater says to wait," Jacob complained to Magdalena. They were sitting at the kitchen table sharing a snack before bed. The boys were already asleep.

"I'm really afraid," Magdalena admitted, "but I don't know where we would flee to if we chose to leave."

"I should have gotten visas and moved us to America back in October," Jacob fumed. "Now we have nowhere to run to, and the enemy is breathing down our backs."

"We honestly have no choice but to wait and hope Hitler invites us to the Reich," Magdalena reasoned. "The other German colonies to the north that the Red Army invaded were invited back."

"But where will Hitler move us to?" Jacob said with frustration. "I cannot imagine him having room to relocate 90,000 people from Bessarabia, not to mention all those Germans who have already been moved back."

"If the Red Army invades and Hitler offers us refuge, I don't see how we could refuse," Magdalena said.

Jacob sighed heavily. "We couldn't. We would have to accept, but we will lose everything we've worked for in the process."

"But our family would be kept safe," Magdalena answered softly.

"Yes, our family would be safe," Jacob agreed. "At least I hope so."

"Let's get some rest," Magdalena suggested, collecting their empty mugs and the plate that had held cookies just moments before.

Jacob rose slowly from his chair and trudged after Magdalena to their bedroom. Crawling between the sheets he waited for sleep to come. He wished he could stop all the thoughts in his head at least until morning, but he could not make that happen. And then there were the many questions. Would the Red Army invade them? Surely that was inevitable. Why else would they be camped out along Romania's eastern border? Would the soldiers of the Red Army treat them cruelly, raping their women and killing their children? There was just too much to consider, and after two hours of running the scenarios through his mind, Jacob finally slipped into a fitful sleep. The rest didn't last long, as he bolted upright in bed in the wee hours of the morning. Magdalena awakened too, though she didn't know if it was Jacob who had caused it or something else.

"What is it, Jacob?" Magdalena asked.

"I thought I heard something," Jacob said, "but maybe it's just my mind tricking me. I haven't been asleep long, and I was dreaming I heard a plane flying low over our house."

"I don't hear anything," Magdalena said after listening for a minute.

"Go back to sleep," Jacob said. "I'm sorry I woke you."

"It's okay," Magdalena said, snuggling back under the covers.

Jacob lay back down beside his wife. He knew it would be another two hours before sleep claimed him again, and then it would be time to get up and start his day. Sighing heavily, Jacob rolled to his side and tried to get comfortable. Five minutes later, he knew a plane flying over had not been in his dream.

"Jacob, I hear a plane," Magdalena said, sitting up in the bed again.

"Yes, I hear it too," Jacob said.

"Why would a plane be flying over Hoffnungstal at this hour of night?"

"There is only one reason," Jacob replied.

"And what is that reason?" Magdalena asked, knowing full well the answer already.

"The pot that has been simmering has finally boiled over," Jacob said. "The Red Army has finally decided to make a move. The planes are probably carrying paratroopers."

"I hope they're not carrying bombs," Magdalena fretted.

"I don't believe they will bomb us," Jacob said. "The Soviets know the Romanians are not powerful enough to keep them from invading. They are smart enough not to bomb a piece of ground they hope to regain unless it becomes necessary."

"What are we going to do?" Magdalena asked.

"Wait until daylight," Jacob said. "We have no way to fight them and no hope of fleeing Bessarabia now."

"We must pray for the safety of everyone here in Bessarabia," Magdalena stated, knowing that was always an option.

"Yes, Magdalena, we will pray," Jacob whispered.

"Should I go start coffee brewing?" Magdalena asked.

"I suppose so," Jacob replied. "I'm sure neither one of us will be getting any more sleep this night."

"I could not possibly close my eyes knowing the enemy is amongst us," Magdalena said.

The morning of June 28th, 1940 dawned clear and sunny. It should have been a day to shock wheat, can green beans, and cut hay in the Hoffnungstal colony. Instead, it was a day of terror and uncertainty. The Red Army marched down the street and hung the Soviet flag from each business, leaving no question of whose rule they were now under. More soldiers came by land the next morning. The Romanians were given four days to pack up their belongings and leave the country. However, the Germans were allowed to stay. The Soviets were not friendly to them, but they weren't hostile either. This treatment just added to the colonist's confusion.

"What does it all mean?" Albert questioned at the town meeting Gottlieb had called.

"I wish I knew," Gottlieb answered, trying to think of words that would calm his village. "We have not been threatened in any way, although the Soviets have hung their flags everywhere. Maybe we will be offered the opportunity to return to the Reich like the Baltic Germans were."

"Where will they put all of us?" the senior Jacob questioned.

"Surely we wouldn't be invited to return if they have no place for us to go," Gottlieb pointed out. "Germany is aware of our plight. Hitler has plans of a Greater Germany. Maybe we will not be forgotten."

"But what if we are?" Albert questioned. "What happens then?"

"I wish I could tell you," Gottlieb sighed. "The only good news is that, for now, we are being left alone and allowed to live the same as before the Red Army invaded."

"But how long will that last?" Jacob inquired.

"They have not given me any information at this time," Gottlieb said. "We will just have to wait. In the meantime, we have grain ready for harvest. We will go about our daily business as usual. We cannot let the crops waste in the fields in hopes we won't be here to have need of them. That would be foolish and leave us starving this winter, should we still be here."

"The Mayor is right," Jacob Grieb senior concluded. "We have all heard the stories from the other side of that "iron curtain". We do not want to subject our families to starvation if we can do anything to prevent it. So, what we can do right now is bring in the harvest."

"I second that," Albert chimed in. "We will do what we can and pray Germany comes to our rescue."

"Let's all go home to our families and try to keep the peace," Gottlieb suggested. "We do not want to do anything that causes the Red Army to fight against us."

With those words, the meeting was adjourned. Jacob made his way toward home, hoping Magdalena would be waiting for him. He needed to talk to her and hear her words of wisdom. Woman or not, his wife was practical and could come up with some good plans. As he neared the house, Jacob could see the lamp burning at the kitchen table. Through the window, he could see Magdalena standing at the stove pulling a batch of cookies from the oven. As he opened the door, the smell of fresh baked cookies made his mouth water.

"Hullo, Jacob," Magdalena said while placing a plate of the fresh cookies on the table.

"Kind of late to be baking cookies, don't you think?" Jacob inquired.

"Well, we were out, and I know how you love your sweet snack each evening," Magdalena said with a smile.

"You know me well, Wife," Jacob chuckled.

"Besides, it took my mind off all that's happening around us," Magdalena admitted.

Snatching the first of many cookies to follow, Jacob took a seat at the table. He savored the flavor and waited for Magdalena to ask about the meeting. He knew she would, but the quietness was nice for the moment. Magdalena watched her husband eat two cookies then wash them down with a drink of cold milk. She decided it was time to glean the details of the meeting and find out the decision the men had come to.

"What was decided?" Magdalena asked.

"We wait and we harvest," Jacob replied dryly.

"So, we do nothing to protect ourselves?" Magdalena asked.

"We are not being threatened at the moment, so we do our daily chores as if the Red Army has not surrounded us."

"Does Vater think Hitler will invite us back to the Reich?"

"He hopes so. He doesn't know how to move our colony if we have no definite place to go. There are the other villages in Bessarabia to consider, too. The number of souls is believed to be over 90,000."

"90,000 people," Magdalena murmured. "We certainly don't want anyone to be left behind, but so many…"

"It would be quite an undertaking to move us all back to Germany," Jacob admitted. "I suppose getting visas to America would be impossible right now."

"I'm sure it would," Magdalena said. "Besides, even if we could leave, we wouldn't. The fate of our families would never be known and we can't leave them at such a time as this."

"Of course, you're right," Jacob admitted. "I just want to get us someplace safe."

"I know you do, Jacob, but we're all so closely knit together here in Hoffnungstal. We need to find a solution that benefits everyone."

"I just pray the solution comes soon," Jacob stated. "Waiting until something happens before having a plan is not how I like to do things."

"I suppose we will just have to be patient," Magdalena spoke softly.

"Yes, patience," Jacob agreed. "I just wish I had more of it."

"We will pray for patience and safety," Magdalena decided. "I know protecting us is at the top of your list, but we will have to go about it the best way. Packing up and leaving without any hope of a destination would be foolish."

Jacob knew Magdalena was right. As he looked at her across the table, he could see she was much too thin after the months of mourning. It seemed, however, that with the invasion of the Red Army five days ago came a new purpose for Magdalena. She could not bring the precious baby girl back, and she found comfort knowing she was safe in Jesus arms. With that thought and the new crisis that had developed, she seemed to focus on protecting the two sons that were alive and well.

****

Rosina had spent the evening reading Isabella's letters again. She was to the last one, the one she had chosen not to read in October. Tonight, however, she was determined to finish them all. Bracing herself for the heartache, Rosina began to read that final letter.

April 1938

Dearest Sister,

We had a small amount of peace for a time here in Kronau and were able to reestablish some symbolism of worship. During that time our Lutheran pastor met with us in our homes, and we were in in constant prayer for an end to this Godless government. Now, the meetings have ceased, because there is not a pastor left in all of Kronau to lead us.

We live on a collective bargain here in the Black Sea region, which means the government takes a portion of everything we grow, even if it leaves us short of food for ourselves. We have tried to comply without complaint just to keep the peace. However, things are changing for the worse again.

Since 1929, there has been an aggressive attack on religion more than ever before. Our pastors are being arrested at an alarming rate. They are being sent to slave labor camps for made up crimes or for not being able to pay the enormous taxes put upon them. We have no clergy left here in our village. All of our schools are now anti-religious instead of just non-religious. They teach the children the ideals of Communism starting at a very young age. The observance of Christmas has even been stripped from us and we work seven days a week, including Sundays. There is a Godless movement here like none I have ever seen. There is actually a newspaper called "The Godless" that circulates everywhere here in Russia.

Men are being deported to slave camps on a daily basis all around us. Their oldest sons are sent along with them. The women and children are being sent to Siberia, separated forever. The women are forced to eke out a living for their children in the harshest of living conditions. This is the fate of all those who cannot produce the amount of grain expected of them.

We suffered another famine in 1933 due to a drought in 1928, 1931 and 1932 and by the deportation of our most skilled farmers to slave labor camps. We have been forced into collectives and the government takes more than their share. All of our storehouses of grain have been wiped out. We will submit to this new way of life or starve fighting against it. Stalin will make sure of it.

Stalin, having starved, deported and beaten the peasants into submission, seems to have turned his attention toward his own government. He had the Leningrad party boss, Serge Kirov, assassinated in December 1934. This has been followed by vast numbers of arrest, believed to be in the thousands. The men most feared by Stalin have been executed while the others waste away their lives in slave camps. He sees everyone as a spy and opposes Hitler most of all. Lenin was a mild form of cruelty compared to the acts of Stalin.

I write this letter in April, 1938. I don't know how I will get it to you, for we are not allowed any contact with the outside world. However, I needed someone on the outside to know the truth of what has happened to the Germans living under the rule of Stalin. If someone doesn't write these events down, no one will believe us later. Of course, at the rate we are being purged, there may be no one left alive to tell the story.

I will not tell you any of my personal information for fear it will be used to trace this letter back to me. It would mean death for me and everyone dear to me here. I pray you and the family are

*well. I am so thankful you are on the outside of the "iron curtain".
At least that gives me hope that some of my family is safe and well.*

*Give my love to everyone. Keep praying for us daily as we
struggle to survive. May peace find us again and God be welcomed
back into our midst. Until then, He will dwell in our hearts and
hear our prayers spoken in whispers.*

Rosina folded the letter and placed it with the others. All of
the letters had reached Rosina, though in different ways. The first
letter was sent out before the Great War, and the second letter was
delivered between the Tsar stepping from power and the new
government being installed. The third letter had been carried out
by a sympathetic German soldier, as the troops were being forced
out. The fourth had found its way to her through the help of an
American Relief Worker who had met Isabella while providing
food for the starving colonists. The last one had been delivered by
a Lutheran pastor, who had escaped from Russia.

The Lutheran pastor had passed through the Black Sea
region and had been hidden by Isabella and her family for a few
days. Along with scraping together food provisions for the
continuation of his journey, Isabella had entrusted the letter to him.
The pastor knew that having the letter on him would not be the
thing that got him killed. The fact that he was trying to escape
would be reason enough.

The pastor was able to sneak into the hull of a ship on the
Black Sea. Upon docking in Bulgaria, the pastor was able to obtain
visas and passage to North America. Before leaving the Bulgaria
region, he had remembered Isabella's kindness and returned the
favor by sending the letter to Rosina. He included a small note of
his own, stating that Isabella, Daniel and their two children were as
well as could be expected, under the circumstances.

It had been almost two years since the last letter had reached
Rosina. She had no idea how her sister was and no way to find out.
The information she really needed to get to Isabella was that, after
over 120 years of their ancestors living in Bessarabia, they may
have to leave. Rosina would lose contact with Isabella forever.
Rosina needed Isabella to know that the Red Army had finally
walked through the "iron curtain".

Chapter Four

Bessarabia remained occupied by the Red Army all through the summer of 1940. The Germans brought in their grain crop, ground their flour and sold any extra. Gardens were planted and harvested, with jars of can goods lining every homes cellar. The future of the Germans living in Hoffnungstal was still uncertain. There had been some propaganda reports that the newspapers had picked up on. They stated that, yes, Germany was aware of the plight of the Germans in Bessarabia. They reported that no harm had come to those Germans and plans were being made to bring them back to the Reich. The reports promised to compensate the Bessarabia Germans for everything they would leave behind. However, there was no definite time of when all this would take place.

The citizens of Hoffnungstal were on edge, to say the least. Men gathered around the short wave radio at the grocery store every chance they could. The reports that came in confirmed that the Soviets had not yet satisfied their hunger to retrieve the territories they had lost as a result of being defeated in the Great War.

On June 14, 1940 they moved troops to occupy the Baltic States, eventually annexing them as Soviet Republics the first week of August. This move by the Soviets did nothing to ease the minds of the Germans in Bessarabia. How easy it would be for Stalin to force them to become citizens of the Soviet Union, taking them back into the country they had been a part of 22 years before.

Reports on the war to the west stated that combat began between Britain and Germany on July 10, 1940. These battles were being fought mostly in the air and from the radio and newspaper reports, it was hard to decide who had the upper hand. Both sides had lost several planes and many soldiers, but Germany's losses were higher. The real concern for the villages of Bessarabia was that Hitler's attention would be focused on those battle plans, and he might forget about them.

"I know we are really not Hitler's concern," Magdalena told her mutti, "but I truly hope he gets us out of this situation."

"Going to Germany may not be a good choice," Rosina replied, "but we have no other options. Who else would even attempt to relocate 90,000 people all at one time? And what will Hitler do with us once we reach Germany?"

Magdalena looked up from the green beans she was snapping while sitting on her porch. Mutti and Emilie had come with their green beans, too. They would can them together to make the work easier. It was the way of the colonies. The women joined together to make their work lighter and to enjoy the fellowship with other women. The men helped one another plant and harvest. Sharing the work was just the Germans way of life here in this village. Magdalena now worried if all that would be lost if they moved back to Germany.

"I think about that, too," Emilie admitted. "Where will we live when we get to Germany? Will we all be separated?"

"Surely if Hitler is inviting us back he has plans for our housing," Magdalena said. "Why would he invite us back if he hasn't figured out where we will live once we get there?"

"I honestly don't see how he can accommodate all of us," Rosina interjected, "and we must remember we are not the only ones. The Baltic Germans have already gone back."

"I wish we could get an eyewitness report about how the Baltic Germans were treated when they returned and where they are living," Magdalena said.

"What difference would it make, Sister," Emilie replied. "Do we really have any choice but to return if Hitler offers?"

"I suppose not," Magdalena admitted. "We are between a rock and a hard place here. If we stay and keep our land and homes we will be forced back into the Soviet Union. If we go back to Germany, we face the uncertainty of where we will live and how we will earn an income."

"We also have to think about traveling all that way back to Germany," Rosina added. "It will be a long journey. I worry about how we will get there."

"You're right, Mutti, we will have to figure out a way for us to travel there," Emilie said thoughtfully. "Do you suppose we will go by wagons?"

"I honestly don't see how we could make the journey any other way," Rosina said. "To get us all on trains would be impossible. Besides, there would not be a train rail that could take us the full distance. We would eventually have to walk. How could we take any belongings if we were to do that?"

"That's true," Magdalena stated. "Though even if we go by wagon, there will only be a few things we can take with us."

"I suppose we should start making a list of what we must not leave behind," Rosina said. "That way, when and if the time comes, we will be prepared to pack the most important things."

"That's a gut idea, Mutti," Emilie replied.

"And now we must work on these beans or we won't get finished today," Rosina said laughing.

Emilie's new baby boy, Klaus, had been asleep in a basket on the porch. He chose that moment to wake up and demand to be fed and changed. Emilie scooped him up and headed into Magdalena's house to care for him. Magdalena followed her with her eyes and her heart ached to be doing the same thing. Rosina watched the scene from her rocking chair.

"I know it's still hard," Rosina began, "but I promise, time will ease the pain."

Magdalena looked at her mutti with tears brimming in her eyes. She knew her mutti had buried a child, too, and her wisdom came through experience. Nodding her head, Magdalena turned her attention fully to the green beans that needed snapping, and Rosina did the same. Magdalena held out hope that there would be another child for her and Jacob somewhere farther down their river of life.

****

Though the war still raged between Britain and Germany, Hitler did not forget the Germans in Bessarabia who had been invaded by the Red Army. On September 5, 1940 a German-Soviet agreement was signed to allow the Germans in Bessarabia the choice to return to the Reich. Jacob came into the grocery store to quite a commotion. Everyone was talking at once and no one was really listening. In their hands they held papers and whatever was written on them was causing the excitement.

"What's happening?" Jacob asked Magdalena, who was standing behind the counter reading the papers, too.

"It seems we are leaving for Germany soon," Magdalena informed him. "German troops are here in Bessarabia and dropped these papers off to be distributed throughout the village."

Jacob knew an agreement had been signed just days ago but did not know any of the particulars of how or when they would leave for the fatherland.

"What's on the papers?" Jacob asked.

"Instructions," Magdalena answered handing hers over to Jacob.

Jacob took the papers offered by Magdalena and plopped down on the stool behind the counter. The papers stated that each family was to list the amount of land they had in Bessarabia and the property they owned. They were promised compensation for these things. Also, each family had to provide a family tree back four generations. The local pastor had to verify that this was indeed their correct genealogy and they were true German descendants. If this could not be proven, then that family would not be allowed to make the journey. Each family was responsible for bringing their required documents with them to Germany. It was mandatory. The journey would be made by land. Each family was allowed to bring one wagonload of goods and absolutely no more. No livestock was to be brought except the animals used to pull the wagon. No exceptions!

"Looks as if we best get to packing," Jacob said to Magdalena.

"Only one wagon load," Magdalena fretted. "How will we ever decide what to leave and what to take with us?"

"I suppose we will take our children, clothes and cooking utensils," Jacob answered. "It states here we will be compensated for everything we leave behind. We will just have to start fresh."

Magdalena looked around the store at her whole family discussing the documents. Vater and Mutti were there along with her younger brothers, Emil and Edward. Albert and Emilie had joined the group with their children. Jacob's parents, along with their younger children Olof, Mathilda, Maria, and Hulda stood grouped together perusing the papers. Along with Magdalena's family, other villagers had stopped in to discuss their documents with Gottlieb, the mayor. They seemed to all be speaking at once as they tried to make sense of all the requirements. Suddenly, Gottlieb's booming voice brought a halt to all the chatter.

"We will have a meeting tonight," Gottlieb announced. "These documents will be read over and explained thoroughly. Every husband will understand exactly what it is he needs to do to get his family to Germany safely. I will make sure our pastor attends so he can help us draw up the required four generation family trees. I will go speak to one of the German officers now to get full instructions."

Everyone nodded in agreement and began to leave for their homes. There were many decisions each family would have to make. Leaving all they had acquired here in Bessarabia would be very difficult. Each family in Bessarabia owned over a hundred years of wealth, which had been added to generation by generation. There was good farm land, not to mention established vineyards. There were businesses that had grown into successful sources of income. The thought of leaving it all and attempting to start over in a country their ancestors had chosen to leave was overwhelming. However, staying in the occupied territory was not an option. No one even suggested they do so.

In the other 149 German settlements throughout Bessarabia, it was much the same as in Hoffnungstal. They mourned leaving this beautiful area they had called home for over 120 years but to stay would be foolish. They had all heard stories of how the German colonies in the Soviet Union had been treated since the end of the Great War and would not take any chances in becoming part of that persecution. The journey would be hard and uncertain but the threat of being trapped here with the Red Army spurred them into action.

That evening, Magdalena was waiting for Jacob to come home from his meeting. Cookies were already on the table and milk was poured in the mugs. Pouring the milk had caused her to consider what would become of the dairy herd upon their leaving. The thought weighed heavy on Magdalena's mind. What would become of all the livestock left behind at their departure? It was definitely a question for Jacob upon his return.

Magdalena slipped quietly out the front door so she didn't wake the boys. Sitting down in a rocking chair on the porch, she took in her surroundings in the waning light. Would they ever find a place as beautiful again? The only thing that took away from the sight was the red flags the Soviet troops had placed all along the road soon after the invasion. It was a constant reminder that they indeed were here in their midst. The Red Army had not shown any aggression toward the Germans in Bessarabia, but the fact the Red Army disliked them was evident on their faces.

Magdalena could make out the men leaving the building where the meeting was held and could hear discussions as they made their way home. She was sure her vater was weary from hearing so many questions this evening, many of which he had no answers for. Magdalena knew her vater was a good mayor and had always given his best to the village of Hoffnungstal. He always said that being a good leader took time and patience, like making a fine wine.

The thought of her vater's comment about wine took Magdalena back to her childhood. She remembered how she loved walking through the vineyard in the spring, when the vines were in full bloom. The bees buzzed a happy tune flitting from blossom to blossom. When summer came and the vines became burdened with grapes, the sweet smell would cause her mouth to water. Magdalena's vater would always press the grapes and bottle grape juice for his children first. This is what they drank until they were old enough to enjoy the "gut stuff". After the juice for the children was canned, the process of making the finest wine in the region would begin. The recipe and knowledge to create the fine wine had been passed from generation to generation, with each one perfecting it just a little. Magdalena's brothers were now being taught the art of making the perfect wine. Sadly, they would be the last generation to do so here in Bessarabia.

The wine the Wallentine family produced was never meant for drunkenness. Magdalena's vater had no tolerance for such things and dealt with it harshly in Hoffnungstal. He always said "drunkenness leads to other sins" and therefore it was not acceptable. No, the wine was not created for such poor behavior. It was created for celebrations and weddings and days of joy. It was made to be sipped around a table with family and friends, thankful for the blessings God had given them. These things, and the income it provided for the Wallentine family, were why so much time and precision were taken in its creation.

Magdalena was drawn back to the present as Jacob approached the house. He and his brother Albert were deep in conversation. The sound of their voices caused Magdalena to startle from her reminiscing.

"So, what do we list as assets?" Albert asked. "Vater will list the mill, grocery store, and dairy herd."

"I suppose just our homes and other livestock, plus the land we own ourselves," Jacob answered.

"What if something happens to Vater on the way back to Germany?" Albert inquired. "Will we be allowed to claim the things on his list?"

"Well, it will probably go to Olof," Jacob said, referring to their younger brother. "He will inherit the land and dairy herd anyway since he is the youngest son. Of course, we will still own one third of the mill and grocery store."

"I suppose that's right," Albert admitted. "I just don't see how Hitler plans to compensate for everything that's left behind."

"Whether he does or doesn't is really not what's pushing us to make this journey," Jacob reminded Albert while nodding to the red flags along the road.

"True," Albert agreed. "I suppose we should just be thankful we have a place to go to instead of being forced back into the Soviet Union."

Jacob looked around nervously, making sure there were no outsiders lurking about. Looking back to Albert he shook his head, indicating that speaking of the Red Army in the open might not be a good idea. Though they had not been mistreated as of yet, the situation could always change. Why Stalin was being so generous and allowing them to flee was still an unanswered question. Albert agreed with a nod and continued on toward his home as Jacob stepped onto the low porch of his own home and he and Magdalena went inside.

"What will happen to the dairy herd?" Magdalena blurted before Jacob could even get sit down to the table.

"I honestly don't know, Magdalena," Jacob sighed.

"Has our departure date been set?"

"We leave in three weeks," Jacob replied. "Each of the families must create their four generation family tree and the pastor will confirm it with his signature. He will bring the record books, in case there are any disputes once we get to Germany."

"So, what will we take?" Magdalena questioned.

"Bare necessities," Jacob answered. "We won't have room for anything else."

"I will start sorting and packing what we will take with us," Magdalena said.

"Remember, it all has to fit in one wagon and you must leave room for you and the boys to ride, too," Jacob informed her.

"120 years here and we all will leave with no more than what our ancestors came with," Magdalena lamented.

"But we will have each other and escape Communism," Jacob reminded softly.

"True," Magdalena agreed, "but I'm not so sure Hitler is the leader we believe him to be. The newspapers reported how harshly the Polish people were treated after the German troops invaded. He may treat his own people well, but he doesn't seem to have any empathy for other ethnic groups."

"Sometimes things get brutal in wartime," Jacob reminded. "We have heard some of the stories those who returned from the Great War told. We both had uncles who were forced into combat during that time. Their accounts of the events during that time did not paint a pretty picture."

"I suppose," Magdalena agreed, but her mind was not at ease. There was something about Adolf Hitler that made her nervous. She just didn't know exactly what that was yet.

Chapter Five

The great exodus began the first week of October, 1940. The German troops led the way. 150 German settlements, totaling 93,000 people, began a journey with horse drawn wagons from Bessarabia, Romania to an unknown destination in Germany. What they would find at the end of the trip was absolutely unknown. In Hoffnungstal the night before, the Lutheran church had been packed as the village held their last service. Communion was taken, using wine created by the Wallentine family. A vintage bottle had been pulled from the cellar for the occasion, one that went back four generations. The service was a very solemn one as the villagers mentally and spiritually prepared themselves for what lay ahead.

Each German family of Bessarabia had packed enough food, water, clothing, blankets, and cooking utensils for the trip and hardly anything else. There just wasn't room to take more than the bare necessities. The trek was long and weary and sleeping on the ground grew old quickly. The travelers were not accustomed to living life out of the back of a wagon and cooking each evening meal over open fires. Tempers flared easily and fights broke out often.

The Grieb and Wallentine wagons, along with a few others, had tarps over them to keep the elements from soaking their packed clothing and blankets. The rest weren't so fortunate. On cold, rainy days, those without tarps had no hope of a dry change of clothes at day's end. They would have to dry out the best they could by the campfire when the wagons stopped for the night. On clear, sunny days, the sides of wagons were strewn with wet clothes, allowing them to dry as the caravan pushed on toward

Germany.

Gottlieb Wallentine, who had been plagued with breathing problems the past several years, was especially troubled by the dust the caravan created. He spent most of his day riding on the wagon with a cloth over his mouth and nose. At night he could be heard wheezing from five wagons away, the labor of each breath evident by the sound. Rosina was particularly worried and tried different remedies, none of which brought much relief.

Magdalena couldn't help but think how they were traveling the 800 miles back to Germany with horse and wagon, the same type of transportation their ancestors had used in 1818. It made no difference that it was over 120 years later and there were now trains, planes, and automobiles. The German colonies had lived off the land and had relied on beasts to help with the work. They used wagons and horses for all their needs and therefore, that was their only means of returning to Germany.

The nights had grown quite cold before the group of displaced Germans reached their destination. Families slept close together wrapped tightly in blankets to keep warm. Jacob and Magdalena kept four year old Ewald and nine year old Erhard between them at night, attempting to ward off the cold. Even so, Erhard had developed a terrible cough that was aggravated by the constant dust. Magdalena prayed that it wouldn't grow worse. There were no doctors or medicine available to help, should that happen.

Finally reaching Germany in mid- December, 1940, everyone was relieved the journey had come to an end. Looking about them for housing, all the Germans saw were long lines of tents. It became clear quite quickly that those tents were intended for their lodging. Winters in Bessarabia had been cold but Germany winters were even colder. How could they be expected to live in tents during the coldest part of the year?

"Tents?" Jacob questioned. "They surely do not expect us to live through the winter in tents."

"It will be so cold," Magdalena fretted.

The murmurings could be heard throughout the group. To think they had been invited back with the promise that everything they left behind would be compensated for. They had traveled nearly 800 miles, through rain, sleet and dust, slept shivering on the ground each night and now they arrived to a field full of tents. It was more than the weary German refugees could stand. Their nice, warm homes in Bessarabia were inviting them back, making them forget why they had fled them. The disbelief of the lodging they were being provided became a roar as angry, road weary people began to protest. It seemed control would be lost, until German soldiers began firing their weapons into the air causing silence to fall immediately.

"This is your home for now," a German commander screamed. "You will not cause trouble about it or you will be faced with imprisonment! Our soldiers are living in tents while they fight to make us a Greater Germany. You do not deserve better treatment than they! You're all just peasant farmers, and you will make do with what's been provided for you."

The harshness of his words was passed back through the crowd to those not close enough to hear them first hand. The German troops had encircled the group, making it very clear there would be no uprising. Every family was made to stand together until a tent could be assigned to them. Each tent would house ten people, no less. Names were taken down and charted as to which tent they occupied. Every man, woman and child was accounted for.

Jacob and Magdalena were joined in their tent by Albert and Emilie. Including the children, it made ten occupants. The boys, Erhard, Ewald, Albert, Richard, and Erwin all slept together in the center. The adults slept on the outside of them to try and keep them warm. Baby Klaus was snuggled close to his mother each night. Gottlieb and Rosina's tent was to the left of Jacob and Magdalena's. It housed Magdalena's parents along with her twin younger brothers, Emil and Edward. Cousins had joined to bring the number to ten. Jacob and Juliana Grieb, Jacob's parents, were in the tent to the right. Along with Jacob's parents, it housed his three sisters Mathilda, Maria, and Hulda and his youngest brother, Olof. Juliana's youngest sister and her husband joined the tent with their two children.

The first night in the camp the Griebs and Wallentines ate the food left in their wagons, which wasn't much. The next day they stood in line to receive the one meal provided for them each day. The meal consisted of one potato, one bowl of soup, and one piece of bread per person. The soup was thin and tasteless and the bread was stale and dry. The meal provided very little nourishment, especially when trying to survive in cold, harsh conditions. The men and women would become weak while the children became ill on such meager rations.

By the fourth day all the names and ages of each German family who had returned had been gone over by the government. Troops came to the camp and began drafting all the young men into the Nazi army. There would be no choice in the matter. They had been taken in as citizens of Germany upon their arrival and would now serve their country. As the troops stopped in front of Gottlieb and Rosina Wallentine's tent, Rosina began to protest. Gottlieb quickly placed his hand on her arm to warn her to stop. Silent tears streamed down Rosina's face as Edward and Emil was taken away. The uncertainty of their fate caused Rosina to collapse in Gottlieb's arms as her sons were led away.

"Rosina, I know you're heartbroken, and I am as well," Gottlieb comforted, "but we must be careful. I believe we have entered a hostile country and must not voice our opinions out loud. It could get us killed."

This warning was whispered in Rosina's ear as Gottlieb held her close. The truth of his words made her shiver. What had they walked into? Had they escaped the clutches of one madman, Stalin, to run into the open arms of another by the name of Hitler? As Rosina buried her face into Gottlieb's shoulder, she could hear other mothers' wailing throughout the camp as their sons were stripped from them. Suddenly, a cry of pain pierced the air, drowning out the sound of the other weeping women. Rosina looked up to see a woman a few tents down being helped up from the ground. Blood dripped from her face, soaking into her coat. Above the woman a German soldier stood sneering, the butt of his gun raised to strike her again if she continued to object. While her son was led away silent tears mingled with the blood on her face, but she did not make another sound. Burying her face once more, Rosina wondered where this journey had taken them, and what price they would pay for coming back to the Reich.

****

It didn't take long for Jacob Grieb to realize the dire situation his family was in. After two weeks of eating only the meager meal provided for them, the children's eyes were sunk in with dark circles surrounding them. The adults didn't look much better. He refused to stand by and watch his family suffer and decided to take matters into his own hands.

"I'm going to walk into town and see if I can find a job," Jacob informed Magdalena.

"But we have been instructed not to leave," Magdalena reminded, fear evident in her voice.

"I know, but we are all going to starve," Jacob stated. "We cannot survive on a potato, bowl of soup and piece of bread!"

"The children are already suffering from the lack of proper nutrition," Magdalena agreed, "but we have been given orders to stay put. Maybe they will move us soon."

"I can't wait, Magdalena," Jacob said. "I will not watch my family go hungry if there is anything at all I can do about it."

"I'm afraid, Jacob," Magdalena admitted for the first time.

"Me too," Jacob said, "but being scared won't stop me from trying to feed my family. I will go to town and look for a job in the morning at first light."

"Jacob, you must eat," Magdalena protested. "If you leave that early the meal will not have been served yet."

"If I wait until after we receive our meal it will be too light out to leave the camp without being seen," Jacob pointed out. "I'll be fine. Missing one meal won't kill me, especially since the meal is barely enough to keep a person alive. Our children and Albert's children need more nourishment, along with everyone else dear to us. I must do this, Magdalena."

"I will pray for your safety," Magdalena replied softly, knowing full well that Jacob was right. She also knew once Jacob set his mind to something, he was going to do it. It would not matter how much pleading she did.

Jacob lay awake long after darkness covered the camp. He had never had to watch his family suffer. With the farm, grocery store, mill, and dairy herd, there had always been enough food. They had never gone hungry. He wished now that they had left more clothes in Bessarabia and brought more food. If only he would have known what they would face here in Germany, he would have come more prepared. So much had been left behind in Bessarabia, so little had been found here in Germany.

Morning light had barely touched the earth as Jacob made his way out of the camp toward town. He prayed with each step that he would not get caught and that he would find a job. He covered the mile to town quickly. The group of Germans from Bessarabia had traveled through the town on their way to the camp. It was how Jacob knew how close it was and that the possibility of finding employment could be as close as a fifteen minute walk. Entering the town, Jacob stopped at the first factory he came to. Jacob slipped into the office door and walked to the counter. The man behind the desk looked up and greeted him.

"I was wondering if you might have any job openings." Jacob inquired.

"Yes, we actually do," the man said with a smile. "How soon could you start?"

"Immediately," Jacob assured.

"Fine," the man said rising from his chair. "I just had a man quit yesterday and need the position filled. It must be your lucky day. Where are you from?"

"I just moved here from Bessarabia, Romania," Jacob said, hoping that would satisfy the man's curiosity.

"You must be part of the Germans who were relocated due to the Red Army invasion," the man said. "Such troublesome times we are in right now."

"Yes, very troublesome," Jacob agreed.

"You look like a hardworking, honest man," the factory owner replied. "Follow me and I'll show you the job I have available. The other men will show you the ropes. I'm sure you will be able to perform the task in no time."

Jacob whispered a prayer of thanks as he followed the man into the loud interior of the factory. It looked as if the production was in full swing and the final product appeared to be metal parts used on tanks. Jacob had never worked with metal but knew he would do his best to learn quickly and do the job well. His family's lives depended on it. By the end of the day, Jacob had caught on to his part in the production. He had also met some other workers who seemed friendly. One was a Jewish man who wore a yellow star on his shirt. The star read Jude and Jacob wondered why he wore it. The man had shared his lunch with Jacob but Jacob did not feel comfortable asking about the star.

Jacob returned to the tent after darkness fell so he would not be seen, and Magdalena greeted him. "I've been worried," Magdalena whispered trying not to wake the children. Albert and Emilie had stepped over to Gottlieb and Rosina's tent to visit awhile.

"I found a job," Jacob told her. "It's in a factory and should pay enough to at least keep us fed."

"I thought the German troops had arrested you for leaving the camp," Magdalena whispered.

"No, no one saw me," Jacob assured. "I will leave before first light and return after dark. It will make it safer that way."

"It's such a long day, though," Magdalena worried.

"Magdalena, I'm used to long days," Jacob reminded. "My day has always started at daybreak with milking cows and the work continued until evening. I will be fine."

"Did you get something to eat?"

"Yes, a Jewish man who works beside me shared his lunch," Jacob told her.

"A Jewish man? We normally don't associate with Jewish people."

"Well, that was in Bessarabia," Jacob said. "The man was very nice, and without his kindness, I would have gone hungry today. The oddest thing, though. He wore this yellow star on his shirt, as did every Jewish man in the factory."

"A yellow star?" Magdalena questioned.

"Yes, like the Star of David," Jacob confirmed. "I didn't feel comfortable asking about it today, but maybe I will tomorrow."

"That is a very strange thing," Magdalena stated. "I wonder what's it's for."

"I don't know," Jacob said. "Maybe it's Jewish pride. Maybe that's why they all wear one."

"Maybe," Magdalena agreed, "but something tells me there's more to it than that."

"You're probably right," Jacob said. "I'm going to bed now. Morning will come early and I didn't sleep well last night."

Magdalena watched as Jacob crawled under the blankets and fell asleep immediately. She was thankful he had gotten a job but was worried for his safety. She never thought she would find herself in such a situation.

Magdalena crawled under the covers beside Jacob and lay in

the dark thinking about home. The last night they were in Bessarabia Jacob had turned the dairy herd to pasture. The next morning as they prepared to leave, they could hear them bawling to be milked. Magdalena had finally covered her ears as they left their home forever. She wondered now what had become of the herd and the other livestock. Was someone living in her home? Would the wheel on the mill ever make music again and if so, for whom would it sing? Who would listen to the buzz of the bees in the vineyard come spring? Who would tend the vines, pruning them just right? The thoughts were endless, and she finally slipped into slumber with the memory of how the sun kissed the ripe grapes in summertime.

Jacob awakened at first light just as his body had been programmed to do his whole life. Slipping from the covers, careful not to wake anyone, Jacob readied himself for work. As Jacob was lacing his boots, Albert whispered from his corner of the tent.

"Jacob, were you able to get a job?"

"Yes," Jacob whispered back. "At least maybe we won't starve now."

"Check today and see if there's an opening for me," Albert requested. "With both of us working, we could feed everyone in all three tents our families occupy, maybe more. Besides, it has to be better than sitting around here all day."

"Okay, I will check," Jacob agreed, and with that he slipped from the tent.

Jacob found his second day on the job to be much easier. He had learned well and his boss was pleased with his progress. When lunchtime came, the Jewish man again shared his food.

"So, what's your name?" the Jewish man inquired.

"Jacob. And yours?"

"Ezra," the man replied.

Jacob could stand it no longer. Before he could think he blurted the question. "Why do you wear the star?"

Ezra looked stunned for a moment. Looking around to see who was listening, Ezra leaned close to Jacob's ear. "Where are you from? I thought everyone in Germany knew why all Jews wear the yellow star."

"I just arrived here from Bessarabia," Jacob informed Ezra. "We were brought here after the Red Army occupied that part of

Romania. Hitler invited us back to Germany where our ancestors came from 120 years ago."

"That explains it," Ezra stated.

Jacob waited for Ezra to continue, but no more discussion of the star came. Upon returning to work, Ezra moved close to Jacob.

"The star is to signify that I am a Jew," Ezra whispered. "Hitler stripped our citizenship in 1936, and we have been treated unfairly ever since. The star has been mandatory since the war began, so we can be arrested and put in a camp on a whim."

Jacob stared at Ezra in horror. Could this really be true? Was Hitler really such a cold hearted person as to treat an ethnic group poorly just because he didn't like them?

"What kind of camp?" Jacob whispered upon finding his voice.

"A concentration camp," Ezra informed him. "Those who are taken away never return."

"What happens to them?" Jacob asked.

"We really don't know," Ezra admitted. "Some Jews have gone into hiding to avoid being put in the camps but that puts good hearted people at risk. When someone is discovered hiding Jews, they are taken to concentration camps, too."

With this said Ezra went back to his work area, leaving Jacob to mull over this new information. The list of things fueling Jacob's concern over how Hitler treated people was growing fast. First, Jacob's family was invited back to Germany and expected to live through the winter in tents. Then, the scarce amount of food provided for them wouldn't keep a rat alive. Now, Jacob had learned that Adolf Hitler stripped a group of people of their citizenship and placed them in prisons for no reason other than the fact they were Jewish. Jacob was coming to realize that Adolf Hitler was a madman and it had only taken two short weeks to figure this out.

Before leaving work for the day, Jacob inquired about a position for his brother, Albert. He was told nothing was available at the moment but he would be informed as soon as something opened up.

"How was your day?" Magdalena asked as Jacob entered the dark tent.

"It was fine," Jacob answered, realizing he would have to

wait until later to tell Magdalena that he had found out what the yellow star meant.

"Vater, Vater," Ewald hollered while running to his father arms.

"Quiet Ewald," Jacob cautioned gently as he scooped him up. "We do not want to bring attention to our tent."

"We've missed you, Vater," Erhard said.

"I've missed you, too," Jacob assured. "I'm glad you waited up for me."

After Jacob spent some time with the boys, Magdalena put them to bed. Emilie had already curled up with Klaus and they were asleep, along with her other boys. Within minutes, Ewald and Erhard slipped to dreamland. Jacob motioned for Albert and Magdalena to follow him. Leaving their tent, they slipped into Gottlieb and Rosina's tent next door. Everyone was still awake and talking quietly. A lamp had been lit to cast a bit of light in the tent. After Edward and Emil had been taken for the Nazi army, no one else was sent to replace their absence. Everyone had already been settled into tents, so moving someone was not necessary.

"Jacob," Gottlieb greeted. "We've been missing you around here."

"Yes, well hopefully I will be able to bring some food before we starve," Jacob answered. "I have obtained a job in town."

"This is what Magdalena told us," Rosina said. "We will welcome the food but we are concerned for your safety."

"I will be fine," Jacob assured them, "much better off than the Jews living here."

"What do you mean?" Gottlieb asked.

"I have made a discovery," Jacob informed them, "one that does not settle well with me."

"Speak softly, Jacob," Gottlieb warned.

"Yes, of course," Jacob agreed, reigning in his anger.

"So, what is this discovery?" Gottlieb questioned, ever the leader he was known for.

"I work beside a Jewish man," Jacob began. "He wears a yellow star on his shirt, as does every other Jew working in the factory. Today I asked him about it."

"What did he tell you?" Magdalena asked, anxious to know the answer.

"It seems Hitler stripped all Jews of their citizenship in 1936. Since the war began, he has required every Jew to wear the Star of David on their chest. It signifies that they are Jewish. Ezra, the man who works beside me, informed me that Jews are arrested and taken to concentration camps, even if they have done nothing wrong. They live in fear at all times."

"This is terrible," Albert whispered. "What is to become of us? Will we be hauled away to a concentration camp, too?"

"I hope not," Jacob answered. "However, it is very clear that Hitler takes not following his orders seriously. Ezra tells me that some Germans have been sympathetic of their Jewish neighbors and have begun hiding them. If they are discovered, the Germans will be hauled to concentration camps, along with the Jews they have been protecting."

"We must be careful of what we say and do," Gottlieb cautioned. "I will spread the word throughout the camp. Have you heard any other information?"

"I've heard how the war is progressing," Jacob confirmed. "It seems the Germans were defeated by Britain at the end of October. Slovakia, Hungary and Romania have joined the Axis powers of Germany, Italy and Japan."

"I wonder where Hitler plans to go from here," Gottlieb muttered aloud.

"Only time will tell," Jacob stated. "With more countries joining him in the fight, you can be sure he is not finished with this war."

"I wonder where Edward and Emil are," Rosina murmured.

"Probably in training," Gottlieb offered. "There are no battles happening at the moment, just Hitler protecting the territory he has acquired so far.

"I pray they remain safe," Rosina whispered.

Jacob tried to stifle a yawn but failed. He was suddenly very tired and weary. His mind had been whirling with thoughts all afternoon, worrying about the cold winter ahead and how they would survive. Added to that was the fear of being caught leaving or returning to the camp. If he was caught, would he be placed in one of the camps Ezra spoke of? If that happened, what would become of his wife and children?

"Go ahead to bed, Jacob," Magdalena said, softly touching

his arm. "I know you must be worn out."

"I believe I will," Jacob replied. "I seem to be especially tired.

"Was there a job opening for me?" Albert asked before Jacob could leave.

"Not at the moment but I will be informed as soon as one becomes available," Jacob said.

With that, Jacob trudged back to his own tent. Albert and Magdalena stayed in Gottlieb and Rosina's tent discussing all Jacob had told them. By the time Magdalena returned to her own tent, Jacob was snoring softly. Magdalena curled up next to him taking comfort in his warmth. She silently prayed for Jacob's safety, not knowing what would happen to him if he was caught outside of the camp. She realized Jacob would not change his mind about going to his new job every day. The thought of his children starving would drive him to take the risk. But what would happen to her and the children if Jacob were caught? She pushed the thought from her mind, not willing to dwell on the "what ifs". Determined to put the matter in God's very capable hands, Magdalena prayed for peace of mind and allowed sleep to overcome her.

Jacob was able to avoid being caught leaving and returning to the camp. Each night, he bought all the groceries his arms could carry the mile back to the tent. The food was hidden in the three tents his family shared, hoping no one would find out. The beginning of Jacob's third week, he arrived at work to find Ezra's place empty. He hoped the man was just ill but the reality of the situation began to take root upon Ezra's third day of absence. At the end of that day, Jacob's boss informed him that he had an opening. Jacob knew Ezra would not be returning and prayed for his friend's safety. Whether Ezra had decided to hide, flee or was put into a camp, Jacob did not know.

The next morning, Albert made the trek to town with Jacob. At least between the two of them more groceries could be carried back to camp. Albert took the position right beside Jacob where Ezra had worked just days before. Albert learned the job quickly as well, and their boss was very pleased with both men's performance.

Christmas came to the camp but there were no presents

exchanged. Gottlieb had packed two of the finest bottles of Wallentine wine before leaving Bessarabia and they all toasted with tin cups, hoping for a better year ahead. The children were gathered and the Christmas story was told of how baby Jesus had come into this world in such a lowly way. He was born in a stable, and after being wrapped in cloth, laid in a manger of hay. His family was far from home, in a town where they knew no one. It caused the Grieb's and Wallentine's to not feel so disgruntled about their situation. At least they had family close. And if God's own son started his life in such a manner, surely they could withstand living in tents for a while.

They were all thankful for the extra food Albert and Jacob provided by finding jobs. Without that, things would be much worse. There had already been several elderly and young children become ill and die from the lack of warmth and food. The food was now being shared with other families, too, though very secretly. If word got out in the camp that extra food was in the Grieb's tent it was sure to cause a scene, as people flocked to get a morsel of bread or anything else. The Grieb brothers would surely be found out.

Things went smoothly until mid-February. Jacob and Albert had let their guard down and were not being as careful about watching for German troops. This error had obviously gotten them followed from the camp to the factory one morning. The Nazi's showed up in the factory demanding the boss fire Albert and Jacob. When he refused saying they were his best workers, a gun was pulled on him. Albert and Jacob could see the whole exchange taking place but did not know they were the cause of it. All work stopped abruptly as every head turned toward the scene.

"You will fire them or you will lose your life," the Nazi informed the boss, a gun to his chest.

"They're referring to us," Jacob whispered to Albert.

"I believe you're right," Albert said, "and we must do something."

The two men made their way toward their boss and the group of Nazi's.

"I believe you may be looking for us," Jacob began.

"You have disobeyed orders," the Nazi officer informed them.

"Yes," Jacob agreed, "you are correct. Please, leave this man alone. My brother and I are quitting immediately."

The Nazi considered Albert and Jacob for a moment, deciding his next course of action. Finally, he buried the butt of his gun deep into the factory owner's stomach, causing him to double over in pain. He informed the owner that he had now been warned and would be arrested if he hired any more relocated Germans. Jacob and Albert were roughly shoved through the door and into the street. Outside the factory, Jacob and Albert feared for their lives as the Nazi soldiers circled them.

"What should we do to them?" the Nazi officer taunted, a wicked smile on his lips.

"Shoot them dead and leave them in the street like the dogs they are," replied one of the other soldiers.

"We were only trying to feed our families," Albert pleaded.

"Against orders," the Nazi officer answered, striking Albert in the face with the gun.

Jacob reached to catch Albert as he slumped to the ground. Anger boiled in him but he knew he had to keep quiet. Any word said could cause the soldiers to make it his last.

"Please, sirs," Jacob began, trying to sound apologetic, "we are refugees from Bessarabia waiting for housing. We did not mean any disrespect."

"Look at you," the Nazi officer spat. "You're filthy and you stink. The whole lot of you in that camp should be taken out and dealt with quickly. You're nothing but wretched farmers, anyway. Why you were brought back to the Reich to eat up our food and take up much needed space is beyond me. The Red Army should have been allowed to deal with the lot of you as they saw fit."

The comment made Jacob's blood boil even more. How dare he call them wretched farmers! Where did he think his food came from? Someone had to grow it. As far as being filthy, it was due to no good way to wash themselves or their clothes. They had been demoted to peasants since coming to Germany. In Bessarabia, they had been the wealth of the community. He and Albert had run three businesses and had done it well. They had been very successful and respected in Hoffnungstal.

The scene had drawn a crowd of onlookers, which was probably Jacob and Albert's saving grace. The Nazis decided the attention was too much and escorted the men back to camp. Jacob half carried Albert the mile from town since his injuries made the task too difficult to walk on his own.

The Nazis confiscated all the extra food Jacob and Albert had brought back and stored. The despair was great but the anger was greater. To be treated this way by your own country was unfathomable, but not surprising. Wasn't this the kind of treatment the Germans in Russia had received since the end of the Great War?

Emilie doctored Albert's wounds but she could not soothe his temper. The treatment he had received at the hands of the Nazis had left a mark much deeper than the gash across his face.

Jacob and Albert were both bitter from the treatment they had received at the hands of the Nazis. They blamed Hitler for all they had been forced to leave behind in Bessarabia and for the poor treatment they had endured since arriving in Germany. The heartache of watching their wives and children go hungry just added more fuel to their fire of anger. Leaving the camp as soon as possible became the fervent prayers of the Grieb and Wallentine families, hopefully before one of their own ended up arrested or dead.

Chapter Six

The next six weeks brought hunger like none the Grieb and Wallentine families had ever seen. The potato, bowl of soup and bread were just enough to keep them in existence, and not much more. Finally at the end of March, the Nazis realized that the camp's men must be allowed to leave the camp for employment. There were too many deaths and everyone was on the verge of starvation. Jacob and Albert were sent to a dye factory to work. Jacob was glad for the income but furious they had made him leave the first job.

After two days at the dye factory, Jacob began to develop a rash. By the fifth day on the job, the rash had covered his whole body. He lay ill in his tent, unable to return to the dye factory because he was allergic to the dye. Magdalena worried Jacob would not survive the severe allergic reaction, and she worked day and night to get Jacob healthy again. Jacob eventually recovered and as soon as he could get back on his feet, Jacob went to the camp officers requesting another job assignment.

"I need a job to help feed my family," Jacob told the officer. "I cannot work in the dye factory because I am allergic to the dye."

"We don't have anything else available," the officer informed him, "but I like your spunk. I need someone to work around my home doing odd jobs."

"Anything, Sir," Jacob pleaded. "I will do any job you have for me."

So, Jacob began to work in the officer's home, which had been seized from a wealthy German who had been kicked out to make a home for the officer. Jacob realized that no one was safe in this country from the Nazis. They took what they wanted and killed at will. They were not required to answer for their actions.

They could even make a whole group of people disappear from their midst by placing yellow stars on them, then throwing them into concentration camps on whims.

The amount of food in the officer's house was more than Jacob had ever seen at any one time in his life. The cellar was full of vast amounts, along with the pantries. He was tempted to take some back to his family, but knew if he got caught he would be a dead man. Besides, Jacob had never stolen in his life. He didn't think he had sunk so low as to start now.

In late April, Hitler decided to send the Germans from Bessarabia to the vacant farms in Poland. Some of the farms had been left when Germany invaded Poland, the owners fleeing to the east. Others had been emptied of their occupants by the Nazis after the invasion. It made no difference to Hitler how the land was cleared of the Poles, just as long as it was vacated. And so the group prepared to move, again. There was no complaining, however. No one wanted to remain in the camp.

The Grieb and Wallentine families were able to remain together and their group was sent to the area of Wartheland. Each family was given a separate farm and they were all near each other. They were thankful to finally have a house of their own after months of living in tents. Each family was given directions to their specific farm. Upon their arrival, they were instructed to wait for relocating representatives to come and show them around.

"This is silly," Jacob said to Magdalena, "why do we need someone here for us to be allowed to look the place over? We've been waiting four hours and still no one has come."

"Those were the instructions," Magdalena reminded. "We're to wait for a representative."

"I'm tired of waiting," Jacob fumed.

"I can see that," Magdalena pointed out. "You're like a wild horse running a fence. Sit down and rest a bit."

The wagon loaded with everything they had brought from Bessarabia had been pulled near the house and Magdalena was sitting on the porch. Erhard and Ewald were busy climbing the tree in the front yard. The tree was showing the first hint of leaves, as buds swelled on its branches. Erhard had made it about fifteen feet up but Ewald, being much smaller, was still on the first limb.

Jacob had unhitched the horses from the wagon and watered

them. He then put them in the paddock beside the large barn. They were now busy munching on the new grass just beginning to show its blades through the rich soil.

Jacob came to the porch and flopped down beside Magdalena. He scanned the farm for the tenth time, and the conclusion was still the same. It was very nice, and whoever had owned it had not been gone long. Things were just too well kept.

"Hear those chickens squawking?" Jacob asked Magdalena.

"Yes, I hear them," Magdalena answered, wondering where Jacob was going with this.

"See how fresh the ruts are in the drive and around the barn?" Jacob asked.

"Yes, they look like they've been made recently," Magdalena agreed.

"Notice how clean swept this porch is?"

"I didn't notice it before but now that you mention it, yes it is quite tidy," Magdalena responded.

"The owners of this farm have not been gone long," Jacob concluded.

Magdalena jerked her head toward Jacob, grasping his meaning for the first time.

"What do you think happened to them?" Magdalena asked.

"I don't know but I'm sure they did not flee when Germany invaded Poland in the fall of 1939. If that had been the case, everything wouldn't be so well kept and those chickens would have been fox food long ago," Jacob said.

"You're absolutely right," Magdalena stated, now wondering what had happened to the owners of this farm.

"I'm tired of waiting," Jacob lamented again.

"You have said that several times," Magdalena reminded.

"No, what I meant to say is, I'm done with waiting," Jacob corrected. "I'm going to at least check out the barn."

"Just go and satisfy your curiosity," Magdalena told him. "You won't be content until you do and your pacing and sighing is about to do me in."

Jacob smiled at Magdalena and headed toward the barn that was a small distance behind the house. As he got closer he could see three Jersey cows in the pasture, and one had a calf at her side. This sight caused him excitement as the thought of fresh milk made his mouth water. Not only that, a fresh cow would mean butter and cheese. What a blessing that animal would be!

Opening the barn door, Jacob inhaled the sweetness of hay, something he hadn't smelled since leaving Hoffnungstal. The ache of leaving there and all they had lost filled him again as he stepped into the barn. Even the interior of the barn was much like the one he had left, though smaller. Jacob noticed a milking stanchion in one corner of the barn where the cow could be confined to milk. Jacob knew that would come in handy very soon. There were a few stalls to keep work horses and some farm implements and tack. Walking to one of the stalls, Jacob noticed there wasn't much manure but what was there was fairly fresh, maybe a week old. He wondered where the horses had gone when the family left. The cows and chickens were here but he did not see any horses.

After checking the first level out thoroughly, Jacob headed for the ladder to the loft. He was sure there was only hay there but wanted to look anyway. Just being in the barn brought him comfort that he hadn't felt for quite some time. He had missed everything about his old life while living in the camp. He had been born a farmer and that would never change.

As Jacob reached the top of the ladder, he stepped into a mostly empty space. The hay that would have filled the loft last fall had been fed to livestock over the winter. Jacob could also tell that the small amount of hay that remained was cut last summer. It was not old, musty hay. Someone had definitely been living and working this farm recently.

Hearing a sound, Jacob walked in the direction of the small mound of leftover hay. As he neared, he realized it was a mother cat with three young kittens. He knew Erhard and Ewald would be excited to know this. The mother cat walked toward Jacob and he reached down to stroke her back. She had definitely been someone's pet and was missing their attention. Jacob reached down and scooped one of the kittens into his large hand. It mewed and fussed but calmed down as he brought it close to his chest. Yes, his boys would be excited over this discovery.

As Jacob placed the kitten back with its mother, he noticed a hole in the hay mound. Walking closer he peered in. To his surprise there was something in the hole. Before giving it a second thought, he reached in and grabbed the thatch of hair he could see.

Upon pulling, the thing the hair was attached to let out a howl. Jacob turned loose quickly and knelt beside the hole. He realized that it wasn't something at all, but someone.

The child crawled back in the hole as far as possible trying to stay out of Jacob's reach. Jacob realized the child was extremely scared and backed away from the hole. Speaking in his native German tongue, Jacob spoke to the child. It only made him shrink further away and cower down. Changing to Russian, Jacob tried again. There was still no response. Being thankful that he had learned ten different languages, Jacob began to use them one at a time. Finally, Jacob got a response from the child.

"Please, come out," Jacob coaxed in the child's tongue. "I will not harm you."

Slowly, the child emerged from the hole. It was a boy about ten years old. He was quite dirty and fear was still evident on his face. Jacob wondered what horrors he had witnessed since the war had begun. Why was he hiding in the hayloft alone?

"Who are you?" Jacob asked.

"I live here," the boy answered.

"Where is your family?"

"Gone," the boy answered, tears welling up in his eyes.

"Gone where?"

"I don't know," the boy sobbed.

Jacob reached out and pulled the child close. He would allow him to grieve the loss of his family and ask questions later. After a minute, Jacob led the child toward the ladder to ascend to the lower floor. The child stopped abruptly, refusing to leave the loft.

"Come on," Jacob coaxed. "I won't hurt you."

"But they will," came the boys reply.

"Who will?"

"The men who took my family. The Nazis."

"The Nazis took your family?"

The boy shook his head yes as tears filled his eyes again.

"What's your name, child?"

"Micah," the boy whispered.

A good Jewish name, Jacob thought. It was becoming all too clear who this farm had belonged to. The thought of where Micah's family might be now filled Jacob's heart with dread. He remembered Ezra saying that when Jewish people were taken away, they did not return. What was happening to all the innocent people being torn from their homes?

"How long have you been hiding in this loft, Micah?"

"About two weeks, I think," Micah replied.

"What have you eaten?"

"I sneak back into the house after dark," Micah informed him. "There's some food in the cellar; potatoes, carrots, and canned goods. I just eat the stuff uncooked."

"Okay," Jacob answered, a plan trying to take shape in his mind. "I want you to stay in this loft for just a little while longer then I will hide you with my family."

"Okay," Micah agreed.

"You might hear me come back into the barn in a little while, but do not make a sound and stay hidden. I will come to the loft and call your name when it's completely safe." Jacob wanted to make sure Micah understood his instructions completely.

Micah shook his head and returned to the hay mound. Jacob concealed the hole in the hay the best he could and still allow some air in. He would do his best to keep the relocation assistant out of the loft.

Returning to the porch, Jacob sat beside Magdalena. He watched his boys now playing a game of tag in the yard and thanked God for their safety. The thought of something happening and either one of them being forced to try and make it on their own made him shudder. It made his resolve to help the boy in the loft that much stronger.

"Find anything interesting?" Magdalena asked.

"There are some Jersey cows, and one of them has a new calf," Jacob informed her.

"Oh, that's good news," Magdalena exclaimed wondering why Jacob was being so sullen.

"Yes and there's a milking stanchion in the barn," Jacob said. "We can start milking in the morning."

"Fresh milk," Magdalena sighed, "it's been so long since we've had that."

"I suppose it's one of those things we took for granted," Jacob said, "like living in peace and not worrying about being arrested and thrown in a concentration camp."

"Are you okay, Jacob?" Magdalena asked with concern.

"You seem distracted and upset since you returned from exploring the barn."

"I'm fine," Jacob assured her, "just anxious for the relocation people to get here so we can unload the wagon and sleep in a real bed tonight."

"A real bed," Magdalena said dreamily, "now that sounds wonderful. You just don't know what you have until it's gone."

"Yes," Jacob said, but he was not referring to the bed at all. His mind was consumed with Micah and all he had lost and endured.

"Look," Magdalena said, pointing up the road, "I see a vehicle coming. It's probably who we're waiting for."

"About time," Jacob grumped, as he rose to his feet to greet them.

The vehicle pulled in the drive and came to a halt. Two men climbed out and Jacob and Magdalena went to meet them.

"It states here that your last name is Grieb and you have two sons," the man with a clipboard noted.

"Yes, that's correct," Jacob confirmed after a brief pause.

Something had passed over her husband's face at the question but Magdalena could not imagine what he was thinking. Maybe he considered adding that they had a deceased daughter and then changed his mind. Whatever the reason, Jacob was acting strange.

"Well, let's take a look around," the second worker announced.

Everyone went into the house first and the men did a thorough check of each room. The home was one story with dirt floors, a kitchen, living room and three bedrooms. One bedroom contained one large bed while the other two had two twin beds per room. The family who had lived here must have had four children, from the evidence of what was left behind. As they went from room to room, the man with the clipboard took notes of everything in the rooms, from the furniture to the clothes in the closets. Going into the cellar, the Grieb's were thrilled to see potatoes and carrots stored there along with a variety of canned goods. Someone had kept very busy the summer before growing and preserving all the food. There were even jars of jams and jellies on the shelves.

After the house had been gone over thoroughly, they all

trudged to the barn. Opening the door, the boys ran in and straight to the ladder that would take them to the loft. Jacob hollered for them to please stay with them and they came back to their parents' side. Magdalena thought it strange that Jacob didn't allow them to explore the loft. It wasn't like they had never been in one. Erhard had been throwing hay down by himself for two years before they had left Bessarabia.

The relocation men looked through every stall in the barn. It was like they were searching for someone, Magdalena thought.

"Who did this farm belong to before we were assigned to it?" Jacob inquired.

"We are not given that information," the man toting the clipboard informed him. "We are just told to show the new occupants around and make sure the place is empty. If anyone is found, we are to take them with us and turn them over to the German soldiers so they can be united back with their families."

"I see," Jacob murmured.

After the men finished on the ground floor they headed toward the ladder. Jacob held his breath. To stop them would raise suspicion; to allow them to go up threatened Micah's hiding place. Deciding to keep his mouth shut, Jacob watched as one of the men climbed the ladder and stepped onto the loft. When Erhard and Ewald attempted to follow, he called them back again.

"We'll explore the loft later," Jacob informed them.

"Hey, there's a mother cat and kittens up here," the man in the loft hollered down.

"The boys will love playing with them," Magdalena answered, watching her sons' faces light up. She wondered why Jacob hadn't mentioned the kittens earlier knowing how excited his sons would be with the discovery.

"That's the least of what's up there," Jacob thought to himself, wanting the man to hurry and come down.

When the relocation representative began descending the ladder, Jacob let out his breath. Just a few more rungs and Micah would be safe. His nerves were on edge and he hoped the men would leave soon. He knew Micah could hear their voices but did not understand a word of what was being said. The child was probably scared to death.

Outside it was noted that three cows and fifteen chickens had been left behind. They asked about the horses in the paddock and Jacob informed them they belonged to him. The beasts had come with them from Bessarabia and had now pulled them to Poland. Satisfied with their search, the men said their goodbyes and wished them well. Then, they climbed back in their vehicle and headed up the road toward the farm Gottlieb and Rosina had been assigned.

Jacob forced down the urge to run back to the barn and check on Micah. It would be best for the relocation representatives to be completely out of the area before attempting to move him to the house, maybe even after dark. He knew the relocation team probably thought they were being helpful by returning anyone found on the farms to the Nazis so they could be reunited with their families. Jacob knew the truth though and feared for Micah's life. People just didn't disappear from their homes never to return unless something bad had happened to them. When this war ended, and he prayed it would soon, he wondered what would be discovered behind the walls of the concentration camps.

Heading to the wagon, Jacob began to unload their belongings. It would be the first time the wagon was completely unloaded since leaving Bessarabia six months earlier. Six months, and it seemed like a lifetime ago. After everything was placed in the house, Magdalena began to prepare supper. She decided on fried potatoes, green beans and biscuits. One of the chickens would have been tasty but she decided not to kill one. The eggs would be good to eat and for every chicken killed, an egg per day would be lost.

Jacob took Erhard and Ewald to the chicken coop and they began to remove all the eggs from the nests so the hens could lay fresh ones there. There were two hens sitting on eggs, and after looking around and noting that there was indeed a rooster, Jacob chose to leave them alone. Hopefully they would hatch little ones, providing meat and eggs for later. Jacob and the boys returned to the house informing Magdalena there would be fresh eggs by the next morning. Erhard also told her of the two hens sitting and wondered when the chicks would hatch.

They all sat down at the kitchen table, something that hadn't been able to do for six months, and Jacob gave thanks for the food. They all ate until they were full, then ate some more. Magdalena had brought up a jar of blackberry jam and each of them mounded the sweet treat on their biscuits.

"Where did you get the ingredients for the biscuits?" Jacob asked.

"There were all sorts of baking supplies in the cabinets," Magdalena said. "You're right. This family has not been gone long."

"About two weeks," Jacob stated.

Magdalena turned toward him abruptly. "How do you know that, Jacob?"

"Um…the manure is still pretty fresh in the stalls," Jacob stammered.

"Only you would notice that," Magdalena laughed.

Jacob nodded and reached for another biscuit. Best to keep his mouth full, it talked less that way. How foolish of him to blurt such a thing. Of course he planned to tell Magdalena about Micah but he couldn't let the boys find out. He realized now the plan of moving him into their house was not a good one. It would put the boys in danger and Ewald was just too young to understand the consequences of telling someone about Micah.

"When will we milk the cow, Vater?" Erhard asked.

"First thing tomorrow morning," Jacob answered. "We'll pen the calf in a stall tonight so the mother will have milk for us come morning. Then we will put the calf back with its mother. We will just milk once a day and share any extra with Oma and Opa Wallentine and Grieb."

"Milking one cow once a day will be easy," Erhard exclaimed. "It won't be nearly as hard as milking twenty twice a day, like we used to with Uncle Albert in Hoffnungstal.

"That's true Erhard," Magdalena said, "and it might be a job you could handle all on your own."

Erhard smiled with pride, knowing how important is was to be a good, hard worker. Even at the age of eight, he had learned much in his father's shadow. Now at the age of nine, he was eager to add to his knowledge and ability.

After night fell and the boys were asleep, Jacob whispered his secret to Magdalena. Upon learning that a small boy was hiding in the barn, Magdalena wanted to run to the loft and rescue him.

"You can't," Jacob cautioned. "First, he will be afraid of you because you can't speak his language. Second, Ewald is too young to keep such a secret."

"Oh, Jacob, this is terrible," Magdalena whispered. "I know you're right, we can't expect little Ewald to understand the seriousness of the situation, but how will we help this child?"

"Fix him a plate of food," Jacob instructed. "Make sure you put jam on that last biscuit we had left. I will take him food and water tonight and allow him to stretch and relieve himself if he needs to. He's made a place for himself in the hay mound but I will take him a blanket for more warmth. It's the best we can do."

Magdalena gathered a blanket and the food with a heavy heart. To think this was all she could offer this little boy caused tears to pool in her eyes. Grabbing a jar, she filled it with water from a crock by the door. Jacob had put fresh water in it earlier from the springhouse that was on the property. The springhouse was a nice discovery, and not just for fresh water. It would also be used to keep things cold.

Handing all the things to Jacob, Magdalena fought the urge to ask to join him. She knew until Jacob explained everything that was happening to the child, she would just scare him more. Watching Jacob slip out the back door, Magdalena sank into a chair to pray. She prayed for her family's safety and thanked God for bringing them to this farm. She thanked Him for His protection and guidance for the rest of their family who had traveled with them. She prayed for the safety of her brothers, Edward and Emil, fighting in the war and as tears streamed down her cheeks, she asked God to protect the child in their barn loft.

Chapter Seven

The Grieb and Wallentine families were thankful for the farms they had been assigned and began work immediately. This way of life had been theirs for generations, and they knew they could make a living here. They all felt as if they had come home, or as close to it as they could hope for.

Jacob and Magdalena worked side by side getting a field ready to plant. Erhard and Ewald helped, too. Jacob would put them on the two horses as he plowed and disc. Their job was to keep the horses going straight. It was also a way to keep them in sight and safe. There were still some Poles living on area farms, and they were not receptive of their new neighbors. It caused concern among the relocated Germans but they just had to make it work the best they could. They had no other choice.

The Germans decided to plant oats because they could be planted in the spring. It seemed to be a crop that the leftover Poles were planting, too, so they were sure oats would do well in this area. All of the farms already had a crop of wheat growing lush and green and the Germans were thankful that they would have it for their livestock and flour. They just prayed that the mill in the nearby town would grind it for them.

Jacob tended to Micah each night after Erhard and Ewald were asleep. Magdalena went with him sometimes but couldn't speak his language. Micah seemed to be comforted by her mothering, however, even with the barrier. The child hungered for affection and security more than the food he was brought. Magdalena wished with everything in her that she could gather Micah in her arms and take him to the house, but she knew it was just not possible. It would put Micah in more danger and risk her sons' lives in the process. Micah would have to remain in the barn loft as long as there were Nazis in the area, and the Nazis didn't appear to be going anywhere.

Jacob took a bucket of warm water out every other night for Micah to use to bathe with, and Magdalena gathered clean clothes from Micah's own closet. At least they could keep him fed and clean, even if they couldn't bring him into the house and treat him as they did their own sons. It was heartbreaking but they honestly didn't know what else to do. Micah was forced to remain hidden in a hay mound while listening to Ewald and Erhard play in and around the barn, with no hope of joining in the fun. It was a lot to ask of such a young boy but Micah seemed to know what was required of him. His parents must have explained the danger of being taken by the Nazis very thoroughly to Micah, so well that he remained hidden no matter the temptation.

Three weeks after arriving at the Polish farm, Ewald and Erhard climbed to the loft to play with the kittens. The little creatures had provided many hours of entertainment, and the boys had been elated with the discovery. They had named all three kittens, as well as the mother cat, and would have moved them to the house, if only their mutti would have allowed it. Their vater had attempted to move the mother cat and kittens to an empty stall where fresh straw had been put down, but the mother cat packed each kitten back to the loft, one at a time.

As Erhard sat with a kitten on his lap stroking its fur, Ewald pulled a piece of hay in front of another kitten, causing it to run and pounce. As Ewald ran backwards laughing at the kitten's antics, he lost track of where he was headed. Before he knew it, he had fallen into the mound of hay and began to laugh even harder. Erhard, wanting to join the fun, jumped into the mound and began covering Ewald with hay. As Ewald squealed, Erhard grabbed large handfuls of hay and let it rain down on his little brother. To his surprise, Erhard came face to face with another boy in the hay and it was not Ewald. Jumping up, Erhard grabbed Ewald by the arm and hauled him from the mound. Pushing him toward the ladder, Erhard instructed Ewald to climb down.

"What are you doing, Erhard?" Ewald protested. "You're hurting my arm!"

"Go, Ewald, get down the ladder," Erhard instructed while looking back toward the hay mound. The boy had disappeared back into the hay but Erhard knew he was still in there.

"Why are we leaving the loft?" Ewald questioned.

"Ewald, get down that ladder or I will shove you out of this loft!" Erhard screamed.

Shaken by his brother's sudden anger, Ewald descended the ladder as fast as he could. Erhard came after him, not even bothering to use the last four rungs. Hitting the ground, Erhard grabbed Ewald's hand and pulled him through the barn doors and to the house.

"Mutti, Mutti!" Erhard hollered, hurling through the back door dragging Ewald behind him.

Magdalena came running from the cellar at Erhard's distressed call, worrying something bad had happened. Topping the stairs that ended in the kitchen, she could see Erhard's pale face and a scared Ewald standing beside him. Neither one appeared to be injured, which slowed Magdalena's racing heart a bit, but something was definitely wrong. The looked as if they had seen a ghost.

"What is it, Erhard?" Magdalena asked.

"There's a boy in the loft of the barn hidden in the hay mound!"

Magdalena was thankful that no one was hurt but now there was a whole new problem. Her sons knew the truth and there was danger that came with that knowledge. What would they do now? Knowing it would do no good to pretend she had no idea what Erhard was talking about Magdalena chose to tell the boys the truth. She knew they would not fully understand why a boy was hiding in the barn but she had to do her best to explain the danger of him being there.

"Erhard, sit down a minute and catch your breath," Magdalena said softly.

"Did you not hear what I said?" Erhard asked emphatically.

"Yes, I heard you and I already know there's a boy in the loft," Magdalena replied.

"You do?" Erhard asked in amazement while sinking into a kitchen chair.

"You about killed me getting me down from that loft," Ewald protested. "I thought you had seen something bad. All you saw was a boy?"

"He surprised me, okay," Erhard retorted. "I didn't expect to find him there in the hay mound."

"Listen, boys," Magdalena began, "I have something to tell you but it must be kept a secret. Do you understand?"

Both boys stared at her wide eyed and nodded that they understood.

"The boy in the loft used to live in this house with his family," Magdalena said.

"Then why did he move to the barn?" Ewald asked.

"Yeah and where's the rest of his family?" Erhard questioned. "Are they all in the loft?"

"No, just the boy is in the loft," Magdalena said quietly. "His name is Micah."

"Then where is the rest of his family?" Ewald asked with concern.

"That's the part I need you to understand," Magdalena said. "The Nazis came and took his family away. Micah was in the barn when they arrived and hid in the hay mound. The Nazis didn't find him."

"Where did the Nazis take his family?" Erhard asked.

"To a concentration camp," Magdalena said.

"Like the camp we were at before we came to this farm?" Erhard questioned.

"No Son, not like that camp. The camp Micah's family went to is like a prison, and they are not allowed to leave."

"Why did they take them away?" Ewald asked.

"Because they are Jewish," Magdalena answered.

"Is that bad?" Erhard asked.

"No, it's not bad," Magdalena said. "It's just that Hitler has decided that being a Jew is some sort of crime, punishable by imprisonment. Jews are being put in camps all throughout the area. Wherever the German soldiers are fighting or occupying, they are arresting Jews. Sometimes they just kill them."

"That's terrible," Erhard said in disbelief. "Do Uncle Emil and Uncle Edward arrest Jewish people?"

The question took Magdalena by surprise as it was honestly something she had not thought of. Her brothers might be forced to commit this crime. How awful they must feel, if that was the case. "I hope your uncles are not being made to take part in arresting

Jews," Magdalena replied quietly.

"So, Micah could be killed if the Nazis know he's here," Erhard said, trying to piece it all together.

"Yes, so it is very important that no one knows about Micah," Magdalena instructed firmly. "Do you understand? You cannot tell anyone that there's a Jewish boy here."

Erhard and Ewald nodded their heads in unison, their faces registering the shock that someone would be so cruel to innocent people. They had never faced such things and had been protected from the evil acts happening around them.

Jacob entered the house and took in the scene around the kitchen table. He knew something had happened but was afraid to voice the question.

"So, what are you boys doing in the house on such a fine afternoon?" Jacob asked cheerfully.

"Erhard found a boy in the barn," Ewald blurted.

Magdalena's eyes met Jacob's and he knew the secret was out. Decisions would have to be made and Erhard and Ewald would have to be kept quiet. The heightened level of danger of Micah being hidden in the barn loft hit Jacob like a hoof from an unruly cow. Sitting down beside Magdalena, Jacob looked at his sons sternly. He did not want to leave any doubts in their minds about how important his next words were going to be.

"Boys, you cannot tell anyone about Micah," Jacob said sternly.

"We know," Ewald replied. "Mutti already told us that."

"I mean no one," Jacob stated again. "Not Oma and Opa Grieb, not Oma and Opa Wallentine, not your aunts, uncles or cousins. Not a soul."

"We can't even tell cousins Albert, Richard and Erwin?" Ewald asked.

"No," Jacob said firmly. "You cannot tell anyone."

"Don't you trust our family not to tell?" Erhard questioned.

"It's not a matter of trust," Jacob said. "It's a matter of safety. It could put Micah's life in more danger or put the lives of our family in danger. For this reason, the fewer people who know the better it is. Do you understand?"

"Yes," Erhard said.

"But we can't even tell Oma Wallentine?" Ewald asked

again.

"Ewald," Jacob said sternly, "if you tell anyone, I will spank you good and hard. Do you understand?"

"Yes," Ewald said, his lower lip trembling.

Jacob felt bad that he had to threaten Ewald but there was no other choice. Ewald had to understand how serious the situation was. There could be no doubt in either boy's mind that it would be alright to tell the secret to anyone.

Jacob got up and headed to the barn to check on Micah. He had to make sure the boy was okay after the encounter. He thought on the way to the barn that he should have forbidden the boys to get in the loft. If the mother cat would have just left the kittens in the stall where he moved them to, everything would have been fine. The boys wouldn't have been up there and Micah would still be safe and unfound.

Climbing the ladder, Jacob called out to Micah. The child emerged from the hay, fear written on his small face. It broke Jacob's heart to think a child so young could understand how important it was for him to stay hidden. His parents must have warned him on several occasions of the danger, which is why he knew to hide when the Nazis showed up at the farm.

"Are you okay?" Jacob asked.

"Yes," Micah answered softly.

"My sons discovered your hiding place," Jacob said.

"Yes, I know," Micah said. "I didn't make a sound. I promise I didn't."

"Oh, Micah, I know you didn't give yourself away," Jacob assured the boy. "I just want you to know this discovery by Ewald and Erhard changes things. We will move you into the house tonight. There's no reason for you to stay in the barn now."

"You're going to move me in with your family?" Micah asked with longing evident in his voice.

"Yes, you will be with my family," Jacob said softly, realizing how lonely Micah must have been out here by himself all the time.

"Okay," Micah said, a small smile playing at his lips.

"Stay in the loft today but you don't have to hide," Jacob said. "Of course, if you hear strange voices you should get back in the hay."

"Okay," Micah said, as a brilliant smile lit up his face.

"I'll send Ewald and Erhard back to the barn to keep you company," Jacob informed him.

"It will be nice to play with someone again," Micah answered.

"Yes, I'm sure it will," Jacob replied softly.

Jacob went back to the house and sent the boys to the barn to play with Micah. He didn't know how they would get past the language barrier but he knew they would figure out a way. Joy and laughter were universal signs of communication and no language was needed to understand them. It had been over a month since Micah had been allowed to run and play, so Jacob was certain he would have fun with Erhard and Ewald, no matter if he could understand a word they were saying or not.

"How is Micah?" Magdalena asked as soon as the boys were outside.

"He was scared that I would be upset with him because he had been found," Jacob replied.

"That poor little boy," Magdalena said as tears pooled in her eyes.

"I told him I knew he hadn't done anything to give away his hiding place," Jacob said. "He's excited about getting to play with Erhard and Ewald."

"I would say so," Magdalena said with a smile. "I can't imagine hiding in a hay mound all day while listening to life going on all around. It must have been so hard."

"I'm sure it was," Jacob stated. "The question is what do we do now?"

"I suppose we just move him into the house," Magdalena said. "If the Nazis come back looking for him, they will find him no matter where he is hidden."

"The relocation representatives made a note that there were two different sizes of clothes in Micah's bedroom," Jacob said. "If the Nazis have kept records of everyone they arrested and where they lived, they will be back to get Micah."

"I already thought about that," Magdalena said. "We will just have to wait and see what happens. Until then, we will treat Micah as one of our own sons."

"Yes, and pray they didn't keep good records," Jacob

replied.

"We will move Micah into the house after dark," Magdalena decided. "He will be able to sleep in his own bed, again."

"I will put a hat on him and take him to the barn after breakfast," Jacob said. "He's about Erhard's height so if anyone is passing by and sees him, they will think Erhard is with me. Ewald and Erhard can go to the barn to play with him when their chores are finished."

"That's a good plan," Magdalena agreed. "I can take lunch to the barn for Micah and the boys so Micah doesn't have to eat alone. Hopefully, we can keep him hidden from our neighbors and family."

"I'll explain to Micah that when anyone comes to the house he needs to hide," Jacob said.

"It's the best we can do," Magdalena said with a sigh. "I am not willing to just hand him over to the Nazis."

"Neither am I," Jacob said. "I'll go tell Micah and the boys the plan we have come up with."

"Okay," Magdalena said. "I hope Ewald is old enough to understand the situation."

"Me, too," Jacob said as he headed toward the back door.

The plan went into action when darkness fell that night. Micah was moved into his own house to live with the Griebs. During the day, the boys played tag and hide and seek all throughout the barn. They messed with the kittens and swung from a rope Jacob had hung from the rafters. Sometimes they played "what's this called in your language", where they showed each other different items and took turns telling the name of it in their own language. In this way, they began to understand one another, one word at a time.

When other family showed up, Micah knew to hide in the loft, if he was in the barn. Jacob had also made him a hiding place in his sisters' closet behind their dresses, for times when he was in the house and needed to disappear. They all ate supper together around the table, making sure to watch and listen intently for anyone who might stop by. Micah seemed to be enjoying becoming part of the Grieb family, and the fear that had been constant in his eyes was slowly fading.

It warmed Jacob and Magdalena's hearts to see Micah smile

and watch him play with Erhard and Ewald. The child had endured so much in his short life. They didn't know how they were going to keep him safe but they planned to do their best. Maybe the war would end soon and Micah's family would be allowed to return home. Of course, that would mean the Grieb's would have to move again but it would be worth it. What could be more important than a family being reunited?

However, the war did not appear to be ending anytime soon, according to the reports that trickled to Jacob's ears. Germany, along with Italy, Hungary, and Bulgaria had invaded Yugoslavia in April, 1941, and Yugoslavia surrendered in a little over a week. The world watched and wondered where Hitler would turn his attention next. What country did he plan to trample across and call his own in his quest of becoming a Greater Germany? All of Europe was on edge wondering if they would be the next to be invaded. Many were already occupied by German or Soviet troops.

Jacob and Magdalena's plan for Micah went smoothly for two weeks and then the unthinkable happened. They had just sat down to supper when a truck with German storm troopers pulled in the drive. Micah immediately jumped up and ran to his hiding place in the closet. He did not have to be told what he should do, for his fear of the Nazis propelled him as fast as his legs could carry him.

The storm troopers barged through the front door and were standing at the kitchen table before Jacob could get all of his instructions whispered to his sons. Magdalena stifled a scream and tears filled her eyes. Ewald and Erhard sat startled by the sudden intrusion, stunned that the troopers didn't even knock and nearly busted down the door.

"Hand over the Jewish boy," the lead trooper demanded.

"Jewish boy?" Jacob asked innocently.

"Don't act like you have no idea what I'm talking about," the storm trooper barked.

"We don't know anything about a Jewish boy," Jacob stated.

"We have records stating that upon your arrival this house had two twin beds in two bedrooms. The closet in one of the rooms contained girls' clothes in two different sizes and the other contained boys' clothes, also in two different sizes. We know now that only a father, mother, two daughters and one son were removed from this house. Where is the other boy?" the trooper demanded.

"Sir," Jacob began but was cut short by a sudden move of the storm trooper. Reaching out, the storm trooper grabbed Erhard from his chair and held a pistol to his head.

"Now, where is the boy?" the trooper demanded again. "You better tell me quick or I will kill each one of your family members until you do."

Jacob's face turned pale. What a situation to be put in! He could not allow the storm trooper to kill his family but to give Micah up? Jacob could hardly take his next breath at the thought. Holding up his hand to hopefully stop the storm trooper from pulling the trigger, Jacob rose from his seat. Knowing he could not keep Micah hidden and save his son's life too, Jacob made the hardest decision of his life.

"Please, give me a minute," Jacob begged. "I will get him."

Jacob headed toward the bedroom, his legs feeling like lead. This was the hardest thing he had ever had to do. The anger he had felt toward Hitler before now turned to a rage inside of him. What had Micah or any of the other Jews ever done to deserve such treatment? Entering the bedroom, Jacob called out to Micah. Two of the storm troopers had followed him but he hoped they could not speak Micah's language. Micah crawled from the closet, his eyes wide with fear. Taking him in his arms, Jacob whispered how sorry he was for what was about to happen. The storm troopers shoved Jacob aside and roughly took hold of Micah. Silent tears slid down Micah's face as he was led away. It was a scene that would haunt Jacob the rest of his life. If only he could have saved the child!

The storm troopers left and Jacob, Magdalena, Erhard, and Ewald stood in a circle weeping for Micah and for all that had just happened. They were thankful that Erhard's life had been spared and that Jacob had not been shot or arrested for his part in it. But they were so sad for Micah. Evil was happening all around them and they felt helpless to stop it. A short year ago, as they lived their peaceful lives in Bessarabia, they could not have imagined where their river of life would take them. Right now, they felt as if they were drowning in the sorrow rushing over them.

Chapter Eight

Edward and Emil Wallentine were thankful they had been allowed to stay together after being drafted into the German forces. They had been through some training and now in mid-June, 1941, they were preparing for battle. Hitler was planning something big, and all the young men who had been drafted from the 92,000 Germans from Bessarabia had been brought together into one unit. Upon receiving their orders, Edward and Emil's division headed southeast, back toward Bessarabia. They had not been told why they were pushing toward the Russian border but figured their knowledge of the territory would be used as an advantage. Other divisions had moved out at the same time, headed toward the northeast and the middle of Russia's border. It seemed they were attempting to form one long line of troops across the Soviet's entire western border. It appeared the Frontier and Friendship Treaty that Hitler and Stalin had signed in the fall of 1939 was about to be broken.

At four o'clock in the morning on June 22, 1941, the Nazi troops, joined by the Finns in the north and Rumanians in the south, invaded the Soviet Union. The German front was broad and the attack was a complete surprise since no war had been declared by either side. Hitler and Stalin were now back to being the bitter enemies they had always been, with the exception of the non-aggression pact signed in August, 1939. The Nazis overran the Soviet Union in an unbelievable way. They pushed through the border and didn't slow down. The Red Army was not prepared for a large-scale war. Unlike Germany, who had been fighting for almost two years now, the Red Army had not engaged in much warfare, except for the winter war with Finland during the winter of 1940. They had basically just taken over territories without much resistance from the occupants.

As the Nazi troops pushed through the western Soviet Union, they came upon German villages. The invasion was celebrated in these villages, for the Russian Germans saw the Nazis as a form of deliverance from the ill treatment they had experienced at the hands of Stalin and the Communist party. As Edward and Emil Wallentine pushed across the Inguletz River with their unit, they couldn't help but think about Isabella, the aunt they had never met but knew so much about. Would they find her in the village of Kronau which lay just ahead?

With the German troops occupying their colonies the Russian Germans began to re-organize their lives. They opened their German schools again and cleaned up their churches so they could have worship services. They spoke their native language and the occupying German troops understood every word! The Fatherland had come to their rescue. They rejoiced in being liberated from the hands of Stalin and the cruel treatment they had suffered the last twenty years. The Greater Germany Hitler dreamed of had arrived for the Russian Germans still in the Black Sea region.

Edward and Emil began to ask every person they came across if they knew Daniel and Isabella Gingrich as they came into the Kronau village. Surely someone would know their whereabouts and if they were still alive. The last letter had been written less than three years before, so they knew they had recently been in this area.

It didn't take long for their inquiries to pay off, as a passing villager confirmed they knew Daniel and Isabella. They were given directions to their home, and as night fell and the soldiers rested for the next day, Edward and Emil made their way to the location.

As they neared the home they had been directed to, Edward and Emil began to slow down. Every house they passed was nothing more than a shack. To think their mutti's sister had been forced to live in such squander made the men feel a bit guilty. They had enjoyed a good life working in their vater's vineyard and on the farm. They had never wanted for food or clothes. Looking about them, they realized how absolutely blessed they had been. The people of this village didn't even own their own outhouse. It appeared there was about one outhouse per five homes. Their homes were such shambles that Edward and Emil had no idea how they kept from freezing to death during the harsh winters. What had Stalin done to this once proud colony of Germans? It sickened the men to the point that they weren't sure if they wanted to visit their aunt after all.

"Is this a good idea?" Edward voiced the question that was bouncing around in Emil's head, too.

"This place is depressing," Emil said, "but if we don't go see Aunt Isabella, she will never know that Mutti no longer lives in Bessarabia. They will lose contact forever."

"That's true," Edward agreed. "I'm just afraid of what we will discover behind the door of one of these shacks."

"Poor, weary people," Emil answered, knowing there was no hope of finding anything different at Aunt Isabella's house than what they saw right now before their eyes.

"Let's just get this over with," Edward decided, picking up his pace.

Reaching the home of their aunt, Emil knocked lightly on the door, afraid it would collapse if he knocked any harder. A woman slightly resembling their mother but much thinner opened the door. Her eyes were sunken into a worn face while bones protruded through the rags that covered her frame. The only thing that kept Edward and Emil from turning and running from the scene was the smile that spread across her face at the sight of the soldiers.

"We are so glad you have come to rescue us," Isabella began. "You have no idea what we have endured here since the Great War ended."

"Actually, we do," Edward began, "because our mutti let us read your letters."

As the words sank in tears sprang to Isabella's eyes. "Are you really Rosina's sons?"

"Yes, we are," Emil answered. "We asked around the village until we found you. We knew our mutti would want to know."

"Wilkum," Isabella exclaimed. "Please, come in and meet your cousins."

Edward and Emil stepped into the home. It was as sad inside as out. Their aunt and her family had been living on the bare necessities and sometimes not even that. Sitting at a rickety table that had been thrown together with scraps of wood was a man. He looked as thin and unhealthy as Aunt Isabella. The sight of the humble abode and its occupants made Emil and Edward cringe. Would they report all of what they were seeing to their mutti? It was not likely.

"This is my husband, Daniel," Isabella introduced while Daniel stood to shake the boys' hands.

"Pleased to meet you, Sir," Emil said.

"I am more pleased to meet you fellows," Daniel said. "You and your troops have delivered us from the clutches of Stalin and his evil ways."

"So we have heard," Edward stated as a smile spread across his face.

A young man and girl entered the kitchen from one of the other two rooms in the house. They were no better off than their parents. They were dressed in rags that hung on frames of skin and bones. The picture the four of them standing before them created was enough to make Emil and Edward shudder. What kind of torment had these people been living through? Not just the fact of being half starved, but not being able to worship or speak their native language. They had been stripped of all dignity and self-worth.

"These are your cousins, Adolf, and Agathe Rosina," Isabella informed them.

It did not surprise Edward and Emil that Isabella had named her daughter after their mother. The fact that they had used the name Adolf caused them concern. The boy would have to live with that name long after all of the truths about Adolf Hitler came out. Yes, Adolf Hitler had moved Edward and Emil's family back to Germany when the Red Army invaded Bessarabia, however, Edward and Emil had witnessed the treatment of fellow Germans and especially Jews since that time. They had been made to take part in the arrests of entire Jewish families and seen the camps they were placed in. They had also seen men shot dead for not honoring Hitler's name when prompted to. There was definitely evil in the leader of Germany, just as there was in the leader of the Soviets. Of course, Daniel and Isabella had no way of knowing this. To them, the Nazis had just become their saving grace.

"How did you boys become part of the German troops?" Daniel asked.

"We were drafted," Emil said.

"After we moved from Bessarabia to Germany," Edward added.

"So, all of my family moved to Germany," Isabella stated.

"All of Bessarabia moved to Germany," Edward corrected. "Hitler invited us back to the Reich after the Red Army invaded us."

"There were over 90,000 Germans who made the trek," Emil supplied.

"How nice of Adolf Hitler to take an interest in your plight," Daniel said.

"Yes," Edward answered, not wanting his aunt and uncle to know their son bore the same name as a madman. That information would probably find its way to them soon enough, but he could always hope it didn't. He was certainly not going to be the one to tell them. The reprieve the German troops had given them from Stalin's iron fist gave them great joy, and he would not be the one to dampen their spirits.

"So, how are my parents?" Isabella questioned.

"They passed away some years ago," Emil informed her. "I'm sorry."

Isabella let that soak in for a moment, thinking how she hadn't even known. Being trapped behind the "iron curtain" all this time had certainly made it impossible to get information from the outside world. She had wondered many times the difference it would have made in her life if she had traveled home with her and Daniel's first child when Daniel had been drafted into the Great War. It had been a point of discussion for her and Daniel when he returned. There had been a small window of opportunity for her to freely leave, but she had not crawled through it. She had chosen to stay in Kronau and wait for Daniel's return. Daniel told her when he came home from the war that she should have left. He would have found a way to get across the border to join her. They could have enjoyed a life in Bessarabia near Isabella's family. Instead, they had lived in this wretched place scraping out a mere existence. Here two children had grown up hungry their whole lives. Why had she not fled? Shaking her thoughts aside, Isabella continued to question her nephews. "And your mutti, how is she?"

"Mutti was fine the last time we saw her," Edward supplied.

"They were put into a camp with all of the other Germans from Bessarabia when we returned to Germany. I've heard Hitler has since moved them to the vacated farms in Poland."

"That's good to know," Isabella said, longing in her voice. It was evident that she would like to join her sister at that farm in Poland. "Please tell her I love her and miss her terribly when you see her again."

"We will," Emil assured her. "Mutti has missed you very much, too."

"If only I would have known what was going to happen here at the end of the Great War," Isabella lamented.

"Well, at least we've been liberated now," Daniel added cheerily, trying to make his wife look on the brighter side of things.

"True," Isabella agreed, "with thanks to the German troops who have shown up. I just pray it lasts."

"We better get going now," Emil said, thinking he had seen all he could stand. "We will be moving east again by morning."

"Push the Red Army all the way to Siberia and leave them there," Daniel cheered.

"Yes, and bring back all the deported Germans from the slave camps," Isabella added.

"We'll do the best we can," Edward assured them, walking out the door.

Waving goodbye, Edward and Emil headed back to join their troop. Maybe they didn't agree with all aspects of this war, but they were proud to play a part in giving these poor German colonies some much needed peace. Living under Communist rule had stripped them of everything: their language, schools, Christian holidays, and even the freedom to worship. To have a hand in giving all that back made Edward and Emil agree with Hitler's scheme for the first and only time. They knew deep down that liberating these oppressed Germans had not been the cause for Hitler invading Russia, but it had happened just the same. The question was could the German troops protect this new found freedom of the German colonies they had liberated?

Pushing eastward the next morning, the German troops again were dominating the battlefield, backing the Red Army up and killing thousands of its soldiers. It was beginning to look as if

Germany might overtake the whole Soviet Union if the Red Army could not get things together and retaliate. Hitler's Greater Germany was growing by the day, as more and more territory was occupied and overtaken by the German troops.

As the Nazis pushed further east, they found fewer and fewer German villages with people in them. It seemed Stalin was evacuating the colonies at an alarming rate and sending the occupants east. The colonists were probably starving in some camp or had been added to the slave labor. With this thought, Edward and Emil fought harder, hoping to rescue more of the Russian Germans who had been mistreated under Stalin's rule.

Chapter Nine

Life continued for the relocated Germans living on the farms in Poland, but the sadness of not being able to protect Micah hung over Jacob and Magdalena like a fog. They had shared the story in whispers with the rest of their family, who also shared in their grief. They all knew in their minds that there had been no choice but to hand Micah over to the storm troopers, but their hearts wondered if they could have saved him somehow.

Erhard and Ewald did not know exactly what had happened just that Micah had been brutally taken away from their home. Jacob tried to explain it so they could understand but he didn't want to tell them the complete truth. There was no sense in adding more pain to them than what had been caused already.

News of the war's progress filtered in to the Germans who now lived on the Polish farms. They had found out that the Nazis invaded the Soviet Union and were quickly pushing the Red Army east. Rosina was excited by the news and couldn't help thinking of her sister living in the area. Would help come for the Germans trapped behind the "iron curtain"? It was a thought that was continually on her mind.

"Do you think your Aunt Isabella has been helped by the German troops?" Rosina asked Magdalena and Emilie as they worked side by side in Rosina's kitchen.

"I hope so," Emilie said. "I know living here is not the best situation, but things could be so much worse."

"Yes, things could always be worse," Magdalena agreed. "I miss Hoffnungstal but I thank God every day that we are not still in that camp."

"Maybe Hitler will offer the Germans who have been trapped in the Soviet Union the choice to return to the Reich like he did for us," Rosina said hopefully.

"It could definitely happen," Emilie assured her mutti.

Magdalena nodded her head, agreeing with Emilie. She couldn't help but notice the glow her younger sister was beginning to have with expecting her and Albert's fifth child. She hoped, for her sister's sake, she would finally get a girl. The baby was due in January, six months away. Magdalena hoped for another child, too and wondered if one would ever come. She had always had difficulty conceiving, leaving five years between Erhard and Ewald. There would have been four years between Ewald and the baby girl who never drew her first breath. Magdalena's mother had been right, that time heals the broken heart, but she knew there would always be a crack in it.

"Maybe the Germans in the Soviet Union will be moved straight to here," Rosina surmised.

"That would make the most sense," Emilie agreed. "There are still empty farms all around us. There aren't many Poles still living here."

"Your vater said that some of the Poles still living in the area have been hostile to some of the Germans living near them," Rosina said.

"Really?" Magdalena asked with surprise. "I knew they didn't care much for us, but hadn't heard they were acting on that dislike. We've been treated cordially so far."

"Is there any danger?" Emilie wanted to know.

"There have been some things happen that they suspect the area Poles of doing," Rosina said. "One family had their horses turned loose during the night and another found their cat killed and nailed to the side of the barn."

"How cruel and heartless," Emilie said. "Who could do such a mean thing as kill innocent animals?"

"Well, we are living among men who take whole families and put them in concentration camps for no reason at all," Rosina retorted. "It seems anything is acceptable in the name of war."

"That's true. The storm troopers barged into our house and took Micah, threatening to kill us all," Magdalena added. "It seems this war has turned men into monsters."

"We are living in a scary time," Emilie admitted.

"Your vater wanted me to tell you girls so you would be

careful," Rosina added. "I would not go anywhere alone until things settle down."

Emilie and Magdalena had walked over together and now would definitely be walking home together, too. It was July and they had been in Poland for three months. Up until this point, there had been cases where the Poles ignored the Germans waving to them or made remarks about the Germans stealing the farms they now lived on. Those actions had been ignored or overlooked by the relocated Germans. To think that the Poles would turn to violence to show their disapproval of the Germans living in their midst was a new concern. Would disgruntled Poles begin attacking the relocated Germans? The thought concerned Magdalena, and that night after Erhard and Ewald were asleep she discussed her fears with Jacob.

"Mutti told Emilie and me that some of the Polish people are doing cruel things to the Germans who have relocated here," Magdalena began.

Jacob looked up from the blackberry pie he had been enjoying, concern on his face. "What kind of things?"

"One family had a cat killed and it was nailed to the side of the barn," Magdalena said.

"Hmm…might have been teens playing a prank," Jacob suggested.

"Another family had their horses turned loose while they were sleeping," Magdalena informed him.

"Still could be teens feeling their oats," Jacob said. "We need to be careful not to blame the Poles without any proof. As for our family, and the rest of the Griebs and Wallentines, we have been allowed to live in their midst without much trouble. We don't want to start accusing them of things we aren't sure of."

"You're probably right," Magdalena admitted, though her nerves were not completely calmed by Jacob's explanation. However, she let the matter drop and allowed Jacob to enjoy the rest of his pie.

No more incidents were heard about in the next few weeks and Magdalena decided Jacob must have been right. Killing a cat seemed like a really cruel thing for teenage boys to do, but the same thing had happened a few times back in Hoffnungstal. Maybe the story of the cat and the horses being turned loose were just rumors. Suppose someone had started spreading the stories to cause more conflict between the Germans and Polish farmers. This could be the case, and for that reason, Magdalena decided not to waste any more time worrying over it.

Late July brought lots of weeds to life, and Magdalena made her way to the garden with a hoe to fight against them. The fact that they had not left Bessarabia until October of last year had been a blessing. The garden plants had matured and produced seed for the next year's garden. Had they left any earlier, that would not have been the case because the seed would not have been mature yet. A good farmer always prepares for the next year's crops by saving seeds. Jacob had placed the seed in jars and Magdalena had packed them safely on the wagon when they left Bessarabia. Now they were thankful they had somewhere to plant them.

After Magdalena finished taking vengeance on the newly emerged weeds amongst the green beans, she checked the potatoes for beetles and larvae, which was a daily routine. The potatoes had been taken from the cellar of the house they now lived in. Thankfully, there had been enough extra to plant a crop. Next, Magdalena moved to the broccoli to check for pests and see if any was ready to eat. It was late in the year for the vegetable, but with not arriving here until mid-April, the seed was started late. It seemed to be doing okay but Magdalena was glad she had saved some seed for a fall planting, too. She had saved some of the cabbage and cauliflower seed for a fall crop, also. Her mouth watered at the thought of turning the cabbage into sauerkraut. She had already located a crock in the cellar for just such a use.

Moving through the rest of the garden hoeing weeds and checking progress, Magdalena was in her element. Again she gave thanks for the farm they had been assigned. She longed for Hoffnungstal but knew it would not have been safe to stay. Of course, the German troops had taken it back over now, so maybe they could return one day. She wondered if they would ever be allowed to leave the Reich, severing their German citizenship.

Of course, Jacob still dreamed of America. He wanted to live in the land of the free; a land where every man could pursue his dreams and where his children could grow up safe. He believed that one day they would go. Magdalena wasn't sure if it would happen, or if she even wanted the dream Jacob clung to. She would miss her family terribly and would have no hope of seeing them again unless they came to America, too. Magdalena was sure her mutti and vater would never make the move but maybe Albert and Emilie could be persuaded to go. It was a small hope Magdalena clung to, in case Jacob ever figured out a way to move them to America.

Being satisfied with the garden's progress, Magdalena went to the barn to put the hoe away. As she entered she could hear Erhard and Ewald in the loft. She was sure they were playing with the kittens like they did every day. Moving closer, she could hear Erhard saying something to Ewald in the language Micah spoke. Looking up, Magdalena could see Erhard holding the kitten and saying the word. Ewald responded with the German word for cat. They were practicing the unknown language. Was it in hopes of seeing Micah again? Magdalena didn't have the heart to tell them it would probably never happen. Quietly, she slipped from the barn and back to the house, her heart breaking all over again.

****

Summer of 1941 moved into fall and everything seemed to be going smoothly. The crops were being harvested and stored for the winter. The hay had been plentiful and the loft was full. The other two Jersey cows had given birth soon after Jacob and Magdalena arrived, and Jacob had given one of the cows and her calf to Albert and Emilie so they would have plenty of milk. Erhard increased his chore to milking two cows once a day and was proud of his accomplishment. With Erhard fully taking the responsibility of milking, Jacob was free to tend to other things. Life seemed to be finding a rhythm again, though the song it created was not nearly as melodious as the one in Bessarabia.

October came and the leaves turned their brilliant colors. It had always been one of Magdalena's favorite months when they lived in Hoffnungstal. April had been the other one, when everything greened up and came back to life. The only problem with the brilliant fall colors was that they didn't last long enough. A week after the leaves turned they began to fall becoming brown and crispy as they covered the ground. When that happened, it foretold of the cold winter months to come.

Jacob brought reports of the war back when he returned from a trip to town. Being able to read the local newspapers was helpful but he received reports by word of mouth, too. The rumor was that the Soviets were on the verge of collapse. The Germans had pushed to Leningrad in the north, were near Moscow in the center and was as far east as Taganrog in the south. It seemed the Germans would get another victory. The Greater Germany Hitler dreamed of was well on its way to becoming a reality.

Jacob shared this report with Magdalena as they sat at the kitchen table having a snack before bed. As they talked of the war and wondered what would happen if Germany actually took control of the Soviet Union, a German military truck rumbled into their drive. Jumping from his chair, Jacob went to the door and opened it before the storm troopers could barge in again. He did not want the storm troopers to wake his children nor have the opportunity to threaten them again. The last encounter Jacob had with the storm troopers was enough to put him in defense mode immediately and expect the worst.

"May I help you?" Jacob asked, trying to be as courteous as possible. The thoughts of all the things he wanted to say floated through his mind, and they were anything but courteous.

"Saddle a horse and be ready to ride in thirty minutes," one of the storm troopers commanded.

"Why?" Jacob asked, stunned.

"No questions, just do as I say," the storm trooper barked.

With that, the storm trooper got back in the truck and headed down the road in the direction of Albert and Emilie's. Jacob stepped back into the house in shock as Magdalena stood in the kitchen doorway, her face as white as fresh fallen snow. Why couldn't they just live on this Polish farm in peace?

"What's going on, Jacob?" Magdalena stammered.

"I have no idea," Jacob admitted. "All I know is I have a horse to saddle."

"Where are you going?" Magdalena asked.

"I have no idea," Jacob admitted.

"Please, Jacob," Magdalena begged, "don't go."

"We both know that's not an option," Jacob replied. "Disobeying an order will end in death, maybe for all of us. I must do as they say."

"Please, be careful," Magdalena whispered, knowing Jacob had no option but to go saddle a horse and be ready in thirty minutes.

"I will," Jacob promised, grabbing his coat and heading toward the barn.

Jacob knew Magdalena was watching through the window as he led his horse to the front yard. Jacob had no plans of going back to tell her what the Nazis had planned for him to do, knowing it would be something very dangerous. It would be better if Magdalena didn't know details. It would just cause her to worry more. Fifteen minutes passed and Albert showed up on horseback. Jacob could tell he was nervous as he fidgeted in his saddle.

"Do you have any idea what's going on?" Jacob asked Albert.

"They want us to steal horses from the Polish farmers," Albert stammered.

"Steal horses?" Jacob asked in disbelief. "Why would they want us to do such a thing?"

"The German soldiers need them to replace ones killed in battle," Albert said.

"This is crazy," Jacob hissed. "We could be killed while stealing the horses, and if the Polish farmers know it was us who did the stealing, we will be hated. It could put all of our families in danger."

"Yes, I realize this," Albert admitted, "but not doing as the storm troopers commanded will result in death or being thrown into a concentration camp. At least we have a chance of not getting caught stealing the horses. We have no chance of outsmarting the Nazis."

Jacob knew Albert was right. To not do what the storm troopers commanded would be just like committing suicide. They would not be given a second chance. Mounting his horse, Jacob muttered, "Lead the way, Brother."

Albert had been told which Polish farm they were to raid. He and Jacob made their way toward the nearest village. They discussed plans as they rode along, neither one sure how to get the job done.

"How will we catch the horses?" Albert asked.

"Did you bring any rope?" Jacob questioned.

"No, I was so nervous I just saddled my horse and rode to meet you," Albert admitted.

"We will have to have rope," Jacob said. "I suppose we will have to steal that, too."

"Sorry," Albert muttered. "I've never done anything like this before."

"Me neither," Jacob replied, "and I hope to never do it again. Why didn't the Nazis steal the horses themselves?"

"I don't know," Albert said. "The Nazis would have had guns to defend themselves. We have nothing, not even a rope!"

"We'll just have to do the best we can," Jacob said. "We have no other options."

"It's that place right there," Albert said, pointing to a house and barn an eighth of a mile off the main road.

"Okay," Jacob said, "let's get this over with."

The two men slowly made their way up the drive and around the side of the house. They could see six horses in a corral to the side of the barn. Deciding the best way to approach, the men circled to the back of the barn so they wouldn't be seen. Dismounting, they made their way into the barn.

"Here's some rope," Jacob whispered. "I'll catch three and tie them together and you catch the other three."

"Okay," Albert agreed, accepting the rope with trembling fingers.

Neither man had ever stolen anything in their lives. The fact that they were being forced to steal from their neighbors was preposterous. If they were caught, the good relationship they had worked so hard to keep with the area Polish people would be destroyed. Was this all in the Nazi's plan? To cause conflict where there hadn't been any?

Slipping into the corral, Jacob and Albert began to work the horses into groups of three. The men had worked with horses their entire lives so the beasts were not afraid of them but knew they were not their owners. They danced and fidgeted as the ropes were put around their necks and then connected to another horse beside them. They did not like being tethered together and snorted in protest. As Jacob and Albert exited the corral with the horses, a gun went off. The sound scared Jacob and Albert's own mounts, which had just been untied, and the horses took off like the bullets that were being shot at them. Jacob and Albert had no choice but to jump on one of the three horses they had tethered with rope and ride bareback. They headed for the woods behind the barn at breakneck speed. As they rode through the darkness trying to stay balanced on their mounts, limbs from trees smacked their faces and tore at their arms. When they could hear the shouts and gunfire no longer, they slowed the horses to a walk.

"That didn't go well," Albert remarked.

"It's because we're not trained thieves," Jacob retorted dryly.

"I hope our horses find their way home," Albert said.

"I hope the Poles we just stole from don't follow our horses to our homes," Jacob stated, causing both men to have a new fear.

"They don't have anything to ride so I doubt they could catch up with them," Albert said.

"Let's pray that's the case," Jacob said.

The men picked their way through the woods trying to figure out the direction they needed to go. Getting back on the main road was out of the question. Every Polish farmer in the area would be searching for six stolen horses.

By the time they wound their way through the back country to the meeting point of the storm troopers it was almost daylight. Jacob and Albert knew their wives would be frantic by now, but there was nothing they could do about it. Dismounting, they walked the last quarter mile to the drop off area.

"Good job, men," the arrogant lead storm trooper sneered.

"We almost got shot," Jacob growled, not able to hide his anger.

"That happens sometimes when you're stealing your neighbor's horses," the storm trooper said with a laugh.

"Here, take these," Albert said, holding out the rope. "We would like to get home before the sun is up and we can be easily spotted."

"You men don't act like you had a good night," another trooper smirked.

"By the way, where are your own mounts?" a third trooper questioned.

"Hopefully back at home," Jacob retorted.

"May we be dismissed?" Albert asked, trying to contain his anger.

"Yes, you may go," the lead trooper said. "We'll know where to find you if we need this service performed again."

Albert and Jacob left quickly, not wanting to allow the storm troopers time to think up another job for them. Keeping to the trees as much as possible, they made their way back home. They were weary from no sleep and their nerves were on edge. The thought of the Polish farmer discovering who had stolen his horses was taking its toll on the men.

Coming to Jacob's house first, they both decided to stop there. Leaving the cover of the woods they crossed a field and slipped into the back door of Jacob's barn. There they found Magdalena brushing the horse Jacob had ridden the night before. Thankfully, the mount had found its way home and it didn't appear that anyone had followed it.

"Jacob," Magdalena gasped running to his open arms. "I thought you were dead. I saw the horse standing in front of the barn as dawn began to lighten the sky."

"It was good that you put him in the barn," Jacob said. "He ran away when we were being shot at."

"Shot at! Why were you being shot at?"

"It seems the Germans needed more mounts for the armed forces. The storm troopers forced us to steal some from a Polish farm near the village," Albert supplied.

"If they find out who did this," Magdalena began.

"Yes, we know," Jacob said. "The fact that my horse is home and the Poles didn't follow it here means they don't know I was involved."

"I need to get home," Albert said. "Emilie will be worried sick."

Just then the barn door opened startling them all. It turned out to be Erhard coming to do the morning milking. He was surprised to see his parents and Uncle Albert in the barn.

"Gut morning," Erhard said. "What are you doing here, Uncle Albert?"

"I just stopped by to borrow something from your vater," Albert lied. To do anything else would put Erhard in danger, and Albert was not about to do that.

"Oh," Erhard said not really believing him. He could tell they were all upset, even if he was just a child.

"Well, I'm headed home now," Albert said as if all was well. "I'm sure Emilie about has breakfast fixed and I'm starving."

Jacob and Magdalena watched Albert exit the barn, praying he made it home safe. What would happen if the Poles found out Jacob and Albert had been the ones to steal six horses? The thought caused Magdalena's stomach to churn, like cream being whipped to butter.

Going to the house, Jacob sank into a kitchen chair as Magdalena began to prepare breakfast. Jacob never wanted to spend another night like the one he had just had. He hoped he was not asked to do anymore raids but knew he couldn't refuse if the Nazis demanded he do so. He felt trapped by the circumstances.

Erhard came in with the milk and washed up for breakfast. The blessing was said and Erhard and Ewald dug in. Jacob and Magdalena ate little, silently communicating their worry for Albert's safety. The whole situation was a nightmare but they were not sleeping.

"I need to visit Aunt Emilie," Magdalena announced as she cleared the breakfast dishes from the table. "Wouldn't you boys like to go see your cousins and play awhile?"

"Yes," Ewald piped up answering for both brothers.

"Okay," Magdalena said. "Go and collect the eggs and I should be ready to leave when you get back."

The boys did as they were told and as soon as they were outside Magdalena turned to Jacob. "Go and get some rest while I go check on Albert and Emilie. I'm sure his horse returned and everything is fine but we need to know for sure."

"I'll go with you," Jacob said.

"No, you need to sleep," Magdalena instructed. "I go to Emilie's all the time. It will not look suspicious at all."

"Okay," Jacob said wearily, "but be alert and don't stay too long."

"Don't worry, Jacob," Magdalena said. "Just rest and try to forget this whole thing."

"That will never happen," Jacob said angrily. "I've been forced to steal from my own neighbor. It sickens me that I have been brought so low."

"You had no choice," Magdalena reminded. "They would have killed you and Albert both if you had refused."

"I know you're right," Jacob admitted, "but it still doesn't change the fact that I've stolen from someone else."

Erhard and Ewald bounded back into the house, a basket of eggs in Ewald's hand. "The new hens that hatched this spring are starting to lay eggs," Ewald announced.

"That's good," Magdalena said, smiling at his excitement.

"See how much smaller the pullet egg is compared to the big hen's egg?" Erhard asked, holding two eggs next to each other.

"Yeah, and look how many pullet eggs we got," Ewald said with amazement.

"We will take a dozen to Aunt Emilie," Magdalena told the boys. "They don't have as many chickens as us and could use extra eggs. Put twelve in a separate basket, please."

"Okay," Ewald answered, grabbing the basket full of eggs up to do the chore.

"We'll be back soon," Magdalena told Jacob who was dozing off in the kitchen chair. Touching his shoulder, Magdalena inclined her head toward the bedroom, silently telling him to go get some sleep.

Magdalena and the boys headed up the road toward Albert and Emilie's. The boys were excited to spend time with their cousins and took no notice of the fact that Magdalena was fretting. Allowing the boys to set the pace, the half mile distance was covered in no time. As Magdalena approached the house she brought the boys back to walk beside her. Scanning the yard and barn lot, she didn't see anything out of the ordinary. Concluding it was safe to go knock, Magdalena headed to the back door. Emilie opened immediately and pulled Magdalena into her embrace.

"What a night," Emilie whispered in Magdalena's ear.

Magdalena nodded agreeing wholeheartedly. She knew better than to speak because the tears choking her would spill out onto her cheeks. Explaining why she was so upset would be difficult. Erhard and Ewald nor her nephews could know the truth. The thought of anyone finding out what Jacob and Albert were forced to do was causing Magdalena's small breakfast to feel like a rock in her stomach. She prayed she could keep from hurling that rock out here on Emilie's kitchen floor.

"Your cousins are playing in the barn," Emilie told Erhard and Ewald. "Would you like to join them?"

Erhard and Ewald bobbed their heads and scurried back out the door to go play. Magdalena and Emilie sank into kitchen chairs, Magdalena gathering one year old Klaus on her lap as she did. The women finally allowed the tears to fall. In a short twelve hours, the Grieb's lives had been changed drastically. It seemed any peace they had found after leaving Bessarabia had been very short-lived.

"I was so scared last night," Magdalena whispered through her tears.

"Me, too," Emilie confessed. "I wish you and I had just spent the night together. At least we could have comforted one another."

"Yes, but then the boys would know the truth about their vater," Magdalena pointed out.

"That's true," Emilie said not wanting her sons to know the truth either.

"When Jacob's horse returned without him, I thought I would faint," Magdalena cried. "I just knew something bad had happened. Jacob never gets thrown from a mount and there was his horse at dawn standing in front of the barn with no rider."

"At least Jacob's horse returned safely," Emilie whispered.

"Sister, what are you saying?" Magdalena questioned as fear enveloped her like a thick fog.

"Albert's horse did not return home," Emilie said. "We don't know where it is."

"This is awful news," Magdalena said, thinking about Albert's horse being seen by neighbors. It wouldn't take long for them to figure out who it belonged to.

"Yes, I know," Emilie admitted. "Albert is getting some sleep before the discovery of his horse is made and he is forced to answer questions. He honestly doesn't know what to tell the neighbors when they come."

"The truth will set you free," Magdalena murmured.

Panic filled Emilie's eyes. "What if they kill us?"

"They are going to know what our husbands did when the horse leads them here," Magdalena pointed out. "We can only pray they will have mercy and know Jacob and Albert were forced by the storm troopers to perform the raid."

"I'm so scared," Emilie sobbed.

"You should probably lie down," Magdalena said, thinking of her sister's pregnancy.

"I can't," Emilie said. "I have to watch for the horse to return and put it in the barn. Albert has trusted me to do that."

"I'll watch," Magdalena assured her. "Go lie down for a little while. I'll keep an eye on the boys and watch for the horse."

"Are you sure, Sister?" Emilie asked.

"Yes, now go get some rest," Magdalena instructed. "You're all done in and you need to keep your strength up for the little one you're carrying."

"You're probably right," Emilie said, rubbing her rounded six month pregnant belly.

"You know I'm right," Magdalena said. "I'm your older sister, and I'm always right."

"You always have been the strong one," Emilie admitted while struggling out of the kitchen chair. "Wake me up if anything happens."

"Okay," Magdalena said having absolutely no intentions of waking Emilie if the Polish neighbors showed up. She would wake Albert immediately but would allow Emilie to sleep through the whole ordeal.

Magdalena watched as Emilie went to her sons' bedroom to lie down. Emilie didn't want to wake Albert by lying in her own bed. Getting up from the table, Magdalena walked to the screen door with Klaus on her hip and looked outside. The boys were in the yard now, taking turns swinging on a rope Albert had hung from a large tree limb in the back yard. They laughed and took turns pushing the one who was swinging on the rope. If she could just freeze that moment in time, Magdalena thought.

Magdalena knew that Albert's horse was going to lead the Polish farmers straight to this farm. The dumb animal didn't know any better. All the horse could remember was how to get home, and eventually he would do just that. The Polish farmer must have the horse in a stall waiting until morning chores were done to let it go, thus allowing the horse to lead the way to one of the thieves. It was just a matter of time.

Magdalena went outside so she could get a full view of the lane leading to Emilie's house and the road beyond. She wanted to be able to warn Albert in plenty of time. She also needed to get the boys to safety, too, should the Polish farmer come. She had no idea how the Polish farmer would react after discovering his German neighbor had stolen six of his horses but Magdalena knew he would be furious. The boys needed to be safely away from the scene.

"Boys," Magdalena called to them, "if I tell you to go to the barn and stay there, I want you to obey immediately and without questions, okay?"

"Okay, Aunt Magdalena," young Albert, the oldest of Emilie's sons, said. "Is something dangerous happening?"

At eleven, Magdalena realized young Albert noticed more than they gave him credit for. She needed to make the boys understand the importance of hiding in the barn without making them too scared. She decided to put Albert in charge of hiding the other boys.

"Come here, Albert," Magdalena instructed.

Albert came to stand in front of his aunt. "What is it, Aunt Magdalena?

"You're the oldest," Magdalena began, "so I need you to take charge if I tell you to go to the barn, okay?"

"I will, Aunt Magdalena," Albert promised.

"If I tell you to go, I want you to take the boys to the loft," Magdalena said. "Keep them quiet and hide in the hay if anyone comes in the barn. Do you understand?"

"Yes," Albert answered seriously.

"And one more thing, Albert," Magdalena whispered. "If something bad happens, take the boys to our house. Uncle Jacob is there and will know what to do."

"Okay, Aunt Magdalena," Albert said, his eyes wide with fear.

"It will probably be fine," Magdalena tried to assure Albert, "but just in case it isn't, I need you to be prepared."

"I will do my best, Aunt Magdalena," Albert promised.

"I know you will, Albert. You may go back and play," Magdalena said smiling, hoping to calm his nerves.

"So much for not scaring the boys," Magdalena muttered to herself but she knew she needed to have a plan. The fact was, she didn't know what the Polish neighbors would do to them after finding out Albert and Jacob was responsible for the raid. They might even kill them and so preparing Albert seemed like a good choice, even if it scared him some. She hoped Emilie wouldn't be mad for how she had decided to handle the situation.

Magdalena went to the garden to see if there was anything she could do while she waited. Seeing a few weeds, she retrieved a hoe from the barn and went to work, keeping one eye on the road. Klaus was happy to play in the dirt at the edge of the garden while his aunt did the chore. After about an hour of hoeing, the evidence came home with the saddle still on its back. The horse was galloping down the road as fast as he could, several Polish farmers keeping pace a quarter mile behind him.

"Albert, it's time to go to the barn," Magdalena instructed. "Remember everything I told you."

"I will," Albert assured Magdalena, scooping up one year old Klaus and gathering the other boys quickly. Magdalena wondered if she should keep Klaus with her and decided to take him from Albert's arms. It would be impossible for Albert to keep one so young quiet.

With the boys safely entering the barn, Magdalena headed in the house to wake Albert. Quickly making her way to the bedroom she shook her brother-in-law's shoulder until his eyes popped open.

"Albert," Magdalena whispered, "your horse is returning."

Jumping to his feet, Albert looked around the room. "Where's Emilie?"

"Sleeping," Magdalena said quietly hoping Albert would leave her that way.

Magdalena went back to the kitchen and looked out the screen door. Albert's horse came trotting up the lane and went straight to the barn door waiting to be let in. Stupid animal, Magdalena thought. He might as well have opened his mouth and spoke, leading the Poles here like he did.

Albert joined Magdalena at the door and shook his head. "I figured they had captured him and were waiting for the opportunity to use him as a compass. What will I say to them?"

"Tell them the truth," Magdalena said. "Maybe they will understand. They know how cruel the Nazis have been to their families and neighbors. There's no use to lie anyway because they know the truth."

"Jacob always did say you have a level head," Albert sighed. "Where are the boys?"

"I instructed Albert to take them to the loft and hide in the hay," Magdalena said.

"Thank you, Magdalena," Albert said, "good thinking. Please, stay in the house with Klaus and keep Emilie inside if she wakes up."

"I will," Magdalena promised.

With that, Albert stepped outside and called to his horse. The animal trotted to his master, glad to be home. Albert loosened the saddle and removed it as the Polish farmers came into the yard.

"So, this horse belongs to you." It was a statement not a question. Denying it would be pointless.

"Yes, this is my horse," Albert admitted.

"Did you know it was used to raid my farm last night?" the Polish farmer in the front of the pack asked.

"Unfortunately, yes I do," Albert said.

"There were two of you," the farmer stated. "Who was the other man?"

"It doesn't matter," Albert said. "I will take the full blame. I do want you to understand that we were forced by German storm troopers, though. We have never stolen anything in our lives and wouldn't have last night if we hadn't been threatened with death."

"I know your brother was the one with you," the farmer said, leaving no room for argument. "We have had no trouble from any of your family since you came here. I don't understand why you would treat us this way."

"We didn't do it by choice," Albert said. "Look around, your horses are not here. We turned them over to the Nazis."

The Polish farmers looked in the corral beside the barn then headed into the barn to check the stalls. Albert followed close behind, just in case the boys were not hidden. Finding nothing, the farmers came back outside.

"Just know that now your family will be treated like all the other Germans relocated here," the farmer who had had his horses stolen informed Albert.

"I truly am sorry," Albert said. "Please, believe me when I say we were forced."

"You are not a good neighbor," the farmer answered. "You should have refused to make the raid."

"You know they would have killed us," Albert lamented.

"I would have killed you too, if I could have gotten a good

shot last night," the farmer reminded Albert.

"Yes, I suppose you're right," Albert admitted.

"As I stated, from this day on, you're just another stinking German to us," the farmer informed Albert again, and with that, they were gone.

"You did what you had to do," Magdalena assured Albert, stepping outside as the Polish farmers left.

"We have put our families in danger," Albert said.

"But you would have been killed or arrested if you hadn't done what the storm troopers told you to do," Magdalena reminded.

"I wish this war would end and we could go back to normal lives," Albert said.

"Me, too," Magdalena agreed.

Albert picked up his horses reigns and walked toward the barn. Opening the door, he called the boys down from the loft. The boys scrambled down the ladder and back outside into the sunshine. They began swinging on the rope again, like there was not a care in the world. Magdalena envied their ignorance for just a moment, but then was thankful they had not a clue how evil people could be, especially Hitler and his group of followers. Young Albert was the only one who realized that his vater's horse had just returned and how odd that was. He looked toward the barn and then back at his Aunt Magdalena.

"Where had Vater's horse been?" young Albert questioned.

"He took a little trip last night," Magdalena answered not wanting to give out any details. "He's back now, and everything is going to be fine."

Young Albert shook his head up and down and walked back to the rope swing. Magdalena was sure he knew there was more to the story but he didn't ask. He had been brought up to respect adults and not question them about things they did not offer up for discussion.

Taking Klaus to the house, Magdalena put a dry diaper on him and rocked him for a bit. It didn't take long for his eyes to droop and close. Carrying him to the bedroom, Magdalena placed him in the small, low bed Albert had constructed just for him. Hoping he would sleep awhile and allow Emilie to do the same, Magdalena headed back outside to gather Ewald and Erhard. They had been gone long enough and Jacob would worry, if he was awake.

Albert senior had stalled the horse and brushed him good. He was now talking to the boys and swinging them higher on the rope than they could possibly hope to go if one of them was pushing. Magdalena watched for a moment then approached the scene.

"We need to get back home, Albert," Magdalena said.

"Okay," Albert answered. "Thanks for everything."

"You're welcome," Magdalena said, knowing they had just begun to see the ill results of the forced raid.

"Tell Jacob I will come by later," Albert said.

"Okay," Magdalena said reading between the lines. What Albert was really saying was that he and Jacob needed to make some plans to keep everyone safe. "Klaus is asleep in his bed."

"I'll check on him in a little while," Albert assured Magdalena. "Be careful going home."

"We will," Magdalena promised, starting back for home with her boys.

Magdalena kept watch for the Polish farmers all the way home but didn't see any. She was glad when they came to their lane and were safe in their house. Jacob was still sleeping, so Magdalena sent the boys out to play in the back yard with instructions to stay close to the house where she could see them. An hour later, Jacob emerged from their bedroom rubbing sleep from his eyes. The four hour nap had given him some strength back and he was anxious to get to work. Finding Magdalena in the kitchen preparing the noon meal, Jacob sat at the table to find out what had happened at Albert and Emilie's.

"Feeling better?" Magdalena asked.

"Yes, the rest felt good," Jacob admitted. "How long have you been back from Albert and Emilie's?"

"About an hour," Magdalena said.

"And..," Jacob prompted.

"It's not good, Jacob," Magdalena said. "Albert's horse was not home when he returned. The Polish farmer had caught it last night."

"Oh, no," Jacob moaned, rising to his feet. "That horse will lead them right to Albert's house. I have to get over there."

"Sit back down, Jacob," Magdalena said. "They've already

been there; came in right behind the horse, like hounds following a fox."

"What did Albert tell them?" Jacob asked.

"The truth," Magdalena stated. "There was really no other option."

"How did they respond?"

"They said we would now be treated "like all the other stinking Germans", Magdalena said, repeating the Polish farmer's words.

"How many came?" Jacob asked.

"Five," Magdalena answered. "Everyone in the area knows what you and Albert did last night."

"Where were the boys when the Polish farmers showed up?"

"I had instructed young Albert to hide them in the barn loft if I told him to do so," Magdalena said. "He did a good job of obeying."

"He's a good boy," Jacob said.

"Yes, he is," Magdalena agreed. "He knows more than the other boys but still doesn't know the truth of what happened."

"It won't be long before they all know the truth," Jacob said mournfully. "There is no way they won't find out now."

"You're probably right," Magdalena agreed, "but we will cross that bridge when there's water under it. No sense worrying about what hasn't happened yet."

Jacob knew she was right, as usual, but he sure wished he could have done something about it. His and Albert's sons knowing their vaters had stolen was almost more than Jacob could bear.

"Albert will be over later," Magdalena informed Jacob.

"I suppose we'll figure out what to do next," Jacob concluded. "Why couldn't that stupid horse just get home before they caught it?"

"It was only doing what it knew to do," Magdalena said. "I'm sure it was scared to death when the bullets began to fly. It probably ran the wrong way at the end of the lane, being so afraid and all."

"I assure you it was frightened," Jacob confirmed. "So were Albert and I. We have never been so scared in all our lives."

"Let's just hope the storm troopers don't make you do it

again," Magdalena remarked.

"If they do, we will be dead men either way," Jacob said, anger boiling to the surface with his words.

Magdalena knew he was right. To refuse to perform the raid would bring death or imprisonment from the Nazis, to do another raid would bring death to both men at the hands of the Polish farmers. They had been pushed into a corner with no way out.

Chapter Ten

The lives of the Grieb and Wallentine families became miserable after the horse raid. A month had passed since the raid and the Nazis hadn't demanded Albert and Jacob repeat the act. However, the Polish farmers living around them were vindictive and showed it in every way they could. Jacob and Albert had tried to protect their sons from the truth of what they had been forced to do but it was impossible. The accusation was screamed at them each time they passed a Polish farmer on the road. The boys were kept close to home for fear of what might happen if a Pole caught them out without any adult protection.

"Jacob said a Polish farmer spit on him today as they passed on the road," Magdalena shared with Emilie while she visited with her.

"Albert won't let me and the boys go anywhere without him," Emilie admitted. "I'm glad you came over with Jacob. This cold November weather has been keeping us cooped up in the house and I'm about to go crazy."

"Maybe the boys will run all their energy out playing in the barn," Magdalena said.

"We can always hope," Emilie laughed.

It was good to hear laughter after the last month of constant worry. Magdalena wondered if happiness would ever become part of their daily life again. She knew she shouldn't worry so but the fear of what the Polish farmers would do next caused her much stress.

"I will be glad when the next six weeks are passed," Emilie said. "This child is getting heavier by the day."

"You are getting quite large," Magdalena noted.

"Thank you, Sister," Emilie retorted, "that statement made

me feel a lot better."

"Just trying to be helpful," Magdalena replied smiling.

"I'll do the same for you the next time you're expecting," Emilie stated.

"I hope that is soon," Magdalena sighed.

"I'm sorry, Sister," Emilie apologized. "I didn't mean to hurt you with my words."

"I know, Emilie," Magdalena said, "don't give it another thought."

"It was so inconsiderate of me, though," Emilie said.

"God will give us another child in His time," Magdalena assured her sister. "It's just hard to wait for that miracle to happen."

"I'll pray it's soon," Emilie told her.

"Thank you," Magdalena said. "Do you think you will finally get a girl this time after having four boys?"

"One can always hope," Emilie said with a laugh.

Jacob and Albert came into the house and Jacob announced it was time to head home. Going back out to the barn, Jacob gathered Erhard and Ewald and the family started walking for home. About half way there, a wagon and team of horses came toward them. It was one of the Polish farmers. Jacob braced himself for the insults, moving his family to the far side of him. As the wagon neared, the man driving reached behind him and picked up a bucket. Before Jacob realized what was about to happen, the Polish farmer flung horse manure all over them. He screamed "stinking Germans" and drove off as fast as his horses could pull him.

"Yuk," Ewald fussed. "I hate horse manure!"

"None of us like it thrown on us, Son," Jacob stated. "I'm sorry all of you have to suffer for my wrongdoings."

"It's not like you wanted to steal," Erhard said. "The storm troopers made you, just like they made you hand Micah over to them."

Jacob was sure the gun that had been pressed to Erhard's temple the day the storm troopers took Micah was forever branded in Erhard's mind. It had not been hard to convince his son that the same men had forced him to steal horses from their Polish neighbors. Erhard had witnessed firsthand the evil the Nazis were capable of.

"We will just have to endure the ill treatment," Magdalena stated. "To retaliate in any way will just put fuel to the fire. Hopefully, with time, things will settle back down."

"Your mutti is right," Jacob confirmed. "We must not hurl insults or allow them to provoke us into a fight. It will do no good and could cause the Poles to physically harm us."

"Look at me," Ewald whined. "I stink and I even have manure in my hair!"

"You will wash, Ewald," Magdalena assured him, wondering where this child had come from. Growing up on a farm should have made him immune to the smell of horse manure. He had always been fanatical about being clean.

Reaching home, the Grieb family washed up and changed clothes. Magdalena scrubbed the soiled garments immediately to prevent staining. She hung the clothes on a line Jacob had strung in the kitchen near the wood stove for winter. It was nice not to have to hang the clothes outside in the freezing temperatures and they dried quickly near the warmth.

The next morning, to the sadness of Erhard and Ewald, one of their kittens had been killed and left hanging on the barn door. It seemed the Polish farmers were not done punishing them yet and they prayed it didn't lead to more violent acts. With the fear that things would escalate past killing pets and throwing manure, the Grieb and Wallentine families chose not to travel anywhere after dark.

****

The war between the Soviets and Nazis continued with Germany still holding the upper hand. Pushing further east, the Nazis were backing up the Red Army all across the Soviet Union. However, German colonies that became occupied as the Nazis overtook them were now empty. They had all been evacuated quickly and it could only be assumed that the colonists had been loaded onto railroad cars and taken north and east. The slave camps that the Germans in the Ukraine had told the soldiers about must be full and overflowing with the mass influx of refugees from the now empty colonies.

Emil and Edward had fought side by side through the entire fall and now winter was approaching rapidly. They had pushed as far as the Don River and were awaiting instructions of how to proceed. They were cold most of the time with no warmth to be found. At night they talked of happier days living in Bessarabia in their vater's vineyard. They wondered if the art of winemaking would ever be of use to them again.

News reached the Nazi troops on December 7, 1941 that Japan had bombed the United States' Pearl Harbor, located in Hawaii. They were sure the act would cause the United States to declare war and it came one day later. By December 13th, Germany and its Axis partners had declared war on the United States. The war had now reached all the way around the world. The Great War, deemed the war to end all wars, would now be known as World War I. World War II had just become a reality.

"You know, we may be fighting against the Red Army successfully now but pulling the United States into this war will change everything," Edward told Emil as they shivered in their tent trying to get warm enough for sleep to come.

"We could have already beaten the Red Army if Hitler didn't have two fronts to hold," Emil replied. "If we had the troops from the Western front join us, we could finish off the Soviets quite quickly then turn our attention back to the West."

"True, but if the German troops pull out of the already conquered territory to the west and south of Germany, those countries will regroup. Germany will just have to fight to gain the same territory twice," Edward pointed out.

"I just wish this war would hurry up and end," Emil muttered. "I'm tired of being cold and hungry. I just want to move back to Hoffnungstal and live a peaceful life again. We just didn't know how good we had it, and now it's all gone."

"I don't see us ever returning to Hoffnungstal," Edward said. "The only way that would ever happen is if Germany can hold on to that Romanian territory after the war ends. With the United States joining the effort for the Allies, I'm afraid all will be lost. There will never be a Greater Germany. The Allies will win back all of the territory to the west and south of Germany and we will be lucky if Germany even ends up with all of its original land."

"Our only hope is to push the Red Army until they surrender. Then, the German troops who have been fighting the Soviet Union can join the Western front," Emil surmised. "That will be the only way Germany will win this war."

"If Stalin had honored the non-aggression pact signed in 1939 with Hitler, we wouldn't be shivering in this tent right now," Edward fumed.

"I don't know all the details of that agreement," Emil said, "but obviously Stalin took more territory for himself than he was supposed to."

"Maybe Hitler should have just let him have it," Edward replied. "Creating two war fronts is going to be what causes Hitler to lose this war. Mark my words, Brother."

"Tonight, as cold as I am, I would almost surrender so I could go home," Emil said.

"But where is home?" Edward pointed out.

"That's a good question," Emil replied. "I just don't know what I'm fighting for. We have no true home anymore. We are just a couple of displaced Russian Germans who really have no loyalty to anyone."

"We're fighting for Aunt Isabella and all those other Germans we liberated in the colonies west of here," Edward reminded Emil. "If we lose the war on this front, those Germans will go back under Communist rule. It will be devastating for them."

"You're absolutely right, Brother," Emil admitted. "I have to remember their plight and fight to keep them free. Tonight, I'm just too cold and exhausted to think rationally."

"That will become our mission," Edward said. "We have to be encouraged to fight for something, and we will make it for the freedom of our fellow Russian Germans."

"It would be a lot easier if it wasn't so cold, though," Emil said, as a shiver ran through him.

"We will pray for some warmer weather," Edward added. "Wrap up as best you can and let's get some sleep. Morning will come soon enough."

"How many days until Christmas?" Emil asked, his mind turning to other thoughts.

"Five days," Edward replied. "The day won't be much cause for celebration out here, though."

"Christmas is always a reason for celebration," Emil reminded Edward. "We will remember the day and all its meaning.

Maybe by this time next year we will be home celebrating with our family."

"That is my hope and dream," Edward mumbled as he drifted off to sleep.

****

Christmas came for the Grieb and Wallentine families. Though there was war all around them, they still celebrated the birth of their Savior. One of the things Rosina Wallentine had made room for in their wagon upon leaving Bessarabia was a crèche. It was small and she just knew she could not leave it behind. The crèche had not been taken from the wagon the previous Christmas because they were in the camp but this year is was displayed in the center of her kitchen table.

All the Griebs gathered at Gottlieb and Rosina Wallentine's farm to recognize the day. Though fear continued to plague them from the conflict with their neighboring Poles, it was not mentioned throughout the festivities. Nor was the fact that there certainly would not be peace on earth this Christmas or anytime soon, from the reports that had reached them.

Each family had killed two roosters and roasted them for the occasion. Along with the birds, there were homemade noodles, green beans, mashed potatoes, and gravy. There were pickles and relishes to munch on, and the dessert table overflowed. The garden harvest had been good!

Gottlieb said the blessing over the food, remembering his two sons who were fighting a war somewhere in the Soviet Union. The two young men were sadly missed on this special day. Rosina wiped tears as Gottlieb said amen and everyone dug in. It was almost like past Christmases in Bessarabia, except there was no Wallentine wine to toast the occasion.

When the meal was finished and the dishes washed and put away, the families sat around the living room singing Christmas carols. As the group finished "Silent Night", Gottlieb asked the children if they knew how that song came about. When they answered no, he began to share the story.

"The story begins in 1818," Gottlieb began, "on Christmas Eve. Each Christmas Eve the St. Nicholas church in the village of Orberndorf, Austria held a special mass. As the priest, Joseph

Mohr, prepared for that year's celebration, it was discovered that the pump organ would not work. No matter what the priest did, he could not fix the organ. The priest, not willing to let the service take place without special music, paused to say a prayer of inspiration. At that moment, a Christmas poem the priest had written two years earlier came to mind. The poem had been inspired by a winter's walk from Mohr's grandfather's house to the church. He now went to locate the poem, thinking it may be able to be put to music."

"Digging through his desk, Joseph Mohr found "Stille Nacht! Heilige Nacht!" and headed out the door to the local school teacher's apartment, Franz Gruber, who was also the church's accomplished organist. Knocking on the door, Mohr said a hasty Merry Christmas then plunged into the predicament they were in. Thrusting the poem into Gruber's hands, he asked if he thought he could put music to the words. Looking it over, Gruber said he thought he could. A few hours later, the choir came to the church to rehearse their songs for that night. Priest Mohr and Franz Gruber told them of the organ's failure to work and introduced the new song they had created together. A guitar was used for music, and the choir quickly learned the song "Stille Nacht! Heilige Nacht!" The congregation loved the new song and its simple melody."

"When Karl Mauracher, an organ builder and repair man, came to St. Nicholas to fix the organ, Priest Mohr told him about the frantic search for a special song for Christmas Eve mass. Mohr showed Mauracher the song he and Gruber had created and sang it for him. Mauracher wrote down the words and shared the song with many churches and towns as he went about fixing organs. By 1832, the song reached the ears of King William IV of Prussia and he requested it be sung by his nation's Cathedral Choir at the annual Christmas celebration. The song's popularity took off like wild fire and it began to be sung everywhere. Sadly, Joseph Mohr would not be recognized as the song's writer until after his death in 1848. He died penniless."

"So, he never got paid for writing the song?" Erhard asked his Opa Wallentine.

"No, Erhard, he never received a penny," Gottlieb answered, "but I don't think he wrote the song to become wealthy. He wrote it as a special celebration song for the birth of Jesus."

"That was a gut story, Opa," Erhard said. "I'll remember to tell it every Christmas."

"You do that, Erhard," Gottlieb answered. "Don't let people ever forget what Christmas really means and why we celebrate."

The sun was sinking low in the western sky and the planet Venus could be seen just above the horizon. The families all said their goodbyes and left together. There was safety in numbers, and so they chose to travel that way. They couldn't imagine someone out on Christmas looking to do evil but they decided to take every precaution.

A week after Christmas, Albert came in Jacob and Magdalena's yard riding his horse. Albert had pushed the beast into a run and was hanging on for dear life. Hardly waiting for the horse to stop, Albert dismounted and burst through their back door.

"It's time!" Albert said breathless. "We've got to go!"

"Time for what, Albert?" Jacob questioned.

"The baby!" Albert replied, exasperated at the wasted time of explaining.

"Let's go," Magdalena said, not thinking for a second.

They had just finished breakfast and Magdalena left the dishes on the table and her family sitting around it. Throwing on her coat, she ran with Albert back to his horse. He hadn't even bothered to saddle it. Albert jumped on the horses back and pulled Magdalena up behind him. They raced back to Albert and Emilie's at breakneck speed. Albert dropped Magdalena off at the door and took the horse to the barn. Finding young Albert in the barn, his father asked him to take care of the horse for him. Not waiting for an answer, Albert headed back to the house.

"What do you need me to do?" Albert asked, entering the bedroom where Magdalena tended to Emilie.

"Get some clean towels and boil some water," Magdalena instructed, "and calm down. It's not like you haven't been through this four times before."

"Okay," Albert answered, grinning sheepishly.

"And after you get the towels and put the water on, go get our mutti," Magdalena instructed. "She won't be happy if she misses this."

"Okay," Albert answered again taking orders from his sister-in-law like she was a drill sergeant.

Turning, Albert ran into the wall, cracking his head. Backing up and holding the place where a goose egg was rising, he tried to exit again. Shaking her head, Magdalena turned her full attention on Emilie.

"Are you close?" she asked knowing Emilie would be able to tell her precisely how much time there was until the little one entered the world.

"Contractions one minute apart," Emilie panted.

"Okay," Magdalena said. "It won't be long then."

Albert returned with the clean towels and Magdalena snatched them from his hands. Taking one look at his pale face she said, "Go get Mutti, and take one of the boys with you. I honestly don't know if you could get there on your own."

"Right," Albert answered. "Go get Rosina and take one of the boys."

As Albert turned to leave, Magdalena hollered after him, "And don't take just your horse. Mutti is not going to ride behind you with no saddle like I had to. Hitch up a wagon." Turning back to Emilie, Magdalena saw a smile spread across her face.

"You always were the bossy one," Emilie said through her pain. "Did he really come get you without a saddle on the horse?"

"Yes, and I just had the fastest ride of my life," Magdalena huffed. "I thought you were dying the way he was acting. Albert couldn't even put a sentence together when he reached our house."

As another contraction gripped Emilie, she screamed like she might really be dying. Magdalena knew she was close and after the contraction eased, she placed some folded towels under Emilie. By the time Albert returned with Rosina, Emilie was holding their new baby in her arms, born January 1, 1942.

"Is it a girl?" Rosina asked hopefully.

"No, Mutti," Emilie said, "come meet your newest grandson, Walter."

"Another boy," Rosina sighed. "Oh, well, at least he's healthy. That's all that matters."

Rosina stayed with Emilie for three days, until she could get back on her feet. With a husband and five hungry boys, Emilie welcomed the help. She had hoped for a girl to lighten the load in a few years, but her mutti was right, having a healthy baby was most important.

Winter of 1942 came and was brutal throughout January and into February. No one went anywhere if they didn't absolutely have to. For this reason, the Poles insults had lost a bit of their sting. Without being taunted constantly, the Germans felt safer and more at peace. They all knew it was a false sense of security but they welcomed the reprieve just the same.

Chapter Eleven

The second week of February warmed a bit and Emilie sent her three oldest boys, Albert, Richard, and Erwin, to play in the barn. They had all been cooped up in the house too long and the boys definitely needed to burn some energy. The boys became involved in a game of tag that led them to the outdoors where there was more room to run. The rope swing became base.

"You run slow, little brother," Richard taunted Erwin who was "it".

"Why don't you turn loose of that rope and we'll see how fast I can run," Erwin spouted back.

"Hey, Erwin, what are you waiting for?" young Albert hollered. "I'm not on base. You can tag me."

"You're way too fast, Albert, but Richard's not," Erwin informed Albert. "Richard's just a chicken roosting on the base."

"He's not now," Albert said pointing at Richard as he began to run toward the barn. "Richard gave you the slip while you were turned around."

Erwin took off after Richard as fast as he could. Richard bypassed the barn doors and ran around to the back. As Erwin come flying around the corner of the barn, he plowed right into Richard. Richard fell to the ground from the blow and stared into sightless eyes.

"Tag," Erwin shouted, triumphant in his victory.

"Erwin," Richard whispered, "go get Vater and hurry."

Erwin stopped his victory dance and looked down at Richard. The involuntary scream that came from him brought young Albert to the back of the barn.

"It's the Polish carpenter's son," Richard said, pointing at the young man on the ground as he scrambled to his feet.

"How did he get behind our barn?" Erwin asked.

"More importantly," Albert said, "how did he get dead?"

"Go get Vater," Richard told Erwin again pushing him in the direction of the house.

Erwin suddenly sprang into action and ran to tell his father. Bursting through the back door, he began to scream. "Vater, Vater, come quick!" Erwin gasped. "There's a dead man behind our barn."

"Slow down, Erwin," Albert senior instructed. "Now, what did you say?"

Erwin took a deep breath to calm his nerves and slow his breathing. "There's a dead man behind our barn. It's the Polish carpenter's son."

"Oh, no," Emilie whispered, turning pale, "as if they didn't hate us enough and now this."

"Stay in the house," Albert ordered Erwin, "I'll go see for myself."

"Be careful," Emilie said, "and send Richard and Albert to the house."

Albert grabbed his coat and headed out the back door. Quickly, he walked to the back of the barn. There he found Richard and Albert at the corner of the barn. Richard had lost his breakfast on the ground and Albert was pale and not speaking.

"Go to the house, boys," Albert demanded.

Numbly, the boys obeyed, trudging slowly to the house. Their usual chatter and bantering was silent as the shock of the discovery took full effect. Albert senior knew it would be vivid in his sons' young minds for a very long time.

Turning his attention to the silent young man, Albert could see a gunshot wound in his chest. There was no pool of blood around the body, and they had not heard a shot fired in the night. He knew from this evidence that the boy had not been killed here behind the barn. Someone had dumped his body behind Albert's barn on purpose. The Nazis were the first suspects that came to mind.

Knowing he had no other choice, Albert went to the barn to saddle his horse. He had to go tell the Polish carpenter that his son lay dead behind his barn. Convincing the man that Albert had no part in it was going to be hard.

Walking to the house, Albert went to check on the boys and explain the situation to Emilie before leaving for the carpenter's home. Albert, Richard, and Erwin were sitting quietly in the living room in complete silence. Emilie had sunk into the rocking chair with baby Walter and was staring out the window. Klaus sat playing with blocks in the living room floor, not old enough to realize what had just happened.

"What are we going to do?" Emilie asked Albert as he entered the living room.

"I'm going to the carpenter's house to tell him," Albert stated.

"You can't," Emilie insisted. "The man may kill you."

"I have to, Emilie," Albert said, "or I will look even guiltier than I already do. If I go myself and tell him about his son, he will know I didn't do it. Why would I kill someone and then confess the crime to that person's father?"

"How was the boy killed?" Emilie asked.

"Someone shot him in the chest," Albert replied.

"We don't even own a gun," Emilie said, knowing this fact would help prove Albert's innocence.

"No, we don't, and we didn't hear a shot," Albert stated. "The young man was not shot here. He was moved here after the crime."

"I hope they believe you, Albert," Emilie fretted. "Please, take Jacob with you."

"Okay," Albert agreed, thinking the suggestion was wise. "I'll be back as soon as I can."

"Be careful, Albert," Emilie pleaded.

"I will," Albert promised, heading back toward the door.

Riding to the end of the lane, Albert turned left toward Jacob's house. Going alone was probably not a good idea, especially under the circumstances, and he was thankful Emilie had mentioned he take his brother along. The Polish farmers already hated them, and now he had to go inform them of such a horrific crime. How would he ever prove that he was not the one who killed the boy?

Knocking on Jacob's back door, Albert tried running the conversation with the Polish farmer through his mind. What would be the best way to break such sad and unbelievable news?

"Albert," Magdalena said, opening the door for him, "you look as if you've seen a ghost."

"Close enough to it," Albert murmured, stepping into the warm house.

"What's wrong, Albert?" Jacob asked coming into the kitchen. "Sit down and have a cup of coffee to warm up."

Albert knew he did not have time for a cup of coffee but felt he needed one. Sinking into a kitchen chair, Albert buried his face in his hands, the full effect of the dead boy finally sinking in. A life had been cut short, a child lost in a violent act, and he was the one who had to notify the parents. It was a nightmare.

"Albert," Jacob said softly, "what's wrong?"

"The boys were playing tag outside," Albert began.

"Did one of the boys get hurt?" Magdalena broke in, alarm evident in her voice.

"No, the boys are fine," Albert assured them, "at least physically. Emotionally, they are probably not too good."

"Albert, what has happened?" Jacob demanded.

"The Polish carpenter's son is dead behind my barn," Albert stated just getting to the point.

"Oh no," Magdalena gasped.

"The boys found him while playing tag," Albert informed them.

"This is awful," Jacob stated, "really awful."

"I know," Albert said, accepting the mug of coffee from Magdalena.

"What are you going to do?" Magdalena asked.

"I'm heading to the carpenter's house to break the news," Albert said.

"I'll go with you," Jacob offered.

"I was hoping you would say that," Albert confessed. "This is going to be the hardest thing I have ever had to do."

"We have to convince them it was not you who killed their son," Jacob said.

"Yes, I know, but it's going to be hard," Albert stated.

"Drink your coffee and then we'll head that way," Jacob instructed. "I'll go saddle my horse while you finish the cup and warm up a bit."

"Thank you, Jacob," Albert said softly.

Five minutes later, Jacob and Albert started for the Polish carpenter's house. They were quiet during the ride, each deep in thought about what lay ahead. How could such a terrible thing happen and who placed the body behind Albert's barn? Were the boy killed by another Polish man and the body placed there because they knew of the hatred between the Polish farmers and Albert Grieb? Or, did the Nazis kill the boy trying to increase the conflict between the Polish farmers and the Griebs? The questions were endless and there were no answers. The position Albert had been placed in seemed hopeless. Reaching the lane to the Polish carpenter's home, Albert turned to Jacob.

"Pray, Brother, please pray," Albert begged.

"I already have been," Jacob admitted. "It's going to take a miracle to make this man believe you had nothing to do with the murder of his son."

"I know," Albert said.

Dismounting from their horses, Albert and Jacob approached the front door. Neither man wanted to be there but knew they had no other option. Slowly, they shuffled onto the porch and approached the door, the dread of what they were about to do pressing down upon them. Albert knocked tentatively, and the door opened abruptly, the frame of the big Polish carpenter completely filling the doorway. The scowl on his face left no doubt that he was not happy to see them.

"What do you stinking Germans want?" the Polish man demanded.

"We've come to tell you some really bad news," Albert began.

"What is it this time? Did you steal more horses for the Nazis?" the Polish man asked brusquely.

"No," Albert said, "it's not about horses."

"Well, spit it out," the Polish man demanded. "It's not like it's warm outside and I'm standing here with my front door wide open."

Albert thought about asking to come in but he knew that would never be allowed. Unfortunately, he would have to tell this man the worst news of his life while standing in his doorway. "I have some sad news," Albert began again. "Your son has been found behind my barn. He's dead from a bullet wound."

"You killed my son!" the Polish man screamed.

"No," Albert defended himself, "I didn't kill him. I don't even own a gun."

"You have come to tell me you killed my son?" the Polish man hollered.

"Please, sir," Albert begged, "would I come tell you about your son's death if I had been the one who killed him? I know all of you Polish farmers hate us. I'm risking my life to tell you the news personally."

A woman appeared beside the big Polish man. "Tolek, what do these men want?"

"Anka, they have brought us some devastating news," Tolek said, putting a big arm around the small woman.

"What is it, Tolek?" Anka asked.

"Our oldest son is dead," Tolek said. "He has been found behind this German's barn. They can't just stop at stealing our horses; they have to murder our children, too."

"Oh, Tolek," Anka sobbed. "I knew something bad had happened when he didn't return home last night."

"Ma'am, please believe me, I did not kill your son," Albert pleaded.

"I know," Anka replied. "It was those wretched Nazis who killed him. They are full of all kinds of evil."

"Go back inside, Anka," Tolek instructed. "I will be there in a moment."

Anka did as Tolek demanded and disappeared back into the house, tears streaming down her cheeks. Jacob and Albert wished they could offer comfort in some way but knew it was impossible under the circumstances. There was too much hatred toward the German men for any condolences to be expressed and heard.

"I will hitch up my wagon and come get my son's body shortly," Tolek told Jacob and Albert. "I will bring witnesses and we will decide if you murdered my boy."

"Yes sir," Albert replied quietly. There was no sense in Albert trying to defend himself again. When Tolek and the other Polish men arrived, they would see for themselves that the boy had been dumped behind the barn after his murder. Slowly, Jacob and Albert made their way back to their mounts. They rode back to Albert's house to wait for the Polish neighbors to arrive.

Emilie had a pot of coffee ready and the men welcomed the hot drink and warm house. Sitting at the kitchen table, they discussed the situation with Emilie.

"What did the Polish man say?" Emilie wanted to know.

"He thinks I killed his son," Albert replied.

"Did you tell him you didn't?" Emilie questioned.

"Of course I did," Albert said. "The man is in deep grief. He is going to blame the person he hates most, and unfortunately, that is me."

"His wife saw reason, though," Jacob inserted.

"Oh, that poor woman," Emilie said. "To get such news would just tear your heart out."

"She was upset," Jacob agreed, "but she blamed the Nazis, not Albert. Maybe they know something we don't. Their son had obviously been missing since sometime yesterday."

"We are not monsters," Emilie whispered. "We would never take the life of someone just for revenge. What kind of people do the Polish believe us to be?"

"The kind of people who steal their farms and their horses," Albert remarked. "What they don't understand is that we did not have a choice in either matter."

At that moment the Griebs heard a wagon pulling into their yard. Jacob and Albert knew the time had come. The Polish men would be their judge and jury. If it was decided Albert was guilty, the Polish men would deal with him, and maybe Jacob, too.

There had been a time when Tolek, the Polish carpenter, had been a friendly neighbor. That had all changed after the horse raid. The Poles might not kill another man over stealing horses but taking the life of one of their son's would be plenty of reason to retaliate in a most brutal way.

Jacob and Albert slipped back into their coats and went out to face the Polish farmers. They knew their lives hung in the balance based on the conclusion the Poles came to about how the young man came to be lying behind Albert's barn.

"He's around this side of the barn," Albert said pointing in the direction.

Tolek, along with three of his neighbors, slowly started toward the rear of the barn. Tolek trudged slowly, as if his feet were lead weights too heavy to lift. As long as he didn't see his son dead, he could still believe he would return home. The reality of his body lying behind this barn would put an end to any hope.

Jacob and Albert followed behind, keeping a little distance between them and their Polish neighbors, one of which they had stolen the horses from. It could mean danger for both of them if the Polish men decided Albert was guilty and took the matter into their own hands, an eye for an eye, so to speak. Albert had to tell his side of the story, though. He had to convince these four men that he was innocent, that he would never kill anyone.

"Yes, that is Dawid," Tolek confirmed, tears welling up in his eyes.

"My sons found him while playing tag this morning," Albert told Tolek.

"Your sons are the ones who found him?" Tolek asked his face softening just a little.

"Yes," Albert confirmed. "They ran to the house to get me and are quite upset, as are my wife and I."

"You have to understand," Jacob began, "Albert would never do this heartless act. Neither of us even own guns. We were not allowed to bring them from Bessarabia when we moved."

"That's probably true," the Polish man who had his horses stolen piped in, "If they owned guns, they would have returned fire on me the night they stole my horses."

"I noticed something else that might help you believe I'm innocent," Albert said. "There's no blood anywhere around your son, no puddle on the ground or spatter on my barn. Also, we did not hear a gunshot last night."

"It must have been the Nazis," another Polish neighbor concluded. "They have placed Dawid behind the Grieb's barn because they know we are feuding."

"Just like it was the Nazis who forced us to steal the horses," Jacob added.

"I am a man of reason," Tolek finally said. "With all the evidence I see here, I don't believe it was you who shot my son."

"I'm very sorry for your loss," Albert said softly.

"I'll go get the wagon and bring it closer," Tolek said, wiping a tear from his cheek.

The men helped Tolek load his son into the wagon. Climbing back in, the Polish farmers prepared to ride back to Tolek's house to help him unload Dawid's body. Dawid would be prepared for burial and a wake would be held the next day. Dawid's body would then be placed in the cemetery behind the church.

"We will come help you dig the grave," Albert offered as the Poles were preparing to leave. "The ground is frozen and it will be very difficult to turn the dirt."

"Thank you," Tolek said. "Do you know where our church is?"

"Yes," Jacob confirmed.

"We will start in an hour," the Pole from whom Jacob and Albert had stolen the horses stated.

"We will be there," Jacob said.

An hour later found Jacob and Albert, along with three Polish men, chipping away at the frozen ground. The job was cold and tedious but once they got below the freeze line, it became much easier. They took turns because five men couldn't dig at once in such a small space. As two men dug, the other three men sipped coffee that had been brought in a crock and nibbled cookies, all provided by Magdalena. She had insisted they load the items in the wagon with the shovels and picks and all the men were thankful for her thoughtfulness.

As the hours of digging passed, Jacob and Albert attempted to mend the relationship between them and the Poles. The Nazis were the ones to blame in all of this, while the Poles and relocated Germans had become pawns in their evil schemes.

The Grieb and Wallentine families paid their respects by attending the wake. They wanted to make sure the Poles understood that they had not wanted to ever cause them grief and that they shared in their pain now. Magdalena, Emilie, and Rosina prepared dishes for the grieving Polish family and brought them along. They were accepted with gratitude, and it seemed that the neighboring farmers might once again live peacefully beside one another as it had been before the horse raid occurred.

Chapter Twelve

Spring of 1942 finally began to arrive for the Germans relocated in Poland. The wheat that had been planted the previous fall sent slivers of green up all around the area. The sun warmed the earth again and the birds began to migrate back from their winter homes. The farmers began to grease their disc and wagon wheels, preparing for the work that lay just ahead.

Things had calmed down between the area Polish farmers and the relocated Germans. A month after his son's death, Tolek had come to tell Albert that he now knew for sure it was the Nazis who had murdered him. A neighbor of Tolek's had overheard some Nazi soldiers bragging about killing the boy and placing him behind the Grieb's barn. It seemed Dawid, Tolek and Anka's son, had ignored a Nazi's order to halt and paid the price of death for it.

The Germans and the Poles now knew the Nazis were plotting to keep discord among them. It appeared boredom was leading to the Nazi soldiers finding ways to entertain themselves, even going as far as killing young men who did not stop on command. There were no battles being fought in Poland at the moment, just territory to be protected as a part of the Greater Germany which Hitler was attempting to create. The idle time was obviously being spent arresting innocent Jews and killing those who did not support Hitler's quest.

Along with fearing the Nazis, there were rumors in the area of Polish bandits committing acts of terror. These men were referred to as Polish underground workers and they were avenging themselves for the farms they had been kicked off of to make room for the returning Germans. Though nothing had happened close by, everyone was being careful as they traveled about and sleeping with one eye open.

As an April day began to warm, Magdalena busied herself making fresh loaves of bread. She planned to take a loaf to Emilie and her family when they had baked. With five boys and a husband to tend to, poor Emilie had a heavy workload. Anything Magdalena could do to lighten it was her pleasure. Just as Magdalena finished kneading the bread for the second time and forming the loaves, Ewald came bounding in the back door.

"Mutti, come quick," Ewald urged, "I have something to show you."

Placing the bread near the warm stove to rise, Magdalena grabbed a jacket and followed Ewald toward the barn. Ewald ran ahead of her dancing around, wanting her to hurry up. Magdalena watched him, wondering how the time had passed so quickly. It seemed just yesterday she was rocking him to sleep and now he would be six years old next month.

"It's in the barn," Ewald said, running back to make his mutti move faster.

"Okay, Ewald," Magdalena said, "I'm moving as fast as I can."

Opening the barn door, Ewald turned to his mutti, "We have to climb to the loft."

"Lead the way," Magdalena instructed.

Grasping the ladder, Ewald scurried to the loft. Hurrying to the mound of hay, he knelt down and waited for Magdalena to catch up. "Look," Ewald pointed, "one of the kittens had babies."

"Yes, she sure did," Magdalena said smiling at Ewald's excitement.

"I know how you hate mice in the house," Ewald said. "These kittens will help keep them killed. I've already counted them and there are three babies. One looks just like its mutti."

"That's right, Ewald, there are three kittens," Magdalena said. "I see Oma Wallentine has been teaching you well."

Rosina, having been a schoolteacher for years before leaving Bessarabia, insisted that her grandsons keep up on their studies. For this reason, she had conducted school at her house three days a week through the winter. Erhard, Ewald, and Emilie's three oldest boys attended together, along with other area German children. It had been something to keep them busy during the cold winter months.

"I know how to count to 100," Ewald informed his mutti, "and write my name and I know all of my letters."

"That's very good, Ewald," Magdalena said. "You will have to show the kittens to Erhard when he gets done helping your vater today."

"I will," Ewald said, "because I found them first. Maybe we could give a kitten to Oma Wallentine when they're big enough. Oma doesn't have any cats and she hates mice, too."

"I'm sure Oma would love to have a kitten, Ewald, but let's leave them alone for now, okay," Magdalena suggested. "They're awful young and the mother cat might move them if we pester her too much."

"I remember Vater moving the kittens that were in the barn when we got here last year," Ewald said. "The mother cat just moved them right back to the loft."

"You're right, Ewald," Magdalena said. "The mother cat didn't like the new home your vater tried to give them."

"No, they didn't," Ewald said, "and Erhard found Micah in the hay while we were playing with the kittens in the loft. What do you think happened to Micah?"

"I don't know," Magdalena said, "let's just hope he was reunited with his family and they are doing fine."

"Yes, that's exactly what I hope for," Ewald said.

Magdalena knew that Micah was probably not doing fine, but she didn't want to think about him in any other way. The day the Nazis took him stilled burned in her mind and made her blood boil. One of the soldiers had jabbed the butt of his gun into Micah's back as they dragged him to the truck. How could anyone treat an innocent child that way?

"I need to go check on my loaves of bread," Magdalena told Ewald. "Why don't you come to the house for a glass of milk and some cookies?"

"That sounds gut," Ewald said, scurrying down the ladder ahead of his mutti.

Magdalena made her way back to the house behind Ewald, still thinking about the Jewish boy that had been hiding in their loft a year ago. Any story that reached their ears about the concentration camps was never good. If the Nazis would shoot a

Polish boy just because he didn't stop when they told him to, they would certainly not think twice about killing a hated Jewish child.

Magdalena had never faced such hatred while living in Bessarabia. There had been times when people disagreed, but no one would have killed anyone over it. The thought of a whole ethnic group being stripped from their homes and thrown into concentration camps was something Magdalena couldn't have ever imagined happening. If she hadn't witnessed the treatment of Micah herself and known that her own family now lived on a farm that used to belong to Micah's family, she might not be convinced that such evil really existed. Sadly, she knew first hand that it did.

Entering the house, Magdalena fixed Ewald's snack and checked her bread. The loaves had not quite doubled but it wouldn't be long. Magdalena turned her attention to tidying the kitchen while the bread finished rising, trying to put the depressing thoughts of Micah from her mind.

****

Mid-April brought busyness to the Grieb farm. The broccoli, cauliflower and cabbage were moved to the garden from the cold frame Jacob had made the previous fall. The lettuce was planted in the garden, along with peas. Potatoes were cut into large chunks leaving eyes on each piece to sprout into plants. The chunks were then planted in deep rows in the garden after the cuts had time to skin over. Tomato seeds were started in the cold frame, and the plants would be transplanted in mid-May when the soil was warm enough. A lot of hard work went into growing enough food for the winter, not to mention the time it took to preserve the harvest.

Magdalena tended her own garden first then went to Emilie's to help her work in her garden. With a sixth month old baby, it was difficult for Emilie to get everything done. Her two oldest sons were needed to help Albert with the field work, leaving Erwin to be Emilie's helper. Erwin was good to entertain nearly three year old Klaus who seemed to be into everything, but was not much help when it came to six month old Walter.

"I am absolutely worn out," Emilie admitted to Magdalena after a warm June morning spent in the garden. "Let's go sit in the shade and have us a drink and a snack."

"Sounds good to me," Magdalena said. "We can sit near the rope swing and watch Ewald, Erwin, and Klaus take turns sailing through the air."

"That rope swing has brought hours of fun," Emilie said. "I'm so glad Albert hung it for the boys."

Making their way to the tree, Magdalena scooped up baby Walter who had been lying in the shade on a blanket taking a nap. Snuggling him close, she again hoped for another baby of her own soon. So far, that miracle had just not happened.

Emilie returned with a pitcher of cool water and some cookies. She placed them on a wooden table Albert had constructed so they could sit outside and enjoy a cool breeze on hot summer days. It made a nice place to prepare fruits and vegetables for canning, too. Returning to the house, Emilie came back with five glasses to pour the water into.

"It's amazing how fast our kids have grown," Emilie said as she filled the glasses with water.

"I know," Magdalena agreed. "It seems like just yesterday I helped bring this little guy into the world and now he's six months old." Magdalena tickled Walter on the bottom of his bare feet, and the baby laughed and cooed up at her.

"Albert, Richard, and Erhard are already old enough to work beside their vaters all day," Emilie said. "Where did the time go?"

"More importantly, where is time going to take us?" Magdalena asked, thinking of all the changes they had endured the past two years.

"Honestly, I try not to dwell on it," Emilie admitted. "It won't do me any good at all to worry about what lies ahead. I've accepted that I can do nothing to change the outcome of this war and for now, I'm going to enjoy this bit of peace."

"That's a good way of looking at it I suppose," Magdalena agreed. "I just wonder where we will end up when the war is over. With the United States joining the Allies, the outcome could definitely be very different than what Hitler hopes for."

"Does Jacob still dream of living in America?" Emilie asked.

"Yes, he does, but he knows there's no way of following that dream right now," Magdalena replied. "Too bad Albert doesn't have the same dream as Jacob. The thought of leaving all our family behind is about more than I can bear."

"Albert has no desire to move so far away," Emilie said. "Maybe Jacob will change his mind when the war is over. It's possible we could move back to our homes in Bessarabia, if the Soviet Union surrenders to the Nazis."

"I suppose that could be a possibility," Magdalen said, thankful for that small bit of hope Emilie had just given her.

"But for now, I'm determined to be content," Emilie said. "There are others facing much more hardships than we have here."

"That's true," Magdalena agreed. "I think about our brothers, Edward and Emil, often. I wonder where they are and if they're all right."

"I think of them too, and pray often for their safety," Emilie said. "We just have to put them in God's hands, along with the future we will face."

"I know and I do put them there. I just seem to have a hard time leaving them there," Magdalena admitted.

Just then Klaus squealed with delight. Emilie and Magdalena were drawn back to the present by the sound. Erwin was pushing Klaus high on the rope swing as Ewald stood close by munching on a cookie, waiting for another turn. The women let the conversation of war drop and enjoyed this peaceful moment. It was hard to imagine battles being fought all around them while sitting under the shade of a large tree on a hot summer day watching their children play. Magdalena and Emilie captured a mental picture of the scene and tucked the memory away. It was something they could recall later, perhaps when times became worse. For today, all was well for the Griebs living in Poland, and the women would be thankful for it.

Chapter Thirteen

The war effort against the Red Army had been going well for the Nazi troops. After invading the Soviet Union in June of 1941, the Nazis had advanced to the outskirts of Stalingrad by June 1942. If Hitler could only free up enough troops from other areas, the Red Army might be pushed to surrender. However, with the British bombing Cologne, Germany the previous month, there was no hope of extra troops being sent to the battlefield to assist and reinforce the Nazi troops fighting against the Red Army. Hitler had now brought the war to his own soil, and the people of Germany were living in fear. The bombs were killing their families and destroying their homes.

Edward and Emil were weary of war. After a year of fighting, they now prepared to take Stalingrad and push further east.

"Do you think we have enough man power to occupy Stalingrad?" Edward questioned Emil as they lay in their dark tent waiting for sleep to come.

"So far the Red Army has not been able to stop our advances, though we have been slowed down considerably," Emil answered.

"Tomorrow we push full steam ahead," Edward said. "I guess we'll know if we have the power soon enough."

"I just want this war to be over," Emil stated. "I want the Red Army to surrender and I want to go back to the lives we had in Bessarabia."

"It's a good thing you don't want much," Edward said, laughing. "I have been thinking about how our family is, though."

"Me too," Emil admitted. "Not seeing them for a year and a half feels like a lifetime."

"Working from sun up to sun down in Bessarabia sounds

like the good life now," Edward commented.

"Yeah, we thought Vater was going to kill us in that vineyard, but now it's the place I would love to be," Emil laughed.

"Funny how circumstances changed our perspective," Edward mused.

"Yes," Emil agreed, "I'm tired of sleeping on the ground every night and eating whatever that stuff is they call food, never getting enough to not still feel hungry."

"The pigs in Bessarabia ate better food than we're getting," Edward chuckled.

"I just can't wait until this war is over," Emil reiterated.

"Looks like that could be awhile," Edward commented, "with the United States entering the war and the British now dropping bombs on Cologne, Germany."

"I think maybe Hitler started something and he's not going to like the way it ends," Emil whispered, not wanting to be overheard.

"I'm afraid you're right, Brother," Edward agreed. "Now, hush up before you get us killed without even facing the Red Army again."

"I'm going to sleep," Emil said with a yawn.

"Sweet dreams," Edward murmured.

"Not likely," Emil retorted, turning over to try and find some comfortable position on the hard ground.

The new launch to take Stalingrad began the next day, on June 28, and by September the Germans had taken Stalingrad, secured the Crimean Peninsula and pushed deep into the Caucasus. The Hungarian and Romanian forces were holding the front line, while the German Sixth Army occupied Stalingrad. It appeared that the Red Army was on the run without the ability to retaliate.

The Nazis held their position in the Soviet Union through October and November, but things were not going well for the Germans on other fronts. In October, the British defeated the Germans and Italians in El Alamein, Egypt, making them retreat all the way to the eastern border of Tunisia. Then in November, the United States and British troops landed on the beaches of French North Africa. The Vichy French could not hold off the Allies invasion, allowing the Allies to move to the western border of Tunisia. This move caused the German troops to back up and occupy southern France.

The Germans losing ground on the Western front may have been what encouraged the Red Army to get motivated and fight. In late November, they counterattacked the Germans advancement. Breaking through the line formed by the Hungarian and Romanian troops to the northwest and southwest, the Red Army pushed into Stalingrad. The German Sixth Army became trapped in Stalingrad by the surge from the Red Army. Hitler refused to allow them to retreat. The survivors of the German Sixth Army were forced to surrender at the end of January, 1943.

The remaining soldiers of Edward and Emil's troop were marched to the railroad station and loaded on empty cars. The ride to the camp was cold and long. By the time the train stopped, it was dark and they had no idea where they were.

The men were assigned quarters and given one blanket. Edward and Emil shivered in their bunks in the cold, dark building. If they escaped, all they knew was to head west and hope they made it to the border before being caught.

"We've just become prisoners of war," Edward muttered to Emil.

"Maybe we should have just allowed them to kill us," Emil suggested.

"We can plan an escape," Edward assured his brother.

"We will freeze to death in this camp," Emil said, his teeth chattering out the words.

"You have to stay positive, Emil," Edward instructed. "We will figure out a way to escape. You have to believe that."

"I told you we should have just let them shoot us," Emil fumed. "We are going to die a slow, painful death in this camp."

"We must pray as we never have before," Edward suggested.

"Yes, I will pray this misery ends soon," Emil stated, turning his back on his brother and trying to sleep in the freezing conditions. Maybe he would freeze to death by morning and his prayer would be answered.

****

The surrender of the Germans in Stalingrad reached the ears of the relocated Germans in Poland by mid-February, 1943. With the British bombing German soil and the Allies on the ground pushing the German troops back, the relocated Germans living in

Poland felt they were in the middle of the conflict.

"Where do you think Emil and Edward are?" Rosina questioned Gottlieb as they ate breakfast.

"I wish I knew," Gottlieb responded.

"I feel they are in danger. A Mutti's intuition, I suppose."

"They probably are in danger," Gottlieb agreed. "How could they not be? They are probably fighting the Red Army and being pushed back west. The Germans had been fighting so well there. What could have happened to cause the Red Army to retaliate so strongly?"

"I don't understand it, either," Rosina admitted. "We must pray for Edward and Emil's safety, though. I feel it so strongly."

"Yes," Gottlieb agreed, "we will pray harder."

"The children will be here soon for school," Rosina said, rising from the kitchen chair to prepare for their arrival.

"Yes," Gottlieb said, "at least you can offer them some normalcy during this war torn time."

"We don't know how long this war will last," Rosina stated. "There's no sense in the children getting behind in their studies, especially since I'm capable of preventing it."

"You've always been a good teacher," Gottlieb said, laughter dancing in his eyes. "Look how you've taught me to agree with everything you say."

"Oh, get on with yourself," Rosina retorted. "Go greet the children as they arrive. I know how you love to spoil them."

"That I do," Gottlieb said, heading toward the living room.

Rosina had just finished the breakfast dishes when she heard the front door open followed by a scream and then laughter. Gottlieb had hidden from the children behind the door and scared them as they shut it. What a child he could be. It had kept their marriage filled with laughter through the years, though.

Rosina entered the living room and after a few minutes of allowing Gottlieb his fun, she cleared her throat loudly. The children stopped abruptly and took their places on the floor. It was not the most ideal way to teach children but it would have to do. They had no other place to go or desks for the children to sit at.

Gottlieb sat down and picked up his Bible. The Bible was read each morning of school, just as it had been done in Bessarabia. Religion had always been taught in the German colony schools, as well as at church. The children learned from a young age to trust God for their daily needs, to rest in His strength. Welcoming God into their midst, taking comfort in His promises, was just the way they had always lived.

"I'm going to read Psalm 91 this morning," Gottlieb said.

As Gottlieb's deep voice filled the room, Rosina let the words of the Psalm wash over. She knew Gottlieb had chosen the passage just for her and it was giving her peace where there had been fear and fretting. She knew Edward and Emil were in trouble but she also knew God was still in control. Somehow, someway, this madness would end.

"He shall cover thee with His feathers, and under His wings shalt thou trust; His trust shall be thy shield and buckler," Gottlieb boomed.

Rosina thought of how a mother hen gathers her chicks under her wings to protect them and keep them warm. She silently prayed that Edward and Emil would feel God's presence, that they would be protected under His wings. She could do nothing for them physically, but she could pray and that was a very powerful thing.

"For He shall give His angels charge over thee, to keep thee in all thy ways. They shall bear thee up in their hands, lest thou dash thy foot against a stone," Gottlieb continued through the Psalm.

Yes, Rosina prayed silently, send your angels to Edward and Emil. Bear them up and give them strength in whatever circumstance they have found themselves in.

"Let us pray," Gottlieb said, finishing the Psalm and bowing his head.

Rosina took over the class as Gottlieb finished the prayer, and Gottlieb left Rosina to her teaching. To stay would just distract the children since he had not one teaching bone in his body where books were concerned. Children, to Gottlieb, were to play with and to have them walk in your shadow, learning to cultivate the earth and produce crops. Sitting still and writing letters and numbers had never really appealed to Gottlieb, though he had endured school at a young age just as the children surrounding his wife were doing now.

Gottlieb headed outside to the barn to busy himself with

repairing a wheel on one of the wagons. Though it was only mid-February, the planting and harvesting season would be here before he knew it. The wagon had belonged to the previous owners of the farm they now lived on. It was in poor shape but having an extra wagon came in handy, especially during harvest. Jacob and Albert always came to help Gottlieb, along with their younger brother, Olof. It was the way the work got done when they all lived in Hoffnungstal as a colony, and the tradition continued here in Poland. Neighbors helping neighbors until all the crops were in.

When it was noon, Gottlieb returned to the house to eat lunch with Rosina and the children. Each child brought a lunch pail but Rosina made sure to have something sweet baked for dessert each day. Gottlieb didn't want to miss out on the sweet treat, so he made sure to always come in at lunch. After the noon meal, Gottlieb returned to the barn until 2:00, when it was time for the children to leave. He would then hitch up the horses to a wagon and pull it close to the door. All the children walked to school each morning, but Gottlieb insisted on piling them in his wagon and giving them a ride home. It gave him something to do during the winter months and allowed him to spend more time with his grandsons. It also provided a way to obtain information on how the war was progressing from his sons-in-laws as he dropped his grandsons off at their homes.

Gottlieb pulled the wagon to the front of the house and entered the kitchen through the back door. The children were pulling on their coats, hats and gloves, preparing for the cold ride home. Gottlieb helped Ewald with his coat, being he was one of the youngest attending the school.

"Did you learn anything today?" Gottlieb asked his grandson.

"I'm learning how to read now," Ewald said beaming up at his Opa.

"That's a good thing to know," Gottlieb said.

"Yes, and Oma is teaching me Russian words, along with German ones," Ewald said.

"Well, we do speak both languages, so knowing how to read both will be good," Gottlieb stated. "Let's get to the wagon first so you can ride up on the seat with me."

"Okay, but I might move down with my brother and cousins

before we get to my house," Ewald answered. "It's colder up on the seat. In the bed of the wagon I can burrow between people to keep warm."

Gottlieb chuckled and led the way to the wagon. Scooping Ewald up and placing him on the seat, he handed the child the reins. "Keep the horses steady until everyone is in the wagon," Gottlieb instructed.

"Okay, Opa," Ewald said, proud that he had been trusted to do the task.

After everyone was loaded, Gottlieb put the horses in motion. Once they were on the road, he handed the reins back to Ewald. "Just keep the horses going straight," Gottlieb instructed.

Ewald held the reins tightly in his gloved hands, hoping nothing spooked the horses. He had witnessed some runaway teams before and knew he did not want any part of that. Opa's team was very calm, though and they knew exactly where they were going. When they got to the location of their first stop, the horses turned automatically. After making two more stops, the only children left in the wagon were Gottlieb's grandsons.

"Your house is next," Gottlieb said.

"Yes and then Albert, Richard and Erwin's," Ewald said. "Do you think we could go to Uncle Albert's first, and drop me and Erhard off on the way back?"

"I don't see why not," Gottlieb said. "Just make sure you keep the horses on the road or they will turn at your house on their own."

As they approached Ewald's house, he gripped the reins tight in his hands. Just like Opa had warned, the horses tried to turn. Ewald pulled back and yelled "whoa", causing the horses to stop abruptly. The sudden stop caused Ewald to pitch forward, and Opa reached out and grabbed his coat just before he flew off the seat.

"You just about went to the ground there, didn't you, Ewald?" Gottlieb said chuckling.

"The horses stopped faster than I thought they would," Ewald admitted.

"What are you trying to do, kill us?" Erwin asked from the back of the wagon.

"Sorry," Ewald apologized.

Taking the reins, Gottlieb coaxed the horses down the road

toward Albert and Emilie's. Albert came from the barn as they pulled into the barn lot.

"Opa let Ewald drive the team," Richard said, jumping out of the back of the wagon.

"Yeah, and he about killed us," Erwin added.

"Goodness, Erwin," young Albert said. "You're making a big deal about nothing."

"Ewald was the one who about died," Erhard chimed in. "Opa had to catch him by his coat to keep him on the seat."

"Did the horses not like the change in their routine?" Albert asked, knowing how horses behave.

"No, they didn't," Gottlieb said. "Ewald wanted to go home last but the horses knew they usually stopped at his house before coming here."

"Creatures of habit," Albert said with a laugh.

Gottlieb turned the team around and headed back to Ewald and Erhard's house. When he pulled in the barnyard Jacob was unhitching his team.

"Hullo, Gottlieb," Jacob said. "I see the boys talked you in to dropping them off last. They sure didn't ask for that last week when it was so cold."

"No," Gottlieb confirmed, "everyone wanted to go home first last week."

"I think your mutti probably has some warm milk and cookies waiting for you boys," Jacob told Erhard and Ewald.

"I'm sure she does," Erhard hollered back while racing Ewald to the back door.

"Do you think her vater could get some of those, too?" Gottlieb asked hopefully.

"I'm sure you can," Jacob said chuckling, "but I need to tell you something first. Step into the barn with me out of the cold. I need to curry the horses and stall them, anyway."

The warmth of the barn enveloped the men as they each led a horse inside. Grabbing brushes, both men went to work.

"I just came from town," Jacob began, the brush in his hand never stopping. "It seems the Polish bandits are getting close to us."

"Oh, really," Gottlieb said with concern.

"Yes," Jacob confirmed. "A German family just east of town

found their oldest son at the bottom of their well this morning."

"That's awful," Gottlieb said softly.

"There's been a lot of livestock found dead in their stalls, too," Jacob added.

"You would think those men would realize that we didn't choose to come here. We are not the ones who threw them off their farms," Gottlieb said. "We only did what we were told to do."

"This is true," Jacob said, "but we are the ones they can take revenge on. The bandits know they don't have enough manpower to fight against the Nazis and get anywhere. They target innocent people instead."

"We will have to be careful," Gottlieb said. "I will pass the word along, starting with Albert. I'll go back and warn them now. We will cancel school until this danger passes."

The Germans who had been relocated to Poland went on high alert. The stories kept pouring in over the next six weeks of the Polish bandits killing German men and dropping them in wells. Horses were found hanged in their stalls and barns and homes were burned to the ground. The report Jacob received in early April forced the Grieb and Wallentine families to take drastic measures.

"Magdalena," Jacob said coming through the back door searching for his wife.

Magdalena looked up from preparing the noon meal. Jacob had just returned from town, and the look on his face was one of concern, possibly even fear. "I'm right here, Jacob."

"The Polish bandits are doing unspeakable evil," Jacob said, getting right to the point.

"What's happened now?" Magdalena asked.

"Let's sit down at the table," Jacob suggested, knowing what he was about to tell Magdalena would be hard for her to hear.

Sinking into a chair, Magdalena prepared herself for the worst. She was thankful the boys were in the barn playing in the loft. Another litter of kittens had been born just days ago, and they were looking for another cat who was also expecting kittens. They were sure the cat was hidden in the barn somewhere. It was a good thing other farmers needed cats or they would be overran by now.

"They found two German women dead yesterday," Jacob began. "They were in a ditch along the road. They had been walking together, heading to a neighbor's house."

"They've started killing women now?" Magdalena asked indignantly.

"That's not all," Jacob said softly. "The women were pregnant. They cut the babies from their muttis' wombs and sliced off the women's breast."

"Oh, Jacob," Magdalena gasped, "how awful."

"Yes," Jacob said. "I don't want you or the boys to go anywhere by yourself."

"Okay," Magdalena said, completely agreeing.

"I think we should take more precautions than we already have been, too," Jacob said. "I'll go talk to Albert, my vater, and your vater. I think we should all spend the night together in one of our homes for a while. The men can take turns standing guard."

"That's a good idea," Magdalena agreed, the horror of what Jacob just told her causing her stomach to churn.

"I'll go now and discuss the matter with the men," Jacob said. "The boys need to come in the house with you while I'm gone and bolt the doors when I leave. I'm sure the bandits are still in this area."

"We have been forced to live in terror," Magdalena said, her voice betraying her fear.

"Yes and we don't have any guns to protect ourselves," Jacob pointed out.

"I'll go call the boys in now," Magdalena said, rising on trembling legs.

"No, I'll get the boys to the house," Jacob stated. "You stay in and make sure you bolt those doors when I leave."

"I will," Magdalena promised. "Be careful, Jacob."

"I'll be on my horse," Jacob assured her. "If I were in a wagon or walking, I would be a much easier target."

Jacob went to the barn to retrieve Erhard and Ewald. The boys were not happy about leaving the barn but did not dare argue with their vater. When Erhard and Ewald were safe in the house with Magdalena, she bolted the door, terrified that things had gotten so bad.

Jacob decided to ride to Gottlieb and Rosina's first. Gottlieb had always been a good leader and decision maker. If Gottlieb encouraged the others to start staying together at night for safety, they would listen. Pushing his mount to a fast trot, Jacob covered the distance between his home and Gottlieb's quite quickly. He did not want to give the bandits a chance to attack him along the road. Reaching Gottlieb and Rosina's home Jacob headed straight to the barn, where he was sure he would find Gottlieb.

"Jacob," Gottlieb greeted him as he stepped into the barn. "What brings you here? Did you bring my grandsons along?"

"No grandsons today," Jacob said. "I've come to give you a sad report and suggest we take more safety measures."

"What's happened?" Gottlieb asked.

"The Polish bandits have killed two pregnant women," Jacob said. "They mutilated their bodies by cutting the babies from their wombs and slicing off their breasts."

"These men are despicable," Gottlieb fumed. "How dare they attack innocent women?"

"I believe we need to start staying together at night," Jacob suggested. "The men could take turns keeping watch. At least it would make us feel safer."

"That's a good idea, Jacob," Gottlieb said. "Since you and Albert live closest to one another and have children, Rosina and I will come to you."

"Okay," Jacob agreed. "I will go tell Albert and my vater of our decision. Everyone may stay with Magdalena and me tonight and Albert's home tomorrow night. We will switch off between the two of us."

"We will be there before nightfall," Gottlieb assured Jacob.

Jacob left Gottlieb's house and headed for his vater's home, Jacob senior. It was a few miles beyond the Wallentine farm, the furthest from Jacob's own home. As Jacob trotted into the yard, he could see his vater and younger brother, Olof, preparing to shoe a horse. There was a fire going nice and hot in the forge and Olof was pounding out the metal to form a shoe for the waiting horse.

"Hullo, Son," Jacob senior greeted. "What brings you all the way out here?"

"Bad news, Vater," Jacob replied, "seems the Polish bandits are becoming more evil by the day."

"What have they done now?" Jacob senior asked.

Jacob retold the story for the third time. Each time he repeated it, it made him furious all over again. The bandits had reached an all new kind of low by attacking innocent women. The part that scared Jacob most was the fact that if they could attack women so violently and without remorse, than children would be their next target.

"That is truly despicable," Jacob senior replied. "We will all have to be extra careful and keep our women close to home."

"I was going to suggest all of you come to our house to spend the night," Jacob said. "Albert and Emilie will be there, along with Gottlieb and Rosina. We men could take turns keeping watch."

"That's a good idea," Jacob senior confirmed. "Your mutti, brother, sisters, and I will be there by nightfall."

"We'll be watching for you," Jacob answered.

Jacob left his parents' home and started toward Albert's. Convincing Albert would be no problem at all, considering he was trying to protect a wife and five children. As Jacob pulled into Albert's yard, Albert rushed out to greet him.

"Jacob, I just heard some terrible news," Albert said. "The Polish bandits have gone from killing German men to attacking innocent women."

"That's why I'm here," Jacob said. "I've heard the same report. I think we should start spending the night at one of our homes as a group. It would be easier to keep everyone protected."

"I agree," Albert said nodding his head emphatically. "We are all in a fight for our families lives."

"I have already talked to Vater and Gottlieb," Jacob replied. "We will meet at my house before nightfall."

"We will be there," Albert confirmed.

As the sun began to sink in the western sky, Jacob and Magdalena's families began to arrive at their farm. It was going to be close sleeping quarters but they would make do somehow. They really didn't have any other choice. Albert and Emilie arrived first with their boys, followed by Gottlieb and Rosina. The sun sank lower and lower and still Jacob and Juliana Grieb were not there.

"Where could they be?" Emilie fretted. "They would not be so careless as to be on the road after dark."

"Give them a few more minutes," Jacob said, "then I'll go look for them."

"It's too dangerous, Jacob," Magdalena said. "You would be an easy target alone and after dark."

"They may need help," Jacob said. "Their wagon may have broken down."

"Olof is old enough to help your vater," Magdalena said, referring to Jacob's youngest brother.

Magdalena knew she should not argue with Jacob, especially with everyone watching them, but the fear of him going out alone compelled her to speak. Looking at Jacob, she knew he understood, but she also realized she was embarrassing him.

"I'm going to go see about my parents and siblings," Jacob stated leaving no more room for argument. Grabbing his jacket, Jacob slipped out the back door. Before taking five steps to the barn, Magdalena called to him.

"Jacob, wait," Magdalena pleaded.

Stopping in his tracks, Jacob waited for Magdalena to close the gap between them. "What is it now, Woman?"

"I'm sorry," Magdalena whispered. "I've been waiting to make certain before I told you this but feel I must tell you now. I'm pregnant. We are finally going to have another child."

Jacob was so delighted with the good news that he forgot he was upset with Magdalena. He took her gently in his arms and held her close as tears streamed down her cheeks. They had waited so long for this day.

"Please, be careful," Magdalena begged.

"I will," Jacob said. "I have to go before it's completely dark. Go back inside where it's safe."

Nodding her head, Magdalena made her way back to the house. Emilie gave her a questioning glance but didn't say anything. Magdalena was sure her sister would ask later because Emilie knew her so well. The fact that Magdalena was not one to cry easily and the evidence of tears was on her cheeks was enough to make Emilie wonder.

Gottlieb gathered everyone in the living room to pray for Jacob and the safety of the family still traveling on the road. Magdalena was thankful her vater had taken this liberty and it gave her some much needed peace about the whole situation. Thirty minutes later, the Grieb's wagon pulled into Jacob's yard with Jacob's horse tied to the back. Olof was driving the wagon and the others were sitting low in the bed. It was impossible to see who all was in the wagon, as darkness had fully fallen.

"I'll go see what's happened," Albert said, grabbing his jacket and heading out the back door.

One look at Olof's pale face told Albert that all was not well. Looking in the back of the wagon, Albert could see his vater's beaten body lying limp. Jacob had placed his vater's head in his lap, and his mutti and sisters cried softly around him.

"The bandits ambushed them about a mile up the road," Jacob said. "They knocked Vater from the wagon seat and beat him to death. Everyone else was in the bed of the wagon. Olof fought the rest of the bandits off with a pitchfork and my arrival scared them away."

"Where are the bandits now?" Albert asked, looking around.

"I don't know," Jacob said. "We need to get everyone in the house and bolt the doors. We will need to prepare Vater's body for a wake tomorrow and bury him."

Albert could tell Jacob was in shock, as he spoke of his vater's death and burial without any emotion. Olof did not utter a word and his pale face held an expression of disbelief. The women were herded into the house and the three brothers carried their vater's broken body in after them.

"What has happened?" Gottlieb boomed, expressing everyone's shock with his voice.

"Polish bandits jumped them about a mile up the road," Albert explained knowing neither of his brothers was able to tell the story again.

"Is he dead?" Magdalena asked.

"I'm afraid so," Albert answered.

Suddenly, the realization of what had happened struck Juliana and she began to wail. Her daughters took her to Jacob and Magdalena's bedroom to allow her to calm down. Jacob looked at Olof and decided he needed to sit down in a kitchen chair immediately. Motioning for Albert to lay their vater's body on the kitchen floor, Jacob gently guided Olof to a chair.

"I'll get you a cup of coffee, Olof," Magdalena said. It was the only thing she knew to do for the boy.

"Albert and I will go to the barn and construct a coffin," Jacob said quietly. "Gottlieb, will you please keep guard?"

"Jacob," Gottlieb began softly wanting his son-in-law to understand reasoning, "the Polish bandits are very near. Why don't we make the coffin in the morning?"

"Gottlieb is right," Albert said, touching Jacob's shoulder, "we should wait until daylight. We will prepare Vater's body and wrap him in a sheet."

"Where will we bury him?" Emilie wondered aloud. "We have no church of our own and no cemetery."

"Maybe Tolek will get permission for Vater to be buried in his church's cemetery," Albert suggested.

"I'm sure Tolek will find a way," Gottlieb added.

The women kept the children occupied in a bedroom while the men prepared the senior Jacob Grieb's body for burial. In a bedroom, Juliana cried until there were no more tears then slipped into a fitful sleep. Her daughters, Mathilda, Maria, and Hulda joined the other women and children, allowing their mutti to sleep and forget the nightmare they had all just witnessed, at least for a few hours. At dawn, Jacob and Gottlieb went to the barn to construct a coffin to place the body in.

While the coffin was being built, Albert rode his horse to Tolek and Anka's house to ask for a plot in the church's cemetery where Tolek and Anka had buried Dawid. Knocking on the door, Albert was reminded of the scene just two months earlier, when he was forced to tell the couple their son had been killed.

"Albert," Tolek said, opening the door. "Come in."

"Thank you," Albert replied, stepping into the Polish man's house.

"What are you doing out so early?" Tolek asked, knowing something was surly wrong.

"I have come to ask a favor," Albert began. "I need a plot in your church's cemetery to bury my vater."

"Your vater died?" Tolek asked, shocked.

"Yes," Albert said. "Actually, he was murdered by Polish bandits last night."

"I'm so sorry to hear that," Tolek said, not agreeing with what the bandits were doing any more than he agreed with the Nazis behavior. "Of course you may lay your vater to rest in our cemetery. Our pastor would probably even say a few words, if you would like."

"That would be so kind," Albert said softly

"I will saddle my horse and we will ride to the church right now," Tolek said. "I will gather some men to dig the grave once we find out where he is to be buried."

"Thank you so much," Albert said, almost overcome with the grief he felt and the kindness of this man who had hated him just months before.

Jacob Grieb, husband of Juliana Grieb, Vater of Jacob, Albert, Olof, Mathilda, Maria, and Hulda Grieb, was laid to rest the afternoon of April 12, 1943. As the Griebs and Wallentines stood around the grave, they were joined by some of their Polish neighbors. They all bowed their heads together as the pastor prayed for God to comfort them in their loss and for a peaceful end to the war. There had been too many graves, too many innocent lives lost in Hitler's pursuit of a Greater Germany.

Chapter Fourteen

The war continued through the summer of 1943 with the Allies taking back German occupied territories a piece at a time on the western front. The Axis forces surrendered Tunisia on May 13th and by mid-August the Allies controlled Sicily. The battles between the Red Army and the Nazis continued in the Soviet Union. On July 5th, the Germans launched a massive tank offensive against the Soviets near Kursk. The Soviets slowed the attack quickly, and within a week launched an attack of their own, sending the Germans fleeing west at a rapid pace. Edward and Emil remained imprisoned in the POW camp, not knowing how the war was progressing.

"We have to get out of here soon," Edward whispered to Emil in the darkness of their quarters after everyone was asleep. "The conditions here are going to kill us or make us too weak to flee if we do get an opportunity to escape."

"Edward, please," Emil whispered back, "we are not going to leave this place until we die or the war is over, whichever comes first."

"Listen carefully, Emil," Edward hissed. "I have a plan and I truly believe it will work. I've been watching things and I know how we can escape."

"I've been watching things, too," Emil replied dryly. "Just today I watched a man eat another man's vomit because the man not vomiting is starving to death. The man who was vomiting will be dead in a few days."

"Emil, I know things seem hopeless," Edward whispered, "but we have to remain positive. It's what is going to get us out of here. We must have hope."

"I have hope, Brother," Emil replied sarcastically. "I hope the fleas don't chew on me so fierce tonight that I can't get any sleep. I also hope the lice take a little break from eating on my scalp. And I really hope the man above me in his bunk shuts up so I can get some sleep."

Edward knew Emil was slipping into depression. He had to tell Emil his plan and they needed to execute it soon. Leaning down from the bunk above his brother Edward whispered, "The dog is crazy and doesn't know his job. He behaves like an idiot every time there is a guard change."

"What do you mean?" Emil asked his interest piqued for the first time in months.

"The dog who sits with the guards," Edward whispered. "He looks fierce, like a wolf, but he's a baby. He only likes the guard that works from eight in the morning until four in the afternoon. Come with me tomorrow and I will show you what I mean."

"Is that where you've been disappearing to?" Emil asked.

"Yes," Edward confirmed. "I can watch from the corner of our building without being seen. They have quit keeping a close eye on us anyway, being that most of us are so malnourished we can hardly put one foot in front of the other."

"We are in pathetic condition," Emil agreed, "but I will die before I eat vomit."

"Me, too," Edward said with a shudder. "Meet me at the latrine at ten minutes to four tomorrow afternoon. We'll go watch the dog show together."

"Okay," Emil agreed. "I suppose if we get caught and they shoot us, it will be a blessing."

"Have some hope, Brother," Edward encouraged.

Emil answered with a grunt and rolled to his side to try and get some sleep. He doubted a dumb dog was their ticket out of this place, but he would watch with Edward just to have something to do besides think about how hungry he was. Seven months in this place had taken a toll on him. The constant hunger made him weak and irritable, and the misery he saw all around him caused his hope to sink to the point he had none. If it hadn't been for Edward encouraging him to keep holding on, he would have succumbed to the conditions long ago. Emil had to give it to Edward, he had remained hopeful of escaping and returning to their family all along. He at least owed Edward the courtesy of showing up and watching the guards change. It wasn't like he had anything else calling for his attention.

Emil met Edward the next day as planned. They made their way quickly to the corner of the building. As the guard for the four to midnight shift arrived, the morning guard prepared to leave. The dog became very agitated and began to whine. As the morning guard began to walk away the dog followed, making the night guard run after him. Grabbing his collar, the guard pulled the dog back to the gate.

"And this happens every day?" Emil asked in a whisper

"Every day," Edward said with a smile. "You would think that the night guard would anticipate that the dog is going to follow the morning guard but he never does. Maybe he just likes to beat the dog into submission daily, as he's doing now. Whatever reason the night guard has for allowing the dog to behave that way is not my concern, just as long as he allows it tomorrow afternoon."

"Tomorrow?" Emil questioned.

"Tomorrow, Brother," Edward answered. "If we don't make it and they kill us, what have we really lost? We're going to starve to death, anyway."

"True," Emil agreed. "Tomorrow it is."

Emil could hardly sleep that night and not just because the vermin were eating him alive. The thought of escaping was terrifying, yet exciting. He really didn't believe the opportunity would ever come, and now here it was less than a day away. The scene played over and over in Emil's mind and at the end, he and Edward always made it out safely. He knew it was because he didn't allow his mind to see it any other way, fearing the small light of hope would be snuffed out. Emil prayed, then begged and pleaded with God to let it be so.

The next afternoon, Emil and Edward were at the corner of the building ten minutes before the guard change. As the night guard approached and began talking to the morning guard, they made their way toward the gate that led out of the camp. When the morning guard began to walk away, the dog barked and followed, just like always. Edward and Emil moved quickly toward the gate as the night guard chased the dog. Slipping through the fence, the men moved in the opposite direction of the guard and dog. A building to the right of the gate was the planned hiding place. Scurrying past the building and crouching down as they rounded the end of it, Emil and Edward slowed to catch their breath.

"What now?" Emil asked. "Its hours before dark and we will be seen sitting here."

"Let's catch our breath then run for that next building," Edward said, pointing to a building fifty feet away.

"Good idea," Emil agreed. "We have to get as far from here as possible before they realize we're missing."

"Yes, I know," Edward said. "Ready?"

Emil nodded his head and the men were off again. Hearing a train in the distance, Edward and Emil looked at each other with the same plan in mind. They had to hop a train to get away from this camp fast. Making their way to the tracks the men watched a train pulling into the station. They were in front of it, just where they needed to be. All they had to do was be patient and wait for the opportunity to come to them. As the train began to roll out again, the men hid behind a building so the engineer wouldn't see them. The train moved slowly, and as the cars began to pass the men they looked for an open one. Finally, four cars from the end of the train their prayers were answered. Running with the little strength they had left, Emil and Edward made their way toward the tracks. Edward grabbed the open door and swung himself in. Emil was struggling, so Edward lay on his stomach and extended his arm to him. At just the last second, Emil gripped Edward's hand. Edward rolled into the rail car, pulling Emil in with him. Both men lay panting on the floor of the car, thankful they hadn't been caught.

"We made it!" Emil hollered, thankful to be leaving the POW camp behind. "Thanks for the help. What's the plan now?"

"We rest," Edward said. "When we feel the train slowing down, we jump."

Hours later, Emil awoke to darkness and Edward poking him. "It's time," Edward said.

"We won't be able to see where we're jumping," Emil worried.

"We have to jump," Edward stated, leaving no room for the discussion of other options because there were none.

"Okay," Emil agreed.

Edward and Emil could hear the brakes being applied and knew the time had come. They had to be off the train before it rolled into the station.

"Ready?" Edward asked.

"Ready," Emil replied.

Edward jumped first, followed seconds later by Emil. The ground was hard and tore the rags they were wearing to shreds. Other than some scrapes and bruises, the men were unharmed. Getting to their feet, they started moving away from the tracks. After walking five minutes, Edward and Emil found themselves in a grove of trees. They decided to sit down and wait until morning to determine what direction they needed to go by the position of the sun. As the morning rays lightened the sky, Edward and Emil slowly opened their eyes. Looking around, it was evident they were in a rural area. To some this discovery might have been disappointing, but to Edward and Emil, it was a welcomed sight. The men had grown up living off the land. They knew the month of August meant food in the garden and food was something they desperately needed.

"We need to find a house," Edward said. "Hopefully, it's laundry day."

"Are you planning to ask the wife of the house to wash your clothes?" Emil asked smiling.

"No, I'm hoping the man of the house is close to our size," Edward said. "The first thing we have to do is get out of these rags."

"And take a bath," Emil added.

"We could find a stream of water for that," Edward said. "At least it's August so we won't freeze to death while we scrub all this grime from our bodies."

"We jumped off on the right side of the tracks," Emil said noting the sun coming up behind them. "We won't have to waste time backtracking since we're headed in the right direction."

"That's something to be thankful for," Edward said taking the lead as the men began their journey home. "The sun looks a lot better not being viewed through a fence, too."

"So, where do you think we should go?" Emil asked. "Do we go back to Bessarabia and hope it's not overtaken by the Red Army again? Or should we go to Poland and try to find Mutti and

Vater there?"

"I believe it would be best to go to Poland," Edward answered. "We need to find our parents first. If we are allowed to return to Bessarabia, we will return with everyone else."

Edward and Emil continued west looking for a house where they might find food and clothing. The progress was quite slow because both men were quite weak. However, they were thankful they could walk normally. Others who were in the camp were not so fortunate. They had lost fingers and toes due to frostbite and some had lost portions of their ears. The men who had bunks closest to the doors leading outside seemed to suffer most. The chances of the men who had damaged feet ever escaping were basically hopeless. They would never be able to run fast enough to get away, and could certainly not hop a train as Edward and Emil had done.

"I think I see a ditch ahead," Emil said after twenty minutes of walking. "We may get clean quicker than we hoped for."

When Edward and Emil got closer they could see there was a stream of water ahead. Reaching the edge, they each took a drink before muddying the water with their bathing. Stripping down, the men stepped into the water and began to scrub. It felt so good to wash the filth off from the POW camp. When they were scrubbed clean, they climbed back on the bank to dry in the sun. The thought of putting the filthy rags back on was not appealing in the least but they had no choice. They didn't have time to wash them and wait for them to dry.

The stream ran at the edge of a field where wheat had been harvested the previous month. Before Edward and Emil stepped into the open field they looked for people. Seeing none, they began to scan the ground for grain. Finding several heads of wheat that had been dropped during the harvest, the men began to eat the grain raw. Anything was better than what they had been fed in the camp, and the wheat actually tasted good after so many months of starving.

With a bit of food in their stomachs, Edward and Emil continued on hoping to take care of the next thing on their agenda, decent clothes. Staying at the edge where the trees offered cover, the men headed around the perimeter of the field. They knew eventually a house would be found on the land. Someone had planted and harvested this field, so it only made since that someone lived nearby.

"I think I see a barn in the distance," Emil said pointing toward a large structure ahead.

"I believe you're right," Edward agreed. "Now, if we can just get to it without being seen."

"We may have to wait until dark," Emil suggested.

"That's not going to get us any clothes," Edward pointed out. "No woman is going to leave her laundry on the line overnight."

"I suppose that's true," Emil said. "Let's see how close we can get. Sure hope they don't have a dog."

"Never thought about that," Edward admitted. "A dog would make it much more difficult to sneak close enough to check things out. Probably wouldn't be any chance of getting clothes off the line, either."

When Edward and Emil got within sight of the house and barn, they dropped to their stomachs. Crawling on the ground, they approached the barn from the back. The barn was built with the middle open. Doors could be opened on each end and a wagon and team of horses could be driven all the way through. It was a good design because a wagon load of hay could be pulled in and unloaded to the loft from each side. It also saved time trying to back a team and wagon back out of the barn. Edward and Emil were just thankful for the back door, no matter what its purpose.

Slipping into the interior of the barn, the men listened for any activity or voices. Hearing no sounds, they made their way into the loft to get a better view of the house and surrounding area. As they peeked between the barn's board siding they could see the back of the house.

"It's our lucky day," Edward whispered. "There's laundry on the line."

"And look at the garden near the clothesline," Emil pointed out.

"I don't see anyone outside," Edward said. "They're probably eating breakfast. You raid the garden while I get us some clothes."

"Okay," Emil agreed. "Be careful."

"You, too," Edward said, heading back to the loft's ladder.

"Meet me back here and we'll change our clothes in the loft."

Scurrying back down the ladder, Edward and Emil headed for the rear barn doors. Opening them a crack they peered all around. Seeing no one, they both hurried to the corner of the barn and scanned the yard and surrounding area. All was clear, so each man ran out to get what they needed, praying they didn't caught. This farm was owned by a Russian farmer, and there would be no sympathy for a couple German soldiers who had escaped a POW camp. The men might be shot on the spot, or worse, returned to the POW camp to die a slow, painful death.

Reaching the clothesline, Edward grabbed two pairs of pants, two shirts, two pairs of underwear and some socks. He realized they were still very wet, but they were better than the rags he and his brother were wearing. Quickly, he ran back to the barn with his stolen items. He felt bad for taking the clothes but there really was no other choice for him and Emil.

Climbing to the loft, Edward waited for Emil to return from the garden. He watched between the boards as Emil filled his ragged shirt with vegetables. Edward just hoped the fabric would hold until he could get back to the barn. Climbing back down the ladder, Edward searched the barn until he spotted a small metal bucket. Hurrying to the back door he opened it just as Emil hurried to the entrance, surprising one another.

"You scared me half to death," Emil whispered.

"I was bringing you this bucket," Edward said quietly. "Here, dump your shirt in here."

Emil dumped the contents of his shirt into the bucket. He had found more food in five minutes than he and Edward had eaten in three days. Edward's mouth watered at the thought of tasting the food. He had the urge to eat the vegetables immediately, dirt and all.

"Let's go back to the loft," Edward suggested. "The clothes are really wet. We may want them to dry before we put them on."

"We better go back to the woods," Emil warned. "When the missing laundry is discovered, we are going to be hunted men."

"That's true," Edward agreed. "I'll got get the clothes."

Edward climbed back to the loft to get the clothes. Looking toward the house through the siding, he made sure no one had come outside. Finding the yard and surrounding area still empty,

Edward hurried to join Emil. As Emil reached to open the barn door, they heard footsteps at the front of the barn. Edward and Emil quickly pushed through the back door and made a run for the tree line. Reaching a safe distance from the house, they sat down to catch their breath.

"That was close," Emil panted.

"Yes," Edward agreed. "I couldn't see the front of the barn when I scanned the yard from the loft."

"Do you think the farmer will wonder why the back door on his barn is open?" Emil asked.

"I'm sure he will but I couldn't take the chance shutting it," Edward said. "He would have heard us for sure."

"We better move further from the house," Emil suggested. "Let's go back to the creek. I need another drink, anyway."

"Me too," Edward said getting up from the ground to follow his brother. Catching up to Emil, Edward reached out and took the pail from him. "Potatoes, onions, carrots, green beans, and cucumbers; we will feast like kings."

"We'll wash the dirt from the potatoes, onions, and carrots when we get back to the creek," Emil said. "Too bad we can't build a fire."

"We have no matches and we will still be too close to the house," Edward replied.

"Yes, I know," Emil said, "but fried potatoes with onions sure sound good."

"Soon, Brother, soon," Edward promised.

The brothers hung the wet clothes on tree limbs to allow them to dry. They feasted from the bucket, saving enough for another meal. As they ate, they made plans for the journey ahead of them.

"We need to travel back through the German colonies," Edward said. "Remember how empty they were as we pushed the Red Army east?"

"Yes, I remember," Emil said. "Those empty villages will give us somewhere to rest as we try to get home."

"And hopefully the cellars will provide us with some food, too," Edward pointed out.

"Some of the cellars probably do still have food in them," Emil said thoughtfully. "We may just make it out of here alive,

Brother."

"We certainly will or die trying," Edward spouted. "I will not be taken back to that POW camp."

"Me neither," Emil agreed.

Edward and Emil continued west, staying in the empty German villages as planned. The going was slow because the men did not want to use the road for fear of being spotted. When they were near a town, they would search for a discarded newspaper to find out the latest on the war. They did not want to run into the Red Army from behind. By November 1943, the Red Army had pushed the Germans troops back to Kiev according to a newspaper Edward had found. The brothers were a mere ten miles behind them.

****

As it became clear the German troops were steadily losing ground, the German villages that had been liberated when the Nazis invaded now feared for their lives. They could not stay and wait for the Red Army to overtake them again. Not one of the Germans was willing to fall under Communist rule again. The decision was made to make a run for the Soviet border and beyond. The colonist's only hope was for Hitler to allow them to take refuge in Poland and make them German citizens.

"Daniel, we must head west," Isabella pleaded.

"Maybe the Nazis will rally and push the Red Army back again," Daniel said hopefully.

"Our neighbors are pulling out in two days," Isabella said. "Please, Daniel, let's go with them. We can go to Poland where my sister, Rosina, and her family are."

"Vater, you don't want to fall back into the hands of the Communists, do you?" Adolf asked.

"No, Son, I do not," Daniel answered.

"Please, for our children's sake, let's go to Poland," Isabella pleaded again.

"Okay," Daniel finally agreed, "we will go. The trip will be a rough and cold one, though. It's already November and winter will be upon us soon."

"We will pack wool blankets and warm clothes," Adolf said.

"We have very few clothes, warm or otherwise," Daniel reminded him.

"We will make it," Isabella said.

"We have to go, Vater," Agathe chimed in. "There is no future for Adolf and me here."

Daniel looked at his too thin daughter and knew she was right. There would never be a future for a German in Russia again.

Isabella, Daniel, Adolf, and Rosina packed their meager belongings and food from their cellar. The harvest had been plentiful, since they had not been forced to share it with the rest of Russia. For the first time in twenty years, what they grew truly belonged to them.

When the wagons pulled out of the German village of Kronau, the Gingrich family was among them. They knew the travel would be rough and they must stay ahead of the retreating German troops. If the troops passed them, they would be overtaken by the Red Army and shipped to slave camps like so many others had been. With this knowledge, the colonists fled as quickly as possible, pushing beast and human strength to its limit.

Chapter Fifteen

The reports of the Soviet troops pushing the German soldiers back out of Russia continued to reach the ears of the relocated Germans in Poland. Where would the Soviets stop? Would they come to the original line in Poland agreed upon by Stalin and Hitler in 1939 or would they push as far as they possibly could? Would the Soviets take back all the territory they had lost during the Great War and then add Germany to it?

"The Soviets have liberated Kiev," Gottlieb told Rosina. "They have pushed the Nazis past the Dnieper River now."

"Do you think the German colonies will flee as the Red Army approaches?" Rosina asked thinking of her sister Isabella.

"If they're smart they will," Gottlieb said.

"Do you think Daniel and Isabella will finally make it out?" Rosina asked.

"We will pray they do," Gottlieb answered.

Juliana Grieb walked into the kitchen where Gottlieb and Rosina were talking. She and her children had moved in with Gottlieb and Rosina after her husband was murdered. They had the most room in their home since their children were out on their own or off fighting in the war.

"Good morning, Juliana," Rosina said. "Did you sleep well?"

"Yes," Juliana answered. "What do you need help with?"

"You could fry the eggs if you would like," Rosina said.

As the two women made breakfast, they talked of the cold weather for November and the plans they had for the day. Since Juliana and her daughters had moved in, Rosina found she had a lot more time to do things she liked rather than things she must. The young women were very helpful, taking care of all the laundry and baking. Juliana had taught them well. Honestly, if it hadn't been for the war disrupting their lives, Mathilda and Maria would probably be happily married by now.

Olof, at sixteen, was a big help to Gottlieb, too. Albert and Jacob had been helping Gottlieb get his crops planted and harvested, but the past summer Olof had taken over for them. Olof and Gottlieb plowed, disc, planted, and harvested side by side. They had moved the horses and farm equipment from Jacob Grieb's farm after his death to Gottlieb's farm. This allowed them to get twice as much done in the same amount of time. Like Juliana had taught her daughters how to work hard, Jacob senior had taught his youngest son, as well. If they had still been in Bessarabia, Olof would have been the one to own the mill, grocery store and dairy eventually because he was the youngest son.

The Polish bandits had moved from the area of Poland that the Griebs and Wallentines occupied for the time being, but the relocated Germans kept a close watch for any sign of their return. Everyone was spending nights in their own homes again but they had all decided to get a dog for protection. The Polish farmers had been more than happy to supply them from their litters of puppies that spring of 1943. The puppies were just now getting big enough to do their job of barking when a stranger arrived at the home.

Rosina had started having school again three days a week. The children had missed out last spring when the schooling had to be stopped for fear of the bandits. She was now trying to catch everyone up on what they had forgotten so they could move forward with new lessons. Juliana's three daughters had also been a big help with teaching the little ones while Rosina worked with the older kids.

****

Magdalena sank into a kitchen chair to rest her aching back for a moment. Her ankles had begun to swell some and she was feeling quite large. The baby kicked constantly in her womb keeping her eyes wide open most nights, long after everyone else had gone to sleep.

"I've taught Stein a new trick," Ewald announced, coming in from the barn. "Want to see it?"

"Yes, Ewald, I will watch," Magdalena said.

Ewald opened the back door and called the dog into the kitchen. Magdalena did not like an animal in the house but Stein had captured all of their hearts with his intelligence and loyalty. The dog watched over her sons like a ferocious bear watches her cubs. For these reasons, Stein was allowed in the house throughout the day and spent each night indoors guarding his family.

"Okay, Stein, speak," Ewald commanded.

To Magdalena's amazement, Stein barked three short, staccato barks. Ewald rewarded him with some leftover biscuit he had crammed in his pocket. The dog ate the treat and waited for more. Ewald repeated the command and Stein barked again.

"That's a good trick," Magdalena laughed. "Now if you can teach him to be quiet on command, we will have it made."

Seven year old Ewald beamed at his mutti, two teeth missing in the front of his mouth. Getting the dog had been the best thing to happen for him since they had left Bessarabia. The kittens in the barn had been nice, but the dog went everywhere with Ewald and his brother, Erhard. Stein even walked with them to school and waited faithfully each day to ride home in the wagon with Gottlieb and the other children. It amazed Magdalena how much even she loved the dog.

"Stein is a smart dog," Ewald said.

"Yes, he is," Magdalena agreed.

Magdalena could hear Jacob and Erhard come into the drive and head to the barn. They had gone to the nearby town for supplies. Getting to her feet, Magdalena began to finish up the noon meal she had been preparing before her aching feet and back had demanded a rest.

As Jacob and Erhard came through the back door, Ewald was prepared to show them Stein's new trick. Ewald made Stein do the trick twice for Erhard, and then Erhard insisted on trying to get the dog to do it. Jacob came to Magdalena's side to talk quietly while the boys were occupied with Stein.

"The German troops are being pushed out of Russia at an alarming rate of speed," Jacob said.

"How far west have they come?" Magdalena asked.

"Past Kiev," Jacob stated.

"Do you think they will stop when they reach the Russian border?"

"Maybe," Jacob said, "but they own half of Poland since Stalin and Hitler invaded from both sides in 1939. They may push the Nazis back to here."

"What will that mean for us?" Magdalena asked concern evident in her voice.

"I don't know. We need to keep informed of what's happening in case we need to move to safety."

"I just wish this war would end," Magdalena sighed.

"Me, too," Jacob agreed. "The farms here in Poland have been nice, much better than the tents, but I'm ready to have a place to call home, again."

"Yes," Magdalena replied, "the sooner the better."

"A place in America," Jacob said.

And there it was. Magdalena hadn't heard Jacob mention his dream for a long time but she could see in his eyes now that it still lived on. Magdalena wanted peace and a home of their own again but she did not want to cross an ocean to find it. She knew they had no hope of leaving for America now but with the first opportunity Jacob could find, they would all be on a boat headed to the unknown. It was a worry Magdalena would just place on a shelf for today and hope she could just leave it there. More pressing things boggled Magdalena's mind today, like how far the Nazis had been pushed back toward the Soviet's border and how far the Red Army would go before deciding they had pushed far enough.

Magdalena put the noon meal on the table and the family sat down to eat. Jacob led the prayer while the rest joined in. It was a rote prayer from the Lutheran church that was said by each family before meals. In this way, everyone gave thanks to God, young and old together.

****

Edward and Emil had been staying just behind the Red Army for months but now it was mid-November. The weather was turning cold and they needed to get to Poland to join their family before winter set in.

"We need to get through the Red Army line," Emil stated. "We don't know how long it will take them to push the German troops back across the Soviet border."

"I agree," Edward replied. "If they stop at their border, we will still have to push past them somehow. There's also the chance the Nazis will retaliate and start pushing them back this way. We do not want to get caught in the middle of that."

"We can't get pulled back into the German troops, either," Emil pointed out. "I've seen enough fighting to last me a lifetime."

"No, we do not want to get drafted back into this war," Edward agreed. "We will just have to travel at night. We can see their fires, so we know where they are camped."

"Let's head south so maybe we can cross back over into Romania," Emil suggested. "At least we would be familiar with the area."

"Good idea," Edward said. "We will start tonight after dark."

When night fell, Edward and Emil headed south, keeping the Red Army fires in their sight to the west. When they could not see any more fires, they traveled another five miles. Finding shelter in an abandoned German home, they rested until daylight when they could get a good look at their surroundings.

"I think this is where we should try to break through," Emil said.

"Yes," Edward agreed. "We are very near the Dnieper River. Let's get to the water's edge and find a good crossing before dark. We will continue west after nightfall."

"Good idea," Emil confirmed.

Heading west, the men soon came to the river. Walking south along the bank, they looked for a shallow place to cross. As they came around a bend in the river they stopped abruptly.

"Is that a small boat tied at the river's edge?" Edward asked.

"I do believe it is, Brother," Emil confirmed with a smile.

"Crossing may be easier than we first thought," Edward said. "We may not even have to get wet, which would be really nice as cold as it's going to be."

Walking closer, the men scanned the area on both sides of the river for any activity. Seeing none they decided the boat must have belonged to a German who used to live in one of the neighboring colonies. All of those colonies were empty now, the Soviet Union deporting the occupants at the start of the war with Germany.

"I say we go ahead and cross," Emil said.

"It would be easier in the daylight," Edward admitted. "We just look like the local peasants and we speak Russian fluently. Maybe we can pass ourselves off as native kulaks if anyone questions us."

"It's worth the chance I suppose," Emil replied. "We need to get on the western side of the German troops somehow."

Climbing down the bank and into the boat, Edward and Emil rowed across the Dnieper River. Reaching the other side, they looked around for people. Seeing no one, they tied the boat to a tree on the shore and climbed the bank. There were houses in the distance but no one seemed to be around.

"The colonies on this side of the river should have people in them," Edward commented. "We should fit right in with these German villagers."

"Yes, if they're still living here," Emil replied. "They may be fleeing for their lives as the Red Army is approaching."

"I didn't think of that," Edward said. "I suppose the Germans here would be accepted back into the Reich just as we were when we fled Bessarabia."

"I wouldn't see why not," Emil answered. "Hitler has invited all Germans back to the homeland, even the ones who moved to America."

Nearing the first village, Edward and Emil could tell no one was still living there. Evidence showed that people had been there recently but had all left in a hurry. Going from farm to farm, Edward and Emil gathered all the food and supplies they could carry. The men then called two horses from a pasture to the barn. It seemed the beasts had been left to fend for themselves. Finding tack in the barn, they put bridles on the mounts.

"Let's not weight them down with saddles," Edward suggested. "It's not like we haven't ridden bareback before."

"I just hope I can stay on its back," Emil laughed.

"The horses will make for much faster travel," Edward said. "We will make it twice as far in a day."

Continuing west, the men rode all day. They slept in empty villages at night. They found peasants along the way, but they did not see any military troops. Three days of riding brought them close to the Russian border.

"Look at that great cloud of dust ahead," Emil said.

"Yes," Edward replied, "what do you suppose it is?"

"I don't know but we should probably proceed with caution," Emil replied. "It might be the Nazis moving equipment toward the front line, or the Nazis fleeing the Red Army's advance."

"Let's stop early today and rest," Edward suggested. "We can get closer to check things out after nightfall."

As darkness fell, Edward and Emil made their way west again. They could see campfires in the distance. When they were within a half mile of the camp, they tied their horses and proceeded on foot. Hiding in the trees along the road, they slowly made their way forward.

"It's a bunch of wagons," Emil whispered.

"Yes, and they're loaded down with household possessions," Edward whispered back.

"Must be the Germans from the villages we liberated when we first invaded Russia over two years ago," Emil said quietly. "They're fleeing from the Red Army while they have a chance."

"We will wait until morning and join them," Edward suggested. "We can blend right in with these folks."

"Yes, we will be hidden in plain sight," Emil said with a smile.

As dawn came, Edward and Emil headed toward the wagon train. The travelers were just getting up to prepare breakfast. Walking their mounts, the men moved into the midst of the wagons. The weary people around the campfires paid them little mind. When the group began to move, Emil and Edward rode along, moving farther to the front of the caravan as they went. Staying in the back would result in eating dust all day.

When the wagon train stopped for the night, Edward and Emil shared campfires with other travelers. No one seemed to notice that the two men were without any other family. They just accepted them as fellow Germans fleeing the Red Army. It was just as Emil had said they were hidden in plain sight. This realization fanned their flames of hope, and they believed now that they would make it to Poland and find their family.

The going was rough and some of the refugee's wagons broke along the way. There was no way to repair them, so they loaded what they could on other wagons and moved on. The horses pulling the wagons were in sad shape and some had to be left to die along the road, too sickly to continue on. Some of the travelers were not strong enough to make the trek either and were buried along the road in quickly dug, shallow graves. They were all desperate to stay ahead of the Soviets and to reach shelter before the weather turned frigid.

As the wagon train came closer to the Reich, they began to get assistance from Germany. It appeared this new wave of Germans fleeing Russia would also be invited back into the Reich. The refugees were loaded onto railcars and taken to western Poland. There, they were to be resettled on the farms alongside the Volhynian, Baltic, and Romanian Germans.

"We have to get away when we get off this train in Poland," Emil told Edward as they shivered together in a railcar. "Otherwise, we will be drafted right back into the German forces upon our arrival."

"We will separate from the group at the first opportunity," Edward promised.

As the train finally pulled into the station in Poland, the railcars were thrown open and the occupants could not exit quickly enough. There had not been many stops for elimination needs and so corners of the cars had become makeshift facilities. Others had gotten sick with the motion of the train on the tracks, vomiting what little food they had in their stomachs. Some had been too ill and old to finish the journey and now lay dead in the railcar. It was a scene everyone wanted to leave behind and not ever remember.

Exiting the railcars, the refugees were made to line up along the tracks. Edward and Emil slowly worked their way toward the back of the line. Already going through this procedure upon arriving from Bessarabia, they knew how it worked. All single men eighteen and older would be drafted into the German ranks immediately. Yes, the men would become German citizens protecting them from Stalin, but they would repay that kindness by fighting for a Greater Germany, maybe with their very last breath.

"Move slowly to the left," Edward whispered.

Emil answered with a nod and began to shuffle left. When they reached a connection of two railcars, they stepped back between them. Single file, they slowly backed and stepped over the buckle holding the cars together. Reaching the other side, the men moved toward the end of the train away from the station. They were not even missed among the thousands of refugees now standing alongside the railcars in the cold mid- December air.

"We will just have to head for the countryside and ask if

anyone knows Gottlieb Wallentine," Emil said jogging alongside his brother.

"It may take us a month to find them, but I know they're here somewhere," Edward replied. "This is where they were all sent before we even left Germany to invade Russia."

As the two men walked along the road, they didn't have to wait long to come across a relocated German. The man knew the general area the Germans from Bessarabia had been sent to and pointed Edward and Emil in that direction. Catching rides along the way, Edward and Emil were near their parent's home by nightfall.

"We must stop for the night," Edward said. "I'm tired, hungry and frozen."

"Me, too," Emil agreed. "Do you think we would be welcomed by one of these German families?"

"We have to try," Edward replied.

Knocking on the door of the next house they came to, Edward and Emil were thankful to see a German farmer on the other side and not a Polish one. The Poles might turn them over to the storm troopers just for revenge on the Germans who had flooded their area. It was difficult to know who to trust.

"We just arrived by train," Edward began, "and need a place to stay one night."

"Come in," the German farmer welcomed. "The wife will get you some food and you can warm yourselves by the fire. My name is Stefan."

"Thank you," Emil said, relieved to find food and shelter. "I'm Emil and this is my brother, Edward."

"Where are you boys from?" Stefan asked.

"Bessarabia," Edward answered, not wanting to give more information. This German farmer was probably just as sick of this war as anyone else but he didn't want to take a chance on being turned back over to the German troops.

"Ah," Stefan said, "me, too. What's your last name?"

"Wallentine," Emil offered.

"Wallentine?" Stefan asked with interest. "Not the Wallentines who made the fine wine, is it?"

"Yes," Edward said, "that would be us."

"Haven't had a wine so fine since leaving Bessarabia,"

Stefan complained.

"Neither have we," Emil chuckled. "Actually, we haven't had any wine at all since leaving. The last wine we partook of was during communion at the Lutheran church just before we left."

"Such a sad thing, this," Stefan said. "We were all uprooted and had to leave fine land and our possessions. Now the German troops are losing ground to the Red Army daily and the Allies are pounding the German troops on the other front."

"Yes, a sad thing," Edward said, hoping to move the conversation away from the war reports.

"Come sit at the table," Stefan's wife offered. "I have some ham, fried potatoes, green beans and slices of bread for you boys."

Edward and Emil's eyes lit up as they gladly did what the lady asked. The hot, nourishing meal was a blessing. They had not eaten this well in a very long time. With their full attention on the food, Stefan let the Red Army's progress drop from the conversation, along with the Allies victories. Instead, he turned the conversation to local happenings. Edward and Emil listened politely as they shoveled the delicious food into their mouths.

After finishing their meal, Edward and Emil were given blankets and allowed to sleep in the living room. The couple had three young children who were sleeping in the extra bedroom so the floor was all they had to offer, unless one of them wanted to sleep sitting in the rocking chair. Edward and Emil didn't complain one bit about the sleeping arrangement. They were just thankful for the food and warmth, something they had been sorely missing for several years.

The next morning, Edward and Emil left at dawn, taking some cheese and a loaf of bread for the road. They had been offered breakfast by Stefan but chose to get an early start. Catching rides at every opportunity, they arrived at their parents' farm by early afternoon.

"Gottlieb," Rosina said, "there are two men in rags headed up our lane."

The dog had started barking the minute it spotted Emil and Edward. The men knew if anyone was home, they had been alerted of their arrival by the dog. Walking to the back of the house, Edward raised his hand to knock. Suddenly, the door swung open surprising both Emil and Edward.

"What are you young men…," Gottlieb's words froze on his tongue. The men were skin and bones, they were filthy with matted hair and beards, but Gottlieb Wallentine would know his own sons anywhere. "How did you find us?" Gottlieb choked out.

"We knew you had been sent to Poland before we left to invade Russia," Edward said. "It was just a matter of asking questions until someone knew you and where you were living."

"Come in, come in," Gottlieb said standing back from the door.

"Who is it?" Rosina asked, coming to the door. "Oh, my goodness, Emil and Edward," Rosina gasped, hugging both boys at the same time.

"You're going to smother them," Gottlieb teased.

"It wouldn't take much," Rosina replied. "You boys are nothing but bones!"

"Nothing some good cooking won't take care of," Emil replied.

"Right after a bath and haircut," Rosina said.

"Absolutely," Edward agreed.

"What a wonderful Christmas gift," Rosina exclaimed. "Tomorrow is Christmas Eve."

"Really?" Emil asked. "We had lost track of the days."

Juliana and her daughters came from the back bedroom and Olof came in from the barn. Edward and Emil looked from them to their parents, their eyes full of questions.

"A lot has happened here just as I'm sure has happened with you boys," Gottlieb said. "We will all sit down and talk later. First, your mutti will heat water and you boys can get cleaned up. I'll cut your hair out in the barn after it's washed."

"It would probably be better if you cut our hair before we wash it," Emil said. "It might get some of the tangles out."

"And some of the critters," Edward added with a chuckle.

Rosina's face became stern. She had just hugged the life out of these boys and now they announce they have lice! She was overjoyed to see them but this new bit of information caused her head to itch immediately, though she knew full well there couldn't have possibly been time for the critters to start setting up house in her hair. "Gottlieb, please shave their heads and beards in the barn, before their baths," Rosina pleaded. "Build a fire outside and burn the hair. We don't want to take any chances of bringing lice into the house. We will throw their clothes on the fire, too, as soon as they take them off."

"That's probably a good idea," Gottlieb said, laughter dancing in his eyes. "We're very thankful both of you safely returned to us but the other guests taking up residence in your hair appear to be unwelcome by your mutti."

Emil and Edward laughed as they followed their vater to the barn. It was so good to find joy again, even if it was over watching their mutti cringe at the thought of having lice. The men had experienced so much sadness the past two years; beginning with being forced to take part in imprisoning innocent Jews into concentration camps and having young men fall dead beside them during battle. The images of watching men starve to death and succumb to illnesses in the POW camp added to that grief. Both men wondered if they would ever be able to close their eyes at night without reliving those past occurrences. So far, it had not happened.

Rosina watched from the kitchen window as her two sons followed their vater to the barn. She whispered a prayer of thanks for their safe return, lice and all. She then said a prayer for all the other soldiers still fighting in the war and for their loved ones waiting for them at home. It didn't matter which side the men were fighting for, the Axis or the Allies, they all had someone waiting for their safe return. Rosina realized how blessed she was that both her sons' lives had been spared and knew there were many soldiers who would never see their families again this side of heaven.

Chapter Sixteen

News of Edward and Emil's return reached the ears of their sisters, Magdalena and Emilie, by nightfall of the day they arrived. Olof rode to both of their houses to deliver the message. There was much to celebrate but all of the family knew the men would have to stay close to their parents' home. The fact that they should still be fighting the Red Army was no secret. Not only did area Poles and relocated Germans know that Edward and Emil would be of age to be drafted into the German troops, the Gestapo patrolling Poland would arrest them on sight and send them back to the front line. For this reason, Christmas day would be celebrated at Gottlieb and Rosina's home.

Magdalena woke at three in the morning on Christmas Eve. Her back had been aching for two days and now the pain would not allow her to get comfortable. Getting up, she shuffled to the living room to sit so she wouldn't wake Jacob with her tossing and turning. Lowering herself in the rocking chair, she attempted to find a position that gave her relief.

As she rocked in the dark, she thought about what day it was, Christmas Eve. Being in her condition at the present time, she was thankful she was not riding on a donkey at the moment. How had Mary done it, being such a young woman and so far from family and friends? Then there was the whole issue of being pregnant before her marriage. It was a miracle she wasn't stoned and probably would have been if Joseph hadn't taken her for his wife. God crossed social and cultural lines to bring his Son to earth.

Magdalena thought of the stable Jesus had been born in and was also thankful for the warm house she was in. To bring a child into the world in such a cold and dirty place would have been terrible.

It all had significance, though. Humbleness was one. The King of Kings coming to earth in such a way was not what the Jews were looking for. Then there was the town of Bethlehem, King David's birthplace, the place where all the lambs were born and raised for use in sacrifices in Jerusalem. How appropriate that the Lamb of God, the supreme sacrifice, would be born in Bethlehem.

Magdalena's thoughts continued through the miraculous story; past the birth, the shepherds and angels, the wise men from the East. She pondered what happened after all that. King Herod demanded all male infants in Bethlehem under the age of two be killed. As Mary and Joseph ran to protect their child, they found themselves in yet another place where they knew no one. What a horrific act evil King Herod committed and the river of tears that must have followed. Thinking about all those muttis having their babies torn from their arms by the calloused soldiers made Magdalena shudder. To think of someone being so cruel was something Magdalena did not want to dwell on.

Suddenly, Magdalena's thoughts settled on Micah. She wondered where he was this Christmas Eve. Had he been placed in the same camp as his mutti and siblings, or had the Nazis just thrown him into the first camp they came to? The thought of Micah being alone in a camp brought tears to Magdalena's eyes. How many Jewish children had Hitler put to death? What were the concentration camps really like? What went on behind the fences and walls of those buildings? Magdalena was pretty sure she didn't really want to know. Did the Allies realize they were not just fighting to help the weaker countries that had fallen to the German troops, but to also free a whole ethnic group who had been imprisoned for no other reason than the fact they had been born a Jew?

Another realization came to Magdalena as she dwelled on Hitler's misdeeds and evil schemes. Hitler and King Herod were much alike. They were both rulers over the Jewish people, and they both chose to persecute them. Nearly two thousand years separated Herod and Hitler but both of their deeds were just as evil.

Magdalena whispered a prayer for Micah and his family, wherever they were this Christmas Eve morning. She prayed that the war would end soon and that the Jews would be allowed to return to their homes, even though the answer to that prayer would mean Magdalena and her family would have to pack up and move again.

Magdalena drifted off to sleep in the rocking chair until the first real contraction woke her at nearly four in the morning. Magdalena knew now that her backache had been part of her labor beginning. Not wanting to wake Jacob yet, she decided to wait until the contractions were closer. This labor had not begun like the last time, hard and furious. Her pregnancy was also full term, giving her full hope of a healthy child.

Magdalena prayed quietly in the darkness for an easy delivery and for the well-being of the new life that would enter the world very shortly. Time ticked on, and at five-thirty Jacob came looking for her. He found her still sitting in the rocking chair.

"Magdalena," Jacob asked quietly, "are you okay?"

"My labor has started," Magdalena whispered back, not wanting to wake the boys.

"Why didn't you wake me?" Jacob demanded. "You need to get back to bed and I need to get your mutti and take the boys to Albert and Emilie's."

"Jacob," Magdalena spoke softly, "you're pacing like a caged animal. Please, sit down and rest a little while. I've only had six contractions in an hour and a half. Let everyone get a full night's sleep. No sense in interrupting their rest."

"Everyone would be out of bed by the time I hitched the wagon and got there," Jacob pointed out.

"That's true," Magdalena agreed, "but let them have a nice breakfast. I think we have a few hours before I will need Mutti."

"A baby on Christmas Eve," Jacob said quietly, "what a blessing."

"It's exactly what I've been thinking about," Magdalena replied, "how thankful I am that I'm not on a donkey and am destined to give birth in a barn."

"Yes," Jacob said with a chuckle, "and that you have others you can depend on to help you when the time comes, besides your husband."

"You would manage if you had to," Magdalena said.

"But today you have your mutti for the task," Jacob replied.

"I wonder if Mary had a midwife in Bethlehem to help her," Magdalena mused.

"The Bible doesn't say whether she did or not," Jacob said, "but I suppose she could have."

"She must have been scared senseless," Magdalena said.

"I'm sure she was," Jacob replied, "but Mary knew she was carrying the Son of God. That had to give her some kind of peace."

Another contraction gripped Magdalena turning her thoughts back to the task that was near at hand. Jacob looked at her with concern but she waved him away.

Jacob went to wake Erhard so he could milk the cow. To sit and watch his wife having contractions was too much for him. He didn't want to wait too long and be forced to deliver the baby himself. It took all the self-control he could muster not to fetch Rosina immediately.

Jacob followed Erhard to the barn as he prepared to do the milking. He decided to go ahead and hitch the horses to the wagon so it would be ready to go the minute Magdalena told him it was time.

"Why are you hitching up the wagon, Vater?" Erhard asked, as milk began to ping in the bottom of the pail.

"It's time for your brother or sister to be born," Jacob answered.

"Oh," Erhard replied his face revealing his fear. He had been old enough to remember the last birth his mutti endured and the sadness that had followed.

"Don't worry, Erhard," Jacob assured, attempting to calm his own nerves along with Erhard's. "It's not like the last time. This baby is full term, so there's no reason to think the child won't be born healthy and strong."

"Okay, Vater," Erhard murmured, not totally convinced his vater was right.

Jacob returned to the house, and an hour later Magdalena decided it was time for her mutti to come. Jacob went to get Rosina with the plan to take Erhard and Ewald to Albert and Emilie's when he returned. The boys would enjoy playing with their cousins and they wouldn't have to endure the painful sounds of their mutti giving birth. From the conversation Jacob and Erhard had just had in the barn, Jacob knew it would be best for the boys to not be present when the baby was born.

By the time Jacob returned with Rosina, Magdalena's contractions were five minutes apart. She was still in the rocking chair but allowed Jacob to help her to their bedroom. Rosina had already prepared the bed for the birth and was excited about the new grandbaby that would soon be born. Rosina had assisted with many births, and Magdalena took comfort in her mutti's presence for this delivery, thankful her family had not been separated after the move from Bessarabia.

"Maybe a girl, Magdalena?" Rosina asked, hopefully. "I have all grandsons. I know it's important to pass on the family name, but what about the family recipes? We need a girl to teach those to, so they won't be lost to the next generation."

"I have no control of whether I have a boy or girl," Magdalena laughed, and then gasped as another contraction took hold.

"Only three minutes apart now," Rosina said checking the bedside clock. "It won't be too much longer."

Two hours later, a baby's wail filled the room. Magdalena smiled, exhausted but happy. Rosina quickly clamped and cut the cord then wrapped the baby in a warm towel. "There won't be any recipes passed down to this one," Rosina said with a smile, passing the bundle to his mutti.

Magdalena opened the towel and peered at the baby. He had ten toes and ten fingers and was full of life. It was another boy but he was healthy, and that was all that mattered. Magdalena whispered a prayer of thanks for the miracle that now lay in her arms. Looking up, Magdalena saw Jacob just outside the bedroom door.

"Come meet your new son," Magdalena invited.

Jacob came into the room and gazed at the bundle in Magdalena's arms. Moisture gathered at the corners of his eyes at seeing his son for the first time. The miracle of life never ceased to amaze Jacob and he silently thanked God for the healthy baby and uncomplicated birth. The wait for this little one had been a long one, but in His time, God had blessed them.

"So, what's my new grandson's name?" Rosina asked, holding out her arms to take the baby.

"Werner," Magdalena said quietly. "Born December 24,

1943; a Christmas blessing."
****

With Magdalena and Werner not being able to travel anywhere, the Grieb and Wallentine families came to Jacob and Magdalena's to celebrate Christmas. Not wanting Emil and Edward to be seen, it was decided they would have a Christmas supper. It would be nearly dark by then and easier for the young men to lay covered in the wagon without detection. There was a small risk but the families refused to miss this Christmas celebration. Edward and Emil had made it home safely and a healthy baby boy had just been born. There was so much to be thankful for.

All of the Wallentine family came, even Jacob and Otto, Gottlieb and Rosina's older sons, with their wives and children. It had been years since the whole family had been together for the holiday. Juliana, her daughters, and Olof also joined the group. The house was packed ready to explode but no one seemed to notice.

Magdalena remained in bed while her mutti and Emilie prepared food in her kitchen. Juliana and her daughters made dishes in Rosina's kitchen, as well, and brought them along. When the meal was ready, the kitchen table was laden with food and desserts lined the counter. If anyone went away hungry, it was their own fault. After the meal, the adults sat around sharing stories of what had happened in Poland while Edward and Emil were away, while the children went to the barn to play hide and seek. They took along one lantern to hang beside "base" with a warning from Jacob to not burn the barn down echoing in their ears.

Jacob told the story of finding Micah in his barn loft and how the storm troopers barged in and threatened his family, taking Micah away in the end. Albert told of how he and Jacob had been forced to steal horses from a Polish farmer and how his horse gave him away when it returned home. Albert also shared the story about the young Polish man his sons had found dead behind his barn. As the stories continued, it seemed everyone had one to tell about the Polish bandits and took turns telling them. Of course, Edward and Emil already knew the bandits were responsible for Jacob Grieb senior's death, since his widow, Juliana and her children lived with Gottlieb and Rosina now. It appeared the dangers of the war were not limited to the front lines where

Edward and Emil had fought the Red Army until their capture.

Edward and Emil shared what had happened to them after being drafted into the German forces. They told of taking part in arresting Jews and placing them in concentration camps. They shared of meeting Aunt Isabella and her family, leaving out the pathetic living conditions they had witnessed and the poor health the villagers were all in. They explained how they had been trapped and captured by the Red Army in Stalingrad because Hitler refused to allow them to retreat. Most of the details of the POW camp were not spoken of, but Edward and Emil told about the poorly trained dog and how it enabled them to escape. They spoke of all the German villagers fleeing Russia ahead of the Red Army and hoped that Aunt Isabella and her family were among them. It seemed the war had left no one untouched, no matter where they had been for the last three years.

The children returned from the barn for more dessert. Everyone found a place to sit down and Gottlieb began to sing Christmas carols and everyone joined in. When they all finished singing "Silent Night", Erhard focused his attention on his Opa.

"Opa," Erhard said quietly, "I remember the story you told us about that song last year."

"Very good, Erhard," Gottlieb replied. "Why don't you try and tell it again?"

So Erhard told the story of the broken organ on Christmas Eve in a small village in Austria. His opa nodded proudly as Erhard correctly remembered each detail. It gave Gottlieb much satisfaction to know that the story would be passed on through the years, long after he was gone.

After Magdalena's kitchen was put back in order, everyone started for home. Rosina wanted to stay and help Magdalena for a few more days but Magdalena assured her she would be fine. They may only have oatmeal for breakfast and simple meals for the next few days but they would survive.

The conclusion was unanimous. It had been the best Christmas since they had left Bessarabia. The war had uprooted and separated them for a time but on this Christmas Day in 1943, they had all been together. It was a good reason to give thanks.

Two days after Christmas, Rosina watched from the kitchen window as Gottlieb pulled into the drive. He had gone to town for some supplies and to glean the most recent report on the war. As he passed by on his way to the barn, Rosina noticed there were people in the back of the wagon. Grabbing her coat she headed out the back door to see who Gottlieb had brought back with him.

"Rosina," the woman in the back of the wagon hollered, "is it really you?"

Stopping in her tracks, Rosina gasped then ran toward the wagon at full speed.

"Isabella!" Rosina yelled. "I thought I would never see you again!"

The two women fell into one another's embrace. Over thirty years had passed since they had seen each other. So many things had happened since the day Isabella married Daniel and left Bessarabia. The river of life had continued to flow for both of them but carving two very different paths. Rosina had enjoyed raising her children and living a peaceful life surrounded by family and friends. Isabella had endured heartache, persecution, and a life of unrest. It had taken a toll on her.

"I can't believe you're here," Rosina exclaimed. "Come in and warm yourselves. How did you get here? Where did Gottlieb find you?"

"Rosina," Gottlieb laughed. "Slow down and let Isabella answer one question before you ask another."

"I'm sorry," Rosina apologized, "I'm just so surprised and excited. Please, come in and warm yourselves. We will talk later."

Rosina led the way into her warm and cozy kitchen. As her sister removed her ragged coat it was everything Rosina could do not to gasp. The young girl and Daniel looked the same way. They appeared to be nothing but bones with skin stretched over them. Rosina couldn't recall ever seeing such a pathetic sight. They were living proof of what years of starvation looked like.

Emil, Edward and Olof came from the barn where they had been working. Juliana and her daughters came to the kitchen from the living room where the girls had been sewing new dresses for themselves. They were not fancy garments, just practical to replace some of their threadbare clothing.

"You have a nice place here," Daniel said as he sat in a kitchen chair.

"It's not quite as nice as what we left in Bessarabia, but it's better than the tent we lived in the winter we arrived in Germany," Gottlieb answered.

"Ah, yes, the vineyard," Daniel said, a pleasant smile appearing on his face. "Isabella and I should have just settled there instead of going back to my home. Life would have turned out much differently for us."

"I have thought that often," Rosina stated. "We just had no idea that a war was going to break out and everything would change. We thought there would always be a Tsar in Russia."

"We did, too," Isabella said sadly. "Who would have thought that the Communist could take over the country? It wasn't always perfect under the Tsar but at least we could govern our colonies, have the freedom of worship, and teach our children as we wished in our own schools."

"I received five letters over the years," Rosina said softly. "I saved them all and even brought them with me to Germany, and then Poland. I didn't know if those letters were the only piece of you I would ever have again or not, Isabella."

"It has truly been a nightmare," Isabella replied, tears gathering in her eyes.

"This must be your daughter, Agathe, who Emil and Edward told us about," Rosina said, attempting to lighten the mood.

"Yes," Isabella smiled, "Agathe Rosina, after you, Sister."

"I'm honored," Rosina said smiling. "How old are you, Agathe?"

"Sixteen," Agathe said quietly.

Rosina could hardly believe the girl was sixteen. She was so pitifully thin she looked as if a puff of wind would blow her completely away. Rosina wondered how the family had made the journey from Russia to Poland without dying along the way.

"Where's your son?" Emil asked. The moment the question escaped his lips he wished he could swallow it back down. Adolf would have been drafted immediately, just as Emil and Edward had been when they arrived from Bessarabia.

Isabella began to sob and Daniel tried to comfort her. "Adolf was drafted into the German troops when we arrived by train in Poland," Daniel supplied.

"Oh, I'm so sorry," Rosina said. "Edward and Emil were drafted too, when we arrived from Bessarabia, along with every other eligible young man."

"I'm sorry, Aunt Isabella," Emil said. "I should have known where Adolf was. Edward and I snuck away when we unloaded from the train. We knew we would be forced back into the German troops."

"We may have been on the same train," Edward said. "We joined with Germans making their way to Poland from Russia ahead of the Red Army. Emil and I escaped from a POW camp where we had been placed after we surrendered in Stalingrad."

"How did you know where to find us, Daniel?" Gottlieb asked.

"When they began to relocate all of us, we asked where they had placed you and Rosina," Daniel replied. "They allowed us to join you because they had so many new families to try and find housing for."

"Yes, and Gottlieb just happened to be in town when we were asking directions to your farm," Isabella added. "What a blessing that was!"

"I'm so glad you came to us," Rosina said. "We will gladly make room for you."

"Maybe we won't have to make room," Juliana spoke up. "Why don't Daniel, Isabella and Agathe move onto the farm that Jacob and I had?"

"That would be a good solution," Gottlieb said. "The farm will still belong to Olof when he's older and takes a wife, but for now it could be Daniel and Isabella's home."

"Thank you for such a generous offer," Isabella told Juliana. "We will take good care of it."

"Did you bring anything with you?" Rosina asked.

"We brought a few clothes," Daniel said. "When we reached the train they only allowed us one bag per person. There was just not enough room for more, considering how many people were trying to escape before the Red Army reoccupied our colonies."

"The number is believed to be over 150,000, with more arriving daily," Agathe supplied.

"I wonder how many Germans have been brought back to the Reich." Gottlieb questioned.

"I don't know," Edward answered, "but what will they do with all of us when the war is over?"

"None of us really know," Gottlieb replied.

"I'll fix all of you a nice hot meal," Rosina said, rising to her feet. "Then we will take you to Juliana's farm where you can get settled in."

"My daughters and I will take care of the meal," Juliana told Rosina. "You just sit and enjoy this time with your sister after so many years apart."

"Thank you so much, Juliana," Rosina replied.

"Maybe we could get some measurements from Isabella and Agathe before they leave and sew them some new dresses," Maria offered.

"Oh, you don't have to do that," Isabella assured them.

"It's no problem at all," Hulda replied. "With winter fully upon us we need something to keep us busy, anyway."

"Thank you so much for your kindness," Isabella replied, knowing she had no way of making any dresses for her and Agathe herself. She didn't even own needle and thread, not to mention material. They were completely destitute but at least they were with family, now.

"Did any of your family come with you?" Gottlieb asked Daniel.

"No," Daniel replied. "As you know, my parents and younger siblings were killed during the Makhno raids and my older brother, his wife, and both children were sent to slave camps. They would not agree to the Communist's way of doing things and therefore were deported. Isabella and I decided that as bad as we had it, a slave camp would be much worse, so we complied with their demands."

"Hopefully, you will have some peace, now," Rosina said softly. "We will pray for Adolf's safe return, too."

"Thank you all for your warm reception and kindness," Isabella replied. "It's been a long time since we have been treated like family and shown such love."

"We have all waited and prayed for this reunion," Rosina said. "We just want you to rest and recover from your long journey and difficult life."

"Why don't I go and help them out until they get rested up and settled in," Maria offered. "Agathe and I are the same age and the company might be nice."

"That's a very nice idea," Juliana agreed. "We have plenty of women's hands for the work here. Isabella and Agathe could use your help for a little while."

"That sounds like fun," Agathe added. "I'm sure Maria and I will keep each other company just fine."

"Then it's settled," Rosina stated. "Maria will go with you back to her own house and help out for as long as you need her."

"We will share our can goods and give you some hens, too," Gottlieb said. "At least you will have eggs and vegetables. We have plenty of wheat to grind for flour and we plan to butcher hogs next week, so there will be extra meat we can share, too."

"We will feast like kings," Daniel chuckled. "It's been a long time since we've had such good food."

"We've noticed", was the thought that went through everyone's mind but was not voiced out loud. Isabella, Daniel, Agathe, Edward and Emil all needed to feast like kings. Starvation's witness of sunken eyes, gray skin, and protruding bones was a very ugly sight, indeed.

Chapter Seventeen

Isabella and Daniel settled onto their new farm and life continued for the relocated Germans. When spring of 1944 came, Olof helped Daniel prepare his fields and plant a crop of barley. Gottlieb and Olof had planted wheat on the farm Daniel now lived on the previous fall, so he at least would have that to harvest. Letting the land grow up would have been a waste of good farm ground and they would not allow that to happen. Seeds for cold weather vegetables were started in cold frames for the spring plantings and gardens were plowed and disc for the coming year's food to be grown in.

By June, warm sunshine glistened off dew kissed heads of wheat. Potatoes were starting to bloom and potato beetles were a constant problem. The beetles and larvae had to be picked daily to prevent an infestation of the nasty pest. There was fresh broccoli and cauliflower to enjoy and cabbage to make into kraut. Green beans were climbing up the poles, stretching their tendrils toward the sky. It appeared all was well with the world but that was far from true. Outside of the Wartheland, there were battles raging all around.

The Allies had liberated Rome and the British and U.S. troops had landed on the beaches of Normandy, opening a second front for the Allies against the Germans. The Soviets continued to push the German troops back westward, and by August 1st, 1944, the Red Army was positioned on the Vistula River across from Warsaw, Poland. By this time, there were also bombs being dropped on eastern Germany by the Allies. The relocated Germans were basically surrounded by war on all sides.

"There has been a Home Army formed by the non-communist to try and liberate Warsaw before the Red Army gets there," Jacob stopped by to tell his brother, Albert, on his way home from getting supplies. "I just heard the news in town."

"So, the German troops are fighting the Red Army to the East and a Home Army at their backs?" Albert asked in disbelief.

"It seems so," Jacob replied. "Not only that, the Red Army is positioned just on the other side of the Vistula River west of Warsaw."

"That close?" Albert asked, astonished.

"Yes, practically at our back door," Jacob confirmed.

"Did you hear of any plans for evacuation?" Albert asked.

"No, and we can't just pack and leave," Jacob replied. "There's bombing all over Germany from the Allied forces and we have no idea where to run for safety."

"This is ludicrous," Albert said. "We are sandwiched between two opposing forces."

"Honestly, I don't see the United States as opponents," Jacob stated dryly. "I hope they come and stop all the persecution and bring some order back to this chaos."

"Careful, Brother," Albert warned. "Statements like that made to the wrong person could land you in a concentration camp far from your wife and three sons."

"I realize that," Jacob replied, "but it's just you and I here. I'm just stating my opinion."

"Just make sure you don't speak out to anyone else," Albert cautioned.

"I can control my tongue," Jacob assured Albert. "I'll come by tomorrow and help you start shocking your wheat."

"Okay," Albert agreed. "We'll do yours when mine's finished."

"It's probably all work done for someone else's benefit, but we can't just leave the crop in the field," Jacob said as he started the horses moving toward home.

"Only time will tell," Albert replied, waving as Jacob moved his team and wagon down his driveway.

The Red Army pushed into East Prussia to the north and towards Belgrade and Budapest to the south but they didn't move across the Vistula River. The relocated Germans lived in fear daily. They believed the Red Army would swoop from the East at any moment, especially with the Home Army rising up against the German troops at their backs. It would have been no problem for the Red Army to crush both the Nazis and the Poland Home Army as they stormed toward Germany. It was almost certain they would not stop until they took Berlin, just as Germany had invaded Stalingrad, the very thing that caused the Red Army to retaliate so fiercely. Berlin was the prize Stalin was after and to think otherwise was just foolishness.

As when the Red Army was sitting just east of Bessarabia in 1940, they now lay just east of the Germans from Bessarabia again. They may be in a different country and four years had passed, but the threat was the same. However, the relocated Germans had no choice but to perform normal, everyday tasks. The garden produced well and canned goods were added to the cellars of the Wartheland Germans. The potatoes were dug and the fields prepared for the planting of winter wheat. There was nothing the relocated Germans could do but go about their lives as usual. They didn't really believe they would be the ones to eat the food they were preserving or harvest the wheat, but they had to perform the tasks just in case they were still on the farms come spring.

"Any news from town?" Magdalena questioned Jacob as he returned one day in early October.

"The Home Army surrendered to the German troops three days ago," Jacob replied.

"What will that mean for us?"

"Well, hopefully the German troops can concentrate all their efforts on the Red Army sitting on the other side of the Vistula River."

"I really don't understand why they stopped at the river in August and have not attempted to come farther," Magdalena replied.

"I don't either but it would suit me just fine if they never crossed that river," Jacob replied.

"Me, too," Magdalena agreed. "I believe we were smart in packing some clothes in a bag for all of us just in case we are forced to run, though."

"Yes, your vater had a good idea," Jacob replied. "I hope we don't have to flee but good that we are prepared to leave quickly."

"Where will we go if we're forced to run?" Magdalena

worried.

"I don't know," Jacob confessed. "The Allies have pushed to the western border of Germany and have liberated France and most of Belgium from German control. The smartest thing might be to run toward the Allies but we would probably get killed trying to reach them."

"I'm scared, Jacob," Magdalena whispered.

"I'm scared, too," Jacob admitted.

The relocated Germans lived with their eyes trained toward the East. The question was not if but when the Red Army would make their move. The Germans felt like mice being stalked by a huge cat, not knowing when they would be pounced upon.

They prepared themselves to flee at a moment's notice. The fervent prayer was that there would be a notice and that Hitler would have a plan of where and how to move them to safety, when the time came.

Christmas 1944 came and the Griebs and Wallentines, along with Daniel, Isabella and Agathe, all celebrated the day at Gottlieb and Rosina's home. It was difficult to focus on peace and the miracle of the virgin birth with all that was happening around them but every adult put forth an effort. The children did not understand the danger that lurked just to the east of them and that was a blessing. It would do them no good to live in the same fear as their parents.

"Did you notice the looks Olof was giving Agathe?" Magdalena asked Jacob when they returned home from the Christmas celebration. "I do believe your brother is in love."

"No, I did not notice," Jacob replied. "Only women notice such things."

"Agathe has turned into a beautiful young woman since she has gained some weight and lost the look of a starving child," Magdalena pointed out.

"I will agree that a year of good food has made all of them healthier," Jacob said, "your brothers included."

"Yes, Emil and Edward look much better," Magdalena agreed, placing a sleeping Werner in his crib.

"I can't believe he's already a year old," Jacob said, coming to stand beside Magdalena and gaze down at his youngest son.

"Time goes by so quickly," Magdalena replied. "Erhard is

already twelve and Ewald eight."

"And we are both over thirty," Jacob said with a laugh.

"You could have left that unsaid," Magdalena said with a smile.

"Ah, well, you're as beautiful as ever," Jacob replied. "I'm sure Olof feels the same way about Agathe."

"Oh, so you did notice Olof not being able to keep his eyes off Agathe?" Magdalena asked.

"Maybe," Jacob replied, "but men don't usually mention such things. We leave that to the gossiping women."

Magdalena just laughed and leaned over to blow out their bedroom lamp. She crawled into bed beside Jacob trying to forget about wars and the threat that lay just east of their home. Instead she settled her thoughts on the celebrated day, Christmas. She pondered what that miraculous birth had brought to all mankind, salvation for all who ask and a peace that passes understanding. It was that peace she was seeking this night.

****

Jacob came into the barn lot with the team of horses and wagon way too fast. Magdalena knew something was dreadfully wrong. Grabbing her coat, Magdalena instructed Erhard to keep an eye on Werner while she went outside.

"Jacob, what's wrong?" Magdalena asked, running up to the wagon.

"Magdalena, you need to get the packed suitcase of clothes," Jacob instructed. "The Red Army has begun to move and the situation could turn dangerous quickly. We have been surrounded on three sides. Hitler has decided it's too dangerous to remain here in Poland."

"So, we're leaving?" Magdalena asked.

"You and the children are leaving," Jacob said, "along with all the other women and children in the area. The men are not being allowed to leave."

"What?" Magdalena gasped. "We are leaving without you, Jacob? I can't do it."

"You can and you will," Jacob said firmly. "You have a good head, a mind to figure things out on your own and a stubbornness that will take you far. This is not up for discussion."

"How will we go?" Magdalena asked.

"By train," Jacob replied. "I will take you and the boys in the wagon to the depot and you will be loaded in railcars."

"But it's so cold," Magdalena said. "We'll freeze in those railcars."

"Pack some blankets," Jacob instructed. "Erhard and Ewald can carry the luggage while you carry Werner. This is the way it has to be done. Now, go and do as I told you. I have to go tell Albert and all the rest."

Magdalena watched Jacob leave as fast as he had come. She stood stunned from what Jacob had just told her. It was the first week of January 1945. The air was frigid and there were eight inches of snow on the ground. Why weren't they evacuated in August when the Red Army first set up camp to the east of Warsaw? Why wait until the dead of winter to make such a drastic move? And why send the women and children alone?

"Mutti?" Ewald asked softly.

"Ewald," Magdalena gasped, coming to her senses. She had not even heard him come outside and approach her.

"Are you okay, Mutti?" Ewald questioned. "You don't look well."

"Ewald we need to get inside," Magdalena instructed. "We have to get Werner some extra diapers packed and gather some warm blankets."

"Okay," Ewald answered, not fully understanding what was about to take place.

Once inside, Magdalena gathered her wits and took charge. Gathering every diaper she could find, she stuffed them into a canvas bag then added four wool blankets. She hoped it would be enough to keep them from freezing to death. She quickly explained the departure that was about to take place to Erhard and Ewald and told them they must remain strong. It was going to be a cold, hard journey, though to where she had no clue.

When Jacob returned to their house, Magdalena and the boys were ready to go. As they hurried to the wagon, Jacob jumped down to help load the suitcase and canvas bag. The boys jumped in the back and Magdalena handed Werner to Erhard. Stein, the Grieb's faithful dog, hopped into the bed of the wagon with the boys.

"Stein, get down boy. You aren't going this time,"

Magdalena said.

"What will happen to Stein?" Ewald asked, tears welling in his eyes.

"Your vater will care for him," Magdalena assured Ewald. "He will come back to the farm after he takes us to the train depot."

"Will you take care of Stein, Vater?" Ewald asked.

"Yes, I will make sure Stein is cared for," Jacob answered, his mind already trying to find a solution for the faithful dog. He could not just leave him behind to fend for himself. Of course, he could not voice this out loud to his wife and sons. They believed he was coming back to stay on the farm until it was safe for them to return. He would not allow them to know the truth and cause Magdalena to worry more.

Stein hopped back out of the wagon and Magdalena climbed in with Jacob's help. She sat down and took Werner from Erhard, wrapping him up in a blanket to keep him warm. As they headed out of the driveway, Stein faded in the distance. He was sitting faithfully at the back door awaiting their return. It broke Magdalena's heart to know he would wait forever but she and the boys would not be back for a long time, maybe never.

They stopped at Albert and Emilie's and all five boys and Emilie joined Magdalena and her sons in the bed of the wagon. Albert scrambled onto the seat with Jacob and they were off. They had chosen to travel together to the train depot so they would not get separated. The women knew they would need one another for what lay ahead.

"What about Mutti, Aunt Isabella, Agathe, Juliana and her girls?" Magdalena asked Jacob as they sped along.

"Your vater and Daniel will bring them," Jacob replied. "We don't have room for anyone else."

"Okay," Magdalena said, wondering how they would find each other in the madness that was sure to be at the train depot.

"This is a nightmare," Emilie whispered, her face the color of the snow covering the fields.

"We will be okay," Magdalena said, trying to reassure both of them with her words.

"How will we find Jacob and Albert again?" Emilie fretted.

"I don't know," Magdalena replied. "We will worry about

that later. Right now, we must get our children to safety."

Two hours later, Jacob turned the team in at the train depot. There were people everywhere. The doors had been thrown open on the railcars and the women and children were being loaded like cattle. It was a frantic, disorganized sight to behold, and Magdalena and Emilie were to become part of it.

The two women looked at one another, a silent conversation passing between them. There was no doubt in either woman's mind that this would be the hardest journey they had ever faced. They also realized this very well could be the last time either woman saw their husbands this side of heaven. These facts caused the women to stall for more time, just one more word, touch, moment, with the men they had pledged their love and devotion to.

"Hurry," Albert instructed. "We want you on this first train. The faster you're away from here, the better it will be."

"How will I find you again, Albert?" Emilie asked. "Please, don't make us leave!"

"You have to go, Emilie," Albert said. "It's too dangerous here."

"Come, Emilie," Magdalena urged, realizing her strength that Jacob spoke of earlier was needed immediately. "At least you and I are together, along with our sons."

Albert quickly hugged his sons and Emilie as Jacob hugged his sons and Magdalena. There was no time for endearing words or long goodbyes. The train would pull out as soon as it was full and Magdalena and Emilie needed to be on it. So many unspoken words lay on each adult's tongue, words that had no time to be voiced but were said silently as tears glided down their cheeks. Magdalena wished someone would pinch her to wake her from this nightmare but no one did, convincing her that it was really happening. She would not eventually wake up safe and sound in her own bed beside her husband.

Magdalena and Emilie loaded their sons and few belongings in one of the railcars. The car was already half full of women and children, so they just found a place on the floor for all of them to sit together. Emilie's older sons, Albert, Erwin and Richard sat close to Magdalena's older boys Erhard and Ewald. Magdalena held one year old Werner on her lap while Emilie placed Walter, who had just turned three, and four and a half year old Klaus close to her. Magdalena spread one of the blankets out so the older boys didn't have to sit on the cold floor. She then wrapped Walter and Klaus in another blanket to keep them warm. By the time the door on the boxcar was shut and the train pulled out, the boxcar was packed with people.

"At least all this body heat will keep us warmer," Magdalena said, trying to lighten the heavy mood.

"There are so many people pressing around me I can hardly breathe," Ewald complained.

"You'll just have to calm down and be patient, Ewald," Magdalena instructed. "There's nothing we can do about this situation we've been forced into."

"It's so dark in here," Erwin said.

"Yes, some windows would be nice," Emilie replied to her son. "We will just have to enjoy light and air each time the train stops. Hopefully, we won't have to be on this journey long."

"Where are we going?" Erhard asked.

"We're traveling in a southwestern direction," Magdalena replied. "They are taking us somewhere inside Germany. The Red Army is coming from three directions, so I don't know how we will be safe anywhere near the border of Germany."

"So, even after we stop we will be in danger?" Richard asked.

"We could be," Magdalena replied. She didn't want to scare the children but they needed to understand the seriousness of the situation.

Three hours after departing the station in Poland, the train began to slow down. Magdalena hoped it was for everyone to have a toilet break. Werner and Walter needed diaper changes, too. There might not be any light in the boxcar but the smell of dirty diapers throughout the enclosed area was evidence enough to that fact.

"Why are we slowing down?" Erwin asked.

"Hopefully for a toilet break," Emilie said.

"I sure hope so," Ewald chimed in. "It smells like some of the breaks have already happened."

"There are a lot of babies in this boxcar, Ewald," Magdalena said. "That means lots of dirty diapers."

"The smell is making me gag," Ewald complained.

"You will be okay," Magdalena assured him.

The train finally came to a complete stop and the doors were opened. Thinking they would see a depot, the occupants were surprised to only see bare trees and knee deep snow. They wondered why they had stopped in the middle of nowhere.

"Everyone off the train! Everyone off!" was the cry all down the line of cars. The women and children began to exit the boxcars. The wind was bitter cold as they huddled along the tracks.

"This is where you will use the necessary," one of the men who had opened the doors announced.

"But there's no place to go," a woman complained.

"There are trees straight ahead," the man gestured, pointing to the barren trees like they were wonderful facilities.

"Come on, boys," Magdalena urged. "Take a blanket and hold it around each other while you take care of business. Emilie and I will take care of Werner, Walter and Klaus, and of course ourselves. Be quick or you'll freeze to death."

"You are a natural born leader," Emilie laughed. "Just like our Vater."

"Well, this is all were getting," Magdalena stated. "Standing around complaining will not get the job done. It is what it is; a forest of frozen outhouses."

Trudging through the knee deep snow, Emilie and Magdalena went to find their tree. Holding the blanket around Emilie, Magdalena allowed her to help Klaus and change Walter. Emilie had no choice but to lay Walter in the snow to remove his diaper. She then grabbed some snow to clean his bottom. Quickly, she placed a dry diaper back on a very unhappy Walter then held the blanket for Magdalena. Werner received the same type of diaper change and they hurried back to the boxcar.

"Did you get them cleaned up?" Ewald asked, wrinkling his nose.

"Yes, they are nice and clean," Magdalena said, "and very cold. We had to use snow to clean their bottoms."

The older boys thought this was quite funny and began to laugh. It was music to Emilie and Magdalena's ears and they joined in. Laughter is always good medicine, even when you feel like crying, which would have done them absolutely no good.

The train began to move again, and the darkness and

boredom caused most to drift off to sleep. Suddenly, the brakes were applied and the train began to lose speed rapidly. The sudden stop jerked the boxcars, waking everyone instantly. After the sound of the cars on the tracks and the screeching of brakes died away, a new sound reached the ears of the women and children. It was the unmistakable drone of planes flying nearby.

"What's going on?" Erhard asked.

"I don't know," Magdalena answered. "I don't think it's been long enough for another toilet break."

The occupants could hear the doors of the railcars being thrown open and hollering up and down the track. As they drew closer the words could be made out. "Get out, go to a ditch, the Red Army is bombing us!"

A wave of terror began to overtake everyone in the railcar. People were on their feet trying to be the first to get through the doors. Babies were crying, women were hysterical and children were scared speechless. The rush to get out was resulting in children being trampled and separated from their families. The horror of what was happening spurred Magdalena into action.

"Stand up and make a circle," Magdalena commanded. "Put the little ones in the middle and the bigger ones on the outside."

Magdalena, Emilie, Albert, Richard, and Erhard formed the outer circle with the smaller children in the middle. They remained this way until the door was opened and everyone else exited. As they made their way toward the door, Magdalena noticed a small girl curled up in the corner of the railcar. She was scared and crying for her mutti.

"Come on, honey," Magdalena spoke. "Come with us."

Erhard was waiting at the opening for his mutti and lifted the small girl down. A woman a few feet away was frantically screaming, letting them know who the child belonged to. Taking the child's hand, Erhard walked the girl to her mutti who hugged her tightly and began to run for a ditch.

"Let's go," Magdalena said leading the way to the closest ditch. There were so many people it was hard to find enough room. As they huddled down with Werner and Ewald, Magdalena felt a blanket drape over them.

"Where did this come from?" Magdalena asked.

"Albert and I brought them out with us," Erhard said. "It

might offer warmth and protect us from debris that may be flying around."

"Smart boys," Magdalena said. "Now get down and stay covered."

The planes could be heard flying in the distance and the ground shook from the explosions. In the ditches, prayers could be heard above the children crying and the women screaming. This group of women and children had never experienced being in the middle of a bombing. The farms in Poland had not been touched by any combat. The fear they felt was paralyzing. They even forgot how terribly cold it was while kneeling in the snow with the bitter wind whipping all around them. All their thoughts were consumed with the threat of a bomb cutting their lives and children's lives short.

Thirty minutes later, everyone was loaded back in the railcars. As they all settled in, Magdalena decided to make an announcement before the clatter of the wheels on the track were so loud she could not be heard. "Please, everyone, listen," Magdalena began. "If we have to stop and run for cover again, could we try to remain a little calmer? A little girl got separated from her family earlier in the chaos. We need to work together and protect one another. Getting hysterical doesn't help anyone."

"She's right," another woman chimed in. "My daughter was the one who got left behind earlier. I lost my grip on her hand when everyone pushed to be the first ones off the railcar. I was shoved out the door but my daughter was left behind. We need to be more careful."

"So, do we agree?" Magdalena asked.

A murmur of agreement floated across the railcar. Magdalena just hoped they remembered what they agreed to when the actual time came. Fear made people do crazy things and this was certainly a time of fear. None of the women knew where they were headed or if they would ever see their husbands again. As with Magdalena and Emilie, other women had also been separated from close family members in the rush to get on the train.

What was to become of all the Germans who had been relocated? Would they ever find their families again? Would they still have homes in Poland when the war ended? If not, where would they live? And now being bombed by the Red Army was a whole new threat to deal with on this journey. Magdalena pondered these things as the train began to build speed again, rolling on to an unknown destination.

Chapter Eighteen

Jacob and Albert made their way back to Jacob's farm. They hadn't told their wives that they were being forced to move to a camp the German forces had set up. They would be required to help the Nazis prepare to fight the Red Army. Gottlieb and Daniel would return to their farms, gather some belongings, and come to Jacob's with Olof, Edward, and Emil. The men would travel to the camp together taking three wagons.

"What do we take with us?" Jacob wondered aloud while standing in his kitchen.

"I suppose just our clothes and some blankets" Albert replied. "We will have no place to store anything else."

"Do you think we will be able to come back before we leave Poland?" Jacob asked.

"Something tells me we will leave Poland with the Red Army breathing down our backs," Albert said. "The Nazis have not been able to stop them so far, so I don't see them being able to stand their ground now."

"Hitler has too many battles going on at once," Jacob stated. "Invading Russia was a bad idea when he already had troops fighting battles in other places or protecting territory the Germans had already taken."

"It was a foolish move," Albert admitted. "The fact that Japan bombed Pearl Harbor didn't help matters any. Bringing the United States into the war for the Allies is proving to be detrimental to Hitler's dream of a Greater Germany."

"I really don't see how the Axis powers can win this war now," Jacob said. "If we get through this, I plan to move to the

United States. It's been a dream of mine for a long time and I plan to follow through with it as soon as this war is over. I have nothing left to call my own now anyway, and Hitler is a madman!"

"You know I agree that Hitler is crazy," Albert said, "but please be careful who you say that to. The problem we face right now is that it's better to run to Germany for safety rather than be dragged back to Russia by the Red Army. At the moment, Hitler is the lesser of the two evils."

"Agreed," Jacob replied. "If we don't make it to Germany and safety, we will never see our families again."

"Then we will run at the first sign of danger," Albert said.

"We need to all stay close together," Jacob replied. "We will tell Gottlieb and the other men of our plan when they arrive here, and hopefully they will agree. Take the wagon to your house and pack your clothes. I will gather my things and be ready when you return."

"Okay," Albert said. "I won't be gone long."

Jacob packed his clothes then wandered through the house they had called home for almost four years. The floors were just dirt and had been packed as solid as rock over time.

Jacob again thought about Micah and his family who had lived here. He didn't believe they would ever return to their home. Jacob wasn't completely certain what happened to all the Jews who had been taken but he feared most of them were dead. From the description Emil and Edward gave of the Russian POW camp they were in, Jacob was sure the conditions in the concentration camps were not much better, or maybe worse.

Walking into Erhard and Ewald's bedroom Jacob noticed a wooden block on the floor. It reminded him of how Ewald loved to build things with those blocks. Many grand designs had come from Ewald's hands as he placed and stacked the blocks just so. Jacob reached down and picked up the out of place piece of wood. Walking back to the kitchen, he packed the block in with his clothes. It would be a reminder of his children, of all he had to fight to live for. He had a deep ill at ease feeling, like his life was about to be forever changed.

Gottlieb and Daniel pulled into the yard followed by Edward, Emil, and Olof in another wagon. Albert came soon afterwards. All of the men stood in Jacob's kitchen and Gottlieb said a prayer for the safety of all the women and children. He then prayed for God's protection on the men as they prepared to go to the camp.

After the prayer, the men discussed their plan for safety. They all agreed that they would flee toward Germany at the first sign of danger. They would not have weapons with which to defend themselves, anyway. To stay would just result in them being captured by the Red Army. They decided it would be better to die trying to get to a safe place rather than being captured and taken to Russia.

"If the Red Army captures us," Daniel said, "we will never be returned. I know were supposedly German citizens now but I am aware of how Stalin operates. We would disappear forever, lost in some slave camp in Siberia. Escape would be our only way out."

"Edward and I did manage to escape," Emil added, "but I would not want to go back to a camp in Russia."

"I would just as soon die before being returned to one of those camps," Edward confirmed.

"So, when the time comes we make a run for it," Gottlieb concluded.

"Yes," Albert said, "that will be our plan. Staying together might be difficult but we will try our best."

"Hopefully they will not have time to check records and notice that Edward and I were part of the German forces that surrendered in Stalingrad," Emil said. "We will be put back on the front line if that happens."

"We'll pray that it doesn't," Gottlieb said. "Staying here is not an option, either. They will be checking every home for men who did not follow orders. It would mean instant death. At least this way you have a chance."

"Gottlieb is right," Jacob agreed. "We must follow their orders. They have no mercy for those who don't."

"Are we ready to go?" Albert asked. "We won't reach the camp before dark as it is."

"Yes, it's past time to go," Gottlieb said, starting for the kitchen door. "I wish we could have brought Jacob and Otto with us. I don't even know where they are right now. I'm sure their wives and children were put on trains, too."

"We can't worry right now, Vater," Emil replied. "You

raised smart sons. They will figure out what to do when the time comes to leave. Maybe we will meet up with them at the camp."

"Yes, maybe," Gottlieb replied, knowing it wasn't likely to happen that way.

Jacob was the last one out, taking a final look around at his home. Where would they live next? How would he ever find Magdalena and the boys when the war was over? Would he make it out of Poland alive? He had so many questions and not one answer. The uncertainty of his future weighed heavy on him as he trudged to his wagon and joined his brother, Albert.

Stein jumped into the back of Jacob's wagon again and Jacob was reminded that he needed to find a safe place for the dog. He would love to just take him along but knew that was a bad plan. There probably wouldn't be enough food for the men, so feeding a dog would not be possible. Such a good, loyal dog deserved to have enough food and a home to protect. Jacob could provide neither for him at the moment.

"I need to stop at Tolek's," Jacob hollered to the men in the other two wagons. "Hopefully he will be willing to adopt Stein."

"Okay," Gottlieb hollered back. "I dropped our dog off at our Polish neighbor's. I couldn't leave him behind, either."

Hurrying in the direction of the camp, Jacob stopped when they reached Tolek's driveway. The other men waited on the road as Jacob and Stein walked to Tolek's door.

"Jacob," Tolek boomed, opening the door wide for Jacob to enter. "How are you doing this cold day?"

"We have to leave," Jacob told Tolek. "Our women and children have been sent by train to the southeast and we are required to report to a camp and help the German troops."

"The Red Army getting ready to make a move?" Tolek asked.

"It's looking that way," Jacob answered. "I came to ask you a favor."

"What do you need, Jacob?"

"I need a home for Stein," Jacob replied, pointing to the obedient dog at his feet.

"I will give him a good home," Tolek said. "He's a very smart dog, one that would come in handy on my farm."

"Thank you so much," Jacob said. "You might have to keep

him in the house until we're gone or he will try to follow us."

"Not a problem," Tolek said, reaching down to pet Stein. "Come Stein, come here boy."

Stein remained beside Jacob, the man who had been his owner since he was eight weeks old. Jacob reached down and patted the dog's head then nudged the dog toward Tolek. Tolek reached down and patted the dog's head, too, reassuring Stein that he would be safe even when Jacob left. Jacob backed out onto the porch and took one last look at the beloved dog. As the door shut, Jacob could hear Stein barking and whining to come with him. Walking faster, Jacob headed toward the wagon trying to get far enough away so he didn't have to hear Stein beg not to be left behind. Not only had he put his wife and children on a train bound for an unknown destination, he had to leave his sons' faithful companion, knowing he would never see the pet again.

Jumping back on the wagon seat, Jacob put the horses in motion. How much would he and his family lose before this war was over? And where were his wife and sons right now?

****

The train carrying the relocated German women and children finally pulled into a station in southeastern Germany. There, they were placed in camps to wait out the war.

There had been little time to prepare for the arrival of the train. Food was in short supply and it was very cold in their sleeping quarters. The only warmth that could be found was the area where the food was prepared and served, but only because of the woodstoves used to cook the food. Everyone lingered in this area as long as they were allowed then returned to their sleeping quarters to wrap up in blankets and shiver.

"We didn't get any more to eat for breakfast than we did for supper last night," Erhard muttered. "Too bad we couldn't have packed some of our food from home."

"Yeah, we could be eating fried eggs, ham slices and fried potatoes," Richard said, his eyes lighting up with the thought.

"Where would we cook it?" Emilie asked. "I don't think they would allow us to use their stoves. Besides, those things would have caused a riot. We would have probably been killed just so they could steal our food."

"Unfortunately, Emilie's right," Magdalena agreed.

"Everyone here is as hungry as we are, not to mention scared and uncertain of their futures. It's made us all on edge and it's difficult to think rationally."

"It's so cold, Mutti," Ewald complained. "I can't feel my fingers or toes."

"It can't be helped, Ewald," Magdalena replied. "There's nowhere else to go."

"Why don't I tell you a story," Emilie offered. "Maybe it will take your mind off your frozen fingers for a while."

"Yes, Emilie, tell us a story," Magdalena said.

Emilie always had been a good storyteller, and she now shared with the boys of growing up in Bessarabia. As she talked, Magdalena realized that the only way their boys would truly remember their heritage was if the adults shared stories about it often. There were a few things Ewald, Erhard, and Emilie's older boys might remember on their own, but not many. As for Klaus, Walter and Werner, they would only know through shared stories.

"One time Magdalena, our brothers Jacob and Otto, and I got into big trouble," Emilie began, building the suspense by changing her voice. "We had been playing hide and seek in the vineyard, which is something we shouldn't have been doing. It was just such a good place to hide from one another that we couldn't resist. At first the game was going fine, but then Otto began to use grapes to tag us when we were found. It led to all of us getting into a huge grape fight with Jacob using his slingshot to send grapes to his wanted targets. When your Opa Wallentine caught us, he set our bottoms on fire. It was great fun while it lasted but we never played in the vineyard again."

"So, Opa Wallentine had a vineyard?" Erwin asked.

"Yes, Erwin," Magdalena replied. "Opa made some of the best wine around. You were only three when we left Bessarabia, so I suppose you don't remember that."

"Do you remember the mill and grocery store?" Erhard asked Erwin.

"Barely," Erwin admitted. "I remember playing behind the counter sometimes."

"Me, too," Ewald chimed in. "I used to play with blocks back there while Mutti worked in the store."

"That's right, Ewald," Magdalena said.

"I can remember shoveling grain at the mill," Albert added. "The water turned the big wheel and caused the stones to spin and grind the grain into flour. I remember the wheel being started one time and a mouse got squished between the stones because it couldn't get away fast enough."

"Ugh," Emilie said. "I really don't want to think about that."

"I helped Vater milk the cows," Erhard said.

"I did that, too," Richard added, "twice a day, morning and night."

"Will we ever move back to Bessarabia?" Ewald asked.

"No, I don't think so," Magdalena answered.

"When will we see Vater and Uncle Jacob?" Erwin asked.

"I don't know, Erwin," Magdalena said.

"Where are Oma Wallentine and Oma Grieb?" Albert asked.

"Hopefully they will be here soon," Emilie said. "Their train may have had to stop more times. They must not have gotten on the first train like us."

"We've only been here two days," Magdalena said. "I'm sure your grandmothers and aunts will be here soon."

Looking over the boys' heads, Magdalena and Emilie silently worried where their mutti was, too. The trip had taken much longer because of the air raids, so maybe the train their mutti was on made even more stops than theirs did. Neither one wanted to mention the fact that the train could have been bombed.

"There will be a meeting in the dining area," a woman who worked at the camp stopped by and hollered out. "Fifteen minutes."

Emilie and Magdalena hurried and gathered the boys. They had no idea what the meeting was about but at least it would be warmer there.

Entering the building, they searched for a seat. It seemed no one wanted to miss the meeting or the few minutes of warmth. Finding seats as close to the woodstoves as possible, Magdalena and Emilie waited for the meeting to begin.

"All of you must head south," a uniformed man informed them loudly. "The Red Army is just three days away."

The murmuring began quietly then swelled into a loud, frantic chatter. Where would they go? How would they get there? How soon would they have to leave? The questions were asked all at one time. Everything was silenced by a gun being fired, the sound ricocheting from floor to ceiling, wall to wall, and settling in the ears of the surprised women and children.

"Silence!" the uniformed man demanded. "You will leave immediately and you will walk! Now, go!"

Women gathered their children and hugged their babies. They all hurried back to the sleeping quarters to gather their belongings and head south. No one was about to ask any more questions. The next shot might not be fired in the air!

"If we leave Mutti will never find us," Emilie whispered to Magdalena.

"We have to go," Magdalena said. "The officer left no room for objections."

"But how will they find us?" Emilie fretted.

"Emilie," Magdalena said gruffly, "you have to be strong. All we can worry about at the moment is getting our sons to safety. The rest will have to wait."

"Yes, you're right, Magdalena," Emilie murmured resolving to be strong and take care of the situation at hand.

"Mutti is a strong woman," Magdalena reminded her sister. "She will find us eventually."

Emilie and Magdalena packed up their belongings and retrieved the diapers that had been drying on a makeshift line. They only had time to wash them out the night before and now they had frozen stiff overnight.

"I hope we won't need to use these anytime soon," Magdalena said.

"I don't see how we could, frozen like they are," Emilie replied.

"Well, at least they're clean," Magdalena said, stuffing the stiff material into a canvas bag. "Are you ready, boys?"

"Yes, Mutti," Erhard replied picking up the one large canvas bag that contained diapers and blankets. He handed the suitcase to Ewald.

Magdalena tied a shawl over her dress and coat to form a sling. She placed Werner inside and they all headed out into the bitterly cold, snowy morning. They were among the first to start down the road toward the unknown and they had no idea where they were going. After two hours on the road, a United States military truck came by and agreed to take some of them. Magdalena didn't want to split up the children from their mutti's, so she told Emilie to take the ride.

"I'll wait, Sister," Emilie argued. "We will get a ride together."

"No one is going to be able to take all ten of us," Magdalena reasoned. "Take this ride, and I'll catch the next one. I'll find you up the road."

"Okay," Emilie agreed, though reluctant.

Emilie handed Walter to Erhard while the three older boys crawled into the back of the truck. Emilie then helped Klaus into the back with his brothers. Climbing in last, she turned to get Walter. The U.S. soldier didn't understand that Walter belonged with Emilie and closed the tailgate. As he went back to the front of the truck to drive away, Emilie began screaming from inside. Magdalena reached over and snatched Walter from Erhard and ran after the slow moving truck. When she got close enough, she threw him in to Emilie, thankful she didn't drop him in the process. Emilie held Walter tight, thankful the baby was back in her arms. She watched Magdalena and three sons fade in the distance as the truck gained speed and left them far behind.

"Now what?" Erhard asked, catching up to his mutti.

"We continue walking," Magdalena answered, adjusting a sleeping Werner in the sling around her body.

"I'm tired, Mutti," Ewald complained.

"Ewald, today we must be stronger than we've ever been," Magdalena told him. "We must walk or be overtaken by the Red Army. I'm sorry to be so harsh but you need to realize we are in danger."

"Okay, Mutti," Ewald agreed, taking steps forward as he spoke.

Other vehicles passed but no one stopped to pick up Magdalena and her boys for two more hours. Finally, when they felt they couldn't take another step on their frozen feet, a US military ambulance had mercy on them. Pulling over to the side of the road, a US soldier hopped out of the passenger side. Hurrying to the back, he flung the door open for Magdalena and her sons. Not being able to speak English, Magdalena hoped the young man knew how grateful she was by her repeating "thank you" in

German over and over.

Settling into the back of the ambulance, it wasn't long before Magdalena and her sons' feet began to tingle as they warmed. Magdalena knew they had been very near suffering from frostbite and being able to get this ride was a true blessing. She had no idea where they were headed but hoped the soldiers knew where the refugees were supposed to flee to. An hour later, the ambulance pulled into a small village and stopped. The soldier opened the door for them to exit.

"Where do we go?" Magdalena asked the soldier.

The soldier shrugged his shoulders and held his hands up. Magdalena could not understand English, and the gesture told her he had no idea what she was saying, either. The young soldier closed the door and climbed back in the vehicle. Magdalena stared after them as they drove away, wondering what she should do next. At least they were in a village and not out on the road with no hope for any warmth or food.

"Where are we, Mutti?" Erhard asked.

"I honestly don't know," Magdalena answered. "This area is obviously occupied by US troops though, so we should be safe."

"Where do we go now?" Ewald asked.

"There's a small motel," Magdalena said, pointing across the street. "Let's see if they will help us."

Dragging their weary feet and hungry bodies, Magdalena led the way to the motel. Upon entering, Magdalena and her sons basked in the warmth and the smell of food cooking. A German speaking voice brought them back to reality.

"May I help you?" the woman behind the desk asked.

"We are looking for a place to stay," Magdalena began. "You see, we are fleeing Poland because of the danger there and came south by train to a camp. Then we had to flee from the camp this morning. A US military ambulance picked us up on the road and dropped us off here, wherever this is. We have been separated from the other women and children and don't know where to go now."

"You poor woman," the desk lady lamented. "My name is Gerda, dear. What is yours?"

"Magdalena and these are my sons Erhard, Ewald, and Werner."

"Come in and sit in the dining area," Gerda offered. "We will get you all a nice hot supper and then a room for the night. Decisions will be easier to make in the morning after a good night's sleep. By the way, you are in Bavaria, a state in the south of Germany."

"Thank you so much," Magdalena replied following Gerda toward the dining area. "You do not know how much this means to me."

"Kindness is meant to be shared," Gerda said with a smile. "Sit down and I will be out with your meal shortly. I could probably even find some hot water for everyone to take a bath, if you would like."

"Please, don't go to any trouble on our account," Magdalena pleaded. "The food and a place to sleep is more than enough."

"No trouble," Gerda assured her. "You will all have a nice warm bath after you eat, I insist."

"Thank you again," Magdalena said, tears welling up in her eyes. She had not realized how incredibly weary she had become until she sat down. Tomorrow would bring its own set of troubles. Tonight, she and her children would eat a good meal, take a warm bath and sleep well. She prayed Emilie and her children were doing the same, wherever they were.

Chapter Nineteen

The camp Albert, Jacob, Olof, Daniel, Emil, Edward, and Gottlieb were forced to move to was much like the one they had lived in when they first moved from Bessarabia to Germany. There were lines of tents and food was scarce. If it hadn't been so cold, the men would have brought their own food from their cellars, but the jars would have frozen in the bitter cold temperatures. They were able to stay together in one tent and had brought plenty of warm clothes and blankets. It was decided that their bags would remain unpacked, so they could leave at a moment's notice. No one had to tell them they were in the middle of a dangerous situation.

The day after their arrival, Jacob motioned for Albert to follow him outside of the tent. After walking a short distance, Jacob turned to Albert. "Gottlieb is not well. He can hardly catch his next breath and he seems very weak."

"I noticed that, too," Albert replied. "He's been having breathing problems for years, but the anxiety from everything that's happened seems to be taking a toll on him."

"We should see if he can remain in the tent when the Nazis send us out to work," Jacob suggested.

"Maybe the Nazis won't notice or ask questions if there are already two men per wagon," Albert said, trying to think the situation through. "It might be better to just leave Gottlieb in the tent and not draw attention to ourselves by asking permission for him to remain behind. The Nazis may just choose to shoot him if he is of no help to them."

"I hadn't thought of that," Jacob replied. "You may have the best plan. Gottlieb will be no help given the condition he is in. It would be easier for the Nazis to just dispose of him."

"The problem will be convincing Gottlieb to remain behind when we are sent to help the Nazi troops," Albert said.

"He can definitely be stubborn," Jacob agreed. "He will not like the thought of not being well enough to do his part. We will just have to make the suggestion and hope he sees it from our point of view."

Albert nodded his head as he gazed around the camp's flurry of activity. Men were still arriving after they, too, had loaded their wives and children on trains to be transported back into the borders of Germany. "Glad we didn't load our wagons down," Albert said, watching other men unload their belongings from the wagons. "I don't know what those men thought they were going to do with all that stuff."

"They probably made the mistake of telling their wives they were being sent to this camp," Jacob replied. "You know how women are. They think you should pack it all."

"Yes, we were smart not to tell our wives that we were being forced to leave our farms. If we had, our wagons would have been loaded down like those poor men's," Albert said with a chuckle.

"I really hate to lose everything we have been able to regain the last four years, but I honestly believe we will be running for our very lives when we leave Poland," Jacob said. "There will be no time to worry with taking any possessions."

"I hope you're wrong, Brother, but I fear you are not," Albert replied. "I'm just thankful our wives and sons have already been sent back to Germany. Fleeing will be much easier without the worry of protecting our wives and children."

"I agree, but I do wonder how we will all find each other again," Jacob said. "We don't even know the destination the train was headed to."

"We will just have to search until we do," Albert stated. "I just hope Rosina and the other women catch up with Emilie and Magdalena."

"Me, too," Jacob said, "but if they don't at least our wives are together. I don't think they will allow themselves to get separated."

"True," Albert agreed, "and my Albert and your Erhard are old enough to be of help. We will just have to trust the Lord for their safety, along with our own."

"I can't believe the turmoil Hitler has caused," Jacob whispered.

"Your tongue is going to get you killed, yet," Albert hissed. "Come on, let's get back to the tent where it's warmer and hopefully no one can hear you."

"Just stating the truth," Jacob muttered as he trudged after Albert.

"Keep it to your own self," Albert whispered, ending the conversation as they entered the tent.

The next morning the men were instructed on how they were to help the German troops. The men in the tent Albert and Jacob were in would be responsible for taking injured soldiers to the train station. From there, the injured men would be transported to hospitals for treatment. There was a tent set up as a triage to give minimal medical care, with hopes it would be enough to carry them through until more could be done. The fact that the closest medical facility could only be reached by train attested to the fact that the German troops didn't think they could hold the Red Army back.

Two days later, the Red Army began to fire on the German troops from across the Vistula River. Albert and Jacob were put into action immediately, along with Emil, Edward, Olof, and Daniel. Gottlieb was left resting in the tent, though he had argued about the plan, and the German troops did not notice the old man missing from the group. Gottlieb was aware of his condition and knew the truth of the matter was that he would slow them down. He also believed the Nazis would just shoot him rather than be bothered with his ailments.

Arriving at the triage tent, the men began transporting injured soldiers immediately. "Lift on three," Jacob instructed. The young German man Jacob and Albert were loading into the wagon screamed from the pain. He was missing his left leg below the knee. A tourniquet had been tied around it and now he was headed for a long train ride. Jacob hoped the man would just pass out to make the journey more bearable.

"That makes five men," Albert said. "Let's head for the train station."

Albert climbed in the back while Jacob handled the team.

They raced toward the train station as fast as possible. The injured men screamed out with every bump and rut hit in the road. Half way to the station, a plane could be heard flying toward them. Jacob and Albert didn't know what was about to happen but the injured men did. Terror filled their eyes as they began to yell, "Find cover!"

"We can't unload all of you," Albert told the men.

The bomb struck the ground behind the wagon. It was not close enough to kill anyone, but dirt pelted and covered everyone in the wagon and the horses went wild. Jacob fought for control as the beasts ran as fast as their hooves would carry them. The snow and ice made the runaway even more dangerous. The wagon bounced along behind the team, the injured men taking a beating to add to their other injuries. Finally, the scared animals slowed and obeyed Jacob's screaming commands. He eventually brought the horses to a complete stop and jumped down from the wagon. Albert checked on the men, but their other injuries were so great that the bruises added from the rough ride went unnoticed. Calming the horses completely and allowing them to rest for a moment, Jacob finally realized what had just happened.

"We were almost hit by a bomb, Brother," Jacob said.

"I realize now why these men were hollering to find cover," Albert replied.

"That pilot was a poor aim," one of the injured men added, "or we would all be dead men right now."

"The next time you hear a plane, get off the road and in a ditch," another injured man added. "They don't all miss."

"Let's get you men to the train station," Jacob said, climbing back to the seat, "and thanks for the instructions."

After delivering the injured men to the train depot, Jacob and Albert headed back to pick up more. Twice they had to tether the horses beside the road and find cover in a ditch. When the bombing was over, they returned to the horses and found them all tangled in their harnesses. It took precious time to calm the horses and straighten the leather, time they felt they didn't have. The fact that they were untrained civilians in a war zone was something the men were not at all comfortable with.

"How long are we going to do this, Brother?" Albert asked.

"Not long," Jacob replied. "We will discuss our plans tonight with the rest of our group."

"Providing all our group returns unharmed," Albert muttered.

"Yes, providing we all are alive when this day ends," Jacob agreed, shuddering at the meaning of his words.

That evening, Jacob and the other men discussed their plan. It was decided that they would transport injured soldiers all the next day but would make a run for the German border after delivering their last load of men before nightfall. Edward and Emil would stop and pick up Gottlieb, along with all the men's bags of clothes, before going to the train station for the last time. They felt guilty about leaving the injured men without enough wagons for a quick transport, but they also wanted to see their families again. They knew the German forces would probably fail at holding the Red Army back. The Nazis had been retreating since they had been overtaken at Stalingrad, and there had not been any troops added to strengthen the line of defense. Hitler just had too many battles and not enough men.

The next morning, Jacob's group headed to the medical tent to get the first load of men. They had stopped transporting the night before at dark, so some of the men had been waiting all night to be moved. It was a sad sight, and it tore at the men's hearts to think of the misery the men were in. Somewhere, someone was waiting for every soldier who was fighting to come home safe and sound. Every man lost was someone's son, brother, husband, or father.

"This man is unconscious," Albert said, stepping up to the next soldier to be transported.

"That may be a blessing," Jacob said, pointing to the bone protruding from his splinted arm. "Let's get him loaded and to the train station while there's still some hope of him making it."

"Maybe we should stick around and do our part," Albert whispered when they got to the wagon.

"Albert, I want to help, honestly I do," Jacob said. "It's just that we both have a wife and sons somewhere in Germany seeking refuge and they need us."

"I know," Albert said, "it's just that these men have families, too. They need us to help them get medical attention."

"And we're going to do our part today," Jacob replied. "We

have a plan and we must stick to it. I admit it will be hard to turn tail and run. It's not in our nature, but we are not equipped or trained to stay and fight."

Albert nodded in reply and they headed back into the tent for another injured soldier. When their wagon was full, they prepared to leave. As they began to move away, a German soldier came out and stopped them.

"You need to put more men in your wagon," the soldier demanded.

"Five is the amount we've been putting," Jacob informed him. "We really don't have room for more, not to mention the extra weight for the horses to pull."

"Things are not going well at the front," the soldier replied. "We need to move as many men as quickly as possible."

"Okay," Albert answered nervously, jumping down from the back of the wagon.

Jacob and Albert went back for three more injured men. They were placed so close that no one could move a muscle. Driving as quickly as possible, Jacob and Albert made their way to the train depot. It was still early morning and the sun had just barely peeked over the horizon. Because of the low visibility, the Russian planes had not started bombing yet.

When Jacob and Albert returned to the medical tent for their next load they were shocked to see how many more injured men had been added in the short time they were gone. They were instructed to place the men on their sides and load them like slices of bread. It did not take a trained military person to notice how desperate the situation had become. The fear was written on every face.

"That's ten men," Albert told Jacob. "Do you think we can squeeze anymore in?"

"Let's fill up the place you usually sit in," Jacob said. "I know you try and assist them during the move but we need to get every man we possibly can to that train station. You can join me on the seat."

"Okay," Albert agreed.

Two more men were loaded and Jacob and Albert were off. They knew they were beating and banging the men terribly, but there was an urgency to get to the train station. The statement from the German soldier that things were not going well on the front was the only thought in Jacob and Albert's minds as they pushed the horses to their limit. How long would it be before the Red Army broke the front line and caused the Nazis to retreat?

"No planes, no bombs," Albert said, leaning over to speak in Jacob's ear.

"That's a good thing," Jacob replied.

"Yes," Albert said, "but it's certainly light enough outside now for the Red Army to see their targets."

"What are you thinking, Brother?" Jacob asked.

"Could be the Soviets aren't bombing because they're getting ready to break through the German line and send them running," Albert said.

"And they wouldn't want to take a chance on bombing their own troops," Jacob finished the thought for him.

"Exactly," Albert agreed.

"We have to get to that train station fast," Jacob said. "I really don't think I can push these horses any harder, though. We have too much weight on this wagon for the poor beasts to pull."

"No, I don't believe the horses can give any more than they are right now," Albert agreed.

"Stay alert, Albert," Jacob instructed. "Things could get dangerous very quickly."

Jacob and Albert made it to the train station and unloaded the men. They started back toward the medical tent at a bit slower pace. The horses needed a rest and they were keeping their eyes trained toward the East for any sign that they needed to flee. As they came around a curve, there was another wagon coming toward them at full speed. The driver began to slow the team as he neared Jacob and Albert.

"Turn around, the Red Army is coming!" Edward yelled as he came up even with Jacob and Albert. Gottlieb was bundled up in the back of their wagon and everyone's bag of clothes and the extra blankets had been loaded as well.

"Where are Daniel and Olof?" Albert hollered.

"They're on their way," Emil replied.

"We'll wait here until they arrive," Jacob said. "We will never find them again if we are separated."

"Then we will wait, too," Edward decided. "You're right, if

we get separated, it will be nearly impossible to find one another."

Jacob pulled his wagon past Edward and Emil's then turned the team around and pulled in behind them. "Where were you told to go," Jacob hollered up to Edward.

"Into central Germany," Edward replied. "There's fighting going on around the border. The Allies are closing in from all sides."

"It will be a miracle if we make it into central Germany," Albert stated.

A wagon and team of horses came barreling from behind them. Jacob quickly followed Edward as they moved off the road to allow the approaching wagon to pass. As the wagon approached, the driver began hollering, "Get out of here! The Red Army is close behind! The German troops are backing up and you will be in the middle of the battle soon!"

"Thanks for the warning!" Jacob hollered back as the wagon flew past.

Looking back, Jacob hoped to see Olof and Daniel headed toward them. Another nearly out of control wagon could be seen approaching with three more in the distance. The first three sped by, yelling warnings as they passed. As the fourth one drew closer, Jacob was sure it was Olof driving the team with Daniel hanging on for dear life.

"Whoa!" Olof called to the team as he neared Jacob's wagon. "We have to run, Brothers. Not only is the war front being pushed toward us but Polish bandits are attacking wagons of Germans as they leave. We have been warned to stay very alert when we come to clearings. The bandits are ambushing the wagons, killing the drivers, and taking the horses."

"Let's go!" Emil hollered and Olof snapped the reins on the horses' rumps and took the lead.

The three wagons took off at break neck speed. Staying on the seat was very difficult but they really had no choice but to hold on and ride it out. Three miles into their flight, the bombs started coming again. There was no time to stop and hide in a ditch. They just prayed that none would drop close enough to harm them. With each explosion, the horses would rear up then try to run away. The men had to fight them back onto the road to keep them headed west.

"There's a clearing up ahead," Olof shouted. "Be prepared for attack!"

"Grab that chain!" Jacob instructed Albert, nodding to the chain that lay in the wagon bed. "Use it if you have to!"

As they entered the clearing, Jacob could barely see Olof and Daniel ahead. The bandits had attacked two wagons directly in front of them and were not ready for the three entering the area at such a high rate of speed.

"Yah! Yah!" Jacob hollered at the team. The horses were frightened by all the commotion. They slowed their pace and side stepped wildly. "Use the chain!" Jacob screamed at Albert.

"On the horses?" Albert questioned.

"Yes, or we will die right here!" Jacob hollered back.

Albert lifted the chain and struck one horse and then the other. He had not even used a whip on any horse before and he felt terrible about striking these now with the heavy chain. However, it was really a life and death situation. The horses bolted forward as Albert struck them several more times. They flew through the clearing like their tails were on fire and they were trying to outrun them.

"Whoa!" Jacob hollered, pulling up beside Edward and Emil a mile past the clearing. Olof and Daniel were just ahead.

"We have to let these horses catch their breath," Edward stated.

"Yes," Albert agreed. "We need to dress the wounds I just put on ours, too."

"We will have to use axle grease," Jacob said, climbing down from the wagon seat. "It's all we have."

"It will have to do," Albert replied quietly.

Jacob and Albert smeared grease from the wagon's wheels into the horses' wounds, talking to them quietly. The horses calmed with the men's touch and voice, though they shuddered every few minutes from the hard run and the bitter temperatures.

"We need to keep moving," Olof said. "We will walk for a little while to allow the horses to catch their breath but not cool too quickly."

The men walked their teams for a mile and then stopped at a stream of water for the humans and the beasts to get a drink. The water had a thin sheet of ice on it but could be seen running underneath. Jacob stomped a small hole with the heel of his boot, being careful not to muddy the water. He cupped water in his hands to drink from, and the rest of the men did the same. Edward and Emil helped Gottlieb from the wagon and back, his wheezing able to be heard from several feet away. Edward cupped his own hands and offered his vater a drink. The feeble man was able to take a couple sips before falling into a fit of coughing. A look of concern passed between the others but no one spoke the obvious; Gottlieb was not well.

The hole was made bigger and the horses were brought to the water for a drink. Hitching the horses back up, the men started on their way toward Germany again. Keeping the horses at a trot, they tried to conserve their energy in case they came upon another ambush.

"There's a clearing up ahead!" Olof hollered back and Emil passed the message back to Jacob and Albert.

"Grab the chain," Jacob told Albert.

"I really hate to strike them again," Albert protested.

"Hopefully, you won't have to," Jacob replied.

As Albert picked up the chain the sound of the links clinking together was enough to alert the horses of what must be done. Without a word from Jacob, the horses bolted into the clearing. About half way through, Jacob and Albert caught a glimpse of the bandits beating a man on the ground. They had no way of helping him and couldn't have stopped the horses if they wanted to. Coming through to the other side, they came upon Olof, Edward, and Emil, with Gottlieb still in the wagon bed.

"Where's Daniel?" Jacob asked.

"He was pulled from the wagon seat by the bandits," Olof responded. "I could do nothing to help him!"

"We saw the bandits beating him as we rushed by," Albert said. "We could do nothing, either. It's not your fault, Olof."

"Why don't you leave that wagon and get in with us?" Jacob suggested.

"Okay," Olof agreed.

"We could just ride the horses bareback but I don't think we would be able to stay on through the ambush areas," Albert said.

"We would have to have at least one wagon," Edward said, nodding toward Gottlieb bundled in the back of their wagon.

"Let's tie the two extra horses to the back of our wagon," Jacob suggested. "We could use them to relieve the ones pulling or in case one goes lame."

"Gut idea," Olof said, quickly unhitching the team.

Throwing the extra tack in the wagon, Olof and Albert tied the extra horses to their wagon. They could hear planes in the distance and bombs exploding. It seemed the Red Army was bombing in front of the German troops to slow their retreat as the Soviet ground forces came from behind them.

"We have to get out of here and fast," Jacob said. "We are dead men if we get in the middle of the battle."

"Yah," Edward hollered, urging his team to a fast trot. Jacob followed close behind.

The men did not encounter any more Polish bandits but the impending danger behind them kept them moving at a fast pace. They came upon broken wagons that had been abandoned and the horses missing. They were sure the occupants were riding toward Germany bareback, fleeing from the danger just as they were. When nightfall came the men decided to keep going, putting more distance between them and the Red Army. Two men manned the wagons while the others took turns sleeping. Thankful that Edward had grabbed all the blankets when he picked up Gottlieb, the men remained wrapped tightly in the wool all through the night. As dawn began to lighten the sky, the group decided to stop at a farmhouse along the road. The horses needed rest and feed, and so did they.

"Let's pray they are friendly," Emil said as they pulled into the barn lot.

"Yes," Edward agreed. "We have to find food for us and the horses or neither man nor beast will have the strength to carry on."

Jacob jumped down from the wagon and walked to the back door. Before he had a chance to knock, the door opened. Standing before him was a mountain of a Polish man. Jacob knew he could strangle him with one hand but he decided to plead their case just the same.

"Good morning, sir," Jacob began. "We have been on the road all day yesterday and all night fleeing the advance of the Red Army. Would you be willing to help us? Our horses need feed and we are quite hungry as well."

"Maybe you should have remained in Germany," the big man replied.

"We are actually from Bessarabia," Jacob said. "We were forced to leave there when the Red Army invaded. We had no choice as to where we were sent after that. We had to go where Hitler told us. I assure you I am no Hitler sympathizer, just a man trying to get back to his wife and sons."

At the mention of family, the big man softened a bit. His wife joined him at the door and he told her to prepare a meal for the men while he showed them where they could feed the horses. Grabbing a coat, the Polish man led the way to his barn. The sweet smell of hay enveloped the weary group and caused Gottlieb to sneeze and cough. The Polish man instructed Emil to take Gottlieb to the house to warm up and have a cup of coffee. Olof scrambled to the loft and threw down hay for the horses. They would give them a bit of grain before they departed.

The men returned to the house to a large breakfast of ham, eggs, biscuits and gravy, all chased down with hot coffee. The warmth and nourishment revived them some.

They thanked the Polish man and his wife and prepared to leave. Though they had traveled almost twenty-four hours without stopping, the men knew they still had miles ahead of them. They would not be safe from the Red Army until they were deep into Germany.

"I have two loaves of bread and some cheese sacked up for you," the Polish woman said. "I also have a gallon of milk in a crock for you to take. The crock might come in handy to carry water along your way."

"Your kindness will never be forgotten," Jacob said, taking the offered sack of food. "May Gottlieb sit at your table until we are ready to leave?"

"Yes, that would be fine," the Polish woman answered.

The German men, led by the Polish farmer, trudged back to the barn. The horses really needed a full day of rest to recover from the long, terror-filled ride they had been forced into, and the men would have benefited from a rest as well. The luxury was not possible, though. They must keep moving west, hopefully staying ahead of the battle.

As they entered the barn, Jacob turned to the Polish farmer.

"What will happen to you and your wife if the battle comes to your front door?"

"I suppose we will lock ourselves in our house and pray," the Polish man replied. "We have nowhere to flee to. We are not German citizens, so we would not be offered refuge there. Running in any other direction would result in getting trapped in the middle of combat. Besides, we have grown children with families close by. We will stay and hope for the best."

"How many innocent lives will be taken or destroyed before this crazy war ends?" Emil wondered aloud.

"We need to get back on the road before we're among those numbers," Albert urged. "Maybe we should take just one wagon for the rest of the trip."

"What about the horses?" Jacob asked.

"We could pull the wagon with two and tie two behind, trading them off as needed," Emil suggested. "We could leave two horses and the extra wagon here, as a payment for this generous man's kindness."

"What if the wagon breaks down?" Jacob asked. "Gottlieb is in no shape to be riding a horse."

"We will just have to take the chance. How long do you think it will take us to reach Germany?" Edward asked the Polish man.

"You won't be able to drive the horses like you did the last twenty-four hours," the Polish man pointed out. "You will probably make twenty-five miles per day and you're about 160 miles from the border."

"So, about a week," Albert said, doing the calculation.

"Yes, if all goes well," the Polish man replied. "Stop at farmhouses along the way. Most of us are friendly enough and will help provide food and fodder for your horses."

"Thank you again for your kindness," Jacob said, helping the men get the team of horses hitched up. "We will keep you and your family in our prayers."

"Thank you for the extra wagon and team of horses," the Polish man said. "I'll fill your wagon bed with hay. It will make the ride more comfortable until it's all fed to the horses."

Edward went back to the house to help his vater to the wagon. Jacob pulled close to the door and Gottlieb was lifted into the back. Wrapping a blanket around him for warmth, Emil helped Gottlieb to the front of the wagon and got him settled in. Waving to the Polish farmer, the group was back on the road for the week long journey.

"Maybe we should find a train depot," Albert suggested after an hour on the road. "We have a little money from selling our extra grain earlier this year. The trip that will take us days could be turned into hours."

"That's not a bad idea," Emil agreed. "I know we will probably need the money for what lies ahead, but spending a week on the road will take a toll on us. Besides, the Red Army might catch up to us before we can get to safety."

"The sooner we get to Germany the better," Olof added, nodding toward Gottlieb who was wheezing in his sleep.

"What do you think, Jacob?" Albert asked.

Jacob was handling the team but turned to look at the group. His eyes rested on Gottlieb and he knew they needed to do something to help the man. Traveling for a week in a wagon would probably be the death of him. It was still bitterly cold and snow had started to fall again. "I say we ask which direction the nearest train station is at the next farmhouse," Jacob answered.

"Do you think we'll have enough money?" Olof asked.

"I had a bit saved back," Jacob said. "If we put what we have together, I believe we can come up with enough. If not, we will get passage for Gottlieb and send someone with him."

"So, it's a plan," Emil concluded.

Stopping at the next farmhouse, Jacob went to the door to ask for directions. Coming back to the wagon, he informed the others that the train depot was five miles away. All they had to do was stay on the road they were already on. They had also been given permission to pull the wagon in the barn and take shelter while they ate the bread and cheese and fed the horses. An hour later the group headed out again. The horses had been switched, and with a fresh team, Jacob pushed them harder.

"We can sell this wagon and the horses to pay for the train tickets," Olof announced, the thought just coming to him.

"That just might work," Albert said. "Surely we can get enough out of four horses and a wagon to buy six tickets."

"Just don't let Jacob do the selling," Gottlieb said with a

laugh. "He would overcharge his own mutti and argue the price until the cows come home."

Jacob laughed along with the rest just because it was good to hear Gottlieb speak with humor. Jacob had been raised a businessman, running a mill, dairy, and grocery store. He knew how to make money and it had served him well. He also knew when to give a good deal and that would be the case today. The horses and wagon would practically be given away just so they had enough money for the tickets.

Reaching the small town where the train depot was, Jacob dropped off Gottlieb and everyone else except Albert. Checking the prices for the cheapest fare, he then drove to the livery and blacksmith shop. He knew what he had to have and it was going to be a steal for the buyer. Entering the shop, Jacob asked the owner if he knew anyone interested in a wagon and four horses. The owner confirmed that he might know of someone and went out to look at what Jacob had to offer.

"How much do you want for all of it?" the blacksmith asked.

Jacob stated a price that would pay for the tickets and leave enough money for the men to eat a few meals.

"Sold," the blacksmith owner said without hesitation.

Jacob and Albert collected the money and hurried back to the train depot. They hoped to catch the last train out that was headed to Germany. The destination didn't really matter as long as they reached German soil. Boarding the train, the group sank down to rest while the train traveled into the night. It was nice to be out of the cold wind and snow. The conversation dwindled down and all the men slipped off to sleep. The next sound they heard was Olof screaming.

"No! Turn him lose! Go faster, faster! I can't save you, Daniel! I can't save you!

"Olof, Olof, wake up!" Jacob hollered, shaking the boy's shoulder. "You're having a nightmare."

"What, what's wrong?" Olof asked, his eyes flying open.

"You were having a nightmare about Daniel being killed," Albert said.

"Oh, sorry," Olof apologized, embarrassed he had woke them.

An hour later the train pulled into the station in Dresden,

Germany, just inside Germany's eastern border. The men knew they would have to move farther to the west, but Dresden would have to do for tonight. They were just thankful to be on German soil. Stepping from the train, they noticed German soldiers milling about. As one soldier approached another, their arms snapped out and upwards as the words "Heil Hitler!" rang out.

"Heil Hitler, indeed," Jacob muttered. "We have spent the last four years moving and running for our lives. That's what Hitler has gotten us. If it weren't for this crazy war, we would be warm in our beds in Bessarabia right now."

"Jacob!" Albert hissed.

The heads of the German soldiers turned toward the group of men who had just arrived on the train. Their eyes bore into Jacob's, and he could do nothing to hide his anger. Hitler had caused him to lose everything in Bessarabia and now he was fleeing for his life as the Red Army closed in around the Nazis. He had no idea where his wife and sons were or even if they had made it to safety. He was weary of this war and his emotions were raw. Jacob had been pushed to his limit and now there was nothing he could do to put the blurted words back into his mouth.

"Speaking out against Fuhrer Hitler gets you killed or arrested," one of the German soldiers said. "I'm feeling generous tonight, so I'll just arrest you. You will die soon enough."

Jacob, knowing things were going to get bad quickly, whispered to Albert, "The extra money is in my bag of clothes. You will need it to travel farther west. Please, if I don't make it out of this alive, tell Magdalena and the boys I love them."

The German soldier speaking to Jacob was joined by another, who shoved the butt of his gun deep into Jacob's stomach. As he doubled over, the other one kicked him to the ground. Jacob was silent and not just because there was no air left in his lungs. He knew he had gone too far, spoken without thought, and there was absolutely nothing anyone could do to help him.

Chapter Twenty

Magdalena woke rested but with very sore feet. The motel had provided a clean room and soft beds for the night, but nothing would heal the blisters on her and her sons' feet but time itself. The long, cold walk had taken a great toll on them. Thankfully, none of them appeared to have frostbite. That would have been a very painful and potentially dangerous condition. Fingers or toes could have been lost and the threat of infection might prove to be deadly. They had no money for medical care, if a doctor could even be found.

Magdalena woke Erhard and instructed him to stay with his brothers while she went downstairs to help in the kitchen. It was the least she could do to repay some of the owner's kindness. Without Gerda, her children would still be hungry and there was no telling where they would have spent the night. She had no money to pay for the room or food, but she knew how to cook and clean well and she would at least offer that.

Upon entering the kitchen, Magdalena was greeted with warmth and a bustle of activity. Seeing dishes piled up in the sink already, Magdalena went to work. Grabbing a kettle of hot water from the stove, she poured some in a dishpan then added cold to achieve a temperature her hands could tolerate. Using a knife, Magdalena whittled soap from a bar into the dishwater and began to scrub away.

"Magdalena, you don't have to do that," Gerda said, coming into the kitchen with a tray of dirty dishes.

"It's the least I can do after the kindness you have shown me and my children," Magdalena replied.

"Well, if you think you must," Gerda said smiling. "It will definitely be a help. When the breakfast crowd leaves, I want you and your sons to eat breakfast, though."

"Thank you so much for your kindness," Magdalena said.

"I think I have a place for you to stay, too," Gerda said. "We will talk about it later, while we rest and enjoy our breakfast."

"Okay," Magdalena said. "I need to find the rest of my family but it would give us someplace to stay until I do."

Magdalena kept the dishes washed, dried, and put away for the next two hours. Finally, Gerda told her the morning rush was over and it was time for them to eat. Magdalena went back to their room to get the boys. After changing Werner's diaper, they all went downstairs for breakfast. Magdalena instructed the boys to sit at the table and Erhard was to hold Werner. She then went to the kitchen to prepare their breakfast.

"You just go out to the dining area and sit down," Gerda insisted. "I almost have your breakfast ready and will be out in just a few minutes."

"Gerda, you have been so kind already," Magdalena protested. "Let me help you finish our breakfast and carry the tray out."

"The way you're hobbling around, I don't think you would make it to the table with the tray without dropping it," Gerda said with a smile.

"So, you noticed my limping around," Magdalena said with a laugh. "I have blisters on my feet the size of Werner's hands. I didn't know a person's feet could be so sore."

"Go sit down, Magdalena," Gerda demanded. "I will be there in a minute and we will discuss your new home I have found for you."

"Okay," Magdalena replied. Magdalena wanted to argue but the blisters on her feet made her agree. The pain was so great she could not take a step without limping, trying not to apply her full weight to the areas of her feet that were the sorest.

Gerda came out of the kitchen with three plates mounded with food. Werner would be fed from his mutti's plate, since he could not feed himself without making a mess. Gerda then went back to the kitchen to get her own plate of food and joined Magdalena at the table.

"The place I have found for you is just up the street," Gerda began. "They're an older couple who has an extra bedroom. They said you are welcome to stay there until you can find where your family has gone."

"I have no idea where my sister, Emilie, was taken," Magdalena admitted. "She was picked up along the road by a US military vehicle a few hours before we were."

"With so many of you trying to find refuge, it's going to be hard to find out where she ended up," Gerda replied.

"Yes, I know," Magdalena said. "I just don't know where to begin."

"I'll keep asking around," Gerda promised. "Sometimes I see US soldiers in town. Maybe they will be able to help you. Of course, communication is sometimes difficult because I can't speak English and most of them don't speak German."

"Thank you again for all you have done for me and my sons," Magdalena said. "I will always remember your kindness."

"It's nothing you wouldn't have done for me if I had been in your situation," Gerda replied. "I'll walk you down to the house you will be staying at when we're finished eating. All of you need to soak your blistered feet in a pan of warm Epsom salt water when you get there. You walked a long way yesterday, and our feet will only take so much abuse before they revolt against us."

"Mine are definitely fighting back," Magdalena laughed. "Erhard and Ewald's feet don't look much better."

"A soaking in Epsom salts will do them a world of good," Gerda said. "I'll send some salt with you, just in case there's none at the house you're to stay at."

"Thank you," Magdalena replied again. It seemed that's the only thing she had said to this kind woman since she and her children arrived the night before. "By the way, where did you say we are?

"You are in the state of Bavaria," Gerda supplied. "The mountains you see are part of the Bavarian Alps."

"It's very beautiful here," Magdalena said. "Why are there US military vehicles in this location?"

"The Nazis fell to the Allies on the western front just recently," Gerda said. "There had been battles going on for months but it seems the air power of the Allies finally won out."

"With so much activity on the Western front, I suppose no extra troops have been sent to Poland to help the German troops hold back the Red Army," Magdalena said, knowing she was correct in her assumption and what that would mean for her family who was still there.

"No, I don't think extra troops have been sent there," Gerda said. "I will ask around and see if I can get any information about the battles in Poland. I know you're worried about your husband, and perhaps other family who are still living there. I would just read the newspapers but they are never allowed to print what is really happening with the war. It's not like all of us living here don't know that Munich has been devastated by bombing from the Allies and we can clearly see that we are now occupied by US military forces."

"Yes, I am very concerned for my husband's safety, along with my vater and other family," Magdalena admitted. "Any information you can gather would be greatly appreciated."

"I will do my best," Gerda promised.

Magdalena finished her breakfast and insisted on washing the dishes. She may not be able to walk well, but she could stand at a sink of water just fine. She sent the boys back to the room to start packing up their meager belongings. When the dishes were clean and put away, Magdalena went up to the room to prepare to leave. Erhard picked up the suitcase while Ewald carried the canvas bag of diapers and blankets.

When they returned downstairs, Magdalena wrapped Werner in a blanket for the short walk. The snow had stopped falling but was still bitterly cold, and the snow was over their ankles. Thankfully, she and the boys had boots on to keep the snow from getting into their shoes. Gerda had placed their boots beside the wood stove to dry overnight, since the long walk in the snow the previous day had soaked them.

Following Gerda, Magdalena and her sons headed toward the house of refuge. Magdalena was thankful she would have somewhere to stay while she searched for the whereabouts of Emilie but felt bad for having to live off someone else's charity. It was not something she was accustomed to doing and she planned to change her situation as soon as possible.

The home was reached in less than five minutes, and Gerda walked around to the back door. She suggested everyone remove their wet shoes after stepping into the house to prevent snow and mud from being tracked in. Gerda knew the couple kept a tidy home and she wanted to do her part to keep it that way, especially since they were being so kind and opening their home to these complete strangers.

"Magdalena, this is Ada," Gerda made the introduction as soon as Ada opened the door.

"It's nice to meet you, Ada," Magdalena said, "and thank you for opening up your home to us."

"You are quite welcome," Ada replied. "Come in out of the cold. I have the room all ready for you."

Magdalena entered the house followed closely by Ewald and Erhard. A man appeared and took the suitcase from Erhard and the canvas bag from Ewald. "I'll just put these in your room," the older man said.

"Thank you," Magdalena replied.

"That's my husband, Gwiden," Ada said. "He will spoil your sons rotten."

"It will be good for them to spend time with him," Magdalena said smiling. "They are missing their Opa Wallentine, and of course their vater, too."

"Such heartbreak this war has caused," Ada said, shaking her head for emphasis.

"I need to get back to the motel," Gerda said. "I think you will get along just fine here until you can locate the rest of your family. Don't forget to soak your feet in the salt."

"Of course, Gerda," Magdalena said. "If you need any help at the motel, you just come and get me. I owe you several hours of work."

"You need to get those feet healed up first," Gerda pointed out.

"Thank you again, Gerda," Magdalena said, "for everything."

Gerda left to return to the motel and Magdalena and the boys removed their shoes at the back door of the house. Following Ada, she led them to a small bedroom with two full size beds in it. It would be perfect for Magdalena and her sons for a short time.

Magdalena removed the blanket from around Werner and set him down. Erhard and Ewald walked to one of the beds and set down on the edge of the mattress. Unsure of what to do next, the boys turned questioning gazes to their Mutti.

"I'll get some water heated for you to soak your feet in the Epsom salt," Ada said. "What happened to them?"

"We had to walk a long way yesterday," Magdalena said. "Our feet were so frozen we didn't feel the blisters until they thawed out last night. The boys have blisters on theirs, too."

"Well, it's nothing a few days rest and a good soaking won't cure," Ada said smiling. "Now, if we could just solve all the other problems you have that easily, we'd be accomplishing something."

"One thing at a time," Magdalena replied with a smile.

Days turned into weeks and still Magdalena could not get any information as to where Emilie might be or what was happening in Poland. Every few days, while Werner was napping, Magdalena would walk to the motel to see if Gerda had any news for her. Ada and Gwiden gladly entertained Erhard and Ewald while she was gone.

It turned out that the couple had never been able to have children, and Erhard, Ewald, and Werner became the grandsons they would never have. The boys enjoyed the attention the older couple lavished on them and Magdalena knew it would be very difficult to leave, when the time came.

"Any news today?" Magdalena asked Gerda as she entered the kitchen to make herself useful. Today it would be kneading bread dough since Gerda already had it turned out on a floured board and was pounding away at the mass, beating it into submission.

"Maybe," Gerda said, dividing the dough and handing half of it to Magdalena.

"Really?" Magdalena asked with surprise as she pressed the palm of her hand into the dough. The answer had been "no" for weeks. A "maybe" piqued her interest as to what Gerda had found out.

"Remember, it's hard to communicate with the US military because of the language barrier," Gerda began, "but the best I could understand, the Red Army crossed the Vistula River not long after you and your sons left Poland. It sent the Nazis and the relocated Germans running. I wish I had better news and more facts, but it's all I could understand."

"At least it's something," Magdalena said, as her anxiety tripled for her husband's well-being. The dough beneath her hands became her outlet for the anger she felt toward Hitler and the war in general. Hitler's dream for a Greater Germany had ruined Magdalena's life, along with countless others. Magdalena just wanted to go home, back to Bessarabia and the village of Hoffnungstal. She wanted to hear the mill wheel sing its song and watch the cows come from the pasture, eager to be milked. She wanted to watch in amazement as gallons of milk were turned into wheels of cheese when just the right heat, ingredients and pressure were applied. She wanted her sons to grow up in a peaceful place and for her and Jacob to grow old together. She had dreams, too, but Hitler's had destroyed them.

"I believe it's dead," Gerda said, lightly touching Magdalena's hands.

"Oh." Magdalena gasped, not realizing how hard she must have been pounding the poor dough.

"It's okay," Gerda said smiling. "Sometimes I take out all of my frustrations on a good piece of dough, too."

"Do you think my husband is alive?" Magdalena could not keep the question she had been pondering from escaping her lips.

"Only the good Lord knows the answer to that question," Gerda replied. "What I do know is that you have three sons who need you to remain strong, and I know you will do that. There will be time enough for tears when this war is over."

"Of course you're right, Gerda," Magdalena whispered, fighting to keep her tears from spilling over. "It's just been such a long, hard road."

"I know it has," Gerda said, "but you're a strong woman. You will find a way to carry on, no matter what the circumstances. Be strong, Magdalena."

"Thank you, Gerda," Magdalena said. "You never allow me to wallow in my own self-pity because you know I will get stuck there."

"You're welcome," Gerda said with a smile. "I will keep asking about your sister. Maybe we will hear something soon and you will be able to find each other."

"Yes, hopefully soon," Magdalena replied, knowing that being reunited with Emilie would boost her morale. Gerda, Ada, and Gwiden had been kind beyond words, but Magdalena still longed for her sister's company.

A month and a half after Magdalena had moved into Ada and Gwiden's home, Gerda came to visit. Magdalena knew she must have important news because Gerda rarely left the motel. Gerda was a very busy woman with many responsibilities. Her husband had been drafted into the German troops and Gerda had been tending to the business ever since. It seemed everyone had someone they were waiting on to return to them.

"I have some news," Gerda began. "A troop of US soldiers stopped in this morning, and they told me there is a camp up on the mountain toward the Bavarian Alps where some refugees are living. Your sister might be there."

"Yes, she could definitely be there," Magdalena replied, excited about the possibility.

"It would be a very long walk," Ada said. "You could leave the boys here and go see if your sister is at the camp."

"I would just have to walk all the way back to get them," Magdalena said. "I will just take them with me and leave early tomorrow morning. Surely Emilie and her boys are there already."

"I sure hope so, dear," Ada replied. "I'm going to miss you and the boys, though."

"We will miss you, too," Magdalena said, "and we can't thank you enough for allowing us to live here the last six weeks. You and Gwiden were an answer to prayer."

The next morning, Magdalena finished packing up their belongings. She had spent the previous day washing all their dirty clothes and diapers before leaving. She had no idea what she would find when she reached the barracks. Not having to worry with laundry for a few days would be one less concern.

Ada fixed a nice big breakfast and packed food to send with them. Magdalena tried to help Ada clean the kitchen, but Ada refused.

"I've cleaned this kitchen plenty of times by myself," Ada informed Magdalena. "You have a long day ahead, and there is no need in delaying you any longer by allowing you to clean my kitchen. I really don't think you will make it all the way to the barracks today, being it's such a long journey."

"Maybe we will catch a ride," Magdalena said hopefully.

"That would be nice," Ada agreed. "If we had a vehicle, we would just drive you ourselves. Of course, we would not be able to get fuel for it, so a vehicle would do us no good."

"It's okay," Magdalena assured her. "We will manage to get there. Thank you for all your kindness."

"You're welcome, dear," Ada said. "Make sure you wear the nice wool socks I knitted for you and the boys. Maybe you won't get blisters this time."

"We will definitely be wearing the socks," Magdalena laughed. "I don't ever want to have my feet be that sore again."

The early March weather was a bit milder than it had been in January when they had arrived. At least they wouldn't be quite so cold on this walk. Magdalena put a large shawl around her neck and placed Werner inside. Erhard picked up the suitcase and Ewald threw the canvas bag over his shoulder. Ada and Gwiden said a sad farewell, and the family started on their way just as the sun peeked over the horizon behind them. Magdalena feared the sun would make its journey across the sky and below the other horizon before they reached their destination.

"I'm really tired, Mutti," Ewald said hours later. "Are we almost there?"

"We haven't even reached the base of the mountain," Magdalena pointed out. "It must be close to noon, though, because the sun is right above us. Let's stop and eat a little and rest for a while."

Magdalena left the road and found a large rock for her and the boys to sit down and rest on. Erhard and Ewald placed their bundles on the ground and sank to the rock, weary from the hours of walking. Magdalena picked Werner up out of the shawl and handed him to Erhard so she could prepare the food.

"Ada has put enough food in here for two days," Magdalena said, pulling out two loaves of bread, cheese, and ham slices.

"It might take us two days to get there," Erhard replied. "That mountain is not getting any closer."

"Well, we're five hours closer to it than when we started out this morning," Magdalena said. "We will have to just keep walking until we get there."

"What if it gets dark before we reach the camp?" Ewald asked.

"Then we hope for a full moon so we can see to keep walking," Magdalena replied.

The boys and Magdalena ate ham and cheese sandwiches and drank from the jar of water Ada had included. The jar was almost empty, since they had already passed it around once while they were walking. Magdalena knew she would have to locate a water source soon.

Ada had also included a jar of applesauce, which Magdalena fed to Werner, and slices of cinnamon strudel for dessert. When they had finished eating, Erhard and Ewald shared the canvas bag filled with diapers for a pillow. Placing a blanket beneath them and covering themselves with another, they stretched out on the rock and were soon asleep. Magdalena knew they needed to get back on the road but allowed them to take a half hour nap to regain some strength for the rest of the journey.

As the boys slept, Magdalena looked toward the mountain in the distance. Erhard was right. It did not look any closer now than when they had started out that morning. They had seen very few vehicles on the road and they had all been heading in the opposite direction of Magdalena and her boys.

Magdalena reached for the dry diaper she had removed from the canvas bag before the boys laid down. She busied herself changing Werner and playing and talking to him. Werner had slept a lot while they walked, so he was not ready for a nap.

Marveling at how much he had grown in a year, Magdalena couldn't help but think what the next year of his life would bring. Would they ever be able to find Jacob again? Was he still alive? Magdalena shook the questions from her mind as soon as they formed. She did not want to think about raising her three sons on her own. Jacob was alive and somehow, someway, they would find each other. This is what she would choose to believe until there was proof that she need not believe it any longer. It was her hope and prayer, and she would cling to it.

Magdalena gently shook Erhard and Ewald awake. The boys were drowsy at first, but when they were fully awake, they seemed to have regained some energy. Erhard picked up the suitcase again while Ewald carried the canvas bag. Magdalena placed Werner back in the shawl and he fussed about it for a few minutes. When he realized it was going to do him no good, he settled in for another long walk.

After thirty minutes back on the road, Magdalena could see a small town in the distance. She hoped she could refill their jar of water at a place in the town when they reached it, since the jar was completely empty. As they entered the town, Magdalena saw a small bar, the only business that might have water. Approaching the entrance, Magdalena handed Werner to Erhard and instructed the boys to wait outside. They sank down on the sidewalk to rest and wait.

Magdalena entered the bar with the empty jar and walked to the counter. "May I get this jar filled with water?" Magdalena asked the bartender.

"Water?" the bartender asked. "Don't get that request much."

"My children and I are walking toward that mountain in the distance," Magdalena said. "There's a camp being used for refugees there, or so I'm told."

"Yes, that's true," the bartender said, handing the full jar back to Magdalena. "However, if you're walking all the way there, you are still about ten hours away."

"Ten hours?" Magdalena asked disbelief mixed with disappointment evident in her voice.

"Afraid so," the bartender replied. "It won't be easy walking up that mountain after walking all day, either. Wish I had better news for you."

"Thank you for the water," Magdalena replied, placing the jar back in the bag of food Ada had provided.

"There are springs to refill your jar when you get to the mountain," the bartender said, hoping this bit of information might smooth a few worry lines from Magdalena's face.

"Well, at least we'll have water," Magdalena said, heading toward the door.

"Were you able to get water?" Ewald asked Magdalena as she stepped back onto the street.

"Yes, our jar is full," Magdalena replied.

"Will it be enough to last until we get to the camp?" Erhard asked.

"Maybe," Magdalena said, not willing to tell the boys they still had ten hours of walking ahead.

"May I have a drink now?" Ewald asked.

"Why don't I go back in and get us a glass of water to

share," Magdalena suggested, "that way we can save our jar of water for the journey."

"Okay," Ewald agreed.

Magdalena went back into the bar for a glass of water. When she returned, everyone took a drink. Magdalena took the container back in and thanked the bartender again. He wished her well on her trip as she headed out the door. The thought of ten more hours of walking made Magdalena weary but she knew she must press on. She just knew Emilie would be waiting at the end of this journey and she was desperate to find her.

"Did you ask how much farther it is to the camp?" Erhard questioned Magdalena.

"No, I didn't ask," Magdalena said. "Let's get going."

Magdalena had not asked, she reminded herself. The bartender had offered the information all on his own. Hopefully, he was wrong about how much farther they had to walk but Magdalena seriously doubted it as the thought came to her mind. The man surely knew the distance since he lived in the area. The only hope of shortening the time was to catch a ride, and that did not appear to be a realistic occurrence. The only ones who appeared to have fuel for travel were the US military vehicles and they weren't traveling in their direction today. All other supply of fuel was being used by the Nazis to fight the war.

As darkness began to fall, Magdalena and the boys had only made it to the base of the mountain. They were all exhausted from walking all day, but Magdalena decided they would not stop until they reached the camp. She had no plans of sleeping out along the road. "Let's stop and eat our supper," Magdalena suggested. "I know you're tired, but things will look better on a full belly."

"I sure hope so," Erhard replied, finding a rock to sink down on.

"Here, take Werner," Magdalena said, handing the squirming baby to Erhard. "You could hold his hand and let him walk a bit."

"Okay," Erhard agreed. "Take his other hand, Ewald, it will make it easier."

As Erhard and Ewald led Werner around, Magdalena prepared their supper. There was still applesauce left and plenty of bread, cheese, and ham. The strudel was gone, but Ada had included cookies, too. Magdalena had kept them back at noon for a surprise now.

After they had eaten, Magdalena instructed the boys to rest awhile. Pulling two blankets from the canvas bag, the boys placed one on the ground and covered up with the other. Soon, they were sound asleep.

Magdalena changed Werner again, who had been changed along the road several times already, and wrapped him back up in the blanket. The air was turning quite cold with the sun down. Cradling Werner close to her, Magdalena leaned back against a rock. As Werner's eyes fluttered and closed, so did Magdalena's. She was just too weary to stay awake.

When Magdalena awoke, the moon was shining full and the stars were bright. She knew she had been asleep several hours. Her back was stiff and she couldn't get up with Werner in her arms. Laying him on the ground, she rose to her feet, stretching to get the kinks from her joints.

Magdalena gently shook Erhard and Ewald and told them it was time to finish their journey. The boys got up and stretched then folded and packed their blankets, preparing to leave. Magdalena didn't have the heart to tell them the sun would be at their backs before they reached the camp on the mountain.

The walk up the mountain was long and slow. They were all thankful for the thick, wool socks Ada had knitted for them. Without those, their feet would surely have been covered with blisters.

Just as the light from the sun rising tinted the eastern horizon, the barracks came into view. Smoke could be seen rising from wood stoves inside the barracks where breakfast was surely being prepared. Magdalena walked toward the building from which the smoke was rising. Opening the door, the smell of oatmeal was carried on the steam coming from the boiling pots on the stove. Several women were cooking while their children sat at long tables.

"Sit here," Magdalena instructed her boys, pointing to one of the tables.

The boys gladly dropped the loads they had been carrying and sank down onto the table's bench. Magdalena handed a sleeping Werner to Erhard then walked toward the women who were cooking. She hoped that even if there was no room for them to stay here, they at least would be allowed to eat.

Magdalena's stomach growled as her nose took in the aromas of the cooking food. The oatmeal had been the most pungent, but the smell of pancakes now added its own scent, along with eggs being fried.

"Excuse me," Magdalena began, "my sons and I just arrived this morning. We were sent to this area by train from Poland about six weeks ago."

"Yes, so were we," one of the women replied.

"Would any of you happen to know a woman named Emilie Grieb?" Magdalena asked hopefully. "She has five sons."

"No, that name is not familiar," the same woman replied. The rest of the women shook their heads no, too.

"Thank you," Magdalena said, trying to keep her tears from falling. Where was Emilie?

"You're welcome to stay, though," another woman offered. "We have all been here quite some time. There's no place else for us to go, since our homes are now under Soviet control."

"We are from Bessarabia," Magdalena offered.

"We are from all over," the woman replied. "We were all invited back to the Reich as the Red Army invaded. We were made German citizens upon our arrival."

"Yes, we were too," Magdalena said.

"The United States has provided food for this camp," another woman informed Magdalena. "We all take turns cooking the meals for the families living here. Take a seat and we will have breakfast cooked soon. We will add your name to the schedule for meal preparation."

"Okay," Magdalena replied. "Is there a place for me and my sons to sleep?"

"Yes," the first woman who had spoken to Magdalena replied. "Go out the door, turn right and go three barracks down. There are some beds left in that barracks."

"Thank you, again," Magdalena replied. "I will go place our belongings in the barracks and return for breakfast."

Magdalena walked back to her sons, her heart feeling like lead in her chest. Emilie was not here. They had left the home of Ada and Gwiden and walked such a great distance in hopes of reuniting with Emilie and her sons. They should have just stayed where they were, but Magdalena had been sure Emilie would be here at this camp. It was that hope that had kept her going, even when she found out how far she must travel. The disappointment threatened to drive her to despair.

"Is Aunt Emilie here?" Erhard asked as Magdalena reached the table.

"No, she is not," Magdalena sighed.

"What will we do now?" Ewald fretted, already considering how far it would be to return to Ada and Gwiden's house.

"There are beds here where we can sleep and our meals will be provided," Magdalena said. "It's not what I was hoping for, but at least we will have food and shelter. Come and follow me to our barracks so we can put our belongings in a safe place."

Magdalena took Werner back in her arms and led the way to the suggested barracks where they found beds beside one another. Erhard chose the top bunk and was a bit excited because he had never slept on a bunk bed before. Ewald was disappointed that he had to sleep on the bottom until Magdalena suggested he sleep on the bunk above her. Werner would sleep beside Magdalena, so hopefully he would not roll off the bed in his sleep. A crib would have been nice but Magdalena knew that was only a dream. Maybe she could locate a large wooden crate that wasn't being used. With some blankets placed in the bottom for comfort, Werner could sleep next to her bed in that.

After placing the blankets they had brought with them on their beds, Magdalena and her sons went back to the dining area to eat breakfast. Finishing their meal, they returned to their sleeping quarters with full stomachs and tired bodies. Erhard and Ewald climbed onto their top bunks to check them out and were soon asleep. Magdalena played with Werner on the bottom bunk for a while until he grew tired and slept, too.

As Magdalena lay beside him, her tears finally began to fall. She was disappointed and overwhelmed by all that had happened. She had been separated from her mutti and sister and had no idea where to look for them. She was in a strange place and knew no one. What would she do now? How could she provide for her children on her own and not be forced to live on someone else's charity? And most importantly, where was Jacob and how would she find him? These questions swirled through her weary mind as she slipped off to sleep, her drying tears leaving a trail of despair on her pretty face.

Chapter Twenty-One

Albert awoke as the first light of morning seeped onto the eastern horizon. It was the second week of February, and he had been in Dresden nearly a month now. After much discussion, Albert had chosen to stay in Dresden in hopes of Jacob locating him, should he escape the concentration camp or be released from it. Gottlieb and the other men had kept traveling west. They had made a plan that as soon as a safe place was found, Olof would call the Dresden train station and leave a message for Albert. The call came a week after the men had parted company. The message Olof had left was that they were in Scheessel, Germany. Emil, Edward, and Olof had found jobs and the men had a place to stay. Albert was to meet them there after he reunited with Jacob.

Albert had been fortunate to be in Dresden before the mass number of refugees flooded the city. The Red Army was pushing the Nazis back and the relocated Germans were fleeing ahead of the combat. Albert had been able to find a job at a factory and a man he worked beside offered him a room in his home. Now, with the unbelievable number of people seeking refuge, there was not an empty room in all of Dresden. Some of the refugees had been forced to live in the allies, all their belongings in carts they had hastily packed and brought along. It was a sad state of affairs, to be sure.

Rolling out of bed, Albert got dressed for work. Following his nose to the kitchen, he was greeted with a warm bowl of oatmeal. Hanna smiled as she handed the bowl to Albert and he took a seat at the kitchen table. He was joined a short time later by Christof, Hanna's husband, who had invited Albert to stay with them. The two men talked of the weather and discussed their job. The factory they worked at built weapons for the Nazis. When they had scraped the last of the warm porridge from their bowls, they prepared to leave for the day. Hanna handed them each a lunch and they headed for the door.

The factory was not far from Christof's house and the men took off at a brisk pace to get their blood pumping, attempting to stay warm as they walked to work. Another man joined them as they trekked toward the factory.

"Good morning, Olis," Albert said. "It's another cold morning."

"Yes," Olis agreed. "I'm ready for spring and warmer weather."

"Me, too," Albert replied. "If I still lived in Bessarabia, I would be preparing all the implements for spring planting right now."

"If you still lived in Bessarabia, it would mean Germany hadn't went to war with all its neighbors and caused the whole world to get involved," Christof said dryly.

"That's true," Albert said, "and I would be with my wife and sons, and my brother wouldn't be in a concentration camp right now."

"Have you heard any news about your brother?" Olis asked.

"No," Albert said. "I just hope Jacob finds a way to escape the camp. It's why I'm still here in Dresden. I know Jacob will look for me here, because he has no idea where else I could be."

"Just look at all these poor people," Christof said as he gazed at the homeless refugees in the allies all along the way. "They have nothing left to call their own. No home, no country, and no future to offer their children."

"And yet they press on," Albert said, "with the faith that things will get better. It's what I do each and every day. I hope and pray that I'm reunited with my brother and we find our wives and children. I have no home of my own, no country to pledge my allegiance to, but if I could just get my family back together, it would be enough. The rest is just stuff that, in time, can be replaced. But my family; they mean everything to me."

"I can't imagine being uprooted from my home like you have been, Albert," Christof said, "and then separated from all of my family. I don't know if I could survive all you have been through."

"I walk by faith, not by sight," Albert said. "It's the only way I have endured the last four years."

The men reached the factory and clocked in for their ten hour shift. The sun would make its way across the sky and be sinking toward the west by the time they were finished for the day. The job was long and tiring but Albert was thankful for the income. He had been able to pay Christof and Hanna for his room and board and save some money to use to locate his family, when the time came. A shoe box under his bed held all his extra money, money that would hopefully help his family make a new start once the war ended.

That evening after a supper of beans and cornbread, Albert passed the time with Christof and his family. Christof and Hanna had three children and it made Albert long for his own sons that much more. He had played checkers with the oldest child, a boy of twelve, and then everyone had joined in a game of rummy. As the time neared ten o'clock, they all prepared for bed.

As Albert lay waiting for sleep that wouldn't come, he thought of Emilie and his boys. Had they made it to safety? Were they warm and well fed? Whispering a prayer, Albert put them back in God's hands, for Albert's hands could not reach or find them. But God knew exactly where they were and what they were in need of. As that comforting thought calmed Albert's spirit, he began to drift off. Suddenly, he could hear a motor getting louder. Bolting upright, Albert shoved his legs in his pants and grabbed his shirt and shoes.

"Christof! Wake up! There's a plane flying overhead!"

"What is it, Albert?" Christof asked coming from his bedroom half asleep.

"I just heard a plane fly very near," Albert said, putting on his shirt and shoes.

"There's been no air raid siren alerting us to go to a bomb shelter," Christof said.

"I know what I heard. Please, get your family and let's take shelter."

"Okay," Christof agreed, "if you think we should."

"Yes, I think we should!"

Albert helped Christof and Hanna get their family woke and bundled up for the walk to the bomb shelter. It was true, no siren had been sounded but Albert felt an urgency to get to safety. He was being led by an unseen force that he could not deny.

Within five minutes of entering the shelter, the ground shook with the first of many bombs. Other Dresden inhabitants came pouring in, panicked by the unforeseen attack.

"Do you think it's the Red Army dropping those bombs?" Christof asked.

"I'm certain of it," Albert said. "Who else would bomb Dresden right here at the end of the war? The US and Britain have already reclaimed most of the territory to the west of Germany. The Soviets are the ones coming from the east. With Dresden being on Germany's eastern border, it must be the Red Army dropping those bombs."

The bombing continued through the night and into the next day. When the families finally emerged from the bomb shelter on February 14th, 1945, they were horrified at what they saw. Not only had the beautiful city of Dresden been bombed mercilessly, but fires could be seen burning all throughout the city. Whole sections of the city had been leveled while others had been consumed by fire.

As Albert, Christof, and his family made their way through Dresden toward their home, there was destruction in every direction. Reaching their street, they found nothing but piles of rubble where their home had been. What hadn't been destroyed by bombs had been consumed by fire. There was not one home left on the entire street where their home had once stood.

"Who would do such a cruel thing?" Albert muttered.

"The United States Air Force," a man standing nearby replied.

"What? Why?" Albert couldn't believe what the man said but the facts trickled to him over the next few hours. It had been the US who had bombed Dresden. Maybe they were trying to stop the railcars from carrying weapons and supplies to the Nazis. Maybe they were attempting to destroy the weapons factory. One thing was for certain, it was a senseless, ruthless act of war. The Nazis were doomed to lose this war that Hitler had started. Bombing Dresden would not do one thing to change that outcome. Albert was sickened by the thought.

Over the next weeks, Albert and Christof, joined by Olis,

worked side by side helping other people try and locate family members. Very few times did the search for loved ones end with someone being found alive, if at all. With the city being overwhelmed with refugees without homes to begin with, it was nearly impossible to reunite families who had been separated during the bombing. More often than not, they were presumed to be among the tens of thousands who lay dead from injuries or charred beyond recognition.

The overwhelming number of unidentifiable corpses were finally piled on railroad ties and burned. There were no other options. The decaying bodies had to be dealt with and there were not enough graves to bury them in. Albert did his part to help, as heart wrenching as it was. He thought he had lived through the worst of this war. He was wrong.

Albert and Christof pulled together some rubble to provide a little shelter for Christof's family. It wasn't much but it was all they had. Any building that was left standing after the bombing and fire was packed full with now homeless people. It would take years to rebuild Dresden, and it would never, ever be the same again. In time, the city would pick up the pieces and its occupants would heal, but the scar left by the bombing would forever be deep and ugly.

****

The entire building where Jacob slept at the concentration camp was full of beds, though many were empty now. The outer walls had beds mounted to them four high all the way around. There was just enough room for a man to slip in between the beds to sleep, but only on his back. Ladders were at the foot of the beds extending from bottom to top, to enable the men to get to their bunk. The rest of the interior of the building was filled with rows of bunk beds that had been crudely nailed together. There was a very narrow aisle to walk between the rows of beds.

Jacob awoke in the concentration camp with the same dread as the previous 60 days. He knew that was the number of days he had been at the camp by the marks he had made on the wall beside him. By those calculations, Jacob knew that it was mid-March. He had been placed on the very top bed on an outer wall because he still had strength to climb up and down the ladder. Everyone else was so malnourished they could barely walk outside for roll call. It was a miserable existence, to say the least. How some of these poor souls had stayed alive for four years in this place was a mystery to Jacob.

Each day, men disappeared from the camp at an alarming rate. According to other men in the camp, as time had passed there had been those who had left and never returned, thought to have taken ill and died. But now, whole groups of men were disappearing. An awful stench had begun to filter into the camp, and smoke could be seen from fires burning about a quarter mile away. Heavy equipment could also be heard running for hours each day.

No one knew exactly what was happening nor did they want to discuss it. Jacob had discovered this the first time he had tried to bring it up and was ignored. If no one talked about the oddities of what was taking place, it seemed easier to ignore the possibility that men were being murdered, burned and buried in mass numbers. He had been avoided like a plague after he questioned the obvious, marked as the person who threw water on the now low burning embers of hope these men had. The only news they had been interested in obtaining from Jacob was how the war was progressing, and would help arrive for them soon, before it was too late to matter.

Jacob rolled over and looked below him. Being able to roll over was one of the luxuries of a top bunk, though there were really absolutely no luxuries to be had in the camp. Peering down, Jacob could see the three men who resembled skeletons sleeping below him.

Jacob might have still been asleep, too, if it hadn't been for the lice gnawing on his scalp. Bed bugs had also left his ankles ringed with bites, making him scratch until he bled. It was hard to believe that as malnourished as everyone was that anything would attempt to feed on them, but the lice and bed bugs persisted, making the men even more miserable.

Rolling to his back, Jacob stared at the ceiling as the first rays of sunlight began to illuminate the room. At least there were a few windows to allow the light in. He wondered what was happening outside the fence of this prison. Had the Allies pushed further into western Germany? Had the Soviets overtaken the German troops and pushed past the border of eastern Germany? If

Germany fell, would everyone in the concentration camps be set free? It seemed Hitler was surrounded with no way out. What would be his next move?

Jacob's thoughts then wandered to Magdalena and the boys. He hated to allow his mind to think about them, for the sadness it brought made his chest ache. He gasped for air, trying to fill his lungs. There was so much he didn't know! Had they made it to safety? Were they being cared for?

There was one thing he did know. Albert had been right. No matter how much he disliked Adolf Hitler, he should have kept his mouth shut. Nothing good had come from him voicing his opinion. Now, he was stuck in this concentration camp and not able to look for his family. He had allowed his temper to boil over, and his loss of self-control had cost him his freedom and perhaps his very life.

Jacob could hear others waking and beginning to stir. Rising from his bed, Jacob lowered himself to the floor to get ready for roll call. Sometimes they would be forced to stand for hours in formations. Jacob supposed the guards had no other way to spend their time, and it made them feel in control to make a group of half-starved men stand in perfect lines for hours at a time. If a man fell to the ground during the long ordeal, he was beaten in front of the rest of the men then dragged away for more punishment. Lately, those men were never seen again. Jacob could not believe the things he saw happening in this camp. He wondered if others would believe the stories he would tell when he left here. Of course, he would have to be alive to tell the stories and that hope was dimming daily.

Almost all of the men in the camp were Jews. Like Jacob, these men had committed no real crimes. They just happened to be born with the wrong Nationality, according to Hitler's way of thinking. To think someone would attempt to wipe out a whole group of people made Jacob shiver. And not just any group. The Jews were God's chosen people. They were the seed of Abraham, Isaac, and Jacob. The Jewish people were proof of God's promise to make Abraham's descendants countless in number, like the stars in the heavens or the sand on the seashore. Judgment would come for Hitler, maybe on earth, but definitely before his Maker.

Jacob shuffled forward as the men formed a line to take their turn at the latrine. When they were finished there, they would be herded back to their barracks to form lines outside for roll call. Jacob had witnessed a few times when a man's name was called and he was not present. The guards would turn the place upside down looking for him. If he wasn't found, those who were listed close to the man in the line were all questioned. Jacob hoped to be one of those men soon, one that the guards did not know where he had disappeared to. He hadn't figured out exactly how to escape but he turned the thought and plan over in his mind daily.

Leaving the latrine, Jacob went to take his place for roll call. It had been bitterly cold to stand outside for the morning ritual during January and February, but the mid-March weather was more tolerable. Today, Jacob noticed there were several more men missing. Since their names were not called off by the guard, Jacob knew they had been disposed of. The men in this camp could mull around in denial all they wanted to, but Jacob knew the truth. The Germans were murdering the inhabitants of this concentration camp. How they were doing it was the question Jacob couldn't answer.

Two hours into roll call, the man in front of Jacob began to waiver. Jacob knew he was on the verge of collapse. Very slowly, Jacob reached out his hand and grasped the man's clothing at his waistline. Jacob knew if the man fell this would be the last sunrise he would ever see. He also knew the man had a wife and three children on the outside somewhere. Yes, they were probably in another concentration camp, but at least it gave the man a reason to fight for every breath he took.

Finally, they were herded like animals to the dining area, or such as they called it. Dining was not how Jacob would describe what happened in that building. There was very little food, and what food there was tasted awful. This morning they were serving oatmeal, as they had every other morning since Jacob arrived. As Jacob took his from the cook he noticed it was mostly water, thin and tasteless as usual. As he sat down at the table to eat, his first spoonful revealed black pieces floating among the oats. Jacob pretended they were raisins as he swallowed the bite whole without chewing. He knew they were really rat droppings, but maybe they would contain some protein. It was humiliating that he had been forced to such a low level of existence but there was no way to turn back the clock.

Sometimes he would close his eyes while he ate and dream of one of Magdalena's many fine meals. It rarely worked to try and trick his taste buds, but every now and then it did, which made the effort worth it. He knew he had to keep pushing on, keeping Magdalena and the boys pictured in his mind. It was the reason he took the next bite and his very next breath.

After breakfast, the men were allowed to be outside for a while. Jacob enjoyed the sunshine even though the air was still chilly. He sank down next to a building with the sun shining full on him, warming his frail body and lifting his spirits. Closing his eyes, he thought of all the things he would have been doing had he still been on the farm in Poland. He envisioned the wheat he had planted last fall beginning to show signs of growth, the slender green blades glistening with dew on a sunny morning. He could smell the hay in the loft and feel the caress of warm breath on his neck from his team of horses as he hooked them in the harness. In his mind's eye, he watched Erhard, now thirteen years old, climb onto the plow seat and set the team in motion, the earth turning over in neat slices as he plowed a field. It was the life Jacob had grown up doing and had been passing down to his sons. Now, it was all gone. There was no farm to return to in Poland, just like there was nothing left for him in Bessarabia.

"Jacob Grieb," the commanding voice made Jacob jerk back to reality.

"Yes, that's me," Jacob replied, standing to his feet.

"You need to come with me," the camp guard informed him.

"Yes, sir," Jacob answered, falling into step right behind the guard. Jacob was led to a building he had never been in before. Once inside, he was taken to a room where about 40 other men waited instruction.

"You all need to strip off your clothing," the guard instructed. "We are going to allow you to take a shower to help get rid of some of the lice."

Jacob knew there was no option. They would do as they were told or they would be killed. Besides, a shower sounded good. Jacob was filthy and vermin infested. Who would be crazy enough to refuse a shower?

Jacob quickly removed his shoes and stripped off the filthy striped uniform. The thought of putting the garment back on after he was clean brought a feeling of revulsion, but Jacob knew the hope of being given a clean one was far-fetched. The uniform hadn't even been clean when he was stripped upon his arrival to the camp and demanded to put it on two months earlier. It looked as if the guards had removed it from a man who had no use of it anymore and brought it straight to Jacob. Perhaps that was exactly the way it had happened. Jacob had tried not to give the uniform much thought or contemplate the fate of its previous inhabitants.

Once the men had stripped, they were led down a hallway with writing and an arrow on the wall that read "To the showers". The thought of being clean compelled the men forward. Coming to a ramp, they began to descend into a chamber. There was a guard standing at the top of the ramp to follow the group from behind. Jacob was the last man to come to the ramp, as he was in the back of the line.

"Jacob Grieb?" the guard asked as Jacob approached.

"Yes," Jacob replied, looking up into a familiar face. "Hullo, Gunter. It's been a few years since we've seen one another."

"I haven't seen you since we left Bessarabia," Gunter said. "What are you doing here?

"I was arrested for voicing my opinion," Jacob replied.

"Listen to me," Gunter whispered. "I'm going to shut this door behind this group of men. When I do, you run back up the hall and put your clothes on. Go back to your barracks and wait for me. I'll explain later. Now, go!"

Jacob tried to question the guard's instructions, but the Gunter turned his back as if he couldn't hear him and closed the door to the chamber. Jacob thought about the shower he had been promised and wanted to argue, but an urgent feeling to run for his life came over him. Something about this whole scene was not right.

Jacob ran back up the hall he had been led down and entered the room where his clothes were still lying on the floor. He quickly pulled the ragged, striped jumpsuit on and slipped his feet back into his shoes. Exiting the room, Jacob made his way back out of the building watching for any guards who might recognize him. Once outside, Jacob quickly made his way back to his barracks and climbed to his top bunk. He lay very still trying to calm his beating heart and not bring attention to himself, not that anyone still in the barracks would notice. Those who didn't take advantage of outdoor time were too ill to care if Jacob Grieb returned to his bunk early.

Thirty minutes later, Gunter showed up. Jacob remembered him well. They had attended school together and the man was a good customer at the mill and grocery store that Jacob had owned with his family. Gunter walked straight to Jacob and demanded he come with him. Jacob obeyed without any questions.

"Meet me at the front gate after dark," Gunter instructed once they were outside and away from other prisoners. "I will help you escape. You cannot be here in the morning for roll call. You're supposed to be dead right now."

"What?" Jacob stammered.

"You were not going to take a shower," Gunter informed Jacob. "You were going to a gas chamber where you would have been killed. Believe me; I know what I'm talking about."

"So, that's where all the men are disappearing to?"

"Yes," Gunter replied. "This war is almost over. Germany will be defeated. They have stepped up the killing of the Jews before the Allies move in to rescue them."

"Oh, dear God," Jacob gasped.

"Be there tonight," the guard commanded. "I won't be able to save you again."

The guard quickly moved away from Jacob. As the reality of his words sank in, Jacob crumpled against the building he was standing beside. He had been minutes from death! There was no doubt in Jacob's mind that God had delivered him from the gas chamber by placing that guard there. Overwhelmed by the realization, Jacob gasped for his next breath. He knew that he needed to pull himself together, and began to make a conscious effort to do so. He had to survive in this camp a few more hours then make sure he was at the gate when darkness fell. It was his final chance at escaping. If he was present in the camp for the next morning's roll call, he would never see another sunrise or his family this side of heaven.

As darkness fell, Jacob climbed down from his top bunk. The man below him asked where he was going and Jacob muttered "not feeling well", and kept walking. He would not be stopping unless a guard demanded him to do so.

Once outside, Jacob stayed close to the exterior walls of buildings to remain in the shadows and made his way toward the front gate. His palms were sweaty and he could not fill his lungs with enough air. The fear of staying, however, was greater than the fear of trying to escape, so Jacob pressed on. When he was almost to the gate, Jacob noticed a guard standing in the shadows. Stopping to watch for a minute, Jacob was relieved to hear the guard whisper.

"Is that you, Jacob?"

"Yes, I'm here," Jacob replied.

Gunter came to stand beside Jacob in the dark. "I have a plan," Gunter said. "I will distract the guard at the gate by telling him he is needed elsewhere and I have been sent to cover his post until he returns. When he leaves, you come and I will let you out."

"Okay," Jacob said breathlessly.

"Here, take these," Gunter said, shoving a bundle into his hands. "They're clothes you can change into once you're outside the gate. It will make it easier for you to get away."

"Thank you," Jacob said, "for everything."

"You would have done the same for me," Gunter whispered.

"I have one more question," Jacob said, needing to know the answer but not really wanting to hear the truth.

"Yes, quickly," Gunter whispered.

"What is the awful smell and where does the smoke come from?" Jacob asked.

"It's the way they dispose of the bodies after they are removed from the gas chamber," Gunter said quietly. "Now, get ready to run from this place or it will be yours we are piling to be burned tomorrow."

Jacob knew he had guessed right about what the awful stench had been, but hearing his friend confirm it did not ease the feeling that followed. To think one man could convince an army of men to kill innocent men, women, and children just because he had deemed them inferior made Jacob shudder, and a cold sweat trickled from his skin. He wished he could do something for the rest of the men in the camp but he was marked for death. There would be no second chance to escape if he missed this one.

Watching from the shadows, Jacob saw the plan unfold. The guard at the gate left his post and Jacob's friend took over. Jacob quickly made his way to the gate and was let out. "Hurry," the guard warned. "Run!"

It was the last words Jacob heard as he began to run from the camp. He had no idea where he was going but knew he couldn't stop until he was far away. His legs cramped and he could feel the weakness throughout his body. Starvation had taken a toll on him but he had to keep moving. Finally, a grove of trees came into view. Jacob quickly ducked into them, hoping to find cover, even though there were no leaves on the limbs yet. Slowing his pace, Jacob moved deeper into the woods. When he could no longer see the road, he stopped to catch his breath.

When Jacob could finally breathe normal, he opened the bundle the guard had given him. Stripping the filthy camp uniform off, Jacob pulled the regular clothes on, along with a coat. At least he would blend in better. The fact that he needed a shave, haircut, and bath would have to wait.

Jacob started walking again, leaving the camp uniform buried under a rock. He looked up at the clear night sky to see the moon and stars. They would have to be his compass. The moon was just making its appearance at the horizon, so Jacob knew that direction was east. He decided to keep the moon at his back, since he had no idea where he was. The Red Army was coming from the east, and the United States was coming from the west. Heading west was his best option.

As the sun rose, Jacob came upon a stream of water. Sinking to his knees, he plunged his cupped hands in and drew them up to his mouth. Drinking deeply, he allowed the refreshment to wash down his dry throat then filled his hands again. He would have to drink enough to last for a while, since he had no container to fill for later.

After drinking his fill, Jacob stood and surveyed his surroundings. As the landscape began to brighten with the sun's ascent, he could make out the roofs of buildings in the distance. He needed to find food, and a town would be a good place to start. Begging would be his only option, which was something Jacob had never done before. The thought made the water he had so enjoyed turn bitter.

The decision made, Jacob started toward the town. When he entered, he considered trying the motel but then decided to find a home instead. If the guards from the camp came looking for him, they were more likely to stop at a business rather than homes. He would be remembered, as disheveled as his appearance was. Taking side streets, Jacob began to scan houses as he walked along. Two boys came out of one of the houses, books under their arms and hands clutching lunch pails. Jacob knew they were headed to school and decided he would try begging at their house. A mutti had prepared those lunches and Jacob knew she would still be home.

Stepping behind a tree on the opposite side of the street, Jacob watched the boys pass. He then crossed the street and headed toward the house's back door. The fewer people who saw him would result in fewer reports to give the searching Nazis. Stepping up on the stoop, Jacob knocked lightly on the door. A woman opened it then gasped at the sight of the unkempt man. Jacob thought she was about to scream, so he spoke quickly. "Please, don't be afraid. I was just wondering if you might have some scraps of food you could spare."

"Who are you?" the woman demanded.

"I am a relocated German from Bessarabia," Jacob said. "My family and I were living in Poland when the Red Army began to attack. My wife and three sons were sent by train to somewhere in southern Germany, but I have no idea where. I had to run for my life as the Red Army began to push the German troops westward. Please, I just need a little food and I will be on my way."

"Wait here," the woman replied and closed the door.

Jacob didn't know whether to wait or run for his life. He had no idea if the woman had a telephone and was calling the Gestapo or gathering him food. Jacob nervously glanced around to see if anyone was watching or coming his way. It would not do for the woman's neighbors to see him on her stoop. Just when he had decided to turn and flee, the door opened.

"This should be enough food for today," the woman said, handing him a canvas bag. "I included a jar of water, too."

"Thank you so much for your kindness," Jacob said, accepting the offered gift. "You have just saved my life."

"You're welcome," the woman replied, "and I will forget I ever saw you."

Jacob looked into her face and knew she understood more

than she was admitting to. Living this close to the camp, she had to know of some of the evil that took place there. Still, he knew she would be shocked if he told her they were killing innocent people in gas chambers. He could hardly believe it himself and he had stood on the threshold of being put to death in one. The thought caused an involuntary shudder to pass through Jacob's body.

"Thank you, again," Jacob said quietly, turning to walk away as quickly as possible. He did not want to bring any harm to this kind woman or her family.

"Wait," the woman called out, disappearing into the house again. She returned a few minutes later with a wool blanket. Handing it to Jacob, she smiled and said, "It's cold out this morning. You may need this."

"Thank you," Jacob replied, tucking the blanket under his arm. He walked out of the town using side streets and keeping out of sight. When he was finally on the road heading west again, he began to look for a place to hide and eat his food. There were some pine trees ahead and he decided that would give him plenty of cover. The ground would be covered with pine needles, making it a soft place to get some sleep. He was truly exhausted after walking all night with no food in his body for energy. Picking up his pace, Jacob headed toward the seclusion of the pines and the much needed sleep his body was craving.

Jacob sat down in the pine thicket and opened the canvas bag. The woman had given him a whole loaf of bread, six cheese slices, a dozen cookies, and a jar of water. It was more food than Jacob had seen at one time in months. He began to devour the cookies first then slowed himself. He would just be sick if he ate too much after such a long time without a decent meal. Allowing himself one slice of bread with a piece of cheese, Jacob ate slowly, savoring every morsel. He then finished the second cookie he had started on and put the rest back in the bag. After taking a long drink of water, Jacob leaned back against the trunk of one of the pines. Replacing the lid on the water jar, Jacob set it aside. Drawing the blanket up over the length of his body, Jacob slipped off to sleep in minutes. His last thoughts were of Magdalena and his sons and how he would begin looking for them as soon as he got some rest and regained some strength.

Chapter Twenty-Two

Magdalena was in the camp five days before she came to a decision. She had no idea where Jacob was and there was no way for her to search for him. He may still be in Poland, though she doubted it.

The reports Gerda had heard confirmed the Red Army had pushed the German troops past where their farm had been located. Jacob would have fled before taking a chance on being captured by the Red Army, or at least Magdalena hoped he had. She prayed he had been able to make it to Germany ahead of the Red Army. If he had gotten caught in the middle of the combat, there was a very slim chance he had survived.

Magdalena would not dwell on the possibilities of what may have happened to Jacob. She had three sons depending on her and she had to stay focused on their needs. She was a strong, capable woman who had always been known to take matters into her own hands and this predicament was no different.

Magdalena had been surveying the land around the camp. It was surrounded by farms and Magdalena knew all about that kind of work. Physical labor was her specialty and she would apply it now.

"We're going to look for jobs," Magdalena informed Erhard just after breakfast. "You're plenty old enough and have experience in farming. We are surrounded by farms and you and I can earn enough to at least feed us. We will have to sleep at the camp but during the day we can work. Ewald will watch Werner."

"Okay," Erhard replied. "I'm ready to do something anyway besides sit around and wait for this war to end. It's like life has been put on hold."

"I agree," Magdalena replied. "Just sitting and waiting will not bring your vater to find us any faster. Maybe when the war is over we will start looking him."

"We could," Erhard said, "but maybe we should just stay here until he finds us. If we keep moving around, it will make it much harder. Vater will know to check refugee camps first."

"That's true, Erhard," Magdalena agreed, proud of how smart and mature Erhard had become. "In the meantime, we will earn our own keep. Ewald, please put your coat on, and get ready to leave."

"Yes, Mutti," Ewald replied, retrieving his coat that had been hanging on the end of the bunk bed.

Magdalena wrapped Werner in a blanket and placed him in the shawl draped around her neck. The weather was warming, but it was still chilly out since it was only mid-March. Leading the way, Magdalena walked out into the cool, sunny day. Just getting outside lifted her spirits. She could not spend all her days stuck at this camp.

Deciding to head west, Magdalena started walking down the mountain in the opposite direction she and the boys had come up. After two miles, they came upon a farm with several goats and thier new kids in the pasture, along with a flock of sheep on a distant hill. Wheat was sprouting in a field near a creek, and someone was plowing the field next to the growing wheat with horses.

"Probably getting ready to plant barley or oats," Erhard surmised, observing the farm. "I've never dealt with sheep, but I suppose I could learn. Any goat I've ever had the displeasure of meeting was a nuisance."

"I think this would be a good place to start," Magdalena said smiling. "It reminds me of Bessarabia and the wonderful life we had there."

"Do you think we'll ever have that life again?" Erhard asked.

"I honestly don't think so, Son," Magdalena replied. "However, I would be happy if we just found your vater and were all together again."

"Yes, me too," Ewald chimed in.

Magdalena led the way down the long lane toward the house and barn that was nestled in the surroundings of pasture and fields. She could hear the cackle of hens announcing an egg they had just laid. Horses nickered from the corral and goats bleated to their new babies. The smell of hay and manure took her back to better days, days filled with wonderful memories. Until that moment, Magdalena had never stopped to consider all the changes the war had forced upon them and the things that had been left behind, never to be obtained again.

Shaking herself from her reverie, Magdalena walked toward the back door of the house. After knocking, she looked around at the scene from close up as she waited for someone to answer the door.

"Maybe we should try the barn," Ewald suggested.

"Yes," Magdalena agreed. "At this time of morning, I'm sure everyone's outside doing something."

Walking to the barn, Magdalena pulled open a small side door. Entering, she scanned the barn for a person. Hearing a woman's voice and the bleating of goats, Magdalena followed the sound. She came upon a small woman milking away, singing to the beat of the stream of liquid hitting the bucket. Not wanting to startle her, Magdalena waited until the song and accompaniment stopped.

"Excuse me," Magdalena began. The woman spun around on her stool, startled by the interruption. "I'm sorry," Magdalena smiled, surprised by how young the woman was. "I didn't mean to scare you. You have a wonderful voice, by the way."

"Why, thank you," the woman replied. "What can I do for you?"

"I was wondering if you need any help on your farm," Magdalena said. "My son, Erhard, is experienced in many areas, such as plowing, planting, disking and harvesting crops. He's a good, hard worker. I can milk, make cheese, and work in the fields as needed. To be honest, I can help with just about anything on a farm."

"You are an answer to my prayers," the woman laughed. "My husband was forced to join the German troops at the beginning of this war. I have been trying to keep this farm running ever since. Teenage boys in the area have helped in the past but as soon as they turn 18, Hitler grabs them up, puts a uniform on their back and a gun in their hands. Where are you from? I've never seen you around here."

"We are from Bessarabia, Romania," Magdalena replied. "We were forced to leave there when the Red Army invaded. Hitler invited us back to the Reich and our family was eventually relocated to Poland. Now, the Red Army has pushed the German troops back all the way to Warsaw, and the women and children were evacuated south by train. We have been at a deserted Army barracks about two miles up the mountain for five days. It's become a refugee camp for some of the women and children fleeing Poland."

"This war has disrupted everyone's life," the woman replied, shaking her head at the sadness of it all. "My name is Lizzy. It would help me more than you can imagine for you and your son to come work for me."

"I'm Magdalena, and these are my sons Erhard, Ewald, and Werner. Ewald will care for Werner while I work."

"I have extra rooms in my house," Lizzy replied. "You and your sons are welcome to stay here. No sense in walking two miles twice a day. I need all your energy used right here on this farm."

"Thank you so much for your kindness," Magdalena replied.

"I can't pay much but there will be plenty of food," Lizzy added.

"Whatever you can pay will be fine," Magdalena said. "It has to be better than living cramped up in those barracks. I need fresh air and sunshine."

"Let me finish milking these goats and then I'll show you around the place," Lizzy replied.

"Erhard and I will help you," Magdalena offered. "The job will be done in no time."

"Have you both milked before?" Lizzy asked.

"Yes," Magdalena replied. "We owned a herd of dairy cows in Bessarabia and a couple milk cows in Poland. We both are experienced at milking."

"Cows and goats should milk the same," Lizzy replied. "Goats just have half the equipment and twice the orneriness. Of course, you won't get near as much milk from a goat."

"The cheese is good," Erhard added, the teenage boy's mind never wandering far from the thought of food.

"Yes, it is," Lizzy said. "With you two to help, maybe I can keep up with the demand, now."

"I saw your goats have little ones," Magdalena said. "Are you milking all of the does?"

"No," Lizzy replied. "I have 50 does and there is just no way for me to milk them all. I've been rotating the herd. The nannies usually birth twice a year and I milk 25 of them in the spring, and the other 25 in the fall. It has actually kept them healthier."

"Maybe with our help you can go back to milking the whole herd," Magdalena suggested.

"We will certainly try," Lizzy replied. "Cheese keeps a long time, so we will make extra as long as I have your help."

Magdalena, Erhard and Lizzy set to work getting the rest of the herd of goats milked while Ewald entertained Werner with a barn kitten he had found. Ewald took great pride in showing Werner all the fun things a kitten could do. The kitten pounced on sprigs of hay as Ewald pulled them along and chased its own tail when Ewald touched the tail to its nose. Werner laughed and chased after the kitten and his brother, toddling clumsily along.

When all the goats had been milked, Magdalena and the boys followed Lizzy into the house with cans of milk in tow. Setting them down in the kitchen, Magdalena and Lizzy went to work straining the milk and getting ready to make cheese. Magdalena felt as if she had come home after months of being gone. To do something so familiar brought a joy she had not felt for some time, and it took her mind from the constant worry of where Jacob was and how they would ever find one another.

"Why don't Erhard and Ewald go back to the barracks and gather your things?" Lizzy suggested. "By the time they return, we should have the noon meal prepared."

"Okay," Magdalena agreed, adding rennet to the warm milk to make it coagulate.

"We will hurry back," Erhard promised, already thinking of the food that would be waiting for him upon their return, "if I can keep Ewald from dawdling."

"Please leave a message with all the women in our barracks and at the office where our name was added to the refugee list. Tell them where we are staying," Magdalena said. "When your vater comes looking, I want him to be able to find us."

"So, you don't know where your husband is?" Lizzy asked.

"No, and we were separated from my sister and her five sons

when a US military truck picked them up on the road a couple months ago. Jacob, my husband, was forced to remain in Poland, along with all the other men. I have heard since that the Germans who had been living in Poland were fleeing toward Germany ahead of the Red Army. The Nazis were not successful in holding the Red Army back as they crossed the Vistula River."

"It seems the Nazis are falling on all fronts. Do you have other family?"

"Yes," Magdalena replied. "I have four brothers who stayed behind in Poland, along with my husband's brothers, Albert and Olof. My vater, Gottlieb, is in Poland too, along with my uncle, Daniel. My mutti, Rosina, and Jacob's mutti, Juliana, left on a different train, along with Juliana's three daughters and Mutti's sister, Isabella, and her daughter, Agathe. We have all been separated."

"So, everyone you love and hold dear is missing from your life, except for your sons?" Lizzy asked.

"Yes, and I came to the mountain in hopes of locating Emilie, but she's not here," Magdalena said, trying not to give in to the despair that threatened to pull her under. "I don't know where else to look."

"Hopefully you will all be able to find each other once the war is over," Lizzy said.

"It will be a miracle if we do," Magdalena admitted for the first time. "We have no home to return to, so we don't even have any hope of reuniting back there. We are like dandelions that have gone to seed and have been blown by the wind in all different directions." She honestly had no idea how any of them would ever find each other again. The joy she had felt just moments earlier making the cheese was snuffed out as she told Lizzy about her family.

****

Emilie had been in Stuttgart, Germany, for over two months now and still had not been able to locate Magdalena. Emilie was living in a displaced persons camp that had been set up for all the refugees who had nowhere to call home. There had been numerous air raids and the city of Stuttgart lay in ruin. The Allied forces had defeated the Nazis in a battle now being referred to as the Battle of the Bulge and were now occupying the city. They were assisting with food supplies and medical attention to those in need.

At least her mutti, Rosina, and the rest of the women had found their way to Stuttgart. It seemed to be the place most of the women and children who had been in Bessarabia originally had ended up.

But where had Magdalena disappeared to? Was she picked up by a passing vehicle? Had she and her sons frozen to death before they found shelter? Why had Magdalena insisted that she get into that first US military truck that offered a ride?

Emilie could answer the last question that had formed in her mind. It because Magdalena was the strong one, plain and simple, and she always had been. She took charge and was a bit bossy as she did so. Magdalena had always met life head on, pushing through whatever circumstances came her way. Emilie was sure she was still alive, but where had she ended up?

"What are you thinking about, Daughter?" Rosina asked, startling Emilie from her thoughts.

"Not what, but who," Emilie admitted. "I was just thinking of Magdalena."

"Magdalena is strong," Rosina reminded. "She will figure things out on her own. We will all find each other when this war ends."

"I know, Mutti," Emilie said. "It's just that Magdalena and I have never been separated before."

"That's true," Rosina said. "Maybe this is a good trial for you. I fear after the war ends you and your sister will be separated by a whole ocean."

"What do you mean?" Emilie asked.

"Jacob has made no secret about the fact he would like to move to America," Rosina replied. "I believe he will go the first chance he gets when this war is over."

"Do you really think Magdalena will move to America?" Emilie asked.

"I think Magdalena will do as her husband says," Rosina replied. "It will not be her choice."

"Yes," Emilie agreed, "she will do as Jacob says."

Even at her strongest, Magdalena would never defy her husband. It was just not the way of German women. The man was the head of the house and his word and wishes were the law. Jacob

Grieb had always had the dream of going to America and the atrocities this war had brought him and his family would just fan the fires of his ambitions. Even if it broke her heart, Magdalena would follow Jacob. They would travel to another continent across a vast ocean. Emilie would be separated from her sister forever if that happened.

Emilie decided to put her thoughts to rest. They all had to find each other, first. There was no sense worrying over the future when the present had so many problems of its own.

****

Magdalena fell into the rhythm of farm life again. She and Lizzy were like kindred spirits. They thought alike and both worked hard until the job was done.

Erhard took over moving the sheep to pasture every morning and bringing them back to the corral at night. He soon discovered that sheep were dumb animals and had to be herded everywhere they went. In the face of danger, they just gave up or ran bleating, guiding their soon to be attacker by sound. For this reason, they had to be kept close to the barn at night.

The boy who had been plowing when they first arrived had to stay at his own farm and help with the spring planting now that Lizzy had some workers. Erhard took over plowing and preparing the field to plant oats. Next, he spread goat and sheep manure on the garden plot and plowed it under followed by disking, preparing the soil for the spring crops.

"What if we put all the kids in stalls at night and milked all fifty nannies in the morning?" Magdalena asked as she and Lizzy worked to move spring vegetable plants from the cold frame to the garden.

"That just might work," Lizzy replied, deep in thought. "We could milk all fifty in the morning and turn them out to pasture with their little ones for the day. It would save some time not having to stop to milk them in the evening."

"That's what I was thinking," Magdalena said. "We could make the cheese in the morning and be pressing it or hanging it all to dry by the noon meal."

"Let's try that tomorrow morning," Lizzy said, quickly coming to a decision.

"Okay," Magdalena replied, scooping broccoli plants out

with the small trowel she was working with.

"We need to put potatoes in the ground tomorrow," Lizzy informed Magdalena. "I looked at the almanac. Today and tomorrow are transplant and plant root crop days."

"I suppose we should cut the potato eyes after we get done here, then," Magdalena replied.

"Yes, they need to have plenty of time to skin over before we plant them," Lizzy said. "I'm so glad I don't have to teach you how to do everything on the farm. It's like you have grown up here."

"Well, I did grow up doing all these things, just on a different farm," Magdalena said with a laugh. "Should we prepare a place to plant carrots, too?"

"Yes, I try to rotate the vegetables to different spots in the garden each year. It seems to help lessen disease and pests. We need to put the carrots on the far end," Lizzy said, pointing to the area she was referring to.

"Okay," Magdalena said. "Do you want these onion starts moved yet?"

"Let's wait until the next transplant day," Lizzy said. "They need to grow just a little bigger."

Magdalena and Lizzy worked side by side transplanting things from the cold frame. Magdalena dug them out and brought them to Lizzy. Lizzy dug the holes and placed the tender plants in the soil. When they were finished, they each grabbed a bucket to get water for the newly moved plants. As they neared the water spigot, which was gravity fed from a spring up on the hill, Magdalena noticed Ewald was standing near it with his little brother. Werner was wailing in protest while standing in a puddle of water, completely nude.

"Ewald," Magdalena scolded, "it's quite chilly out here to have your brother stripped down and spraying him with cold water."

"Look at this mess," Ewald complained. "I laid down with him for his nap and fell asleep, too. When I woke up, his diaper was full and overflowing on me!"

"Oh, Ewald," Magdalena laughed, "you will wash."

"It stinks and it's nasty," Ewald said. "He didn't have to get it all over me."

"I'm sure he didn't plan it that way," Magdalena said with a smile. Ewald was still just a meticulous as ever, never wanting to be dirty.

"Here, you poor thing," Lizzy cooed to Werner as she wrapped the squalling baby in a towel Ewald had brought out with him. She then scooped him up and headed toward the house to warm his shivering little body and put dry clothes on him.

"What am I going to do with you, Ewald?" Magdalena asked, shaking her head. "I'll draw a bucket of water and you can take it in the barn and clean yourself up. I see you've already brought out clean clothes."

"Yes, and I plan to keep them clean," Ewald replied. "Werner will just have to go to sleep on his own from now on."

"Goodness, he's just a baby," Magdalena reminded Ewald. "It's not like he meant for this to happen. I'm sure he didn't enjoy his cold bath any more than you enjoyed his leaky diaper."

"It's disgusting," Ewald complained again, taking the bucket from his mutti. "I probably won't be able to ever wear these clothes again."

"Oh, my," Magdalena laughed. "You'll never know what happened to those clothes after I get done scrubbing them with lye soap. I do want you to rinse them in the bucket of water after you take them off, though."

"Rinse them?" Ewald was disgusted and couldn't believe his mutti had just asked him to do such a thing.

"Yes, rinse them and hang them on the line until I have time to wash them properly."

"Ugh," Ewald said as he trudged to the barn, bucket in one hand and a towel in the other, his clean clothes held under his armpit.

"I already feel sorry for his future wife," Magdalena muttered, heading to the house to comfort Werner.

That evening, they all went to the barn to separate the nannies from their babies. Magdalena placed Werner safely in an empty stall and shut the door. They did not need to worry about the baby being trampled and they needed Ewald's help with the goats.

"Stand here with the stall door open," Magdalena instructed Ewald. "We will run the baby goats toward you. Shut the door if one of the nannies makes it past us or the babies try to get out."

"Okay," Ewald said, assuring his mutti that he had it all under control.

Lizzy, Magdalena, and Erhard corralled the goats and began to separate the nannies from their offspring, herding the babies into the barn. Ewald watched as one baby after another was safely ran into the stall. He moved in front of the opening anytime one tried to escape. When one stall was full, he closed the door and moved to another one. Ten more baby goats had run into the second stall when one tried to come back out. Ewald turned to face the baby goat, closing the stall door to the width of his body. Bending forward, Ewald tried to shoo the kid back, when he was suddenly propelled through the air and head first into the stall. Ewald scrambled back to his feet, goat droppings covering his face and body. Hearing laughter behind him, Ewald turned to see Erhard thoroughly enjoying his predicament.

"That nanny sure gave you a butt," Erhard laughed.

"What's she doing in here?" Ewald demanded, trying to brush off the goat dung.

"She gave me the slip," Erhard laughed, "and she gave you the boot!"

Magdalena and Lizzy came into the barn to see what the trouble was. The baby goats were coming back out as fast as they herded them in. "What happened?" Lizzy asked, taking in Ewald's appearance.

"A nanny got past me and sent Ewald into the stall face first," Erhard chortled.

"I'm covered in manure," Ewald complained, "twice in one day."

"You're going to live," Magdalena assured him. "Brush yourself off and let's get this   finished.

"I need to wash off," Ewald stated.

"When we're done," Magdalena replied, leaving no room for argument.

Erhard had a good laugh again then herded the nanny out of the stall and back outside. Ewald brushed every dropping off and shuddered at the thought of having to wait to wash off. The separating continued until every kid was in a stall away from its mother.

"Lizzy, do you know what you need?" Erhard asked.

"Yes, I do," Lizzy replied. "I need my husband to return from fighting in the war to help me run this farm."

"Well, yes, you do need that," Erhard agreed, "but you also need a good dog to help herd these sheep and goats."

"That's a very good suggestion, Erhard," Lizzy said. "Maybe I'll ask around and see if any litters of puppies have been born. It would certainly make things more exciting around here and the dog would probably make a good companion."

"Not to mention protecting you," Magdalena added. "We had a wonderful dog in Poland. His name was Stein and he protected the boys with every ounce of strength he had. Stein would have given up his life to keep my sons safe."

"I don't know why I didn't get a dog a long time ago," Lizzy said. "My husband didn't see a need for one, but a dog would have been good company these past few years, not to mention making things easier once it was trained."

"We can help you train the dog," Ewald said with excitement, forgetting he was filthy for a moment. "I taught Stein all kinds of tricks."

"Stein was very smart and loyal," Magdalena said, missing the pet all over again and wondering where he was now. There would have been no way for Jacob to take him to Germany with him as he fled. Of course, she would not mention this to Erhard and Ewald. Leaving the dog behind had already upset them enough.

"I will check around tomorrow," Lizzy promised. "You're right, Erhard, a dog is just what I need."

"Erhard, you and Ewald give the goats some grain while Lizzy and I go start supper," Magdalena said. "I'll boil some water so we can take warm baths after we eat. I think we could all use one after this long day of working outside."

Scooping Werner out of the stall, Magdalena followed Lizzy to the house. Magdalena placed Werner on the kitchen floor, with some wooden blocks and empty pans to play with. Lizzy added wood to the stove and opened the damper fully so there would be plenty of heat to boil the water. The stove blazed to life and heat began to build quickly. After a few minutes, Lizzy shut the damper down and the heat increased, making the stove dangerously hot.

A chicken had been simmering in a Dutch oven on the stove

for several hours and Magdalena took it out to debone it. Lizzy began to cut the noodles that she had rolled out earlier and put them in the boiling chicken broth. A quart of green beans had been brought up from the cellar and Magdalena added them to a pan with a small onion and some pepper. Supper would be ready in no time.

With the chicken deboned and waiting to be added back to the noodles when they had cooked, Magdalena busied herself with making biscuits. Putting flour, salt and baking powder in a bowl, she thoroughly mixed the dry ingredients. Next, she cut in lard then added enough milk to make soft dough. After kneading it a few times, Magdalena began to cut the biscuits with a tin cup turned upside down. The biscuits would serve as bread for the meal and dessert, when some of Lizzie's homemade jelly was thickly spread on a buttered half.

Lost in preparing the food, the two women didn't notice Werner leave his blocks and pans and toddle toward them. Just as Magdalena turned with the pan of biscuits ready for the oven, Werner lost his balance and fell face first into the blazing hot stove. A gasp escaped Magdalena's lips as she threw the pan of biscuits back on the counter and grabbed Werner. The baby was screaming from the pain and Magdalena could immediately see the burn was deep. Not knowing what else to do, Magdalena grabbed a towel and dipped it in a crock of cool water. She gently pressed it to Werner's little cheek, praying that he would be okay. Sinking into a kitchen chair with the wailing baby, Magdalena tried to comfort him.

"He's going to need a doctor," Lizzy stated, coming along side Magdalena for a good look at the burn. "That's a very serious burn."

"I know," Magdalena replied, tears pooling in her eyes at the sight of the wound.

"I'll have Erhard hitch up a team to the wagon and we'll take him," Lizzy said. "There's one down the mountain about five miles."

"Okay," Magdalena said, still shocked by what had happened. In an instant, life for Werner had changed forever. Magdalena berated herself for not paying more attention to what he was doing. Her son would forever wear the scar as a result of her not paying attention.

Magdalena wrapped Werner in a warm blanket for the trip to the doctor. The sun was sinking low in the sky and the early April wind was quite chilly. The child had cried to the point that now all he could do was take short, hiccupping breaths as he lay in his mutti's arms.

Erhard brought the wagon close to the house and Magdalena came out with Werner. Lizzy took him from her arms and gently touched her shoulder.

"Magdalena, you need to go put a coat on," Lizzy said softly.

Nodding, Magdalena headed back in the house to do as Lizzy suggested. Returning to the wagon, she crawled up on the seat and Lizzy handed Werner up to her waiting arms. Lizzy then came around to take the seat where Erhard had been.

"Erhard, watch after your brother," Lizzy instructed. "The chicken and noodles and green beans are ready to eat. You can put the biscuits in the oven for about ten minutes and have them, too. When you're finished eating, please put everything in the warming oven and we will eat when we return home."

"Yes, Lizzy," Erhard replied.

With that said, Lizzy tapped the reins against the team's rumps and they were off. Over an hour later, they came to a small town nestled in a valley. It reminded Magdalena of Hoffnungstal in Bessarabia, with one street stretching east to west. Lizzy started down the street and stopped about half way down at a small house that had a sign hanging on a porch post.

"We're here," Lizzy said, hopping down from the wagon and tying the team to the hitching rail.

"I hope he can help," Magdalena fretted, looking down at Werner's seared cheek.

"We will pray he can," Lizzy replied as she reached to take Werner so Magdalena could climb down. Handing Werner back to Magdalena, Lizzy went to knock on the door. An elderly man opened it after a few minutes and peered out at the women.

"What is it this time?" the doctor asked, clearly perturbed at having his evening interrupted.

"My son fell into the wood stove and has been burned," Magdalena said, desperation evident in her voice.

The doctor looked down at Werner's face and a small gasp

escaped his lips. Magdalena knew in the dimming light that he could not see the full extent of the burn, and yet, the seasoned doctor gasped. It was not a good sign. "Bring him in," the doctor ordered.

Lizzy and Magdalena entered the house and followed the doctor to an exam room. The doctor scrubbed his hands thoroughly before turning back to Magdalena. "Lay him on the table," the doctor instructed.

Werner began to cry again as Magdalena place him on the table. The doctor came close to examine the wound. Shaking his head, he began to mutter to himself. He then turned to his cabinet and took out some gauze. "I'm going to clean this burn and cover it," the doctor said. "You will need to be very careful not to let any dirt get into this wound. Keep it covered and change the gauze often."

"Okay," Magdalena answered.

"I won't lie to you," the doctor continued, "this is one of the worst burns I have seen. It will be a miracle if he doesn't get an infection and die."

Magdalena gasped at the doctor's blunt words as tears trickled down her face. How could she have been so careless? Poor little Werner, the baby she had hoped and prayed to conceive, was now lying here with an injury he might not heal from. The thought of losing him threatened to overwhelm her. The room began to spin and spots appeared before her eyes.

"Sit down, Magdalena," Lizzy said, gently pushing her into a chair.

"I'm sorry to be so straightforward," the doctor said, "but I don't want to get your hopes up either. This is a very serious burn. It's so deep I honestly don't know what to treat it with."

"So, we just keep it clean and change the gauze often?" Lizzy asked making sure she knew what had to be done.

"Yes," the doctor replied. "Under no circumstances are you to allow dirt in this wound."

"We will be very careful," Lizzy promised.

"It will be a miracle if he survives," the doctor concluded.

Lizzy wrapped Werner back up for the ride home, attempting to quickly get out of the doctor's house and away from his grim prognosis. Magdalena seemed to have recovered from the shocking words the doctor had blurted and was rising from the chair. The women made their way back to the wagon and Magdalena climbed up then reached for Werner who was cradled in Lizzy's arms. The women knew they were in a fight to save Werner's life and they would work and pray around the clock in order to do it.

"Have faith, Magdalena," Lizzy said as they rode along. "Werner's healthy and his body will fight to heal this wound."

"I just can't believe I allowed this to happen," Magdalena said, tears streaming down her face again.

"Blaming yourself will do no one any good," Lizzy chided. "We just have to concentrate on helping Werner heal."

Magdalena knew in her mind Lizzy was right, but her heart wouldn't accept it. What kind of mutti allows her child to fall into a hot stove? She should have been more attentive to what Werner was doing. She had been engrossed in preparing supper, forgetting to look up and see where Werner was. If only she could turn the clock back, relive that moment in time, she would be able to change the outcome. Werner would not be seriously burned and they would have all been resting after a long day's work, discussing all that needed to be done the next day. If only...

Returning to the house, Lizzy pulled close to the back door. Jumping down, she came around to take a sleeping Werner from Magdalena's arms. As Magdalena clamored down, Erhard came out of the house.

"Is he going to be okay?" Erhard asked.

"We don't know," Magdalena answered truthfully. "We have to be very careful he doesn't get any dirt in the wound. If he gets an infection..." Magdalena couldn't bring herself to finish the sentence. She would work night and day to keep that burn clean. Infection was not going to have a chance on her watch.

"I'll unhitch the wagon and take care of the team," Erhard offered, not knowing what else to say or do.

"Thank you, Erhard," Lizzy replied, heading toward the door with Werner still in her arms. Entering the house, Lizzy went to lay Werner in bed. Magdalena followed close behind, wanting to pick him up and hold him close.

"Let him rest," Lizzy said, seeing the longing in Magdalena's eyes.

"I just want to hold him tight and never let go," Magdalena

admitted.

"I know," Lizzy said, "but rest will help his body work to heal itself."

"Yes, you're right," Magdalena said. "I just can't think straight right now."

"Let's go eat some supper," Lizzy suggested, "and have a cup of hot tea."

Making their way back to the kitchen, Magdalena noticed Ewald sitting at the table for the first time. She supposed she had walked right past him when she came in. She felt like she had a fog around her, not able to see where to go or which way to turn. Life had a way of changing so quickly, like a ball of yarn being unraveled. To Magdalena, it seemed she had spent the last four years winding that ball of yarn up just to see it unravel again.

"How's Werner?" Concern was etched on young Ewald's face.

"Not good, dear," Lizzy answered, saving Magdalena from explaining again.

"Will he get better?" Ewald inquired.

"We will pray that he does," Lizzy said, patting Ewald's hand for assurance. "You may go ahead to bed, now. I know you're tired after getting up at dawn this morning."

"Okay," Ewald replied, giving his mutti a hug before heading off to the bedroom he and Erhard shared. Ewald had even forgotten he needed to take a bath.

Magdalena sank into a kitchen chair. Lizzy dipped plates of food and placed one in front of Magdalena. Bowing their heads, Lizzy gave thanks and prayed a special prayer for Werner's healing. As the women ate, they talked. Lizzy began to open up to Magdalena about her life and struggles and Magdalena did the same. Up until this point, they had been so busy with the farm that they really hadn't had meaningful conversation. Now, in the face of tragedy, they both needed to share.

"I gave birth to a little girl in Bessarabia," Magdalena began. "She was born too early and had no chance of surviving. I was so thankful when I found out I was expecting Werner."

"My husband and I had been married two years before he was drafted into the German troops," Lizzy said. "I got pregnant soon after our marriage but miscarried before I was even three months along."

"I'm so sorry," Magdalena said. "I can see you long for a child each time I watch you with Werner."

"Yes, I do," Lizzy said. "I just pray my husband returns safely and soon. I hope you find your husband, too."

"This is a time when our river of life is flowing heavy with tears," Magdalena said. "My mutti told me that one time, that sometimes tears flood our river of life."

"It's during the flood that we learn how to be strong and swim the swift waters," Lizzy reminded.

"And our faith strengthens," Magdalena added.

Erhard came back in from the barn and announced he was headed to bed. The women finished their meal and cleaned the kitchen. The day had been long and stressful and now weariness had taken over. Tomorrow would bring its own problems, so a good night's sleep was needed. There was nothing more they could do for Werner tonight but allow him to rest. Time would tell the story of the burn's severity and Werner's ability to fight off any infection.

"I think I will head to bed now," Lizzy said. "It's been a very long day. You should rest, too, while you can."

"I will," Magdalena said. "Werner will probably need me during the night."

"That's just what I was thinking," Lizzy replied. "Good night."

Magdalena stood over Werner watching him sleep, tears rolling down her cheeks at the sight of the bandage covering one side of his face. Werner slept on the floor, made soft with several quilts, so he didn't roll off the bed during the night. He seemed to be sleeping peacefully, so Magdalena readied herself for bed. Sinking onto the mattress, Magdalena again whispered a prayer for Werner's recovery. Then she slipped under the blankets and fell instantly asleep, weary from the events of the day.

Werner slept all through that first night but was fitful after that. He cried almost constantly from the pain, waking Magdalena up several times a night. During the day, it was a battle to keep him from removing the gauze covering the burn. By the dawn of the third day, Magdalena was worn out. As the morning's first rays lit the living room where she sat rocking Werner, Magdalena had to admit the truth. Werner's wound was not healing and now his body was too warm, caused by a fever. Magdalena had no idea what to do for him next, but she knew one thing for certain. Her precious baby boy needed a miracle.

Chapter Twenty-Three

Jacob Grieb woke with a much clearer mind than when he had fallen into his exhausted slumber in the pine thicket. Why was he running to the west? He knew that Albert was probably still in Dresden, the place Jacob had been arrested. Albert would have remained where Jacob would be able to find him, should he escape. The others might have traveled farther west but Jacob knew Albert. Albert would have thought the whole situation through. Finding each other would be next to impossible if they didn't know where to begin looking.

The camp he had been taken to was west of Dresden. Jacob knew this because the sun was rising as he rode shackled in the back of the German military truck on his way to the camp and it had been behind the truck. It was something Jacob had taken note of that cold January morning, just in case he found a way to escape. This remembered fact meant he should go east to find Albert and reach Dresden.

Jacob rose to his feet and shook the pine needles from his clothes, hair, and beard. He then stretched out the kinks in his neck and back. Sitting back down, he reached for the canvas bag filled with food. After making a cheese sandwich with two slices of cheese, Jacob began to form a plan. He would go to Dresden and look for Albert and the rest of the men. If he couldn't find them, he would head into southern Germany to begin looking for Magdalena and his sons.

Grabbing the jar of water, Jacob washed down the sandwich. He then grabbed two cookies from the bag to eat as he walked along. Now that he had a plan, he didn't want to waste any more time just sitting here in the pine thicket.

From the position of the sun, Jacob concluded it was early afternoon. He would have several hours of daylight still that would force him to stay hidden from view. Trudging to the edge of the pine thicket, Jacob began walking back in the direction he had just come from.

As darkness fell, Jacob could make out the concentration camp in the distance. He knew he would have to make a wide circle around it as he passed and was glad it would be dark when he did. He would be shot on the spot if they caught him outside the camp.

By the time morning dawned, Jacob felt he had covered a good distance. The ride in the truck from Dresden to the camp had not been a long one, so he was sure he would reach Dresden by the next morning. He had taken the liberty of walking on the road when darkness had completely fallen and felt he felt he was far enough from the camp. This had made the going much faster than tripping over logs and dodging limbs while in the woods.

Jacob made his way back into a grove of trees to get some rest. He would sleep most of the day and walk all night, again. After eating another cheese sandwich, Jacob covered himself with the warm blanket and slept. Waking in early afternoon, Jacob decided to start walking again. At least in the light he could see the tree limbs before they slapped his face. Keeping a fast pace, Jacob came to the outskirts of Dresden by nightfall.

Jacob was not prepared for what he saw as he entered Dresden. The city had been bombed beyond recognition, and rubble lay everywhere. There were people huddled in alleys with just thin blankets for warmth, as their homes had been destroyed and they had nowhere else to go. The fretting Jacob had done about being noticed because of his unkempt appearance had been for naught. Everywhere he looked, Jacob saw people who looked as bad, or worse.

Moving through the town was difficult because of all the debris and the darkness that was now fully upon him. Jacob finally decided to spend the night with a group of people on the street and wait for the morning light. He would get nowhere tonight with the condition the city was in.

"May I sleep here?" Jacob asked a man who had his family

huddled close for warmth and safety.

"You will not find an empty bed in all of Dresden," the man replied. "Sleeping here is probably your only option."

"What happened?" Jacob inquired. "I just arrived in the city today and was shocked by the destruction. Dresden was so beautiful when I glimpsed it two months ago."

"The Allies bombed us on February 13th and 14th," the man stated. "It is known that thousands of people were killed, and maybe hundreds of thousands, being there were so many refugees in the city that no one could account for. Their bodies were finally piled on railroad ties and burned. There was nothing else that could be done."

"I believe my family is among those refugees," Jacob said. "I'm looking for a man by the name of Albert Grieb."

"Albert Grieb?" the man asked. "I worked with him in the factory where weapons were being made. That building is lying in complete ruin now."

"You know Albert?" Jacob asked, knowing that the first person he spoke to being familiar with Albert was truly a gift from God.

"Yes," the man replied. "He had been staying in a home with a family who lived near me and my family. That house now lies in ruin, too."

"Was Albert killed?" Jacob asked.

"No," the man replied. "I'll take you to the place they are all staying when daylight comes."

"Thank you," Jacob said. "God has definitely directed my footsteps this night. Is there anyone else with Albert?"

"No," the man said, "but he did mention a brother being arrested as they stepped off the train here in Dresden as they were fleeing Poland. He said there had been a whole group of men with him, but he sent the rest farther into Germany for their safety. It seems he had a premonition of things to come."

"As bad as the city looks in the dark, I'm sure I will be shocked when the sun sheds light over the destruction," Jacob replied. "By the way, my name's Jacob." Jacob chose not to mention that he was the brother who had been arrested, though he was sure the man had figured that much out on his own.

"I'm Olis," the man said, introducing himself. "The city is

horrifying to see. We were able to make it to a shelter at the beginning of the bombing. When we came out, our whole street had been leveled and part of the city was a blazing inferno."

"Why would the Allies bomb Dresden with the war almost over?" Jacob wondered aloud. "Germany is clearly going to lose. We are surrounded on all borders."

"I asked myself the same question," Olis said. "I suppose they wanted to halt the movement of German troops by bombing the railway. Destroying the factories where weapons were being made was also part of the plan, I'm sure."

"But what of all the innocent lives?" Jacob questioned. "Hitler started this war, not innocent men, women, and children."

"Your brother said you speak out before you consider who might be listening," Olis said. "Did you not learn anything by being sent to a concentration camp?"

"I learned more in that camp than I'm willing to share this night," Jacob replied. "Albert's right, I speak without thought sometimes. It seems to be something I can't control."

"I would try much harder," Olis replied. "You will just be shot now for speaking out. The soldiers have no time to be arresting anyone and moving them to a camp. All of Germany is in a state of panic as the Nazis have already been defeated by the Allies to the west and are losing ground daily to the Red Army to the east."

"Thank you for the warning," Jacob said, wondering how he could have spoken out yet again. Deciding the best way to keep his opinions to himself would be if he was asleep, Jacob curled up under his blanket and drifted off. He awoke the next morning just as light began to creep into the sky, fading the stars from view. As daybreak exploded across Dresden, Jacob took in the scene. Buildings lay in ruin all around. Some had been leveled while others stood partially destroyed, a testament that they once existed, proud and beautiful. Dresden had been a city with museums and wonderful architecture. Now, it was a pile of rubble, never to be the same again.

"It's worse than I could have even imagined," Jacob muttered.

"At least the stench of burning bodies has faded away," Olis whispered. "The destruction will remain forever, at least in the minds of us who lived through it. Come, I will take you to your brother."

Olis and Jacob picked their way through the once beautiful streets of Dresden. In the distance, Jacob could see two large towers still standing where a once large structure had been. He could tell by the fragments that were still left of the building that it was once very unique and magnificent. "What used to be there?" Jacob asked, pointing toward the towers.

"The Frauenkirche," Olis replied. "It was a beautiful Lutheran church resembling a cathedral. I don't see it ever being replaced. It survived the bombing but was consumed a short time later by the fire that swept across the city, burning buildings and people in its path."

"This bombing was an act of cruelty, a war crime," Jacob stated. "There was no legitimate reason to bomb this beautiful city."

"And yet, they did," Olis replied sadly.

They walked farther on, Jacob taking in the scene every direction he turned. He had never seen such a sight and hoped to never see one such as this ever again. It was an unbelievable view of destruction, one no one would think true when he and Albert explained it later. Jacob honestly wondered how anyone had survived the bombing. And it was all pointless. Germany was going to lose this war, and Dresden lying in ruins had nothing to do with that outcome.

"We're almost there," Olis said.

Olis and Jacob found Albert tending a small fire he had built in the street. It was the only means they had to cook their breakfast, or any other meal. When he looked up, he couldn't believe his eyes. "Jacob," Albert exclaimed. "What a surprise. I see you met Olis."

"Yes," Jacob said, embracing Albert. "God has guided my footsteps to you."

"I was preparing to join Olof and the rest within the week," Albert said. "I sent them on for their safety. I knew you would come back here if you escaped, so I stayed. Since the bombing, I've just been busy trying to help families locate each other and bury their dead. It's been such a heartbreaking ordeal."

"I can see that," Jacob said. "This was an unnecessary act of violence. Nothing has been gained by the Allies from this senseless devastation."

"I'll be heading back to my family now," Olis announced. "Best wishes to you and yours, Albert."

"Thank you, Olis," Albert replied. "I will be going to search for my wife and sons now. I pray you and your family rebuild from the ashes that surround you."

"As we will pray you find your family unharmed," Olis replied. With that, Olis turned and left.

"How did you manage to escape?" Albert asked while turning his attention back to his fire.

"It's an unbelievable story," Jacob replied. "I had an angel of mercy show up at just the right time."

"Let's get some breakfast cooked," Albert said, abruptly changing the subject. "When we're finished, we will prepare to travel west and join Gottlieb and the other men."

"Do you know where they are?" Jacob asked.

"I do," Albert replied. "I wrote down the phone number of the Dresden train station and Olof took it with him. Each day I checked at the station to see if a message had been left for me. Two weeks after their departure, Olof called the station and left a message that they are all in Scheessel, Germany, waiting for the war to end."

"At least we can reunite with part of our family," Jacob said. "I wonder where the women and children have ended up."

"I'm sure somewhere in southern Germany, though I have no idea the exact location," Albert said. "We will hunt until we find them. Right now, let's get some food in our stomachs for the journey ahead. You can tell me all about how you found me when were on our way to Scheessel. No sense taking any chances of being overheard by the wrong pair of ears."

"True," Jacob agreed, knowing all too well how quickly that could happen.

Jacob and Albert ate a breakfast of oatmeal and then packed up Albert's few belongings in preparation to leave. Albert thanked Christof and Hanna for their hospitality during his stay in Dresden and they were off.

There was nothing to keep them in Dresden any longer. They had a whole family to locate and lives to rebuild. They had spent nearly five years with constant uncertainties and they were ready for peace and some stability. They realized the dream of returning to their beloved village of Hoffnungstal, in Bessarabia, would most likely never happen, but they would strive to make homes in Germany. The most important thing now was for them to find their families.

****

Lizzy found Magdalena sitting in the rocking chair in the living room with Werner cradled in her arms. Dawn had just spread its light through the windows making the tears evident on Magdalena's face. Lizzy knew that Werner's burn was not healing and she wondered if he had grown worse during the night. They had done everything the doctor had told them to do, and yet, the wound had not begun to heal. If anything, it appeared to look worse.

"Magdalena," Lizzy said softly as she entered the room.

Magdalena turned, wiping at the tears and trying to compose herself. The attempt was futile. The moment her eyes met Lizzy's, a sob escaped and rivulets of tears chased down her weary face. Lizzy came and took Werner out of her arms. Cradling Werner in the crook of one arm, Lizzy hugged Magdalena's shoulders with her other arm, allowing her this breakdown. "He's running a fever," Magdalena sobbed.

Lizzy pressed her lips to the baby's forehead. She could feel it was warmer than it should have been. Fever meant infection, no matter how one looked at it. The doctor's warning echoed in Lizzy's ears again as he had so crudely given his prognosis. Lizzy had tried to forget his warnings and work diligently to bring healing to Werner's burn, but the truth of the matter was the rude doctor had been right. Taking Werner back to him would do no good, for he had as good as told them he had no other treatment to suggest for such a severe burn. "I have a far-fetched idea," Lizzy began.

"Nothing else we have done so far has helped," Magdalena said, "so let me hear the idea you have."

"There's this old woman who lives over on the other side of the mountain. They call her a healer woman. She mixes herbs to make poultices and salves. Maybe she could help Werner."

"Is she crazy or something?" Magdalena asked. "What have

you heard about her?"

"She's a bit, um…eccentric," Lizzy replied. "She's been known to have success where doctors have failed, though. She can look deep into your eyes and tell you things about your health, so I've heard."

"It's worth a try," Magdalena said. "How long would it take to get there?"

"About two hours," Lizzy said. "I don't think it would be wise to take Werner to her but Ewald and I could ride over and bring her back."

"Do you think she can help him?" Magdalena asked hopefully.

"I honestly don't know," Lizzy replied, "but I feel we need to try something. He's not getting any better and the fever is not a good sign."

"Okay," Magdalena agreed. "Go see if she will come."

Lizzy woke Ewald and they left a half hour later. Magdalena fretted and walked the floor with Werner, trying to calm him. He had been crying for the last ten minutes and nothing Magdalena did helped to ease his discomfort. The salty tears just added to the pain as they ran down his cheek. Magdalena attempted to keep them soaked up before they reached the burn, but Werner fought her hand away, crying all the harder. It was the same way every time she and Lizzy cleaned the wound. One of them had to hold Werner down while the other tended the burn. It broke Magdalena's heart to see him in so much pain but she was at a loss of what to do for him. It was that feeling of helplessness that frustrated her most.

Erhard had gone to the barn to do the milking before starting his normal chores. Both Erhard and Ewald had been helping Lizzy with the milking since Magdalena couldn't leave Werner unattended. When Erhard came to the house with the milk, Magdalena had just gotten Werner to calm down and fall asleep. She placed him on some quilts on the living room floor and busied herself with making cheese. It helped to keep her hands working. Idle time just caused her more worry, and she had done enough of that the last three days to last her a lifetime.

"Be anxious over nothing but in prayer and supplication, with thanksgiving, make your desires known," Magdalena whispered, paraphrasing the Bible verse from Philippians. She then began to hum a familiar hymn, calming herself with the peace only God can give. Her life may be turned upside down but God was still in control.

Lizzy and Ewald returned four hours later, the healer woman in tow. She did not appear to be crazy as she examined Werner's wound and applied some salve she had brought along.

"Put this on three times a day and cover the wound with clean gauze after each application," the woman instructed. "Cleanse the wound once a day, just as you have been doing. Make sure he eats plenty of vegetables so his body gets all the nutrients it needs to help aid in the healing. Also, make a tea from this herb and allow him to sip a small amount. It will help with the fever."

"Do you think he will heal?" Magdalena asked hopefully, taking the proffered dried herb from the woman's gnarled fingers.

"I believe he will," the woman replied, "though the scar will be deep and noticeable."

"Thank you so much," Magdalena said. "Please, stay for the noon meal."

"May I stay all night?" the woman asked. "I don't think this old body can handle another two hour wagon ride today."

"Yes, you may stay the night," Lizzy said. "The horses will appreciate the rest as well."

The old woman settled in the living room close to Werner. She watched him sleep, monitoring his breathing. When he was awake, she looked deep into his blue eyes. As Magdalena watched her, she had to agree with what others thought; she was eccentric. The old woman had a way about her that made you feel insecure. Like she knew things about you that you didn't want her to know. Magdalena was thankful she didn't start chanting, because she wasn't sure how she would have handled it.

Lizzy and Ewald returned the healer woman to her home the next morning. The salve had taken some of the pain from the wound and Werner had slept through the night. It was a blessing for Magdalena's weary body, though she doubted she would have tended him if he had awakened. The old woman stayed near him through the night, insisting on sleeping on the floor next to him.

"Mutti, Mutti," Ewald called as he bounded into the house having just arrived back home from taking the healer woman home.

"What is it, Ewald?" Magdalena asked, coming from the bedroom where she had just laid a sleeping Werner down.

"Look what Lizzy found," Ewald said, attempting to hold a squirming black and white Border collie in his arms.

"Oh, my," Magdalena said. "Isn't that something?"

"Yes," Ewald said, his excitement bubbling over, "and Lizzy said we can name him Stein, just like our dog we left behind in Poland."

"I'm sure you and this pup will have lots of fun together," Magdalena said, thankful for the joy this ball of fur would bring to her sons. There had definitely not been many occasions for joy and laughter lately.

"Oh, we will," Ewald assured his mutti. "I will teach this Stein all the tricks I taught our Stein in Poland. He's going to be the smartest dog on this mountain."

"Just remember, Lizzy needs him to herd sheep, too." Magdalena reminded Ewald. "He will have a full time job learning to do that, so there may not be a lot of extra time to teach him tricks."

"I know, Mutti," Ewald said, "but I can tell this pup is really smart. He will learn to herd in no time and learn the tricks I plan to teach him. Lizzy says he will take to herding without much training. It's what he is bred to do."

"Well, Lizzy probably knows these things," Magdalena said, smiling as Ewald headed back outside to find Erhard and show him the new pet as Lizzy came in the back door.

"I see Ewald showed you the farm's newest addition," Lizzy said with a smile.

"Yes, he did," Magdalena said, smiling back. "Where did you get him?"

"I asked the healer woman if she knew anyone who had a litter of puppies," Lizzy said. "It just so happened that her neighbor did and they were old enough to be weaned. We stopped and picked one out on our way home."

"Thank you, Lizzy," Magdalena said. "That puppy is going to bring many hours of fun and happiness for my sons."

"You're welcome, Magdalena," Lizzy replied, "but honestly, the little rascal has already stolen my heart, too. I don't know why

I didn't get a dog before now."

"Dogs have a way doing that," Magdalena said with a laugh. "I believe the puppy will be good for all of us."

"Yes, I believe she will," Lizzy said.

"She?" Magdalena questioned.

"Yeah, it's a girl," Lizzy laughed. "Ewald wanted a "Stein" so bad I told him he could name her that. Ewald doesn't know the dog's a female and the dog doesn't realize she has a man's name. I figured there was no harm in allowing Ewald to think the dog is a boy."

"Oh, my goodness," Magdalena said, laughing all the harder. It felt good to smile after so many days of constant worry over Werner's wound.

"Between you and me, this farm runs quite smoothly with women in charge," Lizzy said with a smile. "I thought the dog should be one of us. Of course, we will never tell our husbands that."

"No, not ever," Magdalena said, a smile still lighting up her face again.

The new puppy instantly became part of the family and it followed Erhard and Ewald all over the farm. When they came inside, the pup came in, too. Magdalena's only concern was that the puppy would play too rough around Werner and open his wound. However, it seemed the pup understood Werner was injured and remained calm around him.

Werner loved the puppy, and it was good to see a smile light up his face after so many days of being in pain. He was improving daily, and within four days of the healer woman's visit, he was almost back to his old self. The wound scabbed over and the burn began to shrink as it healed. It would always be noticeable, but thank God, he was going to live.

****

Albert and Jacob traveled west toward Scheessel, Germany, catching rides with whoever would pick them up. The sight they had left behind in Dresden still haunted their minds and would relive itself in their nightmares for years to come. There was so much destruction, so many senseless deaths. This war had turned men into monsters, with Hitler being at the top of the list. Did Hitler really believe he could take over most of Europe and get away with it?

The two men reached Scheessel the next afternoon. They had seen evidence of bombings all along the way. Germany's landscape would forever be changed after the final shot was fired, which surely would be soon. The German troops had all been pushed back within the original borders of Germany, and farther in some cases. Surrendering seemed to be the only option left, but still Hitler was holding on. How many innocent lives would be lost and German cities destroyed before he came to his senses?

Upon reaching Scheessel, it didn't take long for Jacob and Albert to find the other men. Olof had left the address in his message at the train station of where they were staying, and a few questions to local citizens were enough to bring Jacob and Albert to their location. Upon seeing the structure, they hoped the building looked better on the inside than it did on the outside. It was not at all what Jacob and Albert were expecting.

"Jacob! Albert! What a surprise," Olof exclaimed as he opened the door to the persistent knocking.

Edward, Emil, Olof, and Gottlieb, were surprised to see Jacob and Albert. News had reached them of the bombing of Dresden. They feared Albert had been among the casualties, since the numbers were now believed to be in the hundreds of thousands. As for Jacob, they didn't expect to see him ever again. They were sure he was marked for death and were surprised the fuel had been wasted to haul him to a concentration camp.

"I can't believe you're both alive," Gottlieb said as the men entered.

"We had planned to locate your wives and children ourselves, as soon as the war ends," Emil told Jacob and Albert.

"Yes, we had decided you were both dead. We planned to bring Emilie and Magdalena back here and help them raise your sons," Edward added.

"Well, praise God, these boys will finish raising their sons themselves," Gottlieb boomed. He was sitting in the only chair in the whole place. He might have become fragile during the last five years of trials but his voice still carried the strength and authority of the mayor of Hoffnungstal.

"Is this the only vacant building you could find?" Jacob asked, looking around in disgust.

"This is it," Olof said. "We were lucky that our boss had it to offer."

"Does your boss own livestock?" Albert asked.

"No," Olof replied. "He owns a leather factory where Emil, Edward and I work. This empty slaughterhouse is just another building he owned and he offered it to us."

"It really is the only available building," Emil added. "We have looked everywhere."

"We just need to do some mending and painting," Edward pointed out, attempting to make Jacob and Albert accept the place. "We haven't had time to do much."

"All I know is we had better get it looking better than this before we bring any of the women here," Jacob said. "They will not be as appreciative for "just a roof over their heads" as us men."

"It is very large, though," Albert said trying to imagine it fixed up. "We could make small apartments for each family until we have the means to do something else."

"Yes, it's large," Gottlieb agreed, "but you're right, Jacob. Rosina, Magdalena, Emilie and the rest will not be pleased with these accommodations."

"Any idea where the women are?" Jacob asked.

"The only thing we know is that they are probably in the southern part of Germany," Emil said. "That area is called the state of Bavaria."

"When do we start looking?" Albert asked, ready to leave at that moment.

"We need to wait until the war is over," Gottlieb cautioned. "I'm ready to leave right now, too, but it's just not a good plan. It's too dangerous to move the women and children. We could find ourselves in the middle of a battle and become targets."

"That's true," Jacob agreed. "I'm anxious to get my family back together but I won't risk their lives to do it."

"How did you survive the bombing on Dresden?" Olof asked.

"I made it to a bomb shelter," Albert replied. "I cannot explain to you the devastation that attack left behind."

"We've read some reports in the newspaper," Olof said. "It sounded like not much was left untouched."

"It is a horrific scene to behold," Jacob said. "I could not believe what had happened to that beautiful city when I returned. And then there are the people who died…"

"Thousands of innocent lives cut short," Albert added. "I'll tell you more at a later time."

"How did you escape the concentration camp, Jacob?" Gottlieb asked.

"An angel of mercy," Jacob replied. "The people in the concentration camps are being put into gas chambers and killed. They are told they are preparing to take a shower. By the time they figure out what is happening, it's too late. I was actually on the threshold of one of those gas chambers."

"Why are you not dead?" Olof asked, the surprise of such a thing taking place evident in his voice.

"The guard at the door was Gunter from Bessarabia," Jacob said. "Of all the people who could have been standing there, God made sure it was him. Gunter shut the door with me on the outside and instructed me to run and put my clothes back on. He helped me escape the camp that very night."

"That is an unbelievable story," Emil said.

"If I hadn't lived through it, I would think the same," Jacob replied.

"So, all we can do now is wait for the war to end?" Albert asked, hoping the answer would change somehow.

"Yes, we have to wait," Gottlieb replied, "though I don't think it will be for long."

Chapter Twenty-Four

Gottlieb had been correct about the war not lasting much longer. On April 16th, 1945, the Red Army encircled Berlin. Hitler, knowing surrender was inevitable, chose to take his own life on April 30th. It was the coward's way out. In so doing, a trial before men was avoided, but he would not escape the judgment of his Creator.

A week later, on May 7th, 1945, Germany officially surrendered to the Allies. The war that Hitler had begun by invading Poland on September 1st, 1939, was finally over for Europe. The destruction left behind would forever remind the Germans, and the countries Hitler attempted to overtake, that there had been a madman among them for a season.

"It's time to go find our family," Jacob announced as soon as word had reached them of Germany's surrender.

"I believe it is safe enough now to begin searching," Gottlieb said. "Where do you plan to start looking?"

"I suppose in southern Germany," Jacob replied. "It's the last known location we have to go on."

"You and Albert go search," Emil told Jacob. "The rest of us will stay here and keep working so the women and children have a place to come to. It's not much, but it already looks better with the walls painted and the dividing walls in place."

"Rosina may still refuse to live in an abandoned slaughterhouse," Gottlieb said.

"Like the rest of us, she will probably have no choice," Edward said. "There is no other place to live. At least we have employment. We may not find that anywhere else right now. Mutti will just have to make do with this for a time."

"With all the changes we have faced since leaving Bessarabia, surely this slaughterhouse won't be Mutti's breaking point," Emil added.

"You're probably right," Gottlieb said, "but get ready to do some major cleaning upon her arrival. What we think is clean is not going to be acceptable to Rosina and the other women."

"At least the cooking will improve around here," Olof added with a laugh.

"I'm offended," Gottlieb said smiling. "You boys go off to work and I have a supper waiting for you each evening and this is the thanks I get?"

"Well, the meals have been improving," Emil said, "but a woman just knows her way around a kitchen."

"A warm strudel does sound pretty good," Gottlieb admitted. "It's been a long time since I've had one of those. Meat and vegetables seem to be the limit of my cooking abilities. "

"We appreciate your efforts, Vater," Edward said, "but I think we will all be thankful to have the women back."

"So, we leave tomorrow," Albert stated.

"Tomorrow can't come fast enough," Jacob replied.

The next morning, Jacob and Albert began their journey south in search of their wives and children, along with the other women who had left with them by train from Poland. They had no idea how they would find them but knew they must. They were able to catch rides with several people who were heading south, making their travel much quicker than they had anticipated. Each time a destination was reached by the person who had offered them a ride, Jacob and Albert would continue south on foot, looking for their next opportunity to speed their travel.

As they walked along the road, a US military truck approached from behind. Hoping to get a ride, the men waved the truck down. The driver slowed and came to a stop beside Jacob and Albert.

"May we catch a ride with you?" Jacob asked. He was so thankful he knew so many languages, including English. His vater had been right about the importance of learning to speak more than just German and Russian.

"Yes," the soldier replied. "Where are you headed?"

"We don't know exactly," Jacob admitted. "Our wives and children were put on a train and moved south to Germany from Poland when the Red Army pushed into Warsaw. We haven't seen or heard from them since. We are trying to locate them now."

"There's a displaced persons camp in Stuttgart," the soldier replied. "You might start there. That's where we're headed."

"Thank you for the information," Jacob replied.

"You're welcome," the soldier said. "Just jump in the back. The other men will make room for you."

Jacob and Albert climbed into the covered bed of the military truck. As they rode along, they talked to the young men in the back.

"So, what's it like in America?" Jacob asked the young soldier sitting next to him.

"It depends on where you live," the young soldier answered. "I'm a farm boy from southern Indiana. My parents tend an orchard and have a small dairy herd. It's beautiful there, the rolling pasture land with a creek running through the lower field. I can picture it now, even though I'm thousands of miles away. I'm ready to go home."

"I live in New York City," another soldier chimed in. "There's everything there you can imagine and the town never sleeps."

"What are your plans when you return home?" Albert asked the young farm boy.

"To finish college and become a teacher," the soldier replied. "I hope to teach History."

"Why did you become a soldier if you were in college?" Jacob asked.

"I was drafted," the young man replied. "I was proud to come do my part, though. Freedom comes with a price. It is never free."

"I would like to move to America," Jacob stated.

"It's the best place on earth to live," the young soldier answered. "My name is Dale. What is yours?"

"Jacob Grieb and this is my brother, Albert."

"Nice to meet you," Dale replied, pulling his hand from his coat pocket to shake Jacob and Albert's hands. As he did, a card was pulled from his pocket and fluttered to the floor of the truck. Jacob picked up the card and handed it back to the soldier. As Dale took it in his hands, he smiled down at the words that were written on it.

"Is that a card from home?" Albert asked.

"No," Dale replied, "it's a note to us soldiers from General Patton, and a note to God."

"A note to God?" Jacob asked with surprise.

"It's really a prayer," Dale replied. "See, the weather was extremely rainy last fall. We were bogged down and couldn't move the troops like we wanted to. In early December, General Patton asked our chaplain, James O'Neill, to write a prayer for better weather. After the prayer was written, it was printed on these cards, with a Christmas message from General Patton on the reverse side."

"May I read the prayer?" Jacob asked.

"Sure," Dale replied, handing the card to Jacob.

Jacob surveyed the card. Sure enough, on one side of the card was a Christmas greeting from General Patton, commending his men on their courage, devotion to duty and skill to obtain complete victory. General Patton also asked for God's blessings upon each of the soldiers. Turning the card over, Jacob read the prayer that Chaplain O'Neill had composed:

"Almighty and most merciful Father, we humbly beseech Thee, of Thy great goodness, to restrain these immoderate rains with which we have had to contend. Grant us fair weather for battle. Graciously hearken to us as soldiers who call Thee that, armed with Thy power, we may advance from victory to victory, and crush the oppression and wickedness of our enemies, and establish Thy justice among men and nations. Amen"

"Was the prayer answered?" Albert asked, after listening to Jacob read it aloud.

"In a mighty way," Dale replied. "I received my card on December 13th, and on December 16th the German troops initiated a successful surprise attack. The battle that we now refer to as "Battle of the Bulge" began. The weather was still terrible and we could not perform any air attacks. We were being pushed back from the line we had established on the western front, creating a bulge in the line. We were all praying this prayer, and on

December 23rd, the weather cleared for six days. We began air attacks and it changed the outcome. The battle was won and eventually the war here in Europe."

"That's an amazing story," Jacob said. "I believe you will see just how wicked your enemy is as you move deeper into Germany. Hitler had concentration camps set up for Jewish people and for anyone who did not support his agenda. You will find the people left in those camps are nearly starved to death. Mass numbers have been killed in gas chambers."

"How do you know such a thing?" Dale asked, outraged.

"I spoke out against Hitler," Jacob replied. "The Nazis overheard me at a train depot in Dresden. I was arrested and put in one of those camps. I stood on the threshold of a gas chamber."

"How did you escape?" Dale questioned.

"The guard who was in charge of shutting the door to the chamber knew me," Jacob said. "We had lived in the same colony in Bessarabia, Romania. He helped me escape."

"Hitler was truly crazy," Dale stated certain he was speaking the truth.

"More so than any of us will ever really know," Jacob replied.

As they entered Stuttgart, darkness had already fallen. The US military truck took Albert and Jacob to the displaced persons camp. There, the men were given cots to sleep on. Everyone else was already asleep, so the search for the men's family would have to continue the next morning. It was hard to end the search knowing they might be close to being reunited with their families after months of separation, but they had no choice.

Waking early the next morning, Jacob and Albert made their way to the administration building. A secretary checked a list for the names that Jacob and Albert supplied her with. All the women were on the list except Magdalena and her sons.

"Where might we find them?" Albert asked, thankful he had found his wife and sons so quickly.

"They should be eating breakfast soon," the secretary informed them. The secretary gave Jacob and Albert directions to the building where meals were served.

"Why isn't Magdalena with the rest of the women?" Jacob worried aloud as he and Albert made their way to locate the women.

"I don't know," Albert replied. "Maybe Emilie will be able to help us find her."

"This should be the building we're looking for," Jacob said, pointing to a building a few feet away. Jacob and Albert entered the building and began to scan the huge number of refugees.

"I'll start on one side of the room while you go to the other," Albert said. "We'll make our way toward the middle as we search for Emilie and the rest."

"Okay," Jacob agreed, knowing it was the best way to locate the women and children since the room was so full.

Jacob and Albert began their search down the rows of tables full of women and children. It was unbelievable how many displaced Germans there were at the camp. Jacob wondered how many families had been separated as they fled to safety during this war. How many of those families would never be reunited? Would he ever find Magdalena and his boys? Hopefully, Emilie would know where Magdalena might be.

Albert spotted Emilie in the third row of tables he searched. She was engrossed in conversation with her mutti, Rosina, and the other women as she fed Walter his breakfast.

Walking quietly up behind Emilie, Albert gently tapped her shoulder. Emilie turned to see who had touched her. Tears immediately flooded her eyes as she turned to see Albert smiling down at her. Emilie quickly jumped to her feet and fell into Albert's open arms. Their five sons joined their parent's happy reunion, thankful their vater had found them.

"How did you find us?" Emilie asked.

"Jacob and I were in Scheessel, Germany when the war ended," Albert began. "When it became safe to travel, we headed south to find you. We were able to catch rides and the last one happened to be in a US military truck headed here. They told us of this camp and so this is where we started looking. I can't believe we actually found you so easily."

"Where is Jacob?" Rosina asked.

"He started looking on the other side of the room," Albert said. "He will be here soon."

"Magdalena's not here," Emilie said, tears pooling in her eyes again.

"We know," Albert replied. "We just came from checking the list of everyone who has taken refuge here. Where is she?"

"I don't know," Emilie admitted. "We got separated on the road when a US military truck picked me and the boys up. I haven't seen her since."

"We'll find her," Albert assured Emilie. "I'm sure she's fine."

"That's what I told her," Rosina added. "Where is Gottlieb?"

"We left him in Scheessel," Albert said. "The journey would have been too much for him. I'm afraid he's not well at all."

"What about Emil and Edward?" Rosina asked.

"They are well and are in Scheessel, too," Albert said. "The two of them, along with Olof, decided to stay and work while Jacob and I went to hunt for all of you."

"And Daniel?" Isabella asked. "Is Daniel there, too?"

Jacob had just reached Albert and the women as Isabella asked the question. Albert turned to Jacob, silently asking him how to tell Isabella that Daniel had not made it out of Poland. Isabella had already lived her whole adult life surrounded by heartache and cruelty. Now, her husband was dead and her son had been sent to fight in the war and could very well be dead, too.

"Isabella," Jacob began, "I don't really know how to tell you this. You see, Daniel was killed while we were fleeing Poland."

"What?" Isabella whispered, trying to grasp the meaning of Jacob's words.

"Polish bandits killed Daniel while we were trying to get through their road block," Albert said. "We had the Red Army at our backs, so there was no choice but to push through the bandits and hope for the best. I'm so sorry."

"Did you bury him?" Isabella asked.

"No," Jacob said quietly. "They pulled him from the wagon seat and we never saw him again."

"So, he could still be alive in Poland somewhere?" Isabella asked hopefully.

"Sister," Rosina spoke softly to Isabella. "Daniel is gone. That's what they are trying to tell you."

"No!" Isabella wailed, burying her face in Rosina's shoulder. The other women gathered around to comfort Isabella. Up until that point, Agathe, Isabella's daughter, had been stunned into silence. Now, her sobs mingled with her mutti's, as they bereaved the fact that a husband and vater was gone forever.

"Do you know where Magdalena is?" Jacob asked after the women had composed themselves.

"No," Emilie said, telling the story of how they had become separated.

"So, you have no idea where she could be?" Jacob asked.

"I wish I did," Emilie answered. "I know she was in the southern part of Germany when we were separated, but I could never find her again."

"Maybe the US military could help," Albert said hopefully. "Suppose there are other camps where we could search for her?"

"I'll go ask," Jacob said. "You should take all of the women and children back to Scheessel. We can't drag all of them along while we look. I will make better time on my own."

"That sounds like the best plan," Albert agreed. "I will get us all settled into the home we have in Scheessel and have a place ready for you and Magdalena."

"Thank you, Brother," Jacob said.

Albert left out the information that their new home had once been a slaughterhouse, and it did not go unnoticed by Jacob. Some things are better left unsaid. No sense upsetting the women before they had a chance to see the potential the building possessed.

After the women and children ate breakfast, they went to pack up their meager belongings. They all hoped it would be the last time they had to put their lives in a suitcase for a very long time. In the last five years, they had packed up and moved three times. They had nothing to show for those years they had lived except the clothes they could fit in a suitcase. There were no pots or pans, no dishes that had been passed down through generations, no cooking utensils or bowls to mix bread or batter in; in essence, they were destitute. However, they still had each other and had survived the war, with the exception of Daniel and Jacob Grieb, Sr. They would rebuild their lives and pray for peace.

Jacob said farewell to Albert and the women as they headed north to Scheessel. He had no idea when he would see them all again but knew he wouldn't leave the area until he had found his wife and sons. They had to be here somewhere. Magdalena was a strong, independent woman and would have figured out a way to survive.

Jacob picked his way through the streets of Stuttgart headed toward the US army barracks. Rubble lay everywhere, evidence of the buildings that used to line the streets. The Allies had destroyed over half the city in their quest to make the Germans surrender. At least there had been no fire that killed thousands of souls as there had been in Dresden. Still, it would take years to rebuild all that had been destroyed, and much of the architecture would be lost forever.

Reaching the US Army barracks, Jacob began to ask any soldier he seen for information about other displaced persons camps. He learned that there was a refugee camp up on a mountain in Bavaria. A map was drawn and given to Jacob, since he was not familiar with the area. Jacob thanked them for their help and set off toward the southeast, determined to not waste any time.

Jacob was fortunate to catch rides in several vehicles, most of them being from Allied forces who were in the area. The last truck he flagged down was heading to the displaced persons camp with supplies. He was thankful he didn't have to walk up the mountain. It would have taken him hours to make the steep climb.

When Jacob reached the camp, he immediately began to scan every face for Magdalena. Not seeing her, Jacob headed for the administration building that had been pointed out to him by the driver of the supply truck. Entering the office, Jacob asked the secretary if there were records of everyone who was living at the camp.

"We do have records," the secretary replied. "So many people are separated from their families that we thought it wise to keep a list of everyone in each displaced persons camp. Other camps are adding people daily, mostly from the concentration camps that are being shut down and the people who are being allowed to leave."

"Those who are still alive," Jacob replied sadly.

"Do you know much about the concentration camps?" the secretary asked.

"Yes," Jacob replied. "I spent a couple months in one until I escaped."

"We have been hearing awful stories coming from those who survived the camps," the secretary said.

"They are all true, I assure you," Jacob said then got to the point of his visit. "I'm looking for my wife and three sons. They were sent by train out of Poland, just before the Red Army took Warsaw. I have not heard from them since."

"What are their names?" the secretary asked, picking up a thick book to begin the search.

"Magdalena Grieb is my wife," Jacob said, "and my sons are Erhard, Ewald and Werner."

"Magdalena Grieb," the secretary repeated, running his finger down the list of names. After turning several pages, he finally stopped and looked up at Jacob.

"I have her name written down," the secretary said, "but she's not here. Seems she found a job on a farm a few miles down the mountain. I have written here that the farm has goats and sheep and can be seen from the road. I'll point you in the direction, but I'm afraid that's all the information I have."

"Thank you," Jacob said. "At least I know she's alive and in this area."

"Yes, I suppose that is a relief," the secretary said with a smile. "I hope you find her and your sons."

"Thank you, again," Jacob said and quickly exited the building. There was no time to stand around having conversation. Jacob needed to get to that farm before nightfall.

Jacob made good time down the mountain, though he did not see one vehicle to catch a ride with. He was sure horse and wagon was still the main transportation here in the Bavarian Alps. The scene reminded him of Bessarabia and a wave of homesickness swept across his heart.

So much had been lost in the past five years: his home, his businesses, his vater, and almost his life. The only thing that mattered now, though, was finding his wife and children.

As Jacob rounded a curve in the road, his eyes fell on a beautiful farm nestled in a valley. The sun was casting its last rays of light across the fields, house, and barn. Jacob could see sheep being herded to a paddock for the night and the unmistakable bleating of goats filled the evening air. Jacob could see a boy the size of Erhard behind the sheep and a small ball of white and black fur running all around the sheep's legs, causing chaos instead of being helpful. In the distance, he could see a field of wheat standing tall and oats just beginning to head out. He knew this had to be the farm Magdalena was at. The scene would have torn at her heart strings as much as his.

Jacob began his descent down the driveway toward the farm. As he neared the barn, the door opened and out stepped Ewald. His eyes lit up as he recognized the man standing before him.

"Vater! Vater!" Ewald hollered, running into Jacob's open arms.

After almost five months of separation, Jacob finally allowed the worry for his wife and children's safety to be washed away in the tears streaming down his face. So much had happened since he had put them on that train in Poland headed south. He had been forced to fight and run for his life, driven by the fact that his family needed him to stay alive. He recounted the desperation he felt while trapped in the concentration camp, not knowing if he would ever survive the harsh conditions. Finding Magdalena and his sons safe and alive lifted a burden from Jacob beyond explanation.

Within minutes, Jacob was surrounded by his wife and two other sons. A young woman looked on, tears streaming down her face, too. The puppy Jacob had seen running circles around the sheep earlier was now barking wildly at the stranger who had just showed up.

As Jacob looked all around him at his family, his eyes fell fully on Werner for the first time, held in Magdalena's arms. "What happened," Jacob gasped, gently touching Werner's cheek.

"He fell against the wood stove," Magdalena said. "I'm so sorry Jacob. I should have been watching him closer."

"It looks like a really bad burn," Jacob said.

"We almost lost him," Magdalena admitted, fresh tears trickling down her face.

"But we didn't," Jacob said. "It's not your fault, Magdalena. Accidents happen and we handle them the best we know how. Werner will have a scar but at least we still have his life to enjoy."

"Yes, thank God for that," Magdalena whispered.

Jacob glanced back at the woman who had been standing on the outside of their family circle. She was a small woman but spirit and determination gleamed from her eyes. No one else had joined her, unless you counted the pup who was now sitting at her feet, so Jacob assumed she was alone here on this farm.

"Oh, this is Lizzy," Magdalena said, introducing the woman Jacob was staring at. "She owns this farm. The boys and I have been working for her the last couple of months."

"Nice to meet you, Jacob Grieb," Lizzy said, extending her calloused hand.

"Thank you for taking care of my wife and sons," Jacob said, shaking her hand quickly.

"Well, I believe they were taking care of me," Lizzy replied with a smile. "I needed help on this farm desperately when they showed up."

"Do you not have a husband?" Jacob asked.

"Yes," Lizzy replied. "He was drafted into the war. Now that it's over, I hope for his safe return, soon."

Jacob looked around the farm. There was way too much for one woman to handle alone. She had done the best she could, but Jacob noticed gates that needed repairs and fences that needed mended, among other things. How could he just leave without helping her? She had opened her home to his wife and sons, giving them a place to live in the fresh air and sunshine.

"We could stay until your husband comes home," Jacob offered.

"I could not ask you to do that," Lizzy replied. "You have your lives to rebuild."

"I want to help you," Jacob said, "as a way of saying thank you for your hospitality to my wife and sons."

"Where will we go, anyway?" Magdalena asked. "We have no home to return to."

"We will go north to Scheessel," Jacob said. "That's where everyone else is."

"Everyone is there? Even Emilie and Mutti?"

"Yes," Jacob replied. "They were in a displaced persons camp in Stuttgart. Albert has taken them all to Scheessel. The only ones we haven't located are your brothers, Jacob and Otto, and their wives and children."

"Thank God," Magdalena said. "What about the men who stayed with you in Poland? Are they all in Scheessel?"

"All of them but Daniel," Jacob said. "He was killed by Polish bandits while we were trying to escape to Germany."

"Poor Aunt Isabella," Magdalena sighed. "She has had so

many trials already."

"Yes, she has," Jacob agreed. "Your mutti will make sure she's cared for, though."

"I'm sorry to interrupt, but I must finish the chores before it's too dark for me to see," Lizzy said. "Please, excuse me."

"We'll help," Jacob said. "Come Erhard and Ewald, there's work to do."

"Yes, Vater," the boys said in unison, falling into step beside Jacob.

Magdalena whispered a prayer of thanks, as she watched them disappear into the barn. God had brought them through so many trials the last few years. She was sure she would hear more of Jacob's escape from Poland and the many other things that had happened to him during their separation. She would share with him, too, of all she and the boys had faced after boarding the train to flee Poland. The carefree girl Magdalena had been growing up in a vineyard in Bessarabia had long since vanished. She had been replaced with a determined woman, whose faith had been challenged and strengthened through difficult trials. "What is faith if it is never tested" were familiar words her vater had spoken often. The answer, it is no faith at all.

Chapter Twenty-Five

Two weeks after Jacob showed up at Lizzy's farm, her husband, Gerhardt, returned home. The war had taken a toll on him and he had sustained an injury to his left leg, causing him to limp. After sustaining the injury, he had been sent to work as a guard in one of the concentration camps. There were scenes he relived in his mind's eye and nightmares during the night of the terrible acts he had been forced to take part in, but he did not speak of any of this.

Lizzy was just thankful he was alive and finally home. The mental healing could take years, and Gerhardt might never be the same, but at least he had survived.

Jacob and Gerhardt, along with Erhard and Ewald, worked side by side to put the farm back in proper working order. For a week, they labored from dawn to dusk. When Jacob was satisfied with all the repairs, he decided it was time to go back to Scheessel.

It was a tearful good-bye for Lizzy and Magdalena, who had grown close over the past five months. Erhard and Ewald had come to love Lizzy, too, but the Border collie pup, Stein, was the one they really didn't want to leave behind. The boys had grown quite attached to the fun-loving ball of fur and knew they would miss her terribly.

Jacob had told Magdalena and the boys that Stein had been left in Poland when he was forced to leave. There was just no way to bring him along, so they had no hope of a dog waiting for them at their new home in Scheessel. Jacob promised them that, in time, they would get another dog. He decided not to explain their living arrangements quite yet, knowing that there would be no way of owning a dog until they could afford a place of their own.

Gerhardt thanked Jacob for all the repairs he had accomplished on his farm the previous two weeks and the help for the past week. He had worried about Lizzy trying to run the farm alone but admitted she had done the job well.

Gerhardt had been surprised to see there would be a wheat harvest, along with an oat harvest, later that summer and was thankful that Erhard had been taught so well. The boy's knowledge would mean Gerhardt would not have a year with no grain of his own to feed his livestock, and the two crops would supply straw for bedding, saving him a good deal of money.

Jacob took his family back to Scheessel, and they began putting the pieces of their life back together. Magdalena was not pleased that they would be living in an abandoned slaughterhouse but she and the other women went to work making it a home. The building was very large, so each family had their own living quarters, but there was just one large kitchen and dining area. They ate each meal as a family: Rosina and Gottlieb, Emil, Edward, Isabella, and Agathe, Juliana, her three daughters, and Olof, Albert, Emilie and their five sons, and Jacob and Magdalena with their three sons. Twenty-three people gathered each morning and evening to give thanks and eat their meal together.

Olof married Agathe a few months after they all arrived in Scheessel. It was a joyous celebration after so many years of heartache. Gottlieb made mention that a glass of his fine wine to make a toast would have made the occasion more memorable, but they all knew there would never be Wallentine wine again. The art of winemaking had ended with Gottlieb, never to be passed down to his youngest son, Emil. The recipe could be written down, but the knowledge of the process could not. It was something one had to experience to get it right.

As time passed, word finally reached the group in Scheessel of the whereabouts of other family. Gottlieb and Rosina's sons, Jacob and Otto, had chosen to stay in Poland and keep their families with them when the Red Army invaded. That choice resulted in them living in the East Zone, never able to leave permanently, unless they escaped. Isabella's son, Adolf, settled in southeastern Germany. He married a woman from that area and he found employment in the coal mine.

Edward and Emil Wallentine married about a year after the war ended. Their wives moved into the slaughterhouse with the rest of the family because there was very limited housing. Mathilda, Maria, and Hulda Grieb all found husbands and moved out of the slaughterhouse. Their mutti, Juliana, remarried and moved out, too. The pieces of everyone's lives were being picked up and put back together. Things would never be like they were in Bessarabia, but the Grieb and Wallentine families chose to adapt and make the best life they could.

Gottlieb Wallentine passed away in 1947, due to breathing complications he had been fighting for years. That same year there was a food shortage in Germany, reminding the relocated Russian Germans of the drought years in Bessarabia. Fearing the poor economy would allow Communism to spread into West Germany, the United States stepped in to give support, hoping to prevent that from happening. A plan, called the Marshall Plan, was set up in Europe. It would later become known as the European Recovery Program. It offered food, coal, and loans to those in need.

"Albert and I have applied for loans through the European Recovery Program," Jacob informed Magdalena one evening. "We're going to build houses for us to live in."

"A real house," Magdalena said, excitement blossoming at the thought. "It's been a long time since we've had a house of our own."

"Yes, and I believe it's time to take care of that," Jacob said. "We need a real house to raise our family in. Understand though, I have not given up the dream of moving to America. We have no way to go right now, but I will find a way."

"We don't know anyone in America," Magdalena pointed out.

"I want our sons to have opportunities," Jacob said. "There's not much for them here in Germany. There's no land to farm and hardly any place to live. America offers so much more than we can give them here. Besides, I need to farm. It's what I was born to do."

"We will have to leave all of our family," Magdalena fretted. "We will never see them again."

"Magdalena, we will go to America when I figure out a way

to get us there," Jacob said, leaving no room for any more argument.

Magdalena focused on the excitement of building a house, a place to call home. Jacob may never figure out a way to allow them to move to America, so there was no sense in worrying over it. She would cross that bridge when there was water under it.

The loans were approved and the construction began. Jacob, Erhard, and Ewald dug the basement by hand. The house was not large but would be much better than the slaughterhouse. The first floor had a kitchen, living room and two bedrooms, with a large attic upstairs. The boys would share the attic space and Jacob and Magdalena would have one of the first floor bedrooms. The other bedroom would be shared by Magdalena's mutti, Rosina, and her aunt, Isabella.

The house was completed by the fall of 1948, and Jacob and Magdalena moved their family out of the slaughterhouse. Albert and Emilie's house was finished at the same time and they also moved. Life seemed to be getting better and taking on some normalcy.

Erhard and Ewald went to school each day and Jacob went to work. Magdalena busied herself running the house and caring for Werner. A garden had been plowed behind their new home in the spring and now Magdalena, with the help of her mutti and aunt, preserved the harvest for the winter ahead.

One day after work, Jacob found a dog that had been abandoned, and Jacob carried him home. It made Erhard, Ewald, and Werner's eyes light up and they were the happiest Magdalena had seen them in a long time. It amazed her how the little creature could bring a smile to her sons' faces each day after school and how many hours Werner spent playing with him throughout the day. The dog was not nearly as smart as Stein had been back in Poland, but he was friendly and loyal, and it seemed to be enough. Life was happening as it should, until one Sunday in November, 1948.

"It's good to see you today," the Lutheran minister said, speaking to Jacob as he and his family were leaving morning worship.

"It's a wonderful Lord's day," Jacob said, shaking the minister's hand.

"I have those papers you asked about, if you can wait around for a moment," the minister said.

"Yes, we will wait," Jacob replied.

Magdalena looked at Jacob, the question written on her face. What papers was the minister referring to? Jacob had not mentioned anything about any papers to her.

When everyone had left the church, Jacob followed the minister to his study. He returned a few minutes later with a handful of papers.

"What are those papers for?" Magdalena asked as they walked toward home.

"They are documents we will have to fill out," Jacob replied. "The minister is going to try and find a sponsor for us in the United States."

"A sponsor?" Magdalena questioned.

"Yes," Jacob said. "It's someone who will provide us with a place to live in America until we can get on our feet."

Magdalena wanted to scream and holler and maybe even throw something at Jacob. They had just built a house and were getting settled in to life in Germany. For the past eight years they had been forced to move, flee for their lives, be separated for months, and endure all the heartaches that came with that. Now, when things were finally starting to come together, Jacob was talking of moving across the Atlantic Ocean, to a place they had never been and knew nothing about. None of them could even speak English, except for Jacob.

"What are the chances of a sponsor being found for us?" Magdalena asked, biting back all the words she really wanted to scream at Jacob.

"The minister says it could take a while," Jacob admitted. "Sometimes a sponsor is never found."

There was hope for Magdalena in Jacob's words. Maybe a sponsor would never be found. She knew better than to argue with her husband, but maybe God would prevent them from getting a sponsor. She would pray for that to be the case. The thought of leaving all her family in Germany to travel to America made Magdalena feel ill. Did Jacob not even care about that? Would he really leave Albert behind to follow his dream of moving to America?

Jacob and Magdalena filled out all the forms needed to start the immigration process. Magdalena had saved all of their baptism certificates and packed them every time they were forced to move. She used them now to prove all of their ages. Questions had to be answered about where they were born and their whereabouts during the war. They also had to include a complete health history for each of them. A long list of vaccinations was required and passports were obtained. Everything was in order, except there was no sponsor for them in the United States.

Three years passed and Magdalena decided her prayers had been answered. Then, the Lutheran minister came to their home to inform them their immigration papers had finally been accepted, and they had a sponsor. They would be moving to Cox's Creek, Kentucky, to a cattle farm. Jacob was so excited by the news, and the boys were too, because it was an adventure in their eyes. Magdalena tried her best to hold back the tears, but failed miserably. The thought of leaving her home and all her family was almost more than she could bear. They had been through so much already. Why did Jacob want to uproot them and move so far away?

Arrangements were made for Olof and Agathe to buy Jacob and Magdalena's home. Rosina moved in with Albert and Emilie, while Isabella remained. Isabella would be living with Olof and her daughter, Agathe, once Jacob and Magdalena left.

It gave Magdalena peace of mind knowing her mutti would be well cared for by Emilie, but still she would have preferred to stay in Germany. Magdalena packed up her life yet again, dreading the thought of the long voyage ahead. She had hoped to never move again, but her husband had other plans for them.

In March1952, Jacob, Magdalena, Erhard, Ewald, and Werner Grieb said good bye to Germany and their family, forever. The only thing Magdalena had to remind her of where she had come from was a journal her mutti, Rosina, had kept. Rosina had painstakingly made Magdalena a copy of her personal journal, so Magdalena could tell her children and grandchildren of their German ancestry. Rosina had begun with the migration of her family from Germany to Bessarabia, Romania, in 1818, and had added her own life story after that. The journal had been packed and carried with Rosina as they moved from Bessarabia to

Germany, Germany to Poland, Poland to southern Germany, and finally to Scheessel. Magdalena promised to add her own personal history to the book, too, so the next generation would know all they had endured during WWII.

As they boarded a US military transport ship in Bremerhaven, Magdalena felt as if her river of life had just became a waterfall. She could feel herself falling, plunging into the undertow below. She knew to voice her opinion about the move would do no good. Jacob had decided long ago that they would move to America, and today was the day. She would pull herself together and face this challenge, just as she had all the previous ones she had been forced to endure.

The first few days of the eleven day journey, the water was smooth sailing. Then, the ocean became very rough and choppy. All the immigrants on the ship became ill, hugging the sides of the ship trying to find their sea legs. Magdalena and Ewald became extremely ill, and were not able to do anything but lie down until they were almost to port in New York City.

Upon reaching Ellis Island, they were put through several interviews, followed by physical exams. Finally, they were processed and approved to enter the country. As they passed the Statue of Liberty, Jacob paused to view the statue up close.

It was huge, standing 305 feet tall from the base to the top of the statue. There were seven points on the crown the Lady of Liberty wore, representing the seven seas and the seven continents of the world. A poem was inscribed on a plate attached to the base of the statue. Jacob read the words written there, translating them for his family. ....*"Give me your tired, your poor, your huddled masses yearning to breathe free, the wretched refuse of your teeming shore. Send these, the homeless, tempest-tossed to me, I lift my lamp beside the golden door!"* As Jacob finished the last words, he wiped the tears from his cheeks. Magdalena then realized Jacob's dream fully. Moving was not meant to punish her but to find a better life for her and her sons. She would attempt to grasp that dream, too, and hope that life would truly be better in this "land of the free and the brave."

The foreman of a horse farm in Kentucky was waiting to transport them to their new home. He informed the Grieb family that there had been a change in their sponsor, and they were now going to a horse farm in Anchorage, Kentucky.

When they reached the horse farm, they were provided with a small house in much need of repair. It had no indoor plumbing and the wood floor had cracks in it. There was even a pile of coal in one of the rooms.

Magdalena wanted to cry in despair. With tears filling her eyes she said, "I gave up a brand new house in Scheessel and have come to a place like this to live. If there was any way to walk back to Germany, I would, for I surely would not get on that wretched boat again!"

"Magdalena, you made a slaughterhouse into a home. Surely we can do the same with this house," Jacob soothed.

"I suppose I have no other choice but to do that," Magdalena fumed. She knew she was trying her husband's patience but it had all been too much. She had been uprooted again, leaving behind a new house and all her family. The boat ride had taken a great toll on her. In truth, she was just plain weary.

"We will make this house a home," Jacob said, "and as soon as we have enough money, I promise to get you a nice house again."

Magdalena knew Jacob would strive to do as he had promised. They would work together to fix this house up and hope for a better one. She had to admit the farm was beautiful and she knew Jacob would be in his element working here. He needed the open fields and fresh air, the sweet aroma of fresh mown hay and horseflesh. Farming had always been his way of life. Hitler had taken all of that away, but here in America, the dream was again a reality.

Werner, who was eight, and Ewald, who was nearly sixteen, started school soon upon arriving in Kentucky. Neither one could speak much English, but their vater helped them learn at home while the teachers and other kids taught them at school. Jacob also told his sons that they were no longer to call them Mutti and Vater, but Mom and Dad. They would full embrace this new life in America.

Erhard, who was nineteen, and Jacob helped with the horses and worked in the fields on the horse farm. Magdalena cooked and cleaned for a friend of the farmer's wife. These were all jobs they were familiar with and did well. They easily adjusted to their new home and surroundings, but Magdalena still missed her family terribly.

When the longings got to be too much, Magdalena would read her mutti's journal and sometimes add events from her own life to the empty pages in the back. She hoped the words written on those many pages would one day help others realize the struggles they had gone through. Magdalena had even written about Jacob's imprisonment in the concentration camp and the things he had witnessed there. They had lived through a part of history that many did not survive to tell about. She prayed that those who did survive would tell their stories, in hopes that this part of history would never be allowed to repeat itself.

In 1953, Erhard was drafted into the United States Army and was a tank driver during the Korean War. Magdalena cried as he left for his deployment, knowing it could possibly be the last time she saw him alive. It seemed so unfair that Erhard had lived as a child through one war just to fight in another as a man. However, Magdalena realized that freedom did not come free, and Erhard would do his part to protect those freedoms he was now enjoying.

"Magdalena," Jacob said, "God has brought us this far. He will bring Erhard home safe."

And God was faithful yet again. Magdalena rejoiced the day Erhard returned home unharmed and recalled the words Jacob had spoken on the day he left. Her faith had been tried countless times and God had always remained faithful. Magdalena had added all of those times in her journal to remind her that she was not ever alone in her trials. There, among the lines and scribbles, was the truth she clung to until her dying breath. God is faithful, even unto death.

Epilogue
October 2014

Ewald Grieb sat on his back deck in Georgetown, Indiana. Fall was in the air and God had painted the trees to mark the season. Looking out over the landscape vivid with colors, he thought back over his life.

His dad had made a choice in moving them to America, and Ewald had embraced that choice. Ewald had had a good life, choosing a wonderful wife, who had given him a precious son.

Ewald had married Patricia Blair, and their son, Larry Dale, was born in December, 1961. Larry had grown up healthy and strong. He married Pamela Pierson, and they had a beautiful son, Cameron, in 1995.

Ewald patted the worn leather journal that lay in his lap where all of this information had been added beneath his mother and grandmother's entries. The book would soon be passed to Larry, who would give it to Cameron, when the time came.

Erhard and Werner had married and had families of their own, too. The three brothers had chosen to live within driving distance of each other throughout their adult lives. Werner lived across the Ohio River, in Kentucky. Erhard had lived right beside Ewald in his last years before going to his eternal home. They had visited daily, sharing a cup of coffee and reminiscing about the past. They were sweet memories that Ewald held dear to his heart.

Dandy whined at Ewald's feet bringing him back to the present. The miniature schnauzer looked up at Ewald with his ever trusting eyes. As Ewald reached to pet his head, he thought of Stein, the dog he had to leave behind in Poland. Stein had been the first dog he owned, opening his heart to the furry creatures. And as smart as Stein was, Ewald was certain Dandy was smarter. Ewald talked to the schnauzer often, and Dandy's understanding was nearly human. Of course, he tried not to let the neighbors see his frequent conversations with the black, chunky dog.

Pat opened the back door and joined Ewald on the deck, bringing out glasses of lemonade for them both. Placing the glasses on the table, she sat in a chair beside Ewald. "Did you read anything good?" Pat asked, pointing to the book.

"Just looking through Mom's journal," Ewald replied. "She and Dad went through so much during the war."

"Yes, they did," Pat agreed. "She told me stories about that time. We just never know what we will face in life. We just pray we have the strength to see it through."

"Our life has been a good one," Ewald said, a peaceful smile on his face.

"It sure has," Pat agreed. "We have been blessed more than words can express."

"I'm thinking of passing the journal on to Larry," Ewald said, caressing the journal like an irreplaceable treasure, which it was.

"I believe it's time," Pat agreed.

"I just want him to know about his Oma and Opa Grieb," Ewald said, "and the life they had before Hitler, in his madness, stripped it from them."

"I believe he will enjoy reading the journal very much," Pat said. "Sometimes we have to know where we came from in order to figure out where we're going."

"I couldn't have said it better myself," Ewald said, picking up his lemonade for a long, satisfying drink. God had kept him and his family in His care their whole lives, and Ewald knew He would remain faithful, just as his mom had written all those years ago.

ABOUT THE AUTHOR

Beca Sue makes her home on an organic farm in Southern Indiana with her husband, daughter and son. She also has a grown son who makes his home in a neighboring county. She is a homemaker and enjoys helping out on the farm.

Beca Sue began her career by writing Vacation Bible Schools and has completed six different VBS programs, many of which have been used by churches throughout the region. She has also been involved with several elementary schools as a physical education instructor, director of music, and Christmas Program director.

If you have comments or questions, please contact Beca Sue at becasuebooks@gmail.com

Thank you so much for choosing this book. Please look for other books and EBooks by Beca Sue on the web.

Made in the USA
Middletown, DE
06 September 2021